Lal Kitab

Dr. Ambika Prasad Parashar
Suresh Chandar Parashar

Published by

F-2/16, Ansari Road, Daryaganj, New Delhi-110002
011-23240026, 011-23240027 • *Fax* 011-23240028
Email info@vspublishers.com • *Website* www.vspublishers.com

Regional Offi ce Hyderabad
5-1-707/1, Brij Bhawan (Beside Central Bank of India Lane)
Bank Street, Koti, Hyderabad - 500 095
040-24737290
E-mail vspublishershyd@gmail.com

Branch Offi ce : Mumbai
Jaywant Industrial Estate, 2nd Floor-222, Tardeo Road
Opposite Sobo Central, Mumbai - 400 034
022-23510736
E-mail: vspublishersmum@gmail.com

Follow us on   

All books available at **www.vspublishers.com**

ISBN 978-93-579408-3-2
Edition 2016

Printed at Param Offseters Okhla, New Delhi-110020

Publisher's Note

In Indian astrology, Lal Kitab occupies an important position. It combines knowledge about astrology and palmistry. This book was first published with a hard cover and since then it has been known as Lal Kitab.

Today and tomorrow are two words about which everyone discusses, but no one gets to the truth for sure. Everyone desires to know about fate, fortune, stars etc. Why do people want to know their future? Perhaps to prevent something bad from happening or to avoid an area that might prove to be an impediment. Tensions of family and life, also affects health and disturbs an individual's life. This book on Lal Kitab can help us understand the various aspects of life and in finding out the causes of problems in life.

Lal Kitab is a treatise that expounds the principles of prediction. Looking back a little, we see that astrology, palmistry and numerology had progressed as independent sciences in the Indian subcontinent and there are many books written on each. In contrast, astro-palmistry is the sole subject matter of the book in your hand - Lal Kitab; here astrology and palmistry complement and supplement each other.

Lal Kitab, originally written in poetic verses on Vedic astrology and is believed to have been first published in ancient Urdu language. The 'farmaans' enunciated in that book gave brief hints of destiny with undertones of philosophical nuances. The book gave easy to follow remedies, prayers and mantras. The solutions offered often revolved around temples and deities. Since the book draws concepts from Hindu astrology and palmistry, there are researchers who say it is based on the Samudrika Shastra.

Pandit Roop Chand Joshi of Punjab is widely regarded as having written the currently available version in five volumes between the years 1939 to 1952.

Yet another set of followers of predictive studies attribute the origin of the book to Jyotisha Shastra since the book follows the planetary positions and names of Navagraha used by Vedic people to give predictions and offer remedies. Navagraha includes nine planets, which are ruled by the nine corresponding Gods: Sun is Vishnu, Moon is Shiva, Mars is Hanuman,

Jpiter is Brahma, Venus is Lakshmi, Mercury is Durga, Rahu is Saraswati, and Ketu is Ganesha. Lal Kitab provides simple remedies for various planetary afflictions in the horoscope or birth chart.

We all know that no one can outrun his destiny, no method will solve all our problems, but this volume can help control and lower the degree of our problems by preparing a birth chart based on the birth place, birth time and directions of constellations and stars. This book gives an estimate of upcoming events of a year and also remedies to overcome ensuing problems and the best part is that these all solutions are very simple to perform.

Learn to use Lal Kitab as a protective shield; such as when we use umbrella in rain to protect ourselves but still our foot gets wet, in the same way it will reduce our problems but not necessarily eliminate them completely.

Special Note : we would like to indicate to the reader that at different places certain Hindi words have commonly been used to retain the authenticity of the book. These words given in italics, come under six-seven categories. These are: Names of god & goddesses like, Laxhimi, Serswati, Ganesha, Hanumana, etc.; certain astrological terms like*, upaya, lagna, kundali, jatak*; names of jewels like, *pukhraj, moonga*, etc.; planets' names, *Budha*, *Mangal*; names of trees like, *peepal, bargad, neem*; names of certain food items like, *mooli, saljam*, *kapoor, sonf, haldi, mashoor, batasha (ptasha), roti, chapatti, saonf, mulee*, *alichi*, *chu-aara*etc.; & certain other terms like, *tilak, dan, sadhu, sants, sufi, vaidya, shradha, prashadam* etc. We have also provided equivalent terms to most of these words if they are common but at a few places we have not been able to do so as certain words cannot be exactly translated into English or there is no exact words that commonly stands for them. Hope the kind reader will try to understand these terms to enrich their understanding towards astrology.

New Awareness about Indian Astrology and Lal Kitab

It is not certain when our *rishies* and *munies*, through research and deep involvement with the study of the stars, created the large knowledge about astrology. They achieved this through their deep study of the planets and their movements. That knowledge, duly arranged and communicated in the shape of great books, was provided to the posterity gradually. It was only due to that reason that Indian astrology was known throughout the world. Lal Kitab is similarly a great book written in Farsi language containing the knowledge about the predictive part of astrology that deals the aspects relating children, marriage, number of years one would live, and how one would earn one's livelihood etc. Besides it also provides small tit bits that help one to stay away from the ill-effects of planets and offers certain cures to ailments.

We have also provided certain tit bits time to time to help the reader keep away from the pitfalls in life. But our main concentration has been towards Indian astrology in this book. It is because of that that we have discussed Kalserp Yoga, Manglik Dosh, Gauchara as well as palmistry in this book. It will certainly help the learners to understand the importance of astrology.

We very much hope that the reader will surely take advantage of the knowledge provided in the book for it will not only bring awareness about astrology but also gradually help them solve their own various problems relating life.

–The Author

Table of Contents

What Do the Twelve Houses Predict?

To understand astrology it is imperative that the learner knows about the twelve houses and what these houses predict. For without that knowledge it would be impossible to make any predictions. Therefore, for your convenience and knowledge, we provide what these different houses predict and convey in respect of individual's qualities, short comings and relationships.

Complexion, the physical body & strength, personality, thinking capability, kindness &cruelity

Right eye, family, father's property, manner of talking, death of wife/husband, self-earned money

Right ear, arms, brother & sister, friends, income, short journey, courage

Neck & chest, mother, mother land, resources of enjoyment,servants,support from people &father in law

Lower portion of back & stomach, children, education, love affairs, intelligence level, third wife, participation in games

Right leg, knees, ankles, heel, mother's sister, enemies, loans, father's luck, imprisonment, losing happiness from wife

Wife /Husband's physical and mental state enjoyment, married life, daily work, partners, partnership or business, sex involvement, business partner

Related to death, sexual pleasures, lottery money, physical strength, sexual parts

Luck, religious activities, foreign visits, higher education, spiritual attainment, grandsons, happiness

Father, position in Government, prestige in society, business & relationships, breath, ribs, type of work involved in service,breath, ribs, bubusiness relationships

Luck, next life, religious inclination, left lower side of back & stomach, state of grandsons, reputation

Left eye, foreign tours, expenses, second wife, illness of wife, mokcha, mothers luck

The truth lying behind the fact that some planets are in an exalted sign and some in a debilitated position, is that when planets are in an exalted state in a *kundali* or chart their rays are fully received by the native (*Jatak*) and when they are in a debilitated sign their rays are received timidly or poorly. They are in fact very weak. Some astrologers hold that when planets are in exalted sign and are in retrograding state, they don't provide good results to the native and when they are debilitated and are retrograding, good results are expected. Our experience unfolds that planets that are retrograde in a *kundali*, they don't extend good results to the native. However, there are various opinions on this issue. We would like the advanced (more experienced) readers in astrology to keep a close touch with the Indian Astrological Calendar, usually known as *panchang*, and go on looking and observing the movements of the planets. On the

retrograde also at a particular time. The following chart displays the exalted and debilitated positions of the planets.

Planets	Exalted Position	Debilitated Position
Sun	Aries/ Mesa Rashi	Libra/Tula Rashi
Moon	Taurus/VirashRashi	Scorpio/VrishchikRasi
Mars	Capricorn/MakarRashi	Cancer/ KarkRashi
Mercury	Virgo/ KanyaRashi	Pieces/ MeenRashi
Jupiter	Cancer/ KarkRashi	Capricorn/MakarRashi
Venus	Pieces/ MeenRashi	Virgo/ KanyaRashi
Saturn	Libra/ Tula Rashi	Aries/ Mesa Rashi
Rahu	Virgo/KanyaRashi	Pieces/ MeenaRashi
Ketu	Sagittarius/ DhanuRashi	Gemini/ MithunRashi

Rahu and Ketu are considered shadow planets and they don't possess any *rashi*

good results in Mercury/Buddha's *rashi* and Ketu gives good results in Guru's *rashi*. Ketu, if well placed in a *kundali*/chart, gives good results and leads the *jatak* to *mokcha/*

is considered to be a highly auspicious planet, Ketu in its *rashi*/sign usually provides very good results.

When we ponder over the exalted and debilitated positions of the

jatak, who has served his father or the king or the ruler of his state wholeheartedly, if the *sun* is often rises in an exalted sign. If we go deeper into this aspect, we learn that the *sun* exalts in Aries at 10 degrees. That particular *nakchatra* belongs to Ketu and therefore, Ketu is considered to be auspicious as far as *jatak'smokcha*/ salvation is concerned. The *sun* is the soul of a *jatak*

in Aries (in 10%) is considered highly auspicious as it can provide*mokcha.*

In whose chart the *moon* is in an exalted sign, that *jatak* must have served his/her mother well in his/her previous life. Therefore, the *Moon* inTaurus sign in 3 degrees is considered to be exalted in one's *kundali.* In that degree the *nakchatra* is of *Kritica* which is owned by the *Sun.* As the *moon* is considered to be ruling one's heart or controls one's tender feelings, the *jatak* gets a great success in life by devoting one's total

her attention towards God.

Many astrologers believe that if a *jatak* has served his brothers and relatives well in one's previous life, in his/her*kundali Mars*/*Mangal* is often placed in an exalted sign. Mars/*Mangal* in Capricorn in 28 degrees gets exalted. *Mangal* is considered to be the commander of forces and whenever an individual/*jatak* is surrounded with problems, it helps him/her get out of them victoriously. Being the commander of forces *Mars* helps the *jatak*

of life) courageously.

Mercury is found exalted in one's chart when the *jatak* has served his/her sisters, cousins or aunties well in the previous life. Mercury in Virgo sign rising in 15 degrees in *hastanakchatra* is considered to be exalted. This *nakchatra* belongs to the *Moon.* It bestows lot of intelligence to the *jatak* and leads him/her to create something new or leads one to invent something unusual which may often trouble humanity. That is the reason that such a native often drift away from God as he/she devoted his/her intelligence to odd jobs detrimental to human beings.

Jupiter in Cancer sign in 5 degrees gets exalted. If one possesses Jupiter in an exalted sign in one's *kundali*/chart it is said that such an individual must have served seers or mahatmas in his/her previous life. Jupiter is considered to be auspicious as it bestows riches and huge property to an

desires and losses, Jupiter is known to be giving *gyana*/knowledge and inclines one towards dharma. Therefore Jupiter in *pushyanakchatra* in Cancer sign is considered to be highly auspicious. It always provides the individual sane thoughts with which he/she serves humanity well, helps others and usually leads a simple life.

Venus in in Pieces sign in 27 degrees is considered to be in an exalted position. Venus provides every kind of happiness and pleasure in life. But Jupiter in Pieces provides pleasures that are sacred and

in lower pleasures of life and try to involve with higher (Spiritual) kinds of enjoyment and pleasures and experiences in life utmost happiness.

Saturn is exalted in 20 degrees in Libra/*Tula Rashi*. It is said that Saturn rises in an exalted sign only in the charts or *kundalis*/charts of the people who have served poor and needy people in their previous life. Saturn represents blackness and darkness and is considered devoid of riches, full of ignorance and without any worldly pleasures. If an ignorant person gets money he is likely to waste his life in worldly unwanted pleasures. It is therefore, Saturn in *Visakhanakchatra*, that it is considered to be in an exalted sign as the native born under this sign is highly gifted, intelligent and full of wisdom, inclined to devote his life in good deeds.

The Aspects of Planets

It has been communicated from the ancient times by the mighty astrologers that all the planets have their own aspects and in view of that they all

planets is important, so are their aspects. For example, the *sun*, the *moon*, Venus and Mercury aspect the seventh house from the place they rise in a chart. Mars exerts its aspects on the 4th, 7th and 8th houses, Jupiter aspects 5th, 7th and the 9th

important matters in one's life. It provides children,love, attention towards God, ministerial status, expertise in games, and cultivates the talent in the native to be a good writer. It also provides great wisdom. Seventh house is related to good luck through one's partner daily involvement in a business. The ninth house bestows luck on the native. It helps to get good education, gives chance to visit foreign countries on business or on assignment and cultivates religious leaning. Saturn has 3rd, 7th and 10thaspects from its rising position. Saturn is considered to be serving others and the master of petty or low work. Therefore it has 3rd, 7th and the 10th aspects in a chart.

Rahu and Ketu, though shadowy planets, have their 7th aspect only in a *kundli* from their rising positions in the chart. Some astrologers also consider that these shadowy planets also have their aspects on the 5th and the 9th houses. Any planet having an aspect on its friendly house provides

negative results. It is also a common belief among astrologers that Jupiter always exerts good aspects on the native and Saturn's aspects are usually rises in the 3rd house, it will provide adverse effects on that house making brothers or sisters or if they are there bad relationship will be experienced in a chart but gives ill effects through its aspects.

We would like to advice our learned readers that all most of these predictions relating the aspects of Jupiter and Saturn are subject to a careful observation and only then predictions need to be made. Yes, Saturn certainly has its bad aspect on the seventh house when it is in an exalted position in a chart. So is the case of Jupiter's aspects. If it is placed in an exalted position in a chart, it has its seventh aspect on the Capricorn sign, which is Jupiter's debilitated state of aspect. Therefore it may exert bad effect on the native relating that house only. However, Jupiter's ill effects are not so detrimental like that of Saturn.

What the Planets Predict According to Lal Kitab?

*rashi*usually gives results according to that *rashi*. To explain that point of view we present the following chart/*kundali* for your convenience and understanding.

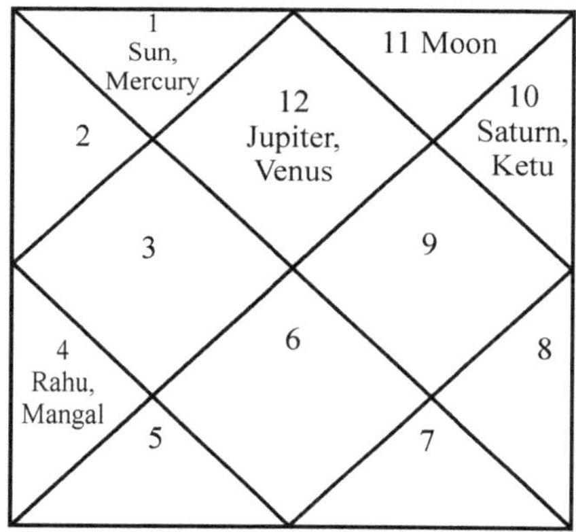

In the above chart Mercury is rising in the Mars/*Mangal's* sign. Therefore, Mercury will provide 50% results according to *Mangal*. It will also provide likewise results in its major and minor *mahadasha* periods. Besides providing results according to *Mangal*, it (Mercury) will also give results pertaining to the house it is placed in the chart. Mercury is rising in the second house along with the Sun. The Sun owns the 6th house, which is not an auspicious house. Therefore, the Sun will not provide good results as far as the native's self-earnings are concerned. Besides, the 2nd house predicts about native's speech and family. These both are going to be affected negatively on account of the Sun being the owner of the 6th house, though exalted in Aries.

Mercury owns 4th and the 7th houses, which predict matters relatingland and property, mother, servants, and wife, partnership, joint business-ventures respectively. In general Mercury also helps a native to get further education. All the above results have been experienced by the native during *mahadasha* of Mercury. Mercury, rising in *Mangal's* sign, in Ketu's *nakchatra* is is also auspicious and therefore has provided good results to the native during its major and minor periods.

If we examine the *kundali* of the *jatak* from *chandra/moon lagna*, we th house and Mercury then owns the 5th and the 8th houses. Therefore, Mercury becomes *yogakarak* th house from the *moon lagna*, the native attained good education during its period.

Lal Kitab also ascertains the results starting from the Aries/ *Mesarashi* in a *kundali*. The logic behind it provided by LalKitab is, that Aries/*Mesa rashi* is the head of a *jatak*/native, Taurus/ *Brash rashi* is considered governing the face and mouth of *jatak* and Pices/*Meenarashi* controls the feet of native. It means in view of *LalKitab* any planet rising in a house contains the same numerical order as it rises in a particular house. For example, starting from Aries/*Mesarashi*which according to *LalKitab* *Meenarashi* which rises in the twelfth house, any planet rising in any house, gives the results according to that house only as it also owns that house. It can well be explained with the help of the already given *kundali*.

According to the above given *kundali* Rahu rises in the 5th house. In view of the traditional Indian Astrology, Rahu rises in Cancer sign, but according to LalKitab it rises in Leo sign (being placed in the 5th house), so it will give results according to the 5th house only and not like that of the Cancer sign/*rashi*. Likewise, Mars/*Mangal* being in the 5th house, according to LalKitab, will provide results only as it owns the 5th house. However, it has aspects from Jupiter, which is its permanent friend in the constellation of the planets. So it may not give adverse results although rising in its debilitated sign, Cancer. Besides in its own period Mars/ *Mangal* is expected to give good results too. Mars/*Mangal*provides courage, children, luck, third child, and good family. All such matters will be affected during the period of Mars/*Mangal* according to *LalKitab*.

All such matters need to be examined very carefully by a learning astrologer. One, who is interested in astrology, should keep one's mind open and decide matters after a lot of thinking and observation. One cannot avoid ancient astrological predictions which are purely based on

dispassionate work, totally dedicated to astrology. Therefore, one must

adhere to those principles too although *LalKitab*
Mangal
the native may have some problems relating 'blood cells'. Therefore, keep in mind that 'ownership of the planets and their placement in the houses' both, are highly important to predict matters. The Sun owns the 6th house and placed in the 2nd, it will create problems and illness in the family. When the period of 6th house owner will operate in the native's *kundali*, the native may work under someone in an unimportant position.

Saturn has the ownership of the 11th and the 12th houses. It also has its aspects on Mars/*Mangal*. Therefore it may give adverse results as far as children are concerned. The wife may bear children but she may also have abortions. Saturn represents villages and country side. Therefore, in Saturn's period the native had to stay in villages or small towns where many facilities for life and enjoyment were not available to the native.

Jupiter and Venus being permanent enemies are placed in the 1st house of the native. Although Jupiter is rising in its own sign and Venus is exalted in Pisces, his combination is going to create certain problems for the native though it will make him highly be imaginative as well as practical. But he will take a lot of time in deciding matters of importance. Indecisiveness on the part of the native is the negative aspect of the combinations of these

observing and examining charts for years to understand the right effects of the planets' placement in a particular house before starting predictions.

At the same time one cannot neglect *nakchatra*in which a planet is rising in a *kundali*. Predictions cannot be fully made or will not be correct if one does not possess good knowledge about *nakchatra*. Just for example, in the above given chart,the native stayed in villages during *mahadasha* of Saturn and during Mars/*Mangal's* period (Mars rising in *Puspanakchatra*) which Saturn rules, he had to work on machines (computer/typing) to earn is livelihood. Therefore, kindly understand thoroughly that predications are made on the following basis: the ownership of the planet, its placement in a house and the*nakchatra* in which it is rising.

Amendments Needed Relating Predictions Indicated by Lal Kitab and Ancient Astrology

Astrology and *LalKitab* contain such kind of knowledge which predicts about man's life according to the signs on the body or the planets that are placed in a *kundali*. While predicting, at times,LalKitabonly considers important planets that are *karaks* or are responsible to provide results—good or bad. But when one starts predicting, one has to consider everything such as the house, the owner of the house and its placement, as well as, *karak*) in a*kundali.* When we consider all these things while predicting, only the right result can be reached.

There are certain *yogas* (combinations) in astrology which cancel one another's positive or negative effect. Man has been constantly trying to seek happiness in life. In that search he/she goes on throughout life. Our *rishis* and *muneis* have said a lot about such things and tried to put some important issues within the framework of religion to help humans to live happily in life. The precepts that would help humans to live happily have been added to the religious practices (*dharama*) so that humans do practice them regularly. Some of those things were added to religious practices so that our uneducated ancestors would practice them and live happily. Just for example, the plant *tulsi* was considered sacred and people were advised to grow it in their houses and water it regularly. Its fresh air if inhaled regularly will help cultivate good health. It was also advised that a couple of leaves of *tulsi* should be taken regularly to ward off so many diseases. In our *Puranas* (Old religious literature) it has been stated that the Goddess Laximi considered *tulsi* as her own sister, so its importance is great.

Similarly, if one offers a tumbler of water to the Sun god, the raysabsorbed by the person offering water, would help him/her to keep away from so many diseases. It also helps one to improve the eye sight. *LalKitab* asserts that the person in whose chart the Sun and Moon are

Vedas. Thus, so many precepts have been developed both by the ancient astrology as well by *LalKitab* which if are adopted and practiced by human beings, they may live happily and keep good health.

When our *Rishi*Patanjali wrote about Yoga, there were not many developed cities in India and people did not lead a lethargic life at that

without exerting ourselves. No physical exercise takes place while one

and happy life, one has to exert and do good things to get results. It will certainly help to lessen their 50% chances to fall ill. To keep healthy one must take good food, indulge regularly with 'yogic' exercises, sleep well and keep his thinking in a positive direction. All that, will surely help a person to keep good health and live happy. Keeping such things in view our *rishies* made certain customs that were needed to be followed at the time of festivals. Behind such activities and the customs was only one aim

physically as those activities make one involve in some kind of exercise.

Moon, in astrology, governs one's heart. As such, when the Moon is

even he/she is unable to sleep in the night on account of such disturbing thoughts. To ward of all such ailments our religious literature unfolds that whatever we experience in life, it happens on account of God's grace and our own deeds. Therefore, we must always indulge in good deeds and help the needy and the poor. Such things will help us think better and keep odd thoughts away from us. Astrology has also suggested certain ways and methods that can help us live better and happy in life. Although all the members in a family eat same sorts of food as others eat, but some out of them keep good health but some get often sick and don't keep good health. Similarly, a teacher, in a class, imparts teaching to all in the same manner, but some pass out in good divisions and some achieve poor marks. Why at all this happens? It gives us the thought that we all are tied down with the nature or God's will and those who try to live in line with the right ways and customs, they surely live happily but others don't. Therefore, it is imperative to be cautious in life and try to live according to the ways suggested by our traditions which contain the ways suggested by our *Rishies*and*Munies*. It will to be useful to blame our luck for bad things that are happening to us in life, rather lead a good life inspired by traditions that certain help us lead a straight life, that would surely provide us happiness.

In view of changes that have come to our traditions and customs recently, it is also necessary that certain changes are required relating the ways and systems suggested by LalKitab and our ancient astrology, so that

lawyer becomes a lawyer after completing a course in certain number of years, astrology also requires a lot of time to conceive its principles properly.If one understands its principles thoroughly once and starts practising containing that knowledge, one will sure be able to advice people better than the one who just reads astrology hurriedly and does not remember its principles better.With all such knowledge, it will also be good to do ' ' time to time in one's house. It will help removing the

that cause illness to the members of the family. In the same manner with the help of the ways suggested by astrology can help us keep off bad things from us and provide happiness in life. Besides, our old religious literature suggests so many good things which help us think in a positive manner. Tulsi Das in the Ramayana has clearly indicated that:

Sunho Bharat bhavipravalbilakhikahat muni nath
Hani, labh, jeevan, maran, yash, upyashbidhi hath

This verse was written at the time when Sri Ram had gone to the forests and the king Dashrath had died.Consequently Bharat is badly sad on account of such unpleasant happenings. At that time, his *guru*
to Bharat that: "O, Bharat, listen to me carefully. That loss, gain, good or bad name, death or life—all these things are controlled by God. Therefore, you must not wail on the things that have been happening to your life." Thus, it suggests that a *jatak* (an individual) must go on doing good things in one's life without caring for bad results.

It also helps us understand that the more you are near the 'Nature', the more you would possess a simple nature, or would be a simple person who is free from any kind of frauds or ill-thinking. He/she will have little jealousy and anger towards others. He/she will like to get up an hour before the Sun rise to keep his luck in good order, keep the house clean before the

If the *jatak* does all that it is expected that the Sun in the *kundali* of such a person starts giving good results. But if someone gets up after the Sun rise, in his *kundali* the Sun brings bad results.

Whether the Predications made by Lal Kitab are true?

Like different faces of people, their luck is also different. Our experience unfolds that ancient astrology and LalKitab both are complements to

other things are well conceived. Similarly certain results and predictions

the other and different places. LakKitab does not provide any predictions about debilitated planets and it also does not predict on the basis of '*Chandra Kundali*'. Instead, it starts predicting from the *mesa rashi*,
kundali. It
also doesn't consider any *mahadasha* or *unterdasha* but it provides results only on the basis of the current movements of the planets in the orbit and also according to the currently running year of the *jatak* about whom any predications are made. For example if *jatak's* 37th year is operating at the
kundai will be
taken care of in view of the planets rising in the sky at that time. But our ancient astrologers would also consider as well as the *Chandra Kundali*for any predictions.

In Lal Kitab two aspects of predictions about a planet have been provided. That is that if a planet is good in a house the results will be like this and if bad then the results will be in that way. But no rules are provided that if a planet is good in a particular house, how could it be bad in the same

after reading such predictions. It is therefore, better to narrate things in a simpler manner so that even an ordinary reader could comprehend all

and*Mangal* *kundali* it is considered good. But with them if Saturn, Rahu and Ketu are also rising, it is considered bad. Even if a planet is rising in its enemy sign or debilitated sign, it is also considered bad. Thus, LalKitab does not consider signs very important but it does consider the houses of great importance and in view of that most of its predictions are based. It is only in a manner of a passing reference that LalKitab has mentioned a few things about *rashis* or signs and considered their importance.

The ancient astrologers have considered the nativity (*janamlagna*) and *Chandra Lagna*very important. At times predictions based on the *Chandra Lagna* come out so accurate that even that much at times cannot be predicted by the *JanamaLagna*. It is, therefore, very important to keep both in mind, the *JanmaLagna*& the *Chandra Lagna* when predictions are made. So many *Yogas*, like *GajKesari* Yoga, *Sunfa&Anfa*yogas as well as and many other unusual *Yogas* are framed by *Chandra Lagna*. However, ancient astrology considers all the three—the *Lagna*, the *Chandra lagna&Suryalagna*, very important.Any predictions are based mostly on the basis of these three *lagnas*in the ancient astrology. With this, it also considers important the *nakchatra* very important as on the basis of *nakchatra* most *dasha* periods operate. Thus, when we make predictions, 40% results are calculated and considered on the basis of *dashas*, 30% on the basis of *gochara* (current positions of planets in the orbit) and 30% on the basis of the year operating in the *Jatak'sKundali* at the time of considering prediction.

LalKitab considers most important *the year which is operating in the jatak'skundali at the time of predictions*. Precautions to lead a happy and safe lifeare also provided by LalKitab. For example, if a statute is placed in the sleeping chamber of a person in whose *kundali*

house, it needs to be removed for the welfare of that person. Better keep that statute in some temple or immerse it into a river so that no ill- effect is experienced by the *jatak*. Likewise, if Saturn is rising in the 8th house in *jatak'skundali*, his feet may get hurt and he/she may suffer a lot. If such a person will indulge in the machinery business, he will sustain losses. All such matters have been concluded after a lot of experience. However, if such results are not experienced or if the predictions don't come true, it means that the *Chandra Kundali* needs to be examined carefully.

many predictions may come true on the basis of the *ChandaraKundali*.

It is really a matter of great concern that because LalKitab contains at times some unusual way of predicting things, so many persons may not understand it properly and hence they may start disbelieving in it. But it is not the case. It contains the best way of providing precautions against

disturb their lives. For example, LalKitabdoesn't approve of giving *dan* (alms) of particular things when certain planets are in the *jatak'skundali*in the 8th house. It will disturb the planets sitting in the 8thhosue and it will create problems for the person. However, if one tries to understand LalKitab properly, one will come to conclusion that all what has been narrated in it as ways to take precautions, all that has been considered

the place where dead are buried or burnt, then one must give away some money to someone at that time or throw away towards some money or rupees towards that place. It may give you some kind of spiritual strength as it is said that at the place where dead are burnt or cremated, Lord Shiva resides.

It is said that Brahma is the creator, Lord Vishnu is the sustainer and Lord Shiva ends all, therefore, 'the place of the dead' (*shamshanghat*) must be honoured and contain a statue of Lord Shiva to please Him. As Lord Shiva gets pleased soon, he will surely help us all if we respect Him properly and install His statue at 'the place of the dead'. Thus, if one throws away a copper coin towards that place, it helps him a lot. In this manner many simple and easy precautions (*upaya*) have been indicated

Many precautions have been listed in such a simple way in LalKitab that it is so easy to perform them or to act upon them. Most precautions are

try to understand all that properly, they would start believing in LalKitab ardently. It is the reason that we have tried to express things in the book most thoroughly and in a simple manner so that people may understand its value and importance.

LalKitab was written from 1939 to 1952. At that time many people used to drink from rivers or springs or canals. LalKitab at that time suggested putting charcoal and copper coins in that drinking water to purify it and make it drinkable. However, people now have various sophisticated ways to drink clean water. Well, certain good acts or precautions like helping the poor by providing medicines, help a poor family to give away their daughter in marriage, help the poor children to get further education, help the blind and physically weak people or help the poor relations in family, are some of the best ways suggested by LalKitab as precautions (*Upaya*) and get happiness and progress inlife. Many of these things can be done very easily and such acts also don't involve much money. If people start taking those precautions and involvewith them, it may provide them great

Lal Kitab contains many simple ways (*totikas/upaya*) to make the Sun favourble in a *kundali.* It says that one should not take much salt to invoke the Sun god's disfavour. Salt represents Saturn or it is governed by Saturn. Both, the Sun and Saturn are deadly enemies and if one eats more salt it may hurt the person in many ways. It may increase his/her blood pressure and also affect the eyesight adversely. Both the Sun and the Moon are considered as the two eyes of a *jatak.* So one should avoid eating more salt to protect one's eyes as well as control blood pressure. Thus, LalKitab suggests using*surma* or white dry medicated powder in one's eyes to please *Mangal* for the protection of eyes.

Our experience unfolds that if in someone's *kundali*Ketu is rising in the 6th house, and Jupiter in the 8th, that *jatak* may not have any son. If the Moon is rising in the 6th house, the *jatak*doesn't take much interest in his routine job/work. In case Venus is rising in the 2ndhouse or if the owner of the 5th is debilitated in a *kundali*
(children). Lak Kitab contains *upayas*(precautions) to ward off problems and if one performs those *upayas*, take precautions and performs acts as suggested, one may lead a very happy life. Its predictions may not be totally effective as it concentrates only on the *karak* (the effective planet in a *kundali*) and does not consider other aspects related to predictions.

may not totally come true.

Lal Kitab and Ancient Astrology Can Help in Redemption of Problems

Ancient Astrology suggests the use of herbs to subside illness in human body. There are few herbs, if used properly, their use may help one to belpatra (a kind of hard fruit that grows on some particular tree) is eaten with black pepper for two months, it can help in lessening diabetes (reduce sugar problem). If a mixture of these two is taken as syrup during summers, it may reduce the effect of heat and provide inside cool to a *jatak.*LalKitab suggests that to get good effect of Mercury, in case it is debilitated or weak in a *kundali*, the *jatak* should clean his/her teeth with (alum, white mineral salt used in medicine) to please Mercury as when white material meet with white teeth it helps pleasing Mercury being white in colour. That would also help improve one's teeth.

In the same way LalKitab has given a lot of importance to *Peepal* tree. It says that if someone eats a couple of *Peepal* leaves regularly, it can help him/her to get well from T.B. or lungs' disease as well as it make one's heart strong and can protect him/her against any heart disease. LalKitab considers *Peepal* as God Brahma who has the power of retaining life. It is also stated in the book that if someone wants to have children, regular use of *Peepal*leaves may help in that respect too. Therefore, *Peepal* tree is of great importance from LalKitab's point of view.

Mangal and *Buddha* (Mercury) rise in one house in a *kundali* these planets may bring bad luck to the native as both the planets are enemies to each other. Therefore, it suggests that *jatak's* kitchen should be made under the stairs of the house for stairs represent *Buddha* and kitchen is represented by *Mangal*. If it happens, both the planets may give odd effects and bring unhappiness to *jatak.*As precautions, the book suggests that *jatak* in whose *kundali* both the planets rise in one house, should remember God regularly, read holy books and drink the water of the river Ganga. It may then bring good results to him/her. LalKitab also suggests that if a *jatak*offers milk and pure water to a *Bargad* tree (a tree that has very long branches which stay for hundreds of years) early in the morning every day, and put some of its dust on his fore-head, it will bring very good results to him. LalKitabholds that if a *jatak* uses milk that comes out of the *Bargad*tree's leaves, it may provide him a lot of physical strength that may protect him against so many diseases. Some persons regularly use *Bargad*tree's leaves oritstender branches. Many indigenous medicines are also made with the *Bargad* leaves and such medicines can cure several diseases which cannot be cured easily by modern medicines. Therefore, LalKitab gives a lot of importance to *Bargad* tree.

If in a*jatak'skundaliBuddha* (Mercury) and Saturn rise in one house, he is advised to plant a mango tree at an auspicious place in his compound. It will not only provide shade but also emit plenty of oxygen, which will provide good effect to health as well as give a lot of wood which can be used in burning and getting charcoal. During rainy season, it helps covering during rainy season. It is also advised by LalKitabthat each religious place should offer food to the needy. At the same time during the full Moon, and at the time when the Sun transits in a new sign, we usually call *Sankranti*, if a yellow coloured vegetable is cooked and distributed to the people to eat, it may protect them against lots of illness. Food supplied along with such vegetables to the passers' by, needy and poor persons, they will bless the house that offers such facilities. As a result their blessings will protect the members of the house (where people offer food) against several illness and diseases. It is advisable that to feed the needy, animals and those who really don't have much food for them, will surely bring good luck to them who offer help and food, as it will subside the bad effects of bad planets in a *kundali.*

LalKitab also suggests to providing food to ants and small insects. It says that eatable material from a ripped coconut fruit, and by adding black *til*, sugar and butter oil to it, if given to ants to eat by placing all that under a *Bargad* or a *Peepal* tree, it will help the *jatak* a lot. That act is considered to be feeding lots of needy and hungry people. It is also advisee in *Lak Kitab* that wheneversomeone constructs a house, a small piece of land should be left out without any construction. Lak Kitab advises to plant a small *tulsi* plant in that open place. If one waters that *tulsi* plant daily and eats a few leaves regularly, it will certainly give good effects to one's health as well luck. In case Ketu is rising in the 12th house in a *jatak'skundali*,LalKitab advises that the *jatak* should shuck his right thumb daily after putting it into sweet milk. It is expected that Ketu will then provide good effects. It is said that a thumb is related to one's mind and health. So bigger is the thumb, better brain the *jatak* will possess. When one will start shucking

one's mind and help it grow positively. When a child or a native wants to improve one's luck, he/she has to work very hard for 15 to 20 years. In

exercise that may help one to grow one's luck.

If one has liver problems, he/she should wear heavy silver rings in one's both the thumbs of feet. It will help improving that ailment. LalKitab considers that *jatak's* feet are governed by Ketu and silver is controlled by the Moon. Therefore, on account of good effect of the Moon the bad effects of Ketu will diminish and life will be easier and happier. In good olden day most Indian ladies, especially those who lived in villages, would wear heavy silver *Kadei*(bangles) to ward off pain in the joints of their legs. It is due to silver which check the ill effect of Ketu that their illness would get reduced. It is also an old Indian custom that while making *chapaties* each time one chapatti should be made extra to be given away to 'a cow, to a crow and a dog'. If you feed animals, it will bring happiness and peace in the family. Thus, the old traditions have some positive meanings and are not made just to practice them without any meaning.

Amazing Precautions

Some people while they show their *kundali* to an astrologer want to know how to ward off the problems and bad days from their lives. Astrology suggests constant prayers (*japs*) and *tap,* meditation and keep engaged with God's prayers, keep fast and make to remove the coming bad days from life. But it has been experienced that even after doing all that bad days still persist. At other places there are suggests to take a dip in the holy waters of the Ganga to keep away the coming bad days. But that too does not help. It is because of that that LalKitab suggests certain simple *upayas* (precautions/activities) that can help in removing the coming

and listening to the *Katha* of SatnarayanBhagwan would help in removing

and those *upayas*
causes why those *upayas* don't affect so much now. Let us clarify it with some example.

If a shopkeeper takes more money than the price of a piece of a thing he sells to a customer, and goes on doing it, he will be considered a cheat and gradually all will know about him. Slowly, as many people learn about him, his customers would start avoiding his shop. Not only that gradually

buy things from his shop. Consequently, his business will be in a great loss. Such a shopkeeper even if he gives alms after cheating his customers, will go on in losses and there will not be any positive effect of the alms if he gives any. But if he charges right price of each article he sells, and goes on like that, his lost reputation will be restored and he will start earning good money through his customers once again. Old customers will also bring new customers and his business will get a new and better jump. By his honest ways and means the shopkeeper has restored his lost reputation and even if he does not involve in or in giving alms, he will earn a lot of good faith which is as good as doing or giving alms.

Similarly, some people when they engage labourers, they don't pay adequately those labourers, then they visit a pandit (Brahman) or to a *tantrick* to check the bad days comig in their lives. But nothing can be done in the real sense by any pandit or by visiting a *tantrick* for the planets will give good results only when the person gives right money to the labourers for the job they have done for him. Thus, those, who don't care for the people and cheat them regularly, planets would never help him/her

upayas

people and respect them in all ways by honest means.Those who indulge

them, they cannot live happily in life for they simply care for themselves and not for their families. These sorts of people even if they indulge in

their duty towards their families adequately.

Therefore, if one does a lot of labour day and night, helps his family to grow in the right direction, then if he does any religious activity, it will

activities as God will also be pleased with him. On the contrary some people cheat their relations, steal their money or property, and later on they

already done something terribly bad by cheating their brothers or relatives. Such people if they take a dip in the holy Ganga, the holyriver will never

own kith and kin. They may talk about their alms and so many good acts, not much and as such they will surely suffer and get punished. Similarly, there are people who don't want to work hardbut take various precautions and believe that various *upayas* will change their luck. But when all the *upayas* fail, they condemn those *upayas* and astrology as well. Likewise, some people do give alms but they give alms from the borrowed money which they never return to the person from whom they have borrowed.

him who has borrowed it and not returned to the owner. Such ungrateful people may involve in any kind of or giving alms, they cannot be

never belonged to them.

Some people claim that they like to receive any *dan* (alms) or money

take it. But such people often take money from others and don't return that to the owner at the right time. Yet there are people who give alms, things or money to the people, but in return they like to inscribe their names on the articles (like a fan or a branch or piece of land or a room) that was given or constructed by them. Is it not the sign of their self-pride which make them think to give to people in that manner so that people may know who gave it? Tulsidasji has rightly indicated in the Ramayana:

Nirmaljal man soimohipawa

That means that 'whose heart is good (clean) and think about others in a positive manner and will not consider others bad nor think about them in a bad manner, only they shall reach God's land'. One who indulges in tricks and wrong deeds, and believes in *tantra* and *mantra* he/she cannot reach unto Him. God says, 'He loves only those, who possess a clean heart'. Tulsidas writes in the Ramayana that Sri Ram while advising Shavri says, 'In all the living beings it is His light and energy which keep them alive. The moment He takes away that light and energy, he/she dies.' Therefore, if anyone tries to deceive a living being, he is not deceiving him but duping God only.' Shri Krishna in Bhagwat has unfolded that 'in all the living beings He is present in the form of *atman*.' Lord Shiva, while narrating some religious *katha* (story), stated once to Devi Parvati, that 'all those who think good of others and wish them live happily he is always pleased with them.' Similarly Guru Nanak Dev devoted his whole life for the good of others without considering any cast, creed or religion. It is thus, so important to do good for others. Our religious testaments unfold that temples, churches, guru-*dwaras* and *masjid* all are made by men, but man himself is created by Him only. So any man must not be overlooked by man. If family women do their duty honestly towards the members of the family, and take care of them, they need not to visit any religious places for salvation. Their duty towards the family is good enough for them than simply visiting any religious or pious place.

To practice *tantra, mantra*

honest and earn their livelihood most honestly. Such activities can help one, if he/she think good about others and also does good for the people,

or *yagya* etc. One who commits atrocities in the name of religion or cast, his/her planets may simply give bad results and he may never stay happy in life. For example, if the President of a country or a Prime Minister wants that his planets in his *kundali*should give good results, he must treat the people of his/her country like his/her children and help them live well. Only then his/her planets in the *kundali* will provide good results. The poor who live in temporary huts and whose children need education, they must be helped by the President or the Prime Minister. Only then the planets in their *kundali* will help them live happily. A poor labour who gets only a meager amount of money in return of his labour, if he/she is helped by you, certainly your planets will help you. If you provide food to a blind

Yet there are people, who don't use things or gifts offered by their relatives as they fear that those gifts must have some kind of ill effects on them if they use them as some sort of magic was connected with those offerings. Is it so easy to control ghosts or bad spirits? It is certainly not. Why do people then think that way? It takes at least 10 to 15 years to get good education. In the same way if one wants to please God, he/she must help the needy and try to provide help to those who are down trodden. Only then God will be pleased with them. It means *tap, dan*(alms) if one gets some kind of strength, then that strength and energy must be used for

pleased with them.

Some professional pundits also advice people wrongly. If a needy and afraid client approach them to take advice to ward off the coming bad days from their lives, the pundit would suggests various ways to keep the ills away from him/her house which has been badly affected by some magic or such a tricky things. He would suggest certain *upayas* and ways. That way the pundit will also extract money from the client's pocket which is the main mission of suggesting various treatment to such coming odds from their lives. Such pundits must fear God and advice people rightly so that they may involve in social service, live with peace with their neighbours, and may be able to invoke God kindness upon them. Deceiving others and create problems for people result on account of Rahu's ill effect on a person. General public is represented by Saturn as well the Moon. If someone plays tricks with them it will create Saturn's anger and consequently the *jatak's* life will be destroyed by Saturn's ill effects.

Certain Upayas Suggested by Lal Kitab

We are narrating certain *upayas* that have been suggested by the LalKitab to reduce one's tension, remove the ill-effect of planets and keep one happy in life. It would be better to get up every day half-an hour before the Sun rises. At that time one must check whether his right or left nostril works. In case right nostril is on, he/she should pray to God 'that the particular day must pass happily without any problem'. Such heartfelt prayers would help him keep courage by God grace just in the manner when the baby is within its mother bomb, hanging upside down for nine months, it is His kind grace that keeps it safe and alive for so many days. It is believed that the baby inside the bomb goes on praying to Him constantly and that saves him from the strain of being in that odd physical state. Similarly, when one gets sick and is unable to eat at all, or when it is very hot and air from a good fan does not cool him down but if God is kind He may send ten minutes heavy rain to cool the temperature of the earth and provide comfort and happiness to people.Therefore, Guru Nanak Dev says that nothing good will come to our lives without God grace. So we must constantly go on praying for His kindness. He should also pray that he would not do any bad to anyone and would go on helping the needy and the poor all the time. He should also take a pledge to earn his livelihood honestly and take care of his family well. Then taking the breath in his hand from the nostril which is operating, and take an appropriate step forward, he goes ahead to work for the day, then he may live happily all that day. For example, if his right nostril works in the morning at the time he gets up, he needs to take

from the said nostril and putting it on his head.

water on the *tulsi* plant and eating a few *tulsi* leaves before getting out for the whole day's work, his day may be very fruitful. Eating *tulsi's* leaves daily will provide good health and if *tulsi* plant should be grown in such a corner of the house where it gets full reverence from all the members of the house, it will be good for all the members of the family. If one offers water to the Sun and to Lord Shiva every day, and wears one *rudrakch* in his/her neck in a chain,prays to the Lord Shiva that he should contain strength to work for eight to ten hours every day to take care of the family, it will help him/her a lot. One who works that much each day, will be able to please Saturn in the *kundali*

as well. It is also advised to help the physically week, the blind and the poor according to one's strength and means. Helping a poor girl to get married, provide medicines to the sick, and help the needy to get further

one's desires in life.

The Effect of Ascendant (Lagnesh) Rising in the First to the 12th Houses

It is highly imperative that a native must learn about all the positions or placement of the ascendant (*lagnesh*) in different hoses stating from the

lagnesh

his/her temperament, behavior, health, physical body, feelings, interests in various things relating life, education as well as visits to foreign countries.

his/her qualities, working capacity, and determination etc.

*jatak'skundali,*it will make him/her very bright, restless, dauntless who is always ready to take risks, and prepared to face any dangers in life. If the Moon is rising in *lagna* in its own *rashi*, it will make him/her very kindhearted, emotional, full of tender feelings, and getting involved in the

Mangal

it will provide the individual unusual strength in the thinking capacity, and it will also own the 8th house, *Mangal* will bestow a lot of physical energy on the individual. In case Mercury (*Budha*) rises in Virgo sign in

very handsome or beautiful, and will be a good orator. In case Jupiter is

servants and such assets in abundance. If Venus is rising in *Tulalagna* or Libra sign, it will make the individual expert in the use of musical instruments and he/she will possess good sense of music. The native will be a good singer too. In case Saturn rises in Capricorn or *MakarLagna*, the native will always stay in a job, will be cool-headed, and his/her capacity to understand problems will be immense. Rahu and Ketu will provide

a *kundali*. The best thing would be to study various or numberless charts to understand their effects in various signs if they rise in the ascendant.

The readers are requested to understand it clearly that except the Sun *kundali*. Only in view of that one should predict on matters of an individual. What we mean is that ownership of both the houses that a planet owns in a chart need to be considered while predicting on various matters. We now start predicting about *lagnesh or ascendant's* strength and qualities when it rises in various

When Lagnesh/Ascendant Rises in the First House

When the *lagnesh* *jatak* shine high (*kuldeepk*) in the family by his excellent progress in life, makes

possess about own-self certain special assessment which will give him success to grow in life. But all that would depend on that which sign rises

native farsightedness and he/she would not be disturbed by small changes or problems. He/she would go on solving the problem that he/she faces. If it is *Mangal*, the native will get excited even with small problems that encounter him/her in life and try to solve them hurriedly. Thus, when

in the native. We try to explain it with the help of an example by providing the native's *kundali*.

The following *kundali* belongs to a person who was born on the 3rd March, 1962. As his *lagnesh/* ascendant is Saturn, the native should possess most of the following characteristics. In the *kundali*only the *lagnesh* has been indicated.

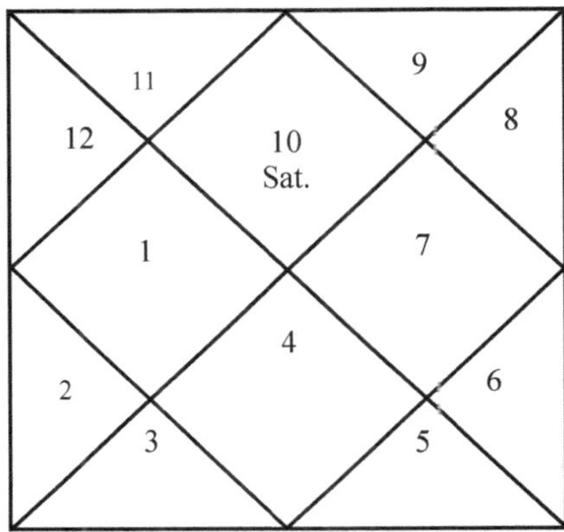

The above native is born in *Makarlagna*/Capricorn. He should have the problem, whether related to education, profession, or family, he would think very deeply and try to solve the problem with utmost care. Consequently most of the time he will be able to solve it quite successfully. Such a person should either be an engineer, a lawyer or a government servant on high position. Now this native is a very successful engineer placed on a high position in a reputed computer company abroad. One of the reasons to support his high placement position is that the *lagnesh* Saturn has its full aspect on the 10th house, which is the house of profession, job and father.

When *Lagnesh* Rises in the Second House

conversation, the way he/she walks (gait), money earned with hard work and dedication, as well as status of family. If *lagnesh* isplaced in this house, it will provide the native a lot of happiness in life, he/she would deal in lending money, possess good family and bestow most of the family relating

both, movable or unmovable property, gain or losses, loans and ways of earning money.If Mercury or Venus rises in this house in their own signs, the native may be a gambler, a good orator, and may involve in money related bats. In view of the positions of the planets rising in this house, the native will be intelligent. His/her conversational talents will be affected by the position and sign of the planet rising in this house. The following *kundali* belongs to a native who was born on the 1st June in 1943. He was a senior government servant and after his retirement he has been enjoying his life very comfortably. As his *lagneshis* Venus and is placed in the second house in a friendly sign, his attachment towards money is great and he has earned money by various means and ways. Money-collection has always been his main aim in life. Therefore, he is the owner of a great fortune and possesses a lot of money. His *kundali*
reader but only the position of the *lagnesh* has been projected.

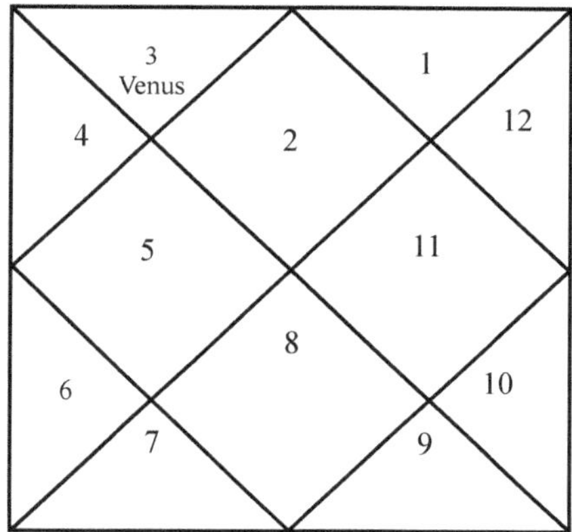

When *Lagnesh* Rises in the Third House

If *lagnesh*/ascendant is placed in the third house, it indicates number of brothers and sisters, friends, relationship with them and whether the native will be effortful, etc. Some astrologers believe that if the ascendant is placed in this house, it makes the native intelligent. He/she may be an educationist and will have several short travels in life. He/she will be a good writer and an orator too. For example the following *kundali*/chart belongs to a person who was born on 10th November, in 1950. The ascendant of the native is the Sun, which is placed in the third house. The native is highly effortful, very honest and lucky in life. As the ascendant, the Sun has its full (exalted) aspect on the 9th house, he travelled a lot in foreign countries, and his children, after achieving good education, reached high position in their lives. Thus, the native has been leading a very happy life.

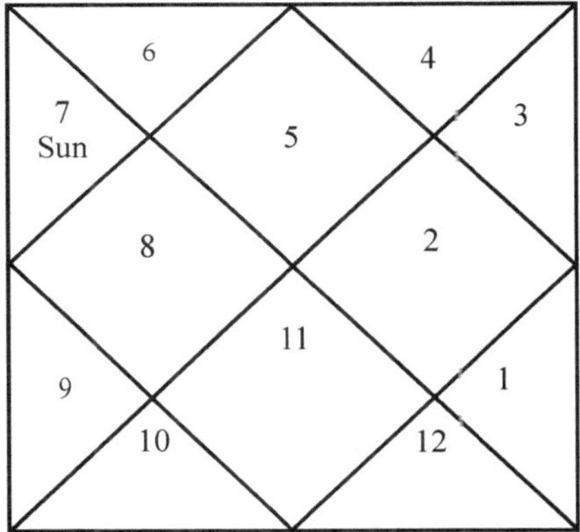

When *Lagnesh* is in the 4th house

If *lagnesh*

relating vehicle, money, land and agriculture etc. Such a native will have

his/her mother. The native will possess his/her own vehicle, servants and

kundali belongs to

a native who was born the 8th August 1941. He has a good house, a car and a couple of servants to serve him. Though his*lagnesh* is placed in the sign before debilitation (*neecchabhilashi*), it has its *ucchabhilashi*aspect on the

10th

in a government job.

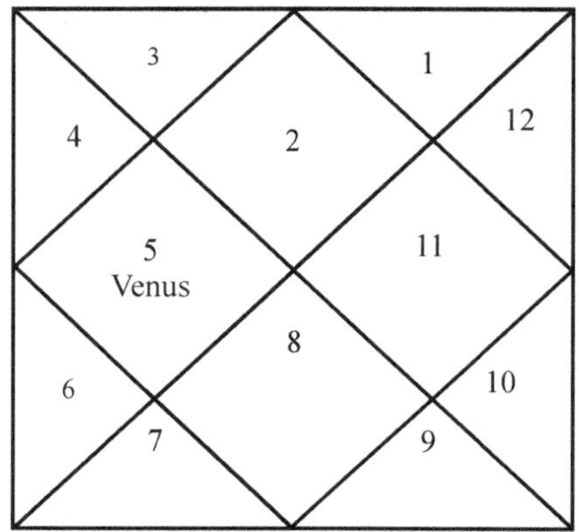

When *Lagnesh* is in the 5th house

When *Lagnesh*

get full respect in the society.

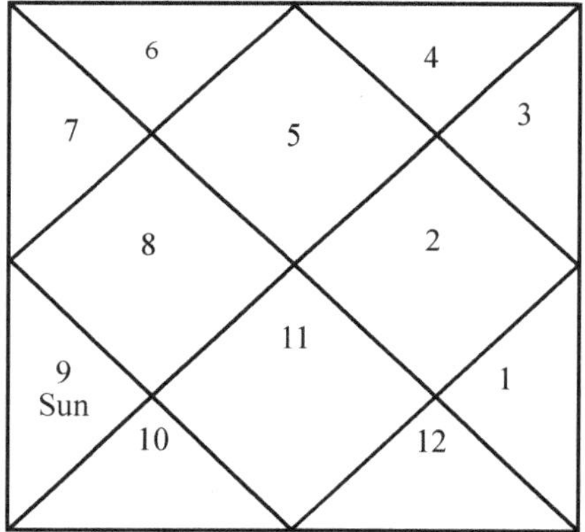

The native will be implicit with wisdom and dedicate his/her life to God. He/she will get good education and possess able children. The native may also be good in writing and may create new books. As this house is related to sports and games, the native will involve with sports or will have

music, arts and singing as well as connected with love affairs. As such the native will have such connections in life. The following *kundali* belongs to a native who was born on the 21st December, in 1939. Most of the above indicated characteristics and experiences the nativeenjoyed during his life time and after retirement from a senior position in Government, he has been living happily with his family and children. The Sun as *lagnesh* is placed in life on high positions.

When *Lagnesh* is in the 6th house

If the ascendant or *lagnesh* is placed in the 6th house, it will go on

planet is the ascendant in the chart/*kundali*. If Cancer sign is rising in the th house, it will provide simple demeanor to the native and he/she will always keep worried on account of others, as well as health related problems will mostly disturb the native. If Libra sign is rising in the *lagna* exalted in the 6th house. As such the native will destroy his/her enemies and will be a great politician. In case the sign Sagittarius is rising in *lagna* and Jupiter sits in the 6th house in its enemy's sign, it will surround the native with enemies and keep sick most of the time. The *kundali* given here below belongs to a native who is a medical doctor but involved with publishing business because his *lagnesh* Mercury (*Buddha*), the owner of ascendant, is rising in its friend's house. The native is also good in conversation and very well behaved.

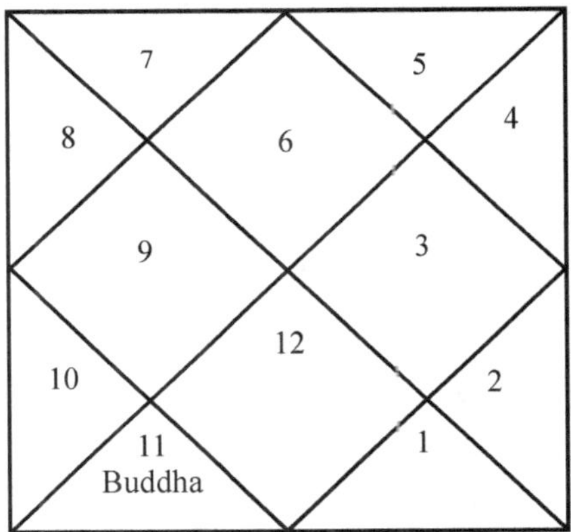

When *Lagnesh* is in the 7th house

The 7th house has so many things to tell about a *jatak* as it is the house which relates to one's wife or husband. Ancient astrology considers it a house that can tell about partnership in business as well as native's end of life or *markesh* can also be predicted by it, especially when the owner of the second house is Venus and seventh house belongs to Jupiter. But in that case if Mercury, being the owner of *lagna* (Virgo), is sitting in the 7th *markesh* yoga until some detrimental *Dasha* starts to end the life of *jatak*.

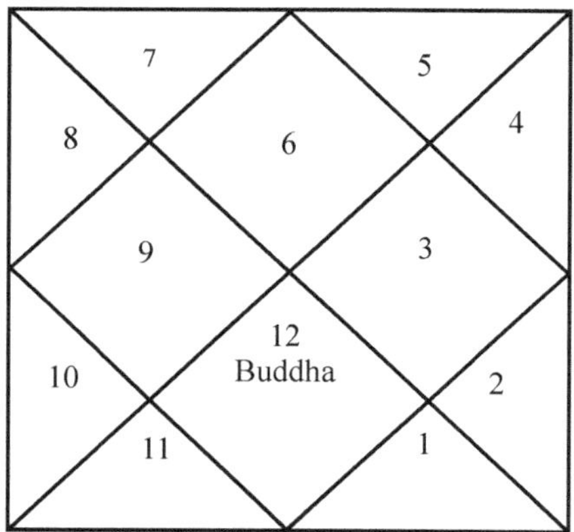

The *kundali* given here above belongs to a famous Indian cricketer who was born on the 24th April in 1975. His *lagneshBudha*, though debilitated and rising in the seventh house, it has its exalted aspects on the *lagna* of the native. Consequently, it gives the native a very positive outlook about life and makes him a kind hearted person.

When *Lagnesh* is in the 8th house

Indian astrologers consider this /house relating to one death. Generally this house can predict about the coming mishaps in an individual's life. But western astrologers take it to be a very positive house that can bestow a strong will and colossal physical strength. However, some astrologers consider it predicting about money through lottery or wealth coming from various hidden and unknown sources. It also predicts native's inclination towards God. It is also believed that if Saturn rises in Virgo sign (*Kanyalagna*) in this house, it can bestow 100 years' life to the native. The following *kundali*/chart belongs to a native whose *lagnesh* is rising in the 8th house. Consequently the native possesses extreme courage, physical

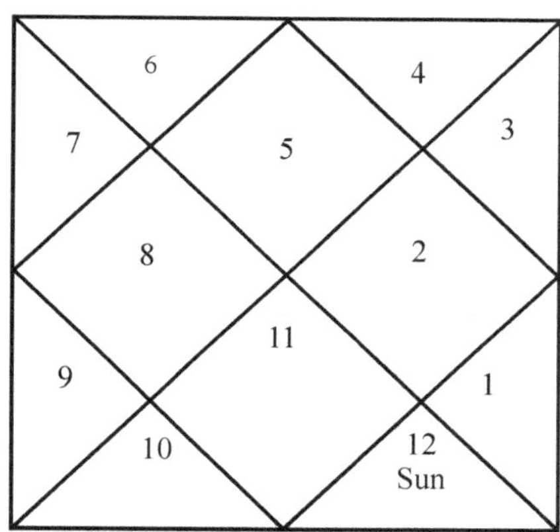

was born on the 23rd March in 1988. Though he had some initial problems

his duties honestly and with full determination.

When *Lagnesh* is in the 9th house

According to astrology, the ninth house is considered to be an auspicious

lagnesh is rising in this house. If the lagnesh rises in a friendly sign in this house, it will bestow lot of good luck to the native, provide good education and give possibilities to go abroad. The native will have a big family and earn lot of money in life. But all this will depend if no adverse aspects as well as no bad conjuncts tarnish this house. The above kundali belongs to a native whose lagnesh rises in the ninth house and is conjunct with the owner of the 4th house. He was born on 6th February in 1957. He has his own house in an important town in the western part of Rajasthan. He obtained good education and performed many journeys to several religious places in the country. He has a government job and is placed on a

other facilities. The meaning of being lucky according to astrology is to possess good education, earn lot of money and have a good family as well as travel abroad fruitfully. Most of these things are available to the native.

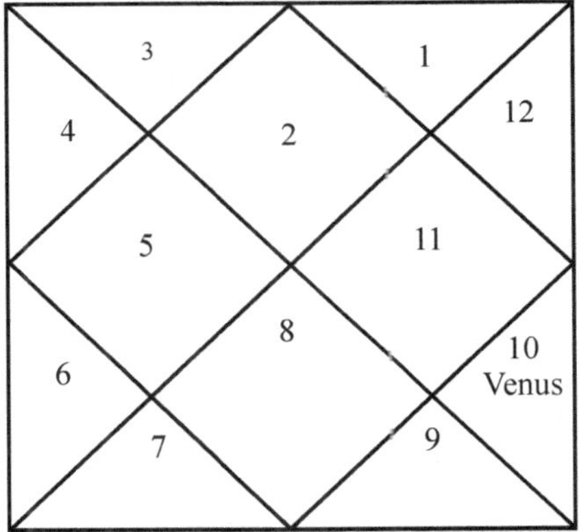

When *Lagnesh* is in the 10th house

This house indicates what type of job a native would do and what will be his/her inclinations towards work. This house also suggests father's

be interested to involve and which jobs will be more suitable for him/her. It also suggests how much he/she will get respect and love from the members of the family. Some astrologers reckon that this house suggests the extent of efforts the native will do at the workplace to go ahead and how much desire he/she possesses to advance in the job he/she is involved. The native whose *kundali*we are quoting here below was born on the 10th January, 1977. His *lagnesh*, Venus, is rising in the 10th most of the predictions given above. The native is employed in a foreign

of wealth and he has been enjoying life greatly.

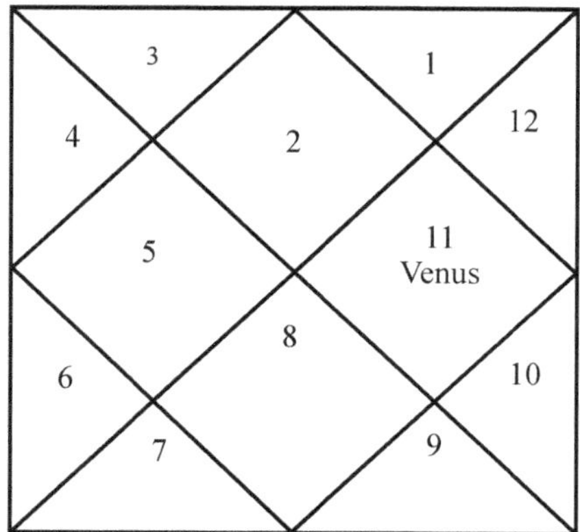

When *Lagnesh* is in the 11th house

According to astrology this house indicates the native's respect in the society. How much money he/she will earn and what kind of gains he/she will have time to time in life –are indicated by this house. If a strong *lagnesh* is rising in this house, the native will never suffer on account of

As he/she will have a strong position I society, hundreds of people will go on seeing him/her time to time. The following *kundali* belongs to a native who was born on 21st March, in 1953. As the native has been employed

status as well as enjoying his life in various ways, though honestly. As his *lagnesh*, Moon, is rising in an exalted sign in the 11th house, he has been

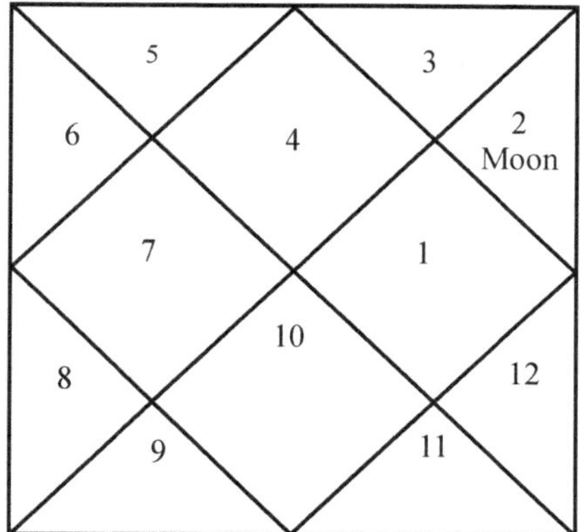

When *Lagnesh* is in the 12th house

The twelfth house indicates various reasons that are responsible to make an individual suffer in life. It also suggests long journeys, expenses, reasons of one's death, and achievement of salvation in life. The following *kundali* belongs to a native whose *lagnesh* is Saturn and rising in the 12th house in the sign Capricorn.

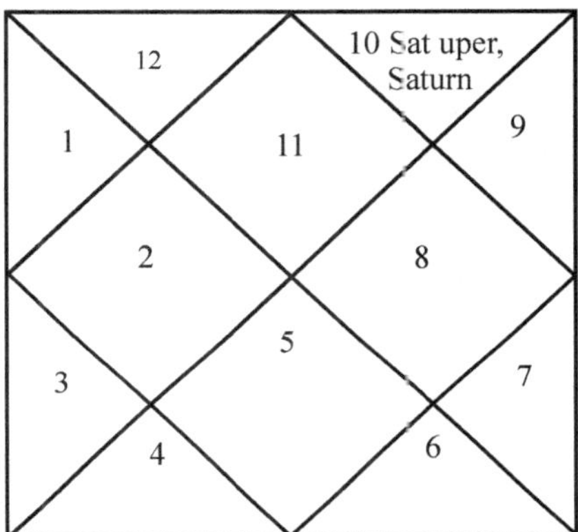

As Saturn is rising in its own sign in the 12th house, the native always consists of a strong desire to earn money in life. Though the *lagnesh* is in its own house, it has its aspect on the 2ndhouse. As a result he has always been spending money on various projects he desires time to time to complete.

The native was born on the 3rd January in 1953. His *lagnesh* is conjunct with Jupiter in the 12th and Saturn's aspects on the 2nd and the 6th houses always involve him in various sorts of expenses time to time. As the *lagnesh*has aspects on the second house, he creates enemies time to time by his sharp tongue which becomes the source of displeasure and unhappiness in life. Most of the predictions indicated so far about the native are true to a large extent.

Professions Predicted by the Nakchatras

According to ancient astrology and Ved Puranas, 9 Planets, 12 *Rashis* (signs) and 28 Nakchatras as well as Abhijeet Nakchatra'are responsible to decide what sort of work/job a person will follow in his/her life.Nakchatras and *Rashis*

moving from one sign to another and they exert their good and bad effect on humans. It is because of that that one needs to study astrology deeply as

attaining a degree of MBBS, that of a medical doctor, or to get a degree in

we consider the effect of a planet in a *kundali*, we need to see the aspects of other planets on a particular house or a planet. Without understanding all this, it would not be possible to reach the right results.

One must keep in mind that a planet rising in a particular Nakchatra provides results according to the *dasha* (period) or *unter-dasha* (sub-period). Likewise, it also gives results relating to the sign (*rashi*) in which it rises in the *kundali.* Besides, it (the planet) also provides results according/relating to the house it controls and has in view of its aspects on the houses. It is the Nakchatra which decides that 'which *dasha* will operate at the time of one's birth'. *Maharshi*Parashar holds that in all the *dashas*, it the *VinshotriDasha* that is supreme while predicting about events happening in one's life. *VinshotriDasha*can only be calculated with the help of the Nakchatras and these Nakchatras have their own qualities and accordingly they affect human beings during their lives. We shall discuss them ahead in this chapter. Out of 27 Nakchatras, 6 are *gandmul*Nakchatras, Out of these six Nakchatras, three belong to Ketu, which are *Aswani, Magha,* and*Mula,* and three belong to *Budha*/Mercury. These are, *Aswaslesa, Jestha,* and . One sign or *rashi* is constituted with two and a quarter Nakchatra.

At the time of birth, the *rashi* of the ascendant or that of the Moon,

are concerned. Therefore, when you decide that a *jatak* should choose a particular profession, you must consider these aspects in a chart/*kundali*, only then right results can be reached. However, you may also consider the Nakchatras that belongs to the tenth house as it is the house that we invariable consider to decide about one's profession or right choice for a job. But out of these three Nakchatras, whichever may be more powerful or possess good degrees, the *jatak's* profession could be decided accordingly. If you decide the profession of a *jatak* accordingly, it is expected that he/she will surely be successful in life.

Now here below we are providing the list of professions that usually belong to a particular Nakchatra. Try to understand all that thoroughly for being as accurate as possible while deciding one's profession in life.

Professions Predicted by the Planets Nakchatra

1. **Aswani :** Police, military, medical, skin treatment, prison, detainees' mansion, crime branch, railway machinery, iron, books, museum, horses' business, digging inspector, leadership, job in a factory, or a respected president of some concern.

   Most natives born in this nakchatra of Ketu are thoughtful, love studies, a teacher or engaged in teaching, an astrologer, honest,

   skin disease or may have moles on the body, get involved in family feuds and very ambitious.

2. **Bharni :** Most of the *jataks* born under the Bharni nakchatra are physically strong, like to subdue their opponents, get victory on enemies and expert in planning to attack enemies all of a sudden. They like to indulge in religious activities, are good photographers, painters or in other art related activities. Such a native could be a deceiver, may indulge in low kind of activities but always desirous to go ahead.

3. **Kritika :** A native born in Kritika nakchatra involves in land purchase, house and building construction, gets parental property, quite active, likes to do things in haste, dauntless, involves in shares, bats and such activities, may be a soldier, or in military services or police department, deals in oil or arms & ammunition industry, works in medical operations, surgery, navy (if born in Moon's period), defense department, works as a travel agent, resignation or retirement departments, or in a chemical industry, may work in a department related to blasting, iron steal, yellow metal, war

   priest or a pundit, a brahman, an astrologer, a potter or a butcher.

4. **Rohini :** A native born in Rohini nakchatra cares for others' rights, may work in hotels or restaurants, may be in-charge of restrooms, students' hostels, works in a bakery, sells lands, deals in fruits, automobiles, petrol, oil, milk, dairy farm, may be an ice-cream seller, deals in glass or plastic material, fragrance, soap, sandal oil, paints, liquids, shipping, navy, may be a judge, a politician, an ambassador, deals in skin material, threads, ready-made garments, sugar, sugar cane, geography or religious rites.

5. **Mrigshira :** A person born under Mrigshira nakchatra may work in a department related to machinery, ammunition or defense related electrical material, skin treatment related equipments, telephones, telegraph, an engineer in a telegraph department, a surgeon, a soldier, mathematician, an auditor, a writer, an ambassador, an accountant, a representative, an expert in distant related work, anexpert in geographic activities, a builder, deals in textiles, engineering, tap-recorder, may be involved in selling radios, minting work specialist,

jewelry, birds, animals, or be a forester, deal in sweet drinks, be a letter bearer or a postman, or a musician.

6. **Aarda :** The native born under Aarda nakchatra will indulge with accounts, may be a book-seller, custodian of food material, post

related departments, with atomic department, areal, advertisement through radio, or engaged in writing, research, excavations, in selling medicines (chemist), may work in a wine industry or engaged with the production of hard drinks, a weaver, expert in hand reading, engaged in a department that deals with general appointments of people, cinema, photography, night watchman, a money lender, one who earns through interests on money, a tourist guide or one who has been tortured by thieves.

7. **Punervasu (born under the third charan of Gemini sign) :** As Punervasu nakchatra belongs to Mercury (*Budha*), the jatak born under this nakchatramay be engaged with media, editing, publishing, corrections, inspections, a story writer, with advertisements, may be an orator, engaged in advertisements of various items through radio or news-papers, head of religious institutions, may be busy with law

civil judge, or a civil engineer, a dental doctor, mayor, counselor, school teacher, an interpreter, a translator, a secretary, registrar, an ambassador, news carrier, a post man, pundit, an astrologer, a mathematician, a calligraphist, one who sells clothes, or sells energy related material.

Punervasu (fourth charan) : A person born under the fourth *charan* of Punervasu nakchatra may work as a banker, physician, may be a religious leader, may be related with a temple or church, may be one who is always invited at auspicious occasions, a (respectful) witness at various occasions, an economist, incharge of accounts, an advocate, a judge, a lecturer, a principal of an institution, a headmaster, one who is a custodian of valuable things, a businessman, may work in navy, or transport department, may work in a general welfare department, work with water related departments, work with the construction of dams, may be a head of women institutions, or head of women departments.

8. **Pusya :** The native born under Pusay nakchatra may deal with mines, work in production department, or*mitte ka tel*, petrol, or petroleum material, coal, land, material related to water production, a coal businessman, or may work at lonely places, wells, mines, canals, cultivation, may be a land distributor, engaged with law departments, may be engaged with responsible positions, a spy, a plumber, a jailor, one who digs for the dead, owner of a place where dead people are buried or burnt, may work at the places of dead people, may be involved with selling of material for the dead, an engineer, a night watchman or a watch man in a building, one who works under lands, a mechanic, an operator, may work with oil related departments, work in navigation department, in air-force, one who collects material for machines, one who collects fees in the department which are related to the dead people.

9. **Aslesha :** The native born under Aslesha nakchatra may be engaged in selling assorted things, a pundit, engaged in cultural and religious activities, a representative, a sales person, an agent, one who likes to work in some business, may be engaged with international trade, work for the trade department, a typist, an in charge of correspondence, a language expert, one who sells ink or ink related material, sells paints, or a dealer of material connected with unexpected events or happenings. Such a native may be in charge of accounts or keep accounts, may work in an examination section, a local teacher, one who is engaged with complicated matters, an interpreter, a temporary translator, an ambassador, engaged with water supply, civil or supply departments, or a cloth merchant or a

with paper related material, a travel agent, a guide, an astrologer, a mathematician, a mathematics teacher, a midwife or may work in such a position successfully.

Besides all that, if a Jatak is born under a nakchatra that is related to Mercury (*Budha*), he/she may deal with bulbs, herbs, fruit-poison, may be an expert of worms related sickness, a copier, one who prepares things from mixed material, may work with plastic material, work to produce rubber, a physician, one who sells fodder and hay for animals and be an expert related to blood sickness.

10 **Magha :** The native born under Magha nakchatra may be a dealer of heavy and rich industry, engaged with chemicals that are related to the production of medicines, an advocate engaged with the physical assault clienteles, work for security or military departments, surgery, be a chemist, work in medical department, government job, engaged in police department, a *tantric*

one who is engaged with electricity related material, deals with operations, instruments, different kinds of business, expert in skin diseases.

Such a native will be well respected by the government. He may

sun beams, engaged with research related with already known things, successful to reach a high position from a low cadre, from a clerk to a minister, or from the position of a fourth-class servant to a minister's status.

11 **Purvaphaguni :** The native born in thisnakchatra will be engaged in a government job, communication department, radio station, may play some sort of musical instrument, may be engaged in a business related to musical instruments, expert in appreciating and assessing the ancient statues and art work on stone, may be a collector of old art and sculptures, in-charge of a museum, representative of entertainment or games & sports. Deal with automobiles, one who will make medicines for the crops and involve in spilling medicines on the crops, involved with cinema, theatre, studio or

and their treatment, protection and keeping animals, connected

hangings of people, skin, hotel, canteen, revenue, building houses for residence, connected with certain kinds of galleries, surgeon of children centers, an expert in love affairs and *kam rogs* (sex related diseases), an educationist, possess great knowledge in the

college, jail, may be an inspector who examines various things, involved with glass business, connected with art and culture, may be a producer, may work in brass material, in a cigar or smoking-items producing company, may be an adviser, or work in as thread ceremony perfectionist, a teacher, an editor, an administrator.

12. **Uttarfaguni :**
engaged in any kind of government job, may be an administrator, a ruler/king, director, doctor, a chemist, a druggist, a chemist, may belong to a security department or work in a shipping company, may be an engineer, or work in navy, be a writer, involve in share market, stock exchange, medical department that deals with pregnancy, hospitals, an expert in heart diseases, an eye surgeon, a

teacher, or a principal.

Either born in the Sun sign (Leo) or born in the nakchatra controlled

hearted. Such a native will be away from narrow-mindedness and hate low & immoral activities. Such a native goes on earning lot of money and be an expert in collecting wealth from an early stage. The native gets honour by government and high-ups. If thisnakchatra is not affected by any ill aspects of a planet, then such a native earns a great name and gets abundant respect from public. He/she is always careful and considerate during conversation, expert in the jobs involved, but careless in spending. He/she loves friends and relatives, and always favours those who stick to the truth, and possesses great memory.

13. **Hasta :** The native born in Hastanakchatra may be salesman, businessman, busy with over-sea communication, correspondence and advertisement, may obtain orders through mails, involve in shopping business, may be a clearing agent, may work in a cloth mill, or deal with the selling of clothes, may be involved in export or import business, be an engineer responsible to construct bridges, maintenance of canals and ditches, involve in ink business or printing press, may work as a lawyer, a cleaner, a stage artist, involved with sculpture work, work as a mason, a painter, an ambassador, may be a carrier of messages, work as a nurse, surgeon, a midwife, be a representative, involve in advertisement, may be a pundit, a poet or a compositor.

14. Chitra : One born in Chitra nakchatra may work as a lawyer, a surgeon, a scientist, a philosopher, involve with religious work or business, work in entertainment division of military or work in military, work in a security department, have partnership in business, expert in building construction, litho press, involve with art related advertisement, caretaker of stage and other matters. He/she involve in beauty enhancement programme, or scent/fragrance making business, work as a marriage mediator, be a marriage registrar, involve with games material, music, telephones, microscope, radio, television or tap-recorder business, be a doctor, a lades doctor, be a dress maker, involve with making cigarettes, involve with petroleum material business, automobile parts, ornaments, toys, paintings, or sculpture business.

15. Swati : A person born in Swatinakchatra may be involve with producing intoxicants or chemicals of any kind,be busy with moving a business,automobiles, travelling and export business, music,stage play, art, painting, photography, x-ray, *tantra-mantra*, electric material, glass, bulbs, tube-lights, air-conditioners, surgery instruments, toilet material, fancy stores, studios, bakery, wine store, be a bar tender, a gangster, a milkman, a milk seller, involve with plastic business, plastic material industry, mica, skin made material, sculpture, one who works in a kitchen or a cook, butler, one who

A jatak born under Vishakhanakchatra ( ) will be connected with international institutions, be a government servant, a business-partner and may earn lot of money through that activity, be a teacher, a professor, a writer of books, letter editor, an editor, one who is involved with critical reviews, a

He/she may be involved with shipping, may work for air travelling agencies, may be involved with keeping contacts with foreigners, a banker, may work in a bank, involve with building construction,

judge, a director, an auditor, a senior teacher, a doctor, a producer, involved with producing coloured papers, cinema, an advertiser, an artist of stage, may be involved with valuable ornaments' business, minting of money, a publisher, may deal with liquid or solid material, one who is involved with well-coming of people, involve with inauguration of programmes, a vice-chancellor, or an actor.

Vishakha (fourth charan) : A native born under the fourth charan of Vishakha may work in a bank, be a judge, a lawyer, work in an insurance company, work in a chemical plant and help produce chemicals, fodder, be an owner of great property, be a cultivator, involved in share business, in horse racing, battery making business, work in customs, industry area, be a defense minister, a village magistrate, work in

treatment literature, be a book publisher, a doctor, a surgeon, or an advisor.

17. Anuradha : One who is born in Anuradha nakchatra, he may be a

in medicinal science, be a surgeon, have interest in instrumental music, be a civil engineer, work in industry, or have business in metal or iron, may work in minting department, be an inventor, be a factory worker, be a dead skin tender, involved in business of woolen and old material, a creator of new things, may work in a rail engine, work as a mason, may be a porter, involve in cleaning of

servant, serve others, be a nurse, an attendant, a watchman, a pilot, a driver, a dacoit, teeth specialist, doctor who takes care of secret illness, a jailor, work in oil department, be a magistrate, a contractor,

make pitchers, may help in making bath-material, be a crane driver,

nut, a *banjara*, or a butcher.

18. Jestha : One who is born under Jestha nakchatra, he may be a chemical engineer, may work at a minting place, be a publisher, produce ink in lots, a typewriter, a shorthand typist, work in a cloth mill, be a weaver, a machine man, involved in the groups of industries, involved in making dams, canals, electricity, digging ponds, preparing musical material, violins, *jaltarangs,* be an insurance agent expert, involved in making surgical instruments, making tonics, work in army, navy, be an accountant, work in advertisement companies, in boilers, may mend pump sets, work in telegraph department, radio, be a mechanic, ply boats in a river or canal, be a representative, a clerk, a writer, an announcer, a serum producer, a mathematician, work as an active announcer for advertisements, expert in accounts and related work, a media personal, be a dancer, an artist, an ambassador (*bidushak*).

19. **Mul :** The *jatak* who is born under Mul nakchatra will mostly involve with religious rites, be a lawyer, a judge, a teacher a *purohit*, a priest, a , and an expert in the explanations of the *Puranas*. He may be a *katha bachak*, an ambassador, leader of a party, be involved in politics, be an expert and appreciator to literary writings and material, be trust-worthy, be an ordinary worker, a secretary, a private secretary to someone, a physician, a , an , a social worker, an elected public nominee to the government (*parshad*), a provision businessman, be involved in horse-racing, one who takes advantage from various sorts of programmes that are planned, be rich through extraordinary plans and programmes, involved in international business, a speaker in *Vidhan Sabha*

selling business man, or sell herbs or underground products, may produce machine tools, work in a spying (intelligence) department, be a writer, an interpreter, or involved in selling things for general enjoyment and pleasure.

20. **Purvaashad :** The native born under Purvaashadnakchatra will be a judge, an advocate, a banker, a cashier, accounts examiner, may work

with sugar, silk, sweets, or biscuits, involved in road construction, may construct Goddess's temple, involve in social service and

awards, be a president, be ananimal doctor, may run a nursery, be involved with cinema, music, radio station, bank, television, be an artist, an actor, involved with foreign trade, making of clothes, may sell dressing (shrangar) material, deal in stock exchange, director of a hospital, be a co-partner, deal with local medicines, children's (birth) hospital, related with health care department.

21. **Uttraashad(Pratham Charan) :**
(Pratham Charan)nakchatra,hemay be an elephant rider & controller (*mahawat*), a wrestler, a horse rider, one who tends elephants, owner of immovable property, likes to involve in skirmishes or battles, be a God fearing person, practice yoga, enjoys life, eager for good behavior, good mannered, like privileges, happy in giving

a judge, a politician, a banker or one who works in a bank, work

work at religious places, may be involved in international trade, connected with embassy, a commissioner, a collector, work in department, or ports, hospitals, *dharmarth* institutions,be an editor, or a publisher, director of administrative services.

Uttraashad (Third Charan) :
(*third charan*) nakchatra may hold any responsible position, owner of property, mines, may work in income tax department, or property

advisor, in charge of a control room, ancient buildings, statues, may be owner of wool stocks, may work as a homoeopathist, a writer, an engineer, may have the knowledge of ancient languages, be a researcher, may be involved with skin trade, be a spy or work in that department, work as a protector or custodian of something, and be a security personal.

22. **Shravan :** The native born under Shravan nakchatra may work in mines, or be the owner of the mines product, work with oil related material, oil, kerosene, petrol, material used in burning or cooking etc, wells, pump sets, tube wells, lifts or work in irrigation department,

cultivator, a plumber, a mines engineer, one who sells ice-cream, may be connected with fridge work, or air-conditioner, be a night watchman, a nurse, a mid-wife, or one who works underground, a driver, be involved in pearl business, work in sub-marine, involve with skin business, be a priest, or one who works in a temple, etc.

The native born under Ghanistha

lohar (work to mend iron instruments), may involve in making utensils, a hunter, a successful engineer to work in mines or under-ground, may work to keep account of the dead, one who sells material for the dead, may work to collect tax on property, keep animals, be in charge of a hostel, work in a *dharamshala* or public guest house. be a chat, a dacoit, a killer, work as insurance agent, be a philosopher, a *sadhu*, a mendicant, *a kaji* (a Muslim magistrate), be a butcher, a surgeon who takes care of fractures, one who collects bones, who takes care of displaced persons, works in an industry, or keeps instruments, deals in spare parts, distillery, wine industry, police, works as a spy, or be a grain or potato business man.

Ghanishta (remaining two charans) : The native born under Ghanistha (the remaining two charans)nakchatra may deal in cultivation, tea or coal business, or iron and steel business, may work in an explosives department, be a researcher, work in mines, in telecasting department, in press, in foundry, deal in machinery,

work in television department, work as an interpreter, in export & imports, as a lab assistant, may take care of poisonous things or poison, or intoxicants, silk, locks & keys, may sell utensils, be a typist, a computer operator, a time keeper, an inspector, or examiner.

24. Shatbhisa : The native born under Shatbhisa nakchatra may be a scientist, a magician, may keep knowledge of extraordinary things, may work in a magnetic related department, a computer operator, work in radio or television departments, be a mathematician, involved in electricity related jobs, energy department, in an air force, may work as an ear-piercing petty worker, work as a geography expert, an astrologer, may be a researcher of ancient culture, the *Purans*, deal in old things, be a psychologist, be a historian,

depart., in stock exchange depart., in taxation department, be a jail superintendent, may work in oil department, be a translator, may work on autobiographies, work in a lab., in a collection house, in a factory, an expert of certain things, may be expert in making maps, be a planner, a photographer, may work to make pots from earth,

One who is born in

space related scientist, or may work as an accountant, be a geologist, an astrologer, be an aurved doctor, work in air, be a head of an urban trust department, work in non-governmental department, in stock exchange department, a dealer in shares, an air-force personal, a pilot, a researcher, be in planning department, may have investments

related printing department, be in a treasury, work in security, a driver, a president of a concern, be a producer,

Purvabhadrapad (fourth charan) : One who is born in Purvabhadrapad (fourth charans)nakchatra,he may be a politician, a professor, a lecturer, a minister, a counselor, or may be a President, Governor, law expert, be related to social or religious work, be a judge, trustee, jail inspector, President of a reform committee, be a superintendent of a hospital, a mayor, a member of Planning Commission, or tourism department, involved in investigations, be a war prisoner, a publisher, a story teller, a book seller or an

26. **Uttarabhadrapad :**
he may be related withHome Ministry, jail- management, be a refugee, in charge of a sanitarium, a bone specialist, related with war prisoners, be a political prisoner, related to mines imprisonment, a mine prisoner, involved with mine digging, be an engineer, connected with export &import business, person related to parental property matters, be a member of a club, concerned with public *nikaya,*
submarine, shipping, foundry work, may be related with espionage, insurance, law work, ship-building, construction of under-ground passages, law, engineering and water related work.

27. **Revti :** The native born under Revtinakchartra may be a publisher, an editor, be related o religious work, may work in civil engineering department, in public works department, be involved in share business, may be related to advertisement section in a press, work in news-papers, be a *pracharak*
something), a drum player, be a steno, may work as a welcome

controller in telecast department, may work in a religious place or department, be a lawyer, a magistrate, a professor, a messenger, work in an embassy, be a telephone operator, be a representative,

in international trade,be an auditor, a trustee, be a governor, a vice-chancellor, work in a university, in a job offering department, be a poetry writer, in water department, work on coast, on a port trust,

work in an income-tax department

In astrology in whatevernakchartra the Moon rises at the time of birth of a native, according to its *charan* (degrees) the parents name the child. There are four degrees or parts of a nakchartra. It is because of that, that four different kinds of names can be made from that *charan* at the time of the birth of a child. One sign (*rashi*) has 30 degrees. But each nakchartra has 13 degrees and 20 *kalas*. Therefore, there are two and a quarternakchartras in one *rashi*. It is because of that, that one nakchartra is divided into two different signs (*rashis*) at times. At such occasions it is imperative to be careful to name a child properly. When a nakchartra is divided into two *rashis* (signs), it may so happen that the *rashi* may fall into the 6th or 12th house which is not considered good.

At the time of marriage both the charts (*kundalis*), that of a boy & of a girl, are compared for their compatibility. In all there are 36 *gunas* such as *NadiVasya* or *Tara gunas* etc. It is important and has been considered important from the ancient times that after comparing both the *kundalies* (charts) ---that of the boy and the girl proposed for marriage, if up to 18 or more *gunas* come up after calculation, they are considered comparable and good. Then a marriage can be approved astrologically.

By matching the *gunas* means considering the conduct of both, the boy and the girl, compatible. If 18 or more than 18 *gunas* come after calculations, it is considered that not only certain characteristic among the boy & the girl proposed for marriage are good, but they will also be able to run their family well. But if *gunas* are not match able, means they are not up to 18 or more at the time of comparing the charts (*kundalies*), it would mean a miss-match of the two charts and two lives. It may result in a quarrel abiding atmosphere in the family and consequently both, the boy and the girl will remain unhappy throughout their lives.

Besides comparing the *gunas*, it is also important to compare the planets in both the *kundalies* as without that the comparison will not be complete. In all, it is only up to 25 % that the *gunas* affect one's life. But comparison of the planets in both the charts (*kundalies*) is very important. The general belief held by most of the astrologers is that the planets affect one's life up to 75 % as more depends on the planets to keep one's life happy and successful. It is also important to compare the *yoni* in the *kundalies*. If the boy is in a 'lion'*yoni* and the girl in a 'cow'*yoni* in the *kundalies*, they both are not compatible. If one is in a (god's) *yoni* the other is in devil (*rakchas*), then the *kundalies* are not compatible.

Most astrologers don't approve such charts while comparing a boy's and a girl's *kundali*. We are providing here under in details about nakchartras and *rashi charans*. With the help of it, you may learn about your nakchartra.

The translation of the charts in English has not been made to avoid any confusion as there are exactly no words in English language of the astrological terms given in the tables. Hope the readers can manage with them.

Nakchatra	Charan	Yoni	Mahaver Yoni	Gan	Nadi
Aswani	चू चे चो ला	अश्व	महिष	देव	आदि
Bharni	ली लू ले लो	गज	सिह	मनुष्य	मध्या
Kritika	अ (प्रथम चरण)	मेढ़ा	वानर	राक्षस	अन्त्या

Aries or Mesa is a *charrashi* and *agni* *tatwa rashi*. It rises from the rear. It is situated in the East, its colour is red, and it possesses an aggressive conduct/attitude. It is hard, manlyand hot in attitude. It belongs to *Chatriya jati*. It becomes strong during the day and lives in hills and forests. *Mangal*
rashi but Saturn is in its debilitated sign in *mesa* or Aries sign.

Nakchatra	Charan	Yoni	Mahaver Yoni	Gan	Nadi
Kritikaa (3 charan)	इ उ ए	मेढ़ा	वनर	राक्षस	अन्त्या
Rohini	ओ वा वी व	सर्प	न्योला	मनुष्य	अन्त्या
Mrigsira (2 charan)	व वो	सर्प	न्योला	देव	मध्या

Tauras *rashi* is like a bull in shape. It is *sam*, well established, a woman like, and has the earth It has a *salral* (simple) conduct, rules the South direction, may get sick easily, and represent *Vaish jati* (community). Its colour is white like yogurt, and is strong during night. It roams in even lands, and is cold by nature. Its owner is Venus, and the Moon is in exalted state in this sign.

Nakchatra	Charan	Yoni	Mahaver Yoni	Gan	Nadi
Mrigsira (2 Charan)	का की	सर्प	न्योला	देव	मध्या
Aarda	कु घ ङ छ	वान	मृग	मनुष्य	आदि
PunarVasu(3 Charan)	के को हा	मार्जार	मूषक	देव	आदि

Thissign represents two sorts of conducts or two faces. It has (air) *tatua*, and is hard hearted, and indicates the West direction. It has a dual shape—a man and a woman, having green complexion. Its impact is hot, liquidity, and is reckoned *sudra* in jati (cast). It is strong during the day, loves to roam in jungles. Its owner is Mercury (*Budha*) and Rahu is considered in exalted sign in this *rashi* (sign), but Ketu is supposed to give bad results in this sign.

Nakchatra	Charan	Yoni	Mahaver Yoni	Gan	Nadi
Punar Vasu (Charan1)		मार्जा	मूषाक	देव	आदि
Pusp	हू हे हो डा	मेढ़ा	नवर	छेव	मध्या
Ashlesha	डी डू डे डो	मार्जा	मूषक	राक्षस	अन्त्या

It is *sam*, womanish, and is water *tatwarashi.* It shape is like a *kekra*, has a civil (pleasant) conduct and it indicates the North direction. Its effect is coldish, and creates cold and cough. It is Brahman by cast, white in colour like milk. It is strong during night, and loves to stay in water. Its owner is the Moon and Jupiter is in its exalted state in this sign, but *Mangal* (Mars) is in its debilitated sign in this *rashi.*

Nakchatra	Charan	Yoni	Mahaver Yoni	Gan	Nadi
Magha	म मी मूमे	मूषक	बिडाल	राक्षस	अन्त्या
Pu Pha	मो टा टी टू	मूषक	बिडाल	मनुष्य	मध्या
	हे	गै	व्याघ्र	मानव	आदि

. It is hardin

jungles. Its owner is the Sun. a

Nakchatra	Charan	Yoni	Mahaver Yoni	Gan	Nadi
	टो पा पी	गै	व्याघ्र	मानव	आदि
Hastha	पू भा ण ठ	महिष	अश्व	छेव	आदि
Chitra(2Charan)		व्याघ्र	गै	राक्षस	मध्या

This sign also represents two sorts of behavior. It has the earth , it possesses even conduct, and rules the South direction. It has an airy fervor in its conduct, is dry and cold. It represents *Veshya jati,* colour *pandu*, green and spotty. It is strong during night. It loves to roam in even lands. Its owner is *Budha* (Mercury) and its conduct is unstable.

Nakchatra	Charan	Yoni	Mahaver Yoni	Gan	Nadi
Chitra (2 Charan)	रा री	व्याघ्र	गै	राक्षस	मध्या
Swati	रू रे रो ता	महिष	अश्व	छेव	अन्त्या
Vishakha (3 charan)	ती तू रे	व्याघ्र	गै	राक्षस	अन्त्या

It is visham male and movable sign (rashi). It has airy , which is cruel in nature. It represents *sudra*cast and its complexion is white like yogurt. It is strong during day and roams in forests. Its shape is like a 'balance', its effect warmish and liquid like and indicates constipation. Its owner is Venus. Saturn becomes exalted in this sign and accordingly provides results, but the Sun gives debilitated effect or becomes debilitated.

Nakchatra	Charan	Yoni	Mahaver Yoni	Gan	Nadi
Vishakha (1 Charan)	ते	व्याघ्र	गै	राक्षस	अन्त्या
Anuradha	न नी नू ने	मृग	वान	देव	मध्या
Jeishtha	यो या यी यू	मृग	वान	राक्षस	आदि

It is *satya, sam* and *istri* *rashi* (sign).It has water , and possesseseven temperament. It indicates the North direction. Its *jati* is Brahman and red in complexion. It enjoys during nights and roams near water as well as at the places where insects reside. Its effect is watery and cold and its sign is Scorpio. *Mangal* (Mars) is its owner and the Moon becomes debilitated in this sign.

Nakchatra	Charan	Yoni	Mahaver Yoni	Gan	Nadi
Muula	य यो भा भी	वान	मृग	राक्षस	आदि
Purvaashad	म ध फ ढ़	वानर	मेढ़ा	मनुष्य	मध्या
	भे	न्योला	सर्न	मनुष्य	अन्त्या

This is a and possesses duel sort of sign. It is *agni* as and possesses a cruel temperament.It is *chatri* in cast (*jati*), is vile predominate, and indicates the East direction. It roams on hills, its effect is dry and its colour yellow. Its owner is Jupiter. According to the ancient astrologers Ketu is exalted in this sign but Rahu provides a debilitated effect in it.

Nakchatra	Charan	Yoni	Mahaver Yoni	Gan	Nadi
(3 Charan)	भो ज जी	न्योला	सर्प	मनुष्य	अन्त्या
Shravan	खी खू खे खो	वानर	मेढ़ा	देव	अन्त्या
Ghnishtha (2 Charan)	ग गी	सिंह	गज	राक्षस	मध्या

It is a *sam* and *istri* (woman) movable sign (*rashi*). Earth is its and it possesses an even temperament. *Vat* predominate is its roaming place, and its effect is dry. It is indicated by a crocodile sign. Its owner is Saturn, Mars is exalted in this sign but Jupiter is debilitated in this sign.

Nakchatra	Charan	Yoni	Mahaver Yoni	Gan	Nadi
Ghanishtaaa (2 Charan)		सिंह	गज	राक्षस	मध्या
Shatbhesha	गो स सी सू	अश्व	महिष	राक्षस	आदि
(3 Charan)	से सो द	सिंह	गज	मनुष्य	आदि

Its *rashi* is airy, and temperament is cruel. Its *jati* (cast) is *sudra* and it indicates the West direction. Its colour is black and effect dry and liquidity. It is strong during the day and loves to roam in forests. Its owner is Saturn.

Nakchatra	Nakchatra	Yoni	Mahaver Yoni	Gan	Nadi
Purvabhadrapad (1 Charan)		सिंह	गज	मनुष्य	आदि
Bhadrapad (3 Charan)	दू य झ ञ	गै	व्याघ्र	मनुष्य	मध्या
Revti	दे दो च ची	गज	सिंह	देव	अन्त्या

It *samistrirashi* as well as it possesses a duel temperament. Its is watery and is civil in temperament. Cough predominant in it and it indicates the North direction. Its *jati* is Brahman, and complexion (colour) *pingla* whitish, yellow. It is strong during night and it loves to roam in

of this sign (*rashi*) is Jupiter and Venus is exalted while Mercury (*Budha*) is debilitated in this sign. Rahu provides low or negative effect in this sign.

An Easy Way to Calculate Mahadasha from the Nakchatras

One Nakchatrahas13*ansh* (divisionsa)and four *charans*. If we divide 13-20 by four, then one *charan* will consist of 3 *ansh* and 20 *kalas*. Now if we want to know that in which *charan* one is born,we would need to see the position and speed of the Moon at that time. On the day of birth of someone we simply consider Moon's Nakchatra that day.

One Nakchatranearly stays for 24 hours but sometimes this duration of time is also reduced. It can be examined from the Hindi *Panchang* (calander)

out the correct time of birth of an individual. Besides, it is also necessary to

its speed depends on the Artic and Mediteranean lines & division (imaginery

According to astrology the Sun and the Moon are very important planets. When the Sun is in Aadra Nakchatra, it is the beginning of rains. Therefore, we make a *kundlai* having Aarda Nakchatra to check for rains.

The Sun stays in one Nakchatra for nearly 12 to 13 days.In Aadra Nakchatra the rains start, but stop when the Sun comes in Hasta Nakchatra. It is because of that,thatour *rishies* and *munies* calculated the beginning of a day from the Sun rise. However, during these days English dates are changed after one minute from the mid-night at 12 O'clock.

Astrology is based on mathematical calculations and it is not based on conjuctors or imagination. It is based on the movements of the Sun and the Moon. Some think that English dates have been initially calculated with

the planest and the nakchatras. If one does not do all that very carefully and seriously, there are chances to commit mistakes. A correct *kundali* can only be made by calculating the correct time of the planets' movement as well that of the nakchatras. Only then correct future of an individual can be predicted.

Though these days a *kundali* can be made by computers, but even then one has to possess right knowledge of astrology and of the movements of the planets etc. Only then right predications can be made. Most *kundalis* made through a computer are not complete as there are so many things in it to predict. The *kundalies* made through computers may not have the complete degrees of *lagna* and neither that of the planets. Which planets are retrograding and which are moving in the right direction-- all these details are also missing from the computer made *kundalies*. Which period in operating at the time of birth and which is running at the time of asking

Our years at someone's birth start from the movements of the Sun. The Sun rises in Aries sign around 13th April and then after its complete circle it completes one year. The Sun is considered in an exalted state while it is in Aries sign and in Aswani Nakchatra. Aswani Nakchatra is owned by Ketu and Ketu provides *mokcha* to a person. This is what an individual desires

God's house, what else he/she would need. The Sun represents soul or Atma of an individual and *lagna* depends on the movement of the Sun and the sign in which it is rising at the time of one's birth. For example if one is born at the time of the Sun rise, in his/her *kundali* the Sun will be rising in the *lagna*

be born during the midnight; if the Sun is rising in the seventh house, it is about to set in the evening; if the Sun is in in the tenth house, the *jatak* will be born during the noon time.

The *Mangal* (Mars) and the Sun in the tenth house are considered very strong (*dig bali*). The Sun and *Mangal*

when it is very hot. Now we will tell you an easy way/procedure which will help you to reckon the movements of the planets correctly. What *dahsha* will operate at the time of one's birth will depend on the Moon's movement in a particular sign or *rashi*.

As the Moon proceeds further so the dashas also starts getting lesser and lesser. For example, Aswani Nakchatra belongs to Ketu. Ketu's *mohadasha dasha* runs for seven years.If Aswani Nakchatra runs for 24 hours, the *madhadsha* will operate according to the time left out of 24 hours of Aswani Nakchatra at the time when one's birth takes place. That means as the Moon will proceed further in 24 hours in Aswani Nakchatra, the period of *mahadasha* will be left out accordingly. It has already been projected in the tables given in the previous chapter. For example, when

Ketu will be left out for 6 years and10 months. In one degree there are 60 *kalas*, which the Moon will complete rotating in 120 minutes or two hours. That also means that the Moon will croos 10 *kalas* in 20 minutes. That also means that the Moon will complete its transit in the Aswani Nakchatra in about two hours. At that time the Ketu's *mahadasha* will be left out for 6 years, 5 months and 21 days only. Likewise we can learn about the transits or movements of all the Nakchatra.

Our earth is like a glove and possesses 360 degrees in its rounded shape. If we divide 360 by 12 *rahies*, the result will be that each *rashi* will be divided into 30 *anshs.* In one *rashi* there are Years*kalas*. Just for your convenience and better understanding we are providing here under all the information contained in the underneath table unfolding which Nakchatra starts from which degree at a particular period of a dasha of a planet, and will it stay up to what time, year, months and days. It also contains for how many years a *dasha* will continue operating in a particular Nakchatra.

Sl. No.	**Nakchtra**	**From which to which Nakchtra**	**Owner of Nakchtra**	**Dasha**
1.	Aswani	0-0-0 froms 0-13-0 to	Ketu	7 Years (Garmul Nakchtra)
2.	Bharani	0-13-20 from 0-26-40 to	Venus	20Years
3.	Kritika	0-26-40 from 1-10-0 to	Sun	6Years
4.	Rohini	1-10-0 from 1-23-20to	Moon	10Years
5.	Mragshira	1-23-26from2-6-40to	Mangal	7Years
6.	ArdaZ	2-6-40 ls 2-20-0 rd	Rahu	18Years
7.	Punarvasuq	2-20-0 ls 3-3-20 rd	Jupiter	16 Years
8.	Pushp	3-3-20 ls 3-16-40 rd	Saturn	19Years
9.	Ashlesha	3-16-40 ls 4-0-0 rd	Budha	17Years (Ganmul Nakchtra)
10.	Magha	4-0-0 ls 4-13-20 rd	Ketu	7 Years (Ganmul Nakchtra)
11.	Purvafaguni	4-13-20 ls 4-26-40 rd	Ketu	20 Years
12.		4-26-40 ls 5-10-0 rd	SunZ	6 Years
13.	Hasth	5-10-0 ls 5-23-20 rd	Moon	10 Years

14.	Chitra	5-23-20 ls 6-6-40 rd	Mangal	7 Years
15.	Swati	6-6-40 ls 6-20-0 rd	Rahuq	18 Years
16.	Vishakha	6-20-0 ls 7-3-20 rd	Jupiter	16 Years
17.	Anuradha	7-3-20 ls 7-16-40 rd	Saturn	19 Years
18.	Jestha	7-16-40 ls 8-0-0 rd	Budha	17 Years (Ganmul Nakchtra)
19.	Mula	8-0-0 ls 8-13-20 rd	Ketu	7 Years
20.	Purva-ashada	8-13-20 ls 8-26-40 rd	Venus	20 Years
21.		8-26-40 ls 9-10-0 rd	SunZ	6 Years
22.	Shravan	9-10-0 ls 9-23-20 rd	Moon	10 Years
23.	Ghnistha	9-23-20 ls 10-6-40 rd	Mangal	7 Years
24.	Shatbhisha	10-6-40 ls 10-20-0 rd	Rahu	18 Years
25.	Purvabhadrapad	10-20-0 ls 11-3-20 rd	Jupiter	16 Years
26.		11-3-20 ls 11-16-40 rd	Saturn	19 Years
27.	Shrevati	11-16-40 ls 12-0-0 rd	Budha	17 Years (Ganmul Nakchtra)

We really want to understand this issue of *dasha* operations

any help is required. In a day including the night, there are 24 hours. That means a day and night have 60 *gharis.* Every hour has two and a half *gharis.* Thus, in 24 hours 12 *lagans* transit one after another or it marks

Moon transits almost one *ansh*
degrees the Moon has travelled in one *rashi* has been clearly given in

time and dasha, you would need to add the Moon's degrees it has already

operating at that particular time. This way, one can calculate the dashas qauite accurately, running currently at the time of a child's birth and there will hardly be any error in the calculation of Mahadasha if you do it this

done can be completed in a few minutes with very little mistakes. Even otherwise, generally people calculate 30 days in a month, whereas almost alternatively, there are 31 days in a month and the entire year contains 365

year. Just for example,ifa child is born on 24th April in 2002, and its *kundali* is prepared, then good or bad period can only be known with the help of Mahadasha. It is because of that that we always keep in view the position of the Moon at 5.30 in the morning. In the above case, it was 3/12/46/44.

it we add as given below:

3 | 12 | 46 | 44

1 *in two hour*

3 | 13 | 46 | 44

45 *add half an hour*

3 | 14 | 01 | 44

Add 15 *ansh*

Moon as 3 | 15 | 01 | 44|. Now if we check this difference at 15 *ansh*, the *dasha* period that remains is 2 years 4 months and 15 days only. It was just one *kala* and 44 more. When we go 4 *kala* further and after subtracting 18 days from the moon's period, the *dasha* that would runwill only remain for 2 years, 3 months and 27 days only.

Now examine the second example. In case someone is born in the evening at 8 o'clock,and if we subtract 5.30 from 20, then 14.30 kala remains of the Moon. Now see the folloing calculations for your reference.

3 | 12 | 46 | 44

7 15

3 | 19 | 93 | 44

ansh and 3 *kalas*. The *Mahadasha* of Budha (Mercury) operates for 14 years and 0 months and 9 days. If we subtract the period of 4 out of that, then after subtracting 1 month and 1 day, the remaining period will be 14 years and 11 months and 18 days.

There is another method too to calculate *dasha* system. It is done with the help of *isthakal*. But it takes a lot of time to calculate that *dasha* system.But with the system explained above, is simpler and takes only a few minutes to reach at the right results as far as the calculations of *dasha* are concerned. We provide a table here under for your convenience and *Dashas* and *Mahadashas* of an individual at the time of his/her birth.

have an easy excess to them. However, we are also providing equivalent English terms of the main Hindi terminology contained in the table for your convenience.

Table -1

चन्द्र स्पष्ट		चन्द्र राशि मेष–सिंह–धनु				चन्द्र राशि वृष–कन्या–मकर				चन्द्र राशि मिथुन–तुला–कुम्भ				चन्द्र राशि कर्क–वृश्चिक–मीन			
अंश	कला	भोग्य	वर्ष	मास	दिन	भोग्य	वर्ष	मास	दिन	भोग्य	वर्ष	मास	दिन	भोग्य	वर्ष	मास	दिन
00	00	केतु	7	0	0	सूर्य	4	6	0	मंगल	3	6	0	गुरु	4	0	0
0	10		6	10	29		4	5	3		3	4	28		3	9	18
0	20		6	9	27		4	4	6		3	3	27		3	7	6
0	30		6	8	26		4	3	9		3	2	25		3	4	24
0	40		6	7	24		4	2	12		3	1	24		3	2	12
0	50		6	6	23		4	1	15		3	0	22		3	0	0
1-1	00		6	5	21		4	0	8		2	11	21		2	9	8
1	10		6	4	20		3	11	21		2	10	21		2	9	18
1	20		6	3	18		3	10	24		2	9	18		2	4	24
1	30		6	2	17		3	9	27		2	8	16		2	2	12
1	40		6	1	15		3	9	0		2	7	15		2	0	0
1	50		6	0	14		3	8	3		2	6	13		1	9	18
2	00		5	11	12		3	7	6		2	5	12		1	7	6
2	10		5	10	11		3	6	9		2	4	10		1	4	24
2	20		5	9	9		3	5	12		2	3	9		1	2	12
2	30		5	8	8		3	4	15		2	2	7		1	0	0
2	40		5	7	6		3	3	18		2	1	6		0	9	18
2	50		5	6	5		3	2	21		2	0	4		0	7	6
3	00		5	5	3		3	1	24		1	11	2		0	4	24
3	10		5	4	2		3	0	27		1	10	1		0	2	12

चन्द्र स्पष्ट		चन्द्र राशि मेष–सिंह–धनु				चन्द्र राशि वृष–कन्या–मकर				चन्द्र राशि मिथुन–तुला–कुम्भ				चन्द्र राशि कर्क–वृश्चिक–मीन			
अंश	कला	भोग्य	वर्ष	मास	दिन	भोग्य	वर्ष	मास	दिन	भोग्य	वर्ष	मास	दिन	भोग्य	वर्ष	मास	दिन
3	20		5	3	00		3	0	0		1	9	0		19	0	0
3	30		5	1	29		2	11	3		1	7	28		18	9	4
3	40		5	0	27		2	10	6		1	6	27		18	6	9
3	50		4	11	26		2	9	9		1	5	25		18	3	13
4	00		4	10	24		2	8	12		1	4	24		18	0	18
4	10		4	9	23		2	7	15		1	3	22		17	9	22
4	20		4	8	21		2	6	18		1	2	21		17	6	27
4	30		4	7	20		2	5	21		1	1	19		17	4	1
4	40		4	6	18		2	4	24		1	0	18		17	1	6
4	50		4	5	17		2	3	27		0	11	16		16	10	10
5	00		4	4	15		2	3	0		0	10	15		16	7	15
5	10		4	3	14		2	2	3		0	9	13		16	7	15
5	20		4	2	12		2	1	6		0	8	12		16	1	24
5	30		4	1	11		2	0	9		0	7	10		15	10	28
5	40		4	0	9		1	11	12		0	6	9		15	8	3
5	50		3	11	8		1	10	15		0	4	7		15	5	7
6	00		3	10	6		1	9	18		0	4	6		15	2	12
6	10		3	9	5		1	8	21		0	3	4		14	11	16
6	20		3	8	3		1	7	24		0	2	3		14	8	21
6	30		3	7	2		1	6	27		0	1	1		14	5	25
6	40		3	6	0		1	6	0	राहु	18	0	0		14	3	0
6	50		3	4	29		1	5	3		17	9	9		14	0	4

चन्द्र स्पष्ट		चन्द्र राशि मेष–सिंह–धनु				चन्द्र राशि वृष–कन्या–मकर				चन्द्र राशि मिथुन–तुला–कुम्भ				चन्द्र राशि कर्क–वृश्चिक–मीन			
अंश	कला	भोग्य	वर्ष	मास	दिन	भोग्य	वर्ष	मास	दिन	भोग्य	वर्ष	मास	दिन	भोग्य	वर्ष	मास	दिन
7	00		3	3	27		1	4	6		17	6	18		13	9	9
7	10		3	2	26		1	3	9		17	3	27		13	6	13
7	20		3	1	24		1	2	12		17	1	6		13	3	18
7	30		3	0	23		1	1	15		16	10	15		13	0	22
7	40		2	11	21		1	0	18		16	7	24		12	9	27
7	50		2	10	20		0	11	21		16	5	3		12	7	1
8	00		2	9	18		0	10	24		16	2	12		12	4	6
8	10		2	8	17		0	9	27		5	11	21		12	1	10
8	20		2	7	15		0	9	0		15	9	0		11	10	15
8	30		2	6	24		0	8	3		15	6	9		11	7	19
8	40		2	4	12		0	7	6		15	3	18		11	4	24
9	00		2	3	9		0	15	12		14	10	6	शनि	10	11	3
9	10		2	2	8		0	4	15		14	7	15		10	8	7
9	20		2	1	6		0	3	18		14	4	24		10	5	12
9	30		2	0	5		0	2	21		14	2	3		10	2	16
9	40		1	11	3		0	1	24		13	11	12		9	11	21
9	50		1	10	2		0	0	27		13	8	21		9	8	25
10	00		9	9	0	चन्द्र	10	0	0		13	6	0		9	6	0
10	10		1	7	29		1	10	15		13	3	9		9	3	4
10	20		1	6	27		9	9	0		13	0	18		9	0	9
10	30		1	5	26		9	7	15		12	9	27		8	9	13

चन्द्र स्पष्ट		चन्द्र राशि मेष–सिंह–धनु				चन्द्र राशि वृष–कन्या–मकर				चन्द्र राशि मिथुन–तुला–कुम्भ				चन्द्र राशि कर्क–वृश्चिक–मीन			
अंश	कला	भोग्य	वर्ष	मास	दिन	भोग्य	वर्ष	मास	दिन	भोग्य	वर्ष	मास	दिन	भोग्य	वर्ष	मास	दिन
10	40		1	4	24		9	6	0		12	7	6		8	6	18
10	50		1	3	23		9	4	15		12	4	15		8	3	22
11	00		1	2	21		9	3	0		12	1	24		8	0	27
11	10		1	1	20		9	1	15		11	11	3		7	10	1
11	20		1	0	18		9	0	0		11	8	12		7	7	6
11	30		0	11	17		8	10	15		11	5	21		7	4	10
11	40		0	10	15		8	9	0		11	3	0		7	1	15
11	50		0	9	14		8	7	15		11	0	9		6	10	19
12	00		0	8	12		8	6	0		10	9	18		6	7	24
12	10		0	7	11		8	4	15		10	6	27		6	4	28
12	20		0	6	9		8	3	0		10	4	6		6	2	3
12	30		0	5	8		8	1	15		10	1	15		5	11	7
12	40		0	4	6		8	0	0		9	10	24		5	8	12
12	50		0	3	5		7	10	15		9	8	3		5	5	16
13	00		0	2	3		7	9	0		9	5	12		5	2	21
13	10		0	1	1		7	7	15		9	2	21		4	11	25
13	20	शुक्र	20	0	0		7	6	0		9	0	0		4	9	0
13	30		19	9	0		7	4	15		8	9	9		4	6	4
13	40		19	6	0		7	3	0		8	6	18		4	3	9
13	50		19	3	0		7	1	15		8	3	27		4	0	13
14	00		19	0	0		7	0	0		8	1	6		3	9	18

चन्द्र स्पष्ट		चन्द्र राशि मेष–सिंह–धनु				चन्द्र राशि वृष–कन्या–मकर				चन्द्र राशि मिथुन–तुला–कुम्भ				चन्द्र राशि कर्क–वृश्चिक–मीन			
अंश	कला	भोग्य	वर्ष	मास	दिन	भोग्य	वर्ष	मास	दिन	भोग्य	वर्ष	मास	दिन	भोग्य	वर्ष	मास	दिन
14	10		18	9	0		6	10	15		7	10	15		3	6	22
14	20		18	6	0		6	9	0		7	7	24		3	3	27
14	30		18	3	0		6	7	15		7	5	3		3	1	1
14	40		18	0	0		6	6	0		7	2	12		2	10	6
14	50		17	9	0		6	4	15		6	11	21		2	7	10
15	00		17	6	0		6	3	0		6	9	0		2	4	15
15	10		17	3	0		6	1	15		6	6	9		2	1	19
15	20		17	0	0		6	0	0		6	3	18		1	10	24
15	30		16	9	0		5	10	15		6	0	27		1	7	28
15	40		16	10	0		5	9	0		5	10	6		1	5	3
15	50		16	3	0		5	7	15		5	7	15		1	2	7
16	00		16	0	0		5	6	0		5	4	24		0	19	12
16	10		15	9	0		5	4	15		5	2	3		0	8	16
16	20		15	6	0		5	3	0		4	11	12		0	5	21
16	30		15	3	0		5	1	15		4	8	21		0	2	26
16	40		15	0	0		5	0	0		4	6	0	बुध	17	0	0
16	50		14	9	0		4	10	15		4	3	9		16	9	13
17	00		14	6	0		4	9	0		4	0	18		16	6	27
17	10		14	3	0		4	7	15		3	9	27		16	4	10
17	20		14	0	0		4	6	0		3	7	6		16	1	24
17	30		13	9	0		4	4	15		3	4	15		15	11	7
17	40		13	6	0		4	3	0		3	1	14		15	8	21

चन्द्र स्पष्ट		चन्द्र राशि मेष–सिंह–धनु				चन्द्र राशि वृष–कन्या–मकर				चन्द्र राशि मिथुन–तुला–कुम्भ				चन्द्र राशि कर्क–वृश्चिक–मीन			
अंश	कला	भोग्य	वर्ष	मास	दिन	भोग्य	वर्ष	मास	दिन	भोग्य	वर्ष	मास	दिन	भोग्य	वर्ष	मास	दिन
17	50		13	3	0		4	1	15		2	11	3		15	6	4
18	00		13	0	0		4	0	0		2	8	12		15	3	18
18	10		12	9	0		3	10	15		2	5	21		15	1	1
18	20		12	6	0		3	9	0		2	3	0		14	10	15
18	30		12	3	0		3	7	15		2	0	9		14	7	28
18	40		12	0	0		3	6	0		1	9	18		14	5	12
18	50		11	9	0		3	4	15		1	6	27		14	2	25
19	00		11	6	0		3	3	0		1	4	6		14	0	9
19	10		11	3	0		3	1	15		1	1	15		13	9	22
19	20		11	0	0		3	0	0		0	10	24		13	7	6
19	30		10	9	0		2	10	15		0	8	3		13	4	19
19	40		10	6	0		2	9	0		0	5	12		13	2	3
19	50		10	3	0		2	7	15		0	2	21		12	11	16
20	00		10	0	0		2	6	0	गुरु	16	0	0		12	9	0
20	10		9	9	0		2	4	15		15	9	18		12	6	13
20	20		9	6	0		2	3	0		15	7	6		12	3	27
20	30		9	3	0		2	1	15		15	4	24		12	1	10
20	40		9	0	0		2	0	0		15	2	12		11	10	24
20	50		8	9	0		1	10	15		15	0	0		11	8	7
21	00		8	6	0		1	9	0		14	9	18		11	5	21
21	10		8	3	0		1	7	15		14	7	6		11	3	4
21	20		8	0	0		1	6	0		14	4	24		11	0	18

चन्द्र स्पष्ट		चन्द्र राशि मेष–सिंह–धनु				चन्द्र राशि वृष–कन्या–मकर				चन्द्र राशि मिथुन–तुला–कुम्भ				चन्द्र राशि कर्क–वृश्चिक–मीन			
अंश	कला	भोग्य	वर्ष	मास	दिन	भोग्य	वर्ष	मास	दिन	भोग्य	वर्ष	मास	दिन	भोग्य	वर्ष	मास	दिन
21	30		7	9	0		1	4	15		14	2	12		10	10	1
21	40		7	6	0		1	3	0		14	0	0		10	7	15
21	50		7	3	0		1	1	15		13	9	18		10	4	28
22	00		7	0	0		1	0	0		13	7	6		10	2	12
22	10		6	9	0		0	10	15		13	4	24		9	11	25
22	20		6	6	0		0	9	0		13	2	12		9	9	9
22	30		6	3	0		0	7	15		13	0	0		9	6	27
22	40		6	0	0		0	6	0		12	9	18		9	4	6
22	50		5	9	0		0	4	15		12	7	6		9	9	19
23	00		5	6	0		0	3	0		12	4	24		8	11	3
23	10		5	3	0		0	1	15		12	2	12		8	8	16
23	20		5	0	0	मंगल	7	0	0		12	0	0		8	6	0
23	30		4	9	0		6	10	29		11	9	18		8	3	13
23	40		4	6	0		6	9	27		11	7	6		8	0	27
23	50		4	3	0		6	8	26		11	4	24		7	10	10
24	00		4	0	0		6	7	24		11	2	12		7	7	24
24	10		3	9	0		6	6	23		11	0	0		7	5	7
24	20		3	6	0		6	5	21		10	9	18		7	2	21
24	30		3	3	0		6	4	20		10	7	6		7	0	4
24	40		3	0	0		6	3	18		10	4	24		6	9	18
24	50		2	9	0		6	2	17		10	2	12		6	7	1
25	00		2	6	0		6	1	15		10	0	0		6	4	15

चन्द्र स्पष्ट		चन्द्र राशि मेष–सिंह–धनु				चन्द्र राशि वृष–कन्या–मकर				चन्द्र राशि मिथुन–तुला–कुम्भ				चन्द्र राशि कर्क–वृश्चिक–मीन			
अंश	कला	भोग्य	वर्ष	मास	दिन	भोग्य	वर्ष	मास	दिन	भोग्य	वर्ष	मास	दिन	भोग्य	वर्ष	मास	दिन
25	10		2	3	0		6	0	14		9	9	18		6	1	28
25	20		2	0	0		5	11	12		9	7	6		5	11	12
25	30		1	9	0		5	10	11		9	4	24		5	8	25
25	40		1	6	0		5	9	9		9	2	12		5	6	9
25	50		1	3	0		5	8	8		9	0	0		5	3	22
26	00		1	0	0		5	7	6		8	9	18		5	1	6
26	10		0	9	0		5	6	5		8	7	6		4	10	19
26	20		0	6	0		5	5	3		8	4	24		4	8	3
26	30		0	3	0		5	4	2		8	2	12		4	5	16
26	40	सूर्य	6	0	0		5	3	0		8	0	0		4	3	0
26	50		5	11	3		5	1	29		7	9	18		4	0	13
27	0		5	10	6		5	0	27		7	7	6		3	9	27
27	10		5	9	9		4	11	26		7	4	24		3	7	10
27	20		5	8	12		4	10	24		7	2	12		3	4	24
27	30		5	7	15		4	9	23		7	0	0		3	2	7
27	40		5	6	18		4	8	21		6	9	18		2	11	21
27	50		5	5	21		4	7	20		6	7	6		2	9	4
28	0		5	4	24		4	6	18		6	4	24		2	6	18
28	10		5	3	27		4	5	17		6	2	12		2	4	1
28	20		5	3	0		4	4	15		6	0	0		2	10	15
28	30		5	2	3		4	3	14		5	9	18		1	10	28
28	40		5	1	6		4	2	12		5	7	6		1	8	12

चन्द्र स्पष्ट		चन्द्र राशि मेष–सिंह–धनु				चन्द्र राशि वृष–कन्या–मकर				चन्द्र राशि मिथुन–तुला–कुम्भ				चन्द्र राशि कर्क–वृश्चिक–मीन			
अंश	कला	भोग्य	वर्ष	मास	दिन	भोग्य	वर्ष	मास	दिन	भोग्य	वर्ष	मास	दिन	भोग्य	वर्ष	मास	दिन
28	50		5	0	9		4	1	11		5	4	24		1	5	15
29	0		4	11	12		4	0	9		5	2	12		1	3	9
29	10		4	10	15		3	11	8		5	0	0		1	0	22
29	20		4	9	18		3	10	6		4	9	18		0	10	6
29	30		4	8	21		3	9	5		4	7	6		0	7	19
29	40		4	7	24		3	8	3		4	4	24		0	5	3
29	50		4	6	27		3	7	2		4	2	12		0	2	17
30	0		4	6	0		3	6	0		4	0	0		0	0	0

Table - 2

कला	केतु		शुक्र		सूर्य		चन्द्र		मगल		राहु		गुरु		शनि		बुध		कला
	मा.	दि.	मा.	दि.	मा.	दि.	मा.	दि.	मा.	दि.	मा.	दि.	मा.	दि.	मा.	दि.	मा.	दि.	
1	0	03	0	09	0	03	0	05	0	03	0	08	0	07	0	09	0	08	1
2	0	06	0	18	0	05	0	09	0	06	0	16	0	14	0	17	0	15	2
3	0	09	0	27	0	08	0	14	0	09	0	24	0	22	0	26	0	23	3
4	0	13	1	06	0	11	0	18	0	13	1	02	0	29	1	04	1	01	4
5	0	16	1	15	0	14	0	23	0	16	9	11	1	06	1	13	1	08	5
6	0	19	1	24	0	16	0	27	0	19	1	19	1	13	1	21	9	16	6
7	0	22	2	03	0	19	1	02	0	22	1	27	1	20	2	00	1	24	7
8	0	25	2	12	0	22	9	06	0	5	2	05	1	28	2	08	2	01	8
9	0	28	2	21	0	24	1	11	0	28	2	13	2	05	2	17	2	09	9
10	1	01	3	00	0	27	1	15	1	01	2	21	2	12	2	26	2	17	10

Predictions about Different Houses and Planets' Placements in them in view of Lal Kitab.

The First House

Kundali.

Kitab gives lot of importance to this house. This house is just like the soul in human body and soul is totally related to God. It is considered God Vishnu's *ansh* or part.

The owner of the second and the seventh houses in a *Kundali*/chart, is Venus. Venus worships the Goddess Laxhimi or in other words a man always runs after Laxhimi/money, which according to the old legends is true because both Laxhimi as well as God Vishnu also want to meet each other quite earnestly. It is because of that that each individual runs after money and wants to get it at all costs. Therefore, Lal Kitab says that for whole life an individual runs after achieving, *zar, zoru* and *zamin* i.e. money, woman and property. So most individuals go on running after money doing good or bad acts, without understanding that the soul inside is the *ansh* or part of God Vishnu.We usually calculate or try to know about a *jatak's* health, courage, power to act and take initiative, capability to complete a task, personal strength and power to rule, oppositions, posts one will hold in life, complexion, facial make up, the power implicit in

achievements, name and fame, etc. In case the Sun is rising in the *lagna*, as Lalkitab considers 1st house having the sign Aries, then the Sun is in an exalted position or sign. The Sun represents one's soul as well as it also bestows longevity to life. If there was no Sun, there would have been no light on the Earth. With its light and heat as well energy, the Sun helps to live all kinds of creatures. It also helps the plants and every kind of animal

with the *kundali* in general.

Astrologically which ever month the Native is born at the time of the *lagna* is considered as everything to an individual. *Mangal*/Mars represents blood, because of that if in one's *kundali* Mangal is placed in a good *rashi*, the person is considered having good blood. Such a *jatak* generally don't get different kinds of sickness in life. Both, the Sun and Mangal, control administration. It is because of that if these both are placed in *lagna*, they are considered very auspicious. Both the planets are also hot and represent energy. They also provide hot temperament to the *jatak*. If only the Sun rises at *lagna* it affects individual's hair which start falling at an early age. It may also be possible that such an individual may possess a thin physique. In case Saturn Rahu or Ketu are with the Sun, the Sun may not give good results as these three are detrimental to its company. Even if they aspect the Sun sitting at *lagna*, the results will not be conducive. For such a combination, one must do some kind of *upayas* (precautions). Only then the bad effects of these may be reduced to some extent. Saturn is considered debilitated in *lagna*. It is known to be black in colour, it is because of that it makes delays in every kind of work. If it has no aspects of good planets, it may check one's progress in education. Saturn rising in *lagna* may make the *jatak* suffer with gas problems, but may give him/her advantage in oil business, or as a builder of houses and roads, and may also lead the *jatak* to involve in machinery business, but if the *jatak* gets losses, he/she needs to do some *upayas* for Saturn so that his/her health may be good and may get gains in business.

These *upayas* are to give alms to *sadhus* certain things like 'the iron disc on which one toasts *chapaties*', 'a small knife', and 'a fork (*chimta*)' as well. Lal Kitab also suggests that a spoonful of *surma* may be put into the soft earth and a riped coconut after opening its mouth and putting into it some black mustered, *khaskas*, and sugar may be put into the earth during evenings each day for seven Saturdays at a place where ants are in abundance so that they may feed on that. It will help Saturn to provide good results. If Saturn is sitting in *lagna,* it aspects the seventh house also besides the third and the tenth houses. If good planets are sitting in *lagna* and have their aspects on the seventh, they are likely to provide good results. If unpleasant planets like Ketu, Rahu or Saturn are rising in *lagna*, their aspects may give ill effects to the husband and wife relationship. Consequently, constant discussions, quarrels and other sorts of disturbances like regular sickness in the family etc., are bound to occur in their lives. It is because of that, as well as considering family peace and smooth job involvement by both or either of them, it is imperative to *lagna*.

If there are no planets in *langna,* it is considered in a low state or in a sleeping state. If it is so, then some *upayas* (precautions) need to be taken or done for Mangal to wake up the slept *lagna*. One of those *upayas* suggested by Lal Kitab is to wear in one's neck a silver necklace/ chain having a piece of silver which is 2 inches wide and 20 grams in weight on Tuesday and keep it constantly as long as one can wear it. Silver represents the Moon and the piece of silver of 20 grams and 2 inches broad, represents *Mangal*. Thus, both *Manga*l and the Moon will become auspicious and provide good results.

The *jatak* in whose chart the Sun Lagna (Leo) is rising will grow in life more and more if he/she does good things for needy the people, be kind to them be helpful to those who need help. The Moon is considered auspicious in *langna*, but it is also stated about the Moon that the *jatak* should not drink milk or water in a pot made of glass. Instead he/she should drink it in a silver glass. Glass is related to Rahu and Mercury which are enemies to the Moon. Silver represents the Moon so drinking water in a silver glass will always be auspicious to the native as it will strengthen his/her physically as well as mentally. It is because of this that many people wear gold or silver ornaments and also take gold or silver powder (*bhasam*) s a medicine to get physical strength. It is also suggested that if in a *jatak'skundali* the Moon *rashi* (Cancer/*kark*) is rising, he should not involve in selling milk. Instead he/she can offer milk free to the needy. If the Moon and *Mangal* sit in *langa* or have their aspects on *lagna*, it is advisable that such a *jatak* should wear silver ornaments and keep a red coloured handkerchief in one of his/her pockets.

It is believed astrologically that if *Mangal* is inauspicious in one's *kundali* then its effect continues for 28 years in a *jatak's* life. Such a *jatak* is advised not to marry for 28 years. After that *Mangal* may not be so inauspicious and the Moon may start bestowing good effects in one's life. In order to provide strength to the Moon, it is stated in Lal Kitab that a *jatak* should nail all the four corners of his/her *chrpai* or cot with copper nails or tie these corners with the copper thread. It will help to put down the ill effects of Ketu if at all such effects exit in the chart. Consequently, the *jatak* may have a good sleep in the night. It is also stated in Lal Kitab that if Jupiter couples with the Moon in *lagna*, it will provide good results. But if Ketu, Rahu or Saturn risesin *lagna*with the Moon, they will provide bad results to the *jatak* and disturb his/her life in many ways. Consequently he/she will be changing houses and jobs.

We have already stated it that Lal Kitab considers starting from the sign Aries. It is therefore Mars becomes the cause of incurring loans if Mercury is rising at the *lagna*. In order to ward off the ill effects of Mars one has to give a lot of alms or money after purchasing property or other things to the needy relatives or needy people. Any action done to help others

act which would provide positive effect and reduce the ill effects of the planets. Some may question how parental obligations can be reduced by giving alms. It happens in the same way as when a parent has some kind of disease, it continues one generation to the other.

Likewise, giving alms may reduce the ill effects of malignant planets and go on reducing their ill effects if continued *dan* (alms) is given to the needy. If one may get property from his elders or forefathers and get illness from the senior parents like grand-father or grandmother, one can also get redeemed from good acts and *dans.* If one can suffer on account of ill acts done by our parents or grandparents, why not then bad effects of planets can be redeemed by giving alms. From Lal Kitab's point of view if Mercury or *Buddh* rising in *lagna* provides good effects. It helps the *jatak* to think better and act intelligently. Such a *jatak* is usually highly educated. Even if he/she is less educated, he/shewould possess some kind

According to the ancient astrology *Budha* (Mercury) is considered Lord Vishnu's form. That means it acts kindly like Vishnu provided it should be placed well in the chart (*kundali*

may not own the 8th or the 12 houses and it may not have aspects from Mangal and Ketu. Lal Kitab expresses that if a *jatak's Budha* is rising in *lagna*

and should not wear clothes of green colour. Lal Kitab says Jupiter rising at *lagna*

affairs, position of a minister, as well deep interest in *mantra sadhana.* The seventh house is concerned with daily business, partnership, spouse (wife/husband). The ninth is concerned with luck as well as acts of *dharma.* Jupiter sitting at the *lagna* when has its aspects on all the three places, it does great good to a *jatak* relating to these three houses provided these houses don't belong to its enemies. Jupiter rising at *lagna* makes the *jatak* individual to get good education, Even if he/she is less educated, he/she may reach a respectable position in life through God grace and prayers.

houses belong to Jupiter. In case Venus, Mercury or Rahu are placed in these houses which are considered Jupiter's enemies, then it incurs loans on the *jatak*. Therefore it is advised that the *jatak* must try to ward of Jupiter's ill-effects caused by Mercury, Vensu or Rahu. For that the *jatak* has to do some *upayas* (take precautions) so that it may give good results.

To get good results from Jupiter one has to offer a pot-full of gram pulses in front of the statue of the god Ganesha on Thursday, and should pray to Ganesha to get relieved from Jupiter's inauspicious effects. In

by the Sun, and the ninth has Aquarius sign in it, how then the eleventh house could be controlled by it as the sign rising in it belongs to Saturn. According to astrology wealth, property and family are controlled by the

money by the ninth house—all these are Jupiter's concern according to Lal Kitab. But if Venus, Mercury or Rahu are not rising with Jupiter, only then it will provide good results. Besides, a person in whose chart Jupiter

drink hard drinks. On the top of that if he indulges in people's service, helps them in need or any time, and pays respects to elders, only then Jupiter will provide good results.

In case Venus is in *lagna* *jatak* should avoid marrying upto 25 years. If he/she does it may be disastrous. But if he/she marries after that period, then his/her business will run very well and successfully. If Venus controls the *lagna*, it will help grow the *jatak* in his/her lifebut the *jatak* will also be a great enemy if he/she comes to that stage with anyone in life. Over all he/she will like to be friendly with everyone. Lal Kitab suggests that if Venus controls the *lagna* the *jatak* should try to get advantage of that planet and after taking bath should always wear clean *lagna*, and the seventh house is without any planets, then to get advantage of that house (seventh house) he should keep a woman servant, take up a good job and serve cows as much as one can. Rahu is considered bad if it is rising in *langa.* In that case Ketu will rise in the seventh house.It is because of that that one needs to invoke Venus' positive effect. To get good results from Venus, one has to go on pleasing it constantly if one desires to lead a happy married life. For that, the *jatak* needs to prepare 100 *chapaties* and on Fridays, one *chapti* needs to be given to feed cows for several years. It is also advised that the *jatak* should not accept any electricity related material of black or blue colour from any one if someone gives that to him/her. If by chance he/she gets it, then it should be given to someone who needs it and help the poor in their hour of need constantly. If Rahu is rising in *lagna*, it may make the individual travel a lot and may take his/her to foreign tours several times. Rahu does not let the individual to take right decisions and to work in the right direction. It may also affect his/her education and interrupt it in between. It may cause to change houses and jobs frequently. It also leads to getaccusations from others without any reasons. It does not permit the *jatak* to take advice from others and the native gest losses in every kind of work he/she does.

worries and little displeasures and disappointments. But in case bad planets have their effect on the *lagna* and Rahu, then they provide bad experiences and unhappy life. It has been a matter of experience that if Rahu rules the *lagna*, the *jatak* often works as a driver, or in military or police in an ordinary position. Such natives don't stay at one place to work because Rahu goes on suggesting many things to them and consequently they go on changing jobs frequently. Rahu also makes the native hefty in body. It frequently creates gases in one's body and keeps him/her disturbed on

ninth aspects on the respective houses if Rahu is rising in the *lagna*, will always bring bad effects on these houses. Rahu gives negative thinking and consequently the native stomach is badly adversely affected giving constant constipation to the *jatak*, resulting ill health. So to be safe against

the native likes. Besides, the native may also 4 kilogram barley and four

canal.The native should also serve the physically weak individuals whose hands and feet are broken or who are lame. He/she should help the poor and assist them to wed their daughters. The native should not misuse the electricity and steal energy from the government.

Ketu rising in *lagna* has its aspects on the seventh house.Therefore, both, Venus and *Mangal* need to be smoothed down as they may provide bad effects to the native. In order to shun down *Mangal's* ill effects, the native should provide free medicines to a medical store to be given to the needy.Bad effects may also be created by Rahu which is rising in the seventh house if Ketu is rising in *lagna.* Therefore at the time of such a native's daughter, it is advisable to give 60 grams of a 5 inches squire piece of silver, which the bride should place in her bedroom to ward off Rahu's ill effect from life. In order to ward off Venus' ill effect the native should offer 100 *chapaties* to 100 cows once in a year. It will help the couple to lead a happy life. If Ketu is in *jatak's lagna*, it will make him/her travel a lot and may give him a chance to work as an agent, a representative of a company, an agent, a driver, a CID in police etc.,

usually if Ketu is rising in a native's *lagna*, that native usually does not get a very high position in life although such natives may be simple persons and may offer their money and things of utility to the needy and

them ordinarily rich in life.

Ancient astrologersconsider that the Sun is considered in an exalted sign in a *kundali* in Ketu's Aswani Nakchatra. It can bestow *mokcha* or salvation to the individual. It is usually the last wish of an individual that

mokcha only if one is ready to help the needy people who too have been created by God. Just like Meera, Sant Nam Dev, Sant Ravi Das, Sant Kabir, Guru Nanak Dev Ji,---who did all for the society and served the people but did not think about their own life at all. It is because of that, that if a person leads a simpler life, he/she is nearer God. On the contrary if he/she is showy and leads an

Rahu is considered a planet which likes to be among people and desires to lead a comfortable and enjoyable life in this world. It is also a very

it considers Mercury/*Budha* as one its best friends and because of that it work in any way *Budha* desires it to do. As *Budha* controls intelligence and native's mind, it can control Rahu with those ways and methods suggested by it (*Budha*/Mercury). Ketu is considered in anexalted state in Sagittarius as well as in Pisces signs which are owned by Jupiter. But Ketu has no 'head' so it has no thinking capability.Because Jupiter is an auspicious planet, it helps people in different ways. It is because of that Jupiter makes Ketu to do good things for the people and get them *mokcha.* As an *upaya* (precaution or a way to help get redeemed from an ill-effect) if Ketu is rising in *lagna*, that the *jatak* should distribute regularly small bananas to children to eat. Such a native should also worship the god Ganeshaand tie a silken thread in the right thumb of both the feet. It will help to get Ketu's ill-effect redeemed.

Our experience suggests that if Saturn is rising in *lagna* and Rahu in the eighth house, or Rahu may be in *lagna*,then that particular year of *jatak's*
Normally the planet that sits in *lagna*, turns bad the planet that sits in the eighth house from *lagna*. Ancient astrologers have also suggested that the rising of planets in the 1st house (*lagna*) and the eighth house makes a yoga known as *shadashak* yoga, which is considered very inauspicious. Lal Kitab also follows the same because planets rising in *lagna*are in the sixth house when counted from the eighth.

Thus, the planets rising in *lagna* make the planets inauspicious that are sitting in the eighth. These eighth house planets cannot get any help

house) unless these are not friendly planets to the eighth house owned planets. But if friendly planets are rising in the twelfth house, every kind of assistance can be provided to the eighth house planets. To remove the problems created by the planets rising in the eighth house, the *jatak* would

the bad effects of the eighth house planets which are not auspicious. In fact, the eighth house represents the place where dead are buried or burnt(cremation ground). In order to lessen the bad effects of the eighth house the *jatak* would need to do many activities to satisfy the ill effect of the bad planets rising in the eighth house. In case Jupiter rises in the eighth, the *jatak* needs to grow a *peepal* plant in the cremation ground. The wood of that *peepal* tree as well as the shadow of it will diminish the ill-effects Jupiter rising in the eighth house.

If two or three planets are rising in the *lagna*, they generally give good results. But if there are one or two bad planets in *lagna* along with good ones, let the *jatak* do some *upyas* to reduce the bad effect of the bad planets. They can be made favourable by giving alms or offering water to gods. Lal kitab advises to give alms to the poor and needy and help the down trodden as well. Those who are unhappy in life due to any reason, may it be lack of

they must be helped to reduce the ill effects of the eighth house planets that are inauspicious. Such kind of help will also improve the society as it will lead reducing the cases of theft and dishonest living in the society.

Lal Kitab says that if there are good planets rising in *lagna*, in the seventh house as well in the eleventh house, they will help *jatak* to lead a very happy and prosperous life, but if bad or inauspicious planets rise in these houses

jatak's life.

The Second House

Lak Kitab considers that in the second house of a *kundali* the sign Taurus rises. Its owner is Venus. But Lal Kitab considers Jupiter as the owner of this house, because, riches, family education, and savings are counted from this house. Lal Kitab considers this house related to *dharma* but ancient astrologers reckon the ninth house as the house related to *dharma*. Because the second house is considered related to dharma, people put a *tilk* at their forehead. It keeps one's head cool and helps to think better comparatively. If Venus is placed in the second house of a man or a woman, it does not

In case Mercury/*Budha* is placed in the second house it does not

that while predicting on various issues or problems related to a person, one must think carefully and keep into consideration *gaucher* (day to day movements of the planets) as well as *dasha* also for without considering them, predictions may not come true. Lal Kitab indicates that if *Budha* rises in the second house in a *kundali*/chart, it does permit the *jatak* to enjoy the married life, yet he/she will be highly educated and exhibit politeness during conversing with the people. He will also earn a lot of money from involving either in a lawyer or teaching, astrology, or from being an advisor or in oratory profession. *Budha* is an auspicious planet

these two matters. Therefore, it will be of great help to the native if *Bhdha* rises in the second house in a *jatak's* chart. But if Budha rises in the second house, Jupiter becomes inauspicious. Therefore, to please Jupiter *jatak* should offer to the god Ganesha plenty of grams on Thursdays and pray for happiness and peace in the family.

lot. But if it is in an enemy sign, it will give him/her lots of familyproblems, leading to losing of property and tax related problems. The Sun is a hot and dry planet and because of that it may create some problems. In case Venus is the owner of the second house, it may give spouse related problems. So to enhance the family happiness the *jatak* should distribute 100 *chapaties* to cows and if almond oil offered at a religious place or at the place of dharma, one may get relieved from the Sun's ill effects. Saturn being friendly to Jupiter as well as to Venus. Therefore, giving almonds in alms to the needy and may go on helping the needy, may diminish the ill effects of different planets including Saturn and Jupiter, including Venus. The Moon is considered in an exalted state if it is rising in the second

Moon is rising in the second house and Ketu in the twelfth house, Then Ketu will exert its ill effects on the Moon, says Lal kitab. To lessen that ill effect of the Moon one should serve the mother and elderly people to

Lal Kitab considers *Mangal*/Mars rising in the second house very auspicious because *Mangal* is a friend to Jupiter and Venus. If such a *jatak* opens kitchen to offer free food to the hungry and needy, it would bring

experienced that *Mangal* rising in the second house also gives bad results. *Mangal* thus placed may disturb family relationship and also detrimental for children. *Mangal* is hot by nature and is also a cruel planet. South Indian astrologers consider *Mangal* in the second house creating *Manglik Dosha*, which is harmful to family and life of husband/wife as well as their relationship. *Mangal* sitting in the second house has its aspects on the eighth house, and its fourth aspect is detrimental to children. However, if it has aspects on its own sign/*rashi* or on a friendly *rashi*, it gives less problems, but if has aspects on the enemy signs, it is going to give lots of troubles.The seventh house refers to husband/wife. In case we consider the seventh house as *lagna*, then the second house (though the eighth) becomes highly inauspicious for the native. To lessen the ill effect of Mangal the *jatak* must open *langars* (kitchens offering free food to all whether needy or anybody else). Besides, husband and wife should take a few drops of honey in lemon water everyday. It will lessen the ill effects of *Mangal.*

Jupiter rising in the second house usually give good results. From that position it has aspects on the sixth, eighth as well as on the tenth houses. The tenth is related to job and different kinds of work. All that will be

jatak's kundali. It will also help lessening illness in the family. It will also remove poverty from the family and extend education opportunities to the *jatak*, but such a *jatak* must not keep things such as a conch, money-plant, pitcher made from black soil, for all these are related to *Budha*, which is Jupiter's

the people who require help in the society. The more he/she will serve the

According to Lal Kitab Taurus sign is rising in the second house. As Jupiter is the *karak* (controller) of this house, it becomes inauspicious as Venus is rising in this house. In order to lessen the bad effects of Jupiter, the *jatak* is advised to offer to god Ganesha a full pot of grams on Thursdays and pray to help him/her and reduce problems from life. Such a *jatak* can also offer butter oil/*ghee* at a religious palce (which is considered usually Jupiter's abode). It will lessen the ill-effects of Venus. But Venus is an

will be helpful in presenting him/her in a respecvtble state before others in the society.

If Saturn is rising in the second house it is considered subordinating Jupiter as the second house is ruled by Jupiter according to Lal Kitab. So Lal Kitab suggests some *upayas* to go under Jupiter's protection by walking bare feet in a public resthouse (*dharamshala*) and bow down before gods to seek their forgiveness. He/she should also apply raw mustard oil and apply milk tilak on the forehead and go on seeking gods' forgiveness to give a happy life. However, in Taurus sign Saturn is considered auspicious as it is its friend Venus's sign. It is also expected as a consequence that usually wife or husband of such a *jatak* is very crafty. But Lal Kitab has simply considered individual planets in different houses. It is our experience on the contrary that if Saturn is rising in the second hosue in its enemy sign, it will give family problems, affect income adversely and also affect educational career to a great extent. Saturn is likely delay in every kind of matter giving disappointments and failures. If it is so, it is better to make upayas for redeeming Saturn.

Astrologically Saturn is the source of unhappiness and physical ailments. According to ancient astrology every planet rising in a particular house gives results according to the house it is rising in. Lak Kitab suggests two sides of each planet—one good and the other adverse. When the planet is rising in its own or in a friendly sign and also has aspects from friendly planets, it gives good results but if rising in a bad sign or in its enemy's sign or seen by its enemy, it provides bad results. Saturn becomes an inauspicious or a bad planet when it rises in its enemy's sign or in the sixth, eighth or twelfth house as their owner and is also has aspects from enemiy planets. Saturn then certainly gives bad results.If Saturn has aspects on the eleventh house having Aquarius sign, it will give good resulst. Lal Kitab

give good resulst. If a *jatak* devotes time in religious activities, Saturn will surely provide good results to the *jatak*.

Rahu in the second house does not provide good results. Rahu is considered enemy of both, Jupiter and Venus. As Rahu is a *papi*/ inauspicious planet, it needs to please Venus and Jupiter as well, by different kinds of public service and *upayas*. When we match a girl's kundali with that of a boy, it is necessary to see that Rahu is not rising in the second house as it will always create family related problems.It will also make the *jatak's* tongue bitter unnecessarily creating enemies. It will create quarrels in the family and will check family happiness adversely. It may make the *jatak* alcoholic, a heavy smoker and provide other kinds of character ailments or problems. The second house represents one's mouth, and if Rahu is rising there, the *jatak* will indulge in bad habits and use intoxicating things in abundance resulting giving bad health and peace less state of life.It has also been observed that if Rahu or Ketu rise in the second house, they are likely to give problems to the native in his/her 18th year by not permitting him/her to get education further. That means these planets (shadowy planets) often disrupt one's education at that particular time. But these planets also help in getting a chance to go abroad by the age of 32 years. It happens because bad planets like Rahu or Ketu often directs a *jatak* to stay away from the family. In order to calm down Rahu's ill effect, the *jatak* is advised to make a very small ball of silver and keep it in the pocket forever and similar small round ball may be tugged in a chain and wear in one's neck. Roundness represents *Budha* and silver represents moon. Rahu gets calm down by the use of silver. It will also help the *jatak* to keep his/her tongue bridled.

Ketu in the second house also provides results like Rahu. But Ketu has to satisfy/please Venus not Jupiter as it is friendly to Jupiter. The *upaya* suggested by Lal Kitab to calm down the ill-effects of Venus, is to wear a silver chain in neck, and put a *tilak* of *haldi* and *kesar* on one's forehead. Such a *jatak* must watch one's conduct strongly and keep it good. Only then Ketu will not give any bad effect.

The Third House

The third house has the third *rashi*/sign according to Lal Kitab. Its owner is *Budha*/Mercury. We consider from this house about 'the younger brothers & sisters, hands, throat, information, writing capability & quality,

Mangal provides courage, small journeys and how to drive a vehicle, etc. are considered/calculated by this house. Ancient astrologers considered this house relating one's income; that means the 3rd, 6th, and the 11th houses are helpful in having good income if the possess auspicious signs in them. It is also mentioned in Lal Kitab that the 3rd house is also the 8th from the 8th house. Therefore, the 8th house is considered detrimental to life, and refers to life and death as well as poverty. Some people think that three people in a company are not considered good or auspicious. Normally life is divided into three parts—childhood, youth, and old age. Most men think that they should never grow old. Therefore, any house having three corners in it is not considered auspicious. Likewise the third child is also not considered good. Lal Kitab reckons that when we

rising in the 3rd, 6th and the 8th houses, that indicates illness and misfortunes in the family. But if there are planets in the 12th house, it can redeem the ill effects of the 3rd
and illness in the family may be ward off on that account. Thus, ancient astrology and Lal Kitiab at times are complementary to each other.

The Sun is considered good if it rises in the third house. This house, according to Lal Kitab, belongs to *Mangal* and *Bhdha*. But we believe that the Sun being a hot planet may create problems related brothers and sisters, and lead to misunderstanding between them. The Sun from the third house will aspect the 9th
good luck to *jatak*.

The Moon is considered good if it rises in the third house as it is controlled by *Mangal*. But according to Lal Kitab this house is owned by Mercury/*Bhdha*, which is not considered a friend to Moon. Therefore, the *jatak* has to do something to satisfy *Budha*. For that he/she has to feed 100 unmarried girls and give them some money at that occasion. Instead the *jatak* may distribute pen or pencils and note books to the poor school children to pacify *Budha*. The school children are considered *Budha* and Jupiter, so if poor children are helped in their education the bad effect of *Budha* will be reduced. When the Moon is rising in the 3rd house, Mars will be very favourable as both are friends. As the Moon is an auspicious planet, it will help keeping good relationship with brothers and sisters. It will also make the *jatak* to keep good relationship with the neighbours. All good planets rising in this house will be very helpful as they will have their aspects on the 9th house which is the house of luck.

Mars/*Mangal* is always considered good in the third house as it provides courage to *jatak*. From the third house *Mangal* will have its aspects on the 9th and the 10th houses. As *Mangal* provides courage, it may also create some problems with family and neighbours. When *Mangal* rises in the third house, and if Jupiter rise in the 10th and *Budha* in the 9th, they give good results to *jatak*. In that case there is no need to make any *upayas* for *Mangal*. But if Mangal is rising in *Budha's* house/sign, one has to make some *upayas* for *Budha*. For that the *jatak* need to feed very small girls or help the poor children in their further education.

In case *Bhdha*/Mercury rises in the third house in Mars *sign* it may not be considered good and may bring bad results. Lal Kitab unfolds that such a *jatak* may be a leper and rejected by the society. It also has its aspects on the 9th house from the 3rd. The ninth is governed by Jupiter and therefore it will bring bad results to one's luck as Jupiter and Mercury/*Budha* are not friendly to each other. Lak Kitab considers that 10th house is also governed by Jupiter so Mercury will also adversely affect this house. To ward off the bad effects of Jupiter, the *jatak* is advised to clean one's teeth with alum. Not only it will keep the *jatak's* teeth tidy and strong if cleaned by alum it will also help bringing good results as far as one's luck and job status is concerned. As a second *upaya* Lal Kitab suggests that the *jatak* must get the nose pierced to wear a small silver ring for 100 days in it. This *upaya* has been chosen from

Our *rishis* and *munies*
called sixteen *sanskars* (holy activities to be performed), which can help

make one cool, it has been proposed so. If one wears a silver *nath*/ring in one's nose, it keeps one's mind cool as one of the arteriesgoes to the mind from the nose. It is because of that that most women in India get their nose pierced and they wear a *nath*/ring in it traditionally after their

nose and going into one's teeth. It will also inspire*Budha* to support the native. As an *upaya* it is also stated in Lal Kitab that *mung*/a kind of pulse, after keeping it in a glass of water in night, may be given in the morning to birds to feed. It will certainly help one's work go well and the *jatak* will go on improving his/her life gradually leading towards success in projects, business, and work. But our experience betrays that birds don't eat all that many times. If it is so, then the *jatak* should put a lot of *moong dal* (a kind of pulse easily digestible) into water on each Tuesday give it to

the life of the *jatak*. As Venus is a great friend of *Budha*/Mercury, when these two combine positively by certain *upayas*, the Sun also gives good results. Since Lal Kitab contains lots of *tits bits* and *tantras*, it suggests such *upayas* for a *jatak* to to ward off problems and bad times. It suggests that twice to the age of a *jatak*, he/she after washing the *dhak* leaves into milk should put between two pieces of stones. Though it is not any kind of

Mangal and *Budha* and in order to pacify *Budha*, Lal Kitab suggests some *upayas* such as serving unmarried young girls by different ways to please Jupiter and *Bhdha*. Our experience unfolds that Jupiter rising in the third house is extremely good. From that position it has aspects on the 7th, 9th and the 11^{th}houses. It is like giving abundence of happiness (rain of nectar/*amrit*) to the native and brightens his/her house. Since Jupiter is an auspicious planet, it will keep happy relations with sisters and brothers and also with the neighbours.

Venus is considered very helpful if it rises in the third house according to lal Kitab.Because Venus is friendly to *Budha* and *Mangal*, it is extremely favourable. As Venus is rising in Mangal's hosue, the *jatak's* wife will support him like one's brother to a large extent. Venus being an auspicious

good only the placements of the planets in a house for predictions, but it has not considered other things such as rising of different planest in the same hosue or their combined aspects on that particular house or other houses, or the effect of mahadasha as well.On the contrary when we provide predictions about certain matters, issues or existing problems, we need to consider all these different things when giving any predictions. Therefore, anyone who is involved or who provides predctions on certain matters from astrological point of view, he/she must consider every aspect important astrologically, or his/her predictions will nmot come true.

If Saturn is rising in the third house, it is considered to be rising in the house of *Mangal* or *Budha*. Therefore, it is not considered auspicious in the third house. From the third house Santurn has its aspects on the 3rd house so it may bring good results relating that house. Consequently,

and the eighth houses are controlled by Mars so Saturn does not provide good results if it has aspects on those houses. If a *jatak*, in whose *kundali* Saturn rises in the third house, involves himself in the gas selling business, or if he is involved with oil business, becomes a contractor, sells stones or dry & rough soil (*bazri*), or deals with machinery, sells iron or wood, he will ultimately get losses in all these business activities. As satrun is a rough & hard-hearted planet, it is bound to bring bad relationships with brothers and neighbours. It may also bring losses in short journies. Lal Kitab suggests that the *jatak* must not keep dry wood on the roof of his house, as Saturn will have its unproductive tenth aspect on the twelfth house, which astrologically represents the roof of a house. It is better to keep the roof of the house clean to get good results from Saturn. In order to please Saturn and be away from its bad effects, Lal Kitab suggests to feed dogs and avoid drinking, eating meat or using tobacco. All these things will surely bring bad effect on the *jatak's* life.

Rahu in the third house is considered auspicious according to the ancient astrology as well as Lal Kitab. The third house, represents courage & strong arms. If Rahu rises in this house, it bestows energy and strength to the *jatak's* arms. According to Lal Kitab as well as in view of the ancient astrology, Rahu rising in the signs of Mercury---Gemini or Virgo, will always give good results because it is considered to be exalting in these two signs of Mercury. But it provides bad results if it has its aspects on Sagittarius or Pisces signs which are governed by Jupiter. However, Rahu being friendly to Mercury and Ketu to Jupiter, these shadowy planets always provide good results if they have their aspects on the respective signs of Mercury & Jupiter. Lal Kitab suggests that Rahu in the third house is always considered good and there is no need to do any *upayas* for it. But if Rahu from the third house has its bad aspects on the Sun or Moon, the *jatak* should serve physically crippled and insane people and help a poor girl in her marriage. Only then Rahu will not give inauspicious results.

Lal Kitab considers rising of Ketu in the third house as inauspicious as it brings bad results to the native. Therefore, such a *jatak* should always avoid living in a house which is made on the land having three corners, or avoid keeping company of three cousins etc. But if Ketu rises in its friendly signs (that of Venus, or Jupiter's *rahies*/signs), it will provide good results to the *jatak*. It will give bad results if it rises in Mercury's signs or if it is in the company of the Sun or Moon. As the third house represents short journeys, the *jatak* will earn his livelihood by a business that involves short journeys. But in case Ketu is not auspicious in the third house because it rises in its enemy signs, the *jatak* should wear silver reigns in the thumbs of his feet and always help his nephews to ward off the ill effects of Ketu.

The Fourth House

In a *kundali*/chart the fourth house consists of the sign Cancer.Its owner is

in this sign. The Moon is considered like human heart and it represents happiness as well as unhappiness. If a person has to do something against the wishes of his/her heart, he/she gets unhappiness. Astrologically Saturn usually causes unhappiness and problems to human beings. When Saturn has its aspects on the planet moon or rises along with it, then the Moon is

when seven and a half years' period starts when Saturn transits one sign before the sign in which the moon is placed in a *kundali*, usually people are unhappy because they are unable to do or act what they really desire to take up. On the contrary just opposite the desired effect is created by their acts. That makes them totally unhappy.

The fourth house represents mother, property & house, vehicle,

breast, land, animal that produces milk, in-laws, a fruit garden, family environment etc. It is also believed that 'in case the moon is better placed in a *kundali*, the native will live for more number of years. Lal Kitab considers the 4th house to be the central point in a *kundali*or equivalent to the 1st house. Because of that Lal Kitab considers that all the planets bow themselves before that house. Therefore, not to disturb this house, one needs to lead a fairly clean life and never indulge in low activities and eat or drink things which are socially not approved or which provide harm to one's health. If one does so, it will be just like wearing warm or woolen clothes during summer season or eating ice-cream during hard winters.

In case the sun rises in the fourth house, the *jatak* is born in the middle of the night. If the sun rises in the tenth house, the *jatak* is born during noon. But if he/she is born during the evening time, the Sun will be placed in the seventh house. If the sun is placed in the *lagna*, the *jatak* should be born during early morning hours. As there is no sun in the sky during the middle of the night, it has no *digbal* or does not possess any harmful power. However, the Sun is a very hot and a harsh planet, it may create some problems to the *jatak*. But being in the house of the Moon (according to Lal Kitab) it may not give troubles to the native for this house is owned by the moon and from the 4th it has aspects on the tenth house. If Saturn, Rahu or Ketu have aspects on it or are with it, it may be inauspicious then and may create troubles. So, in order to ward off its ill-effects the native would need to serve the blind or crippled or insane peoplefor Saturn is blind, Rahu is mad and Ketu is crippled. It is because of that that serving cripples, blind or insane people will help the native to restore happiness by

The moon placed in the fourth house in a *kundali* is in its own house (Lal Kitab). Fourth house represents the native's heart or soul, so it will provide peace and happiness to the native. Such a native will not bear an agitated attitude and mostly lead a peaceful life provided the moon is strong in degrees and has no aspects from Saturn, Rahu or Ketu. Lal Kitab indicates that if the moon is in the fourth house (in its own sign) and has aspects from Jupiter rising in the tenth house then such a native must not feed *sadhus*, seers or mendicants for it will ultimately bring him/her dishonor for Jupiter in the tenth will rise in Capricorn sign, and its aspects on the Moon will get him/her defame and dishonor. Therefore, to be away from the ill-effect of the debilitated Jupiter, one must be away from such acts like feeding the mendicants etc. However, if we examine the moon *lagna*

forms *Gajkeshari Yoga*. Such a *jatak* will be highly religious and will keep his home environment clean and pious and will be involved in religious activities and God's prayers constantly. Such a native if gives milk and

Mangal/Mars is considered in a debilitated sign in the fourth house according to Lal Kitab. Such a placement also forms Manglik Yogs which is detrimental for one's marriage or brings unhappiness in marriage unless both the charts (that of the boy & girl) are properly matched. It also makes one agitated and keeps in angry moods constantly. If Moon is water, Mars *jatak*

may live away from home or may have constant quarrels in the family. Mars from the fourth house will have its aspects on the seventh house. It will affect adversely husband/wife relationship, but if it is placed in the tenth or eleventh house, it will bring good results and becomes *digbali*

land & property. Even if a weak moon is placed in the third house, Mars will not provide bad results. On the contrary Mars will give good results. A native having such placements of Mars and the Moon must keep away from petty quarrels and unholy activities. In order to keep Mars in control one needs to offer sugar into the running water (river/canal). If such a *jatak* keeps good relationship with brothers and sisters, he/she will be spared from the ill-effects of Mars then.

Mercury, if placed in the fourth house in a chart, is highly auspicious. It is also because Mercury considers moon as its close friend.On the contrary the moon does not consider Mercury as its friend. However, Mercury is an auspicious planet and represents business, education & intellect.It is because of that one may earn a lot of money through business. But such a *jatak* is forbidden to keep a parrot as a pet in the house and should not cultivate a thorn plant or need not plant a money-plant in his/her house to get good results from Mercury.

If Jupiter rises with the moon in the fourth house, it would make the native kind-hearted, who will always go on helping others. In the fourth house it will be exalted and will aspect the tenth house as such the *jatak* will be hard-working and honest as well. He will also be helping his friends, serve the mother and will like to serve others in their need. Therefore, Lal Kitab considers Jupiter's placement best in this house provided any of its enemies are not reducing its good effects. Rahu, Ketu, Venus and Mercury are Jupiter's enemies. Their ill-effect, if any, must be reduced by giving alms to the needy and poor and such a native must not use eggs, meat or drinks and should not be envious to others.

Like Jupiter, Venus is also considered good and strong in this house. But Lal Kitab unfolds that if it is coupled with the moon, it will give ill-effects. Such a native may marry twice in life because moon and Venus both are considered female planets. To avoid a second marriage, such a native may marry his wife once again and call her with two different names so that bed effects of Venus' placement in the fourth with the Moon may be reduced. The native should also offer curd to the poor on Fridays. It will help reducing bad effects of Venus if it is ill-placed with the moon in the fourth house.

Lal Kitab holds that if Venus is coupled with the Moon in the fourth house, it may lead to producing black insects in the *jatak's* house. It may also be troublesome to mother. Such a *jatak* may have an old house at a remote place or in an abandoned village. In case serpents appear in the *jatak's* house they must not be killed. It will help riches to grow. Such a native may also keep a serious bearing on account of Moon & Venus being combined in the fourth house.

To get good effects from Saturn, the native should pour milk and rice (sweet pudding) into a well if it is near the house of the *jatak*. He should also offer rice pudding to crows and insects if he wants to reduce the bad effect of Saturn.

Rahu & Ketu in the fourth house normally don't bother the native with their ill-effect.But our experience unfolds that Rahu being in the Moon's house, may send the *jatak* away from his parents. He may also go abroad. He may not be able to get parental affection on account of any reason. Besides he may not have his own house but usually will live in a rented house, which he may go on changing several times in life. He may also not have any vehicle to rise &enjoy, but if such a *jatak* demolish his bathroom by chance, it will create several kinds of problems for him & his family.

Our experience betrays that to construct a new house is equal to start a new life. We have also experienced that when a native starts constructing a house, it is almost customary that quarrels erupt. To be away from such happenings the native should always pay the labourers regularly. If Rahu is rising in the fourth house, the native must not keep raw coal in his house & neither should start breaking the house from different sides for

he should offer 400 grams dry *dhania* into running water (river etc.) to ward off Rahu's ill-effect if any. He should also keep his house clean to invoke good effect of rahu but various kinds of toys, wine or any kind of intoxicants whether in the form of medicines, must not keep in his house to keep away Rahu's bad effect.

If Ketu is in the fourth house, it will surely create problems for the *jatak* as it will be adversely affected by the Moon.

Our experience betrays that the Moon in the sixth house always leads the native to have a hard life. Native's education is badly affected and his work also suffers. The Moon represents *jatak's* heart or soul and if the moon is placed in the sixth house, it will not make the native work seriously. It happens as the sixth house belongs to Ketu & both Ketu and the Moon are enemies. To ward off Ketu's ill-effect the native should offer every year a lot of rise to running water. If he puts four kilograms of rice into running water, it will give better results. It will further be good if the native collects money from the entire family members to buy rice & to put it into running water. Though to put silver into running water could be a better *upaya*, but as it is dearer, rice would be equally good for that act. Lal Kitab considers Ketu important as far as children are concerned. So, one should not worry about children if one does not have them for long as Ketu generally gives children when the *jatak* reaches 36 to 48 years of age. In order to have children at the right age, the native should get the blessing from his family *purohit*/pundit, and give yellow coloured clothes or other eatables as offerings. Whenever he visits the *purohit*, he should offer him blankets, bananas, gold, gram pulses etc. The more he gives to the *purohit*,

the *jatak*

having children. Such a native may go to foreign countries, but that would mean getting separated from parents to get jobs.

The Fifth House

Lak Kitab considers that in a *knudali* *rashi* rise.

consider about children, education, position in state, intellect, belief in God & dedication towards Him, stomach, entertainment, shares, lottery, love affairs, cinema, music & singing and sports etc. from this house. As the Sun represents government & Jupiter intellect & science, so we consider that a *jatak* in whose *kundali*
own or friendly sign, he will get a good position in the government. This is the second *trikona* *trikona*is the ascendant, which represents the entire *jatak*
her children & the third *trikona* is the ninth house that represents his/her

jatak does not get any sickness. If food that goes to stomach gets digested properly, one gets proper blood circulation which also affects one's wisdom & intellect positively. It will help him/her to get proper rise in life. But if someone does not possess good mind/wisdom, he is not considered a sane

Ancient astrologers reckon that one's luck should also be considered from

In whose chart/*kundali*

monkey to ward of the ill-effects of the Sun.But the sun is a hot planet

considers that before calculating all such effects of the Sun, one needs to consider the Moon's periods or *dasha* or *Mahadasha*
dasha are operating in a *kundlai*, such ill-effects from the Sun may not be experienced by the native.

to the Sun & Jupiter ultimately. Therefore, the *jatak* will be religious

Kitab also considers that the Moon will have its aspects on the eleventh should keep reading regularly & religiously & worship God Shiva & keep Him in his/her mind most of the time so that he/she may be

not favourable in the chart.

Mangal
Ancient astrology reckons *lagna*
Mangal

jatak will be sharp & wise and will use the reasoning power when taking decisions. But if Mars rises in its enemy sign it may give odd results. Lal Kitab indicates that such *a jatak*

will constantly worry to get more and more wealth. Lal Kitab suggests certain *upayas* to satisfy *Mangal*. One of these is to put a small copper pot full of water near one's head before he/she goes to sleep. He/she should drink it every morning after getting up. *Mangal* is a great friend of Jupiter and the Sun. So it will provide good children to the native and after their birth the native will get a lot of progress in life. Lal Kitab unfolds that the planets that are good in one's *kundali* may do wonders to the native if he/she uses things or makes *upayas* in line with them. *Mangal* being the planet of children will help the *jatak* tremendously if he takes up a job of a doctor or a physician.

If Mercury/*Budha*
and the Sun. *Budha* bestows knowledge and controls one's speaking power (throat). Therefore, the *jatak* may be a good singer. But *Budha* is also Jupiter's enemy, so certain *upayas* need to be done to satisfy Jupiter. The native should offer a glass-full of gram *dal*/pulse to god Ganesha on Thursdays. It will give happiness and progress to the native if he/she prays for it before the god. Lal Kitab also suggests the *jatak* to wear a copper

but then Lal Kitab also considers avoiding wearing such a coin. The native whose chart rises with Aries, Cancer, Leo or Scorpio *lagna*for him/her wearing a coin will not be favourable. As *Budha* is rising in this house, it will inspire the native a lot to do some work related to mind and full of wisdom.

to Lal Kitab. If it rises in this house it has its aspects on the 9th, 11th&*lagna* (1st house). All this will provide a lot of wisdom and intelligence to the native. But at times it is also observed that such a native may not have children. To have children, the native should regularly go on remembering

Sri Rama as well as Lord Shiva& need to do regular *japs*(read from the religious books) of Om Namo Shiva & offer *kesher* on Shiv Linga. It may give the *jatak* children& lots of happiness as Lord Shiva will be pleased with him.

Jupiter which are the enemies of Venus. So certain *upayas* for the Sun & Jupiter need to be done to satisfy those planets to get good and favourable results. As an *upaya* the native should do *yagya* but all may not be able to do so there are other ways &*upayas* to ward off the ill-effects of the said planets. As an *upaya* the native should listen to the story/*katha* Bhagwan Satya Narayana & may do some sort of & feed 5 to 7 needy people. It will serve and help getting good results. To satisfy Jupiter the native should offer to god Ganesha a pot full of gram *dal* on Thursdays & par to get rid of Jupiter's ill-effects. Venus being an auspicious planet will provide the native a lot of respect from people provided it is not debilitated or weak in degrees.

Rahu & Ketu, if well placed in a *kundali,* may bring good results to the native. If Jupiter & Saturn rise in one house, Venus gives bad results. As Venus represents female, the native may have more number of girls as children, but Venus may provide good education to the native. If a native, in whose *kundali*

he will live well but he should not make a love-marriage if he wants to be happy further in life.

belongs to the Sun according to Lal Kitab. Both Saturn & the Sun are enemies so the native may not have any children. So certain *upayas* need to be done to satisfy Saturn. The *jatak* should build or construct houses which will satisfy Saturn and the native will have good children but the *jatak*

start business relating gas, oil, raw material like *bajri*/rough soil, stone,

of business. But if *kundali* becomes strong due to the *Chandra Lagna*, ill-effects of Saturn may be reduced to some extent.

Certain good *upayas* are suggested by Lal Kitab to reduce the ill-effects of Saturn. It says that the native should offer almonds at some religious place but half of that should be offered to running water after

during a particular year in *gauchara* (movements of the planets in the orbit). But it should only be done when there are no planets in the eighth & the second houses in the native's *kundali.* He should visit the religious places only when such combinations don't occur in his *kundali.* As Saturn

Saturn, the native should offer to people some almonds in religious places.

should keep some sharp but small and clean weapons of iron in his house. The native should never thresh labourers, but serve the blind and crippled

it creates problems to wife/husband. Saturn is considered as salt in Lal Kitab, therefore, it suggests that when a child is born to the native, instead of distributing sweets, he should give salt to people to satisfy Saturn.

Jupiter, so such a native need to satisfy both the Sun & Jupiter by several *upayas*. First of all Rahu will not give any children to the native. It may also happen that there may be abortions & Rahu would not permit children

It is also harmful for the husband & wife of elder sister & elder brother. The eleventh house represents elder brother and Rahu has its aspects on it. Just opposite to Rahu, Ketu will also be placed, so both these inauspicious planets will not let the native get any help from friends or relatives. But if auspicious planets like Jupiter have their aspects on Ketu, some of its ill-effects may be reduced. As an *upayas* for Rahu Lal Kitab unfolds that the native should get a silver elephant as a toy having its nose downwards and place it in sleeping room & he should also marry his wife twice. It will satisfy Rahu. Lal Kitab also suggests that the native should give away his daughter/ or a girl in marriage. If he cannot do so then he should help a poor girl in her marriage by giving utensils or clothes etc. It may help satisfy Rahu & its bad effects. As an *upaya*
wire under the threshold of his house. It will work like *Laxhman Rekha* and would not permit bad things happen to the native. As silver represents the Moon and the silver elephant whose nose is downwards is placed in the native's sleeping room, all this will save the native from bad things happening.

Certain *upayas* are mentioned to stay away from Ketu's ill-effects.The native is advised to give away a milk-giving cow and its calf to a poor *brahman*. As Ketu is an enemy to the Sun, it may affect mother's health

Rahu will be rising in the eleventh, it will affect adversely and he may not *upaya* mentioned in Lal Kitab against all such odds is to keep away from bad habits, drinking and eating meat etc. and by keeping one's conduct good.

The Sixth House

Ancient astrology considers the sixth house representing sickness, incurring loans, enemies, subordination, involvement in competitions and hard work etc. Saturn &*Mangal* *Budha* and Ketu. This house represents the underneath world, where demons live. Human beings live on the earth 7 gods stay in the Heaven. Human feet are also controlled by the sixth house. Rahu is considered as an exalted planet in this house. Lal Kitab suggests the native should put 4 kilos coins into a well to satisfy Rahu. Since this *upaya* *upayas* should be altered according to times and place.The native is advised to serve the needy & the poor to satisfy Rahu if it has ill-effects on the native. The sixth is somehow related to the second, eighth & the twelfth houses. Ketu is supposed to control the twelfth house & Jupiter is considered to air which gives life to all. It is because of that that Ketu is considered friendly to Jupiter. But Jupiter is always considered an enemy to Rahu. As the sixth house becomes the third house from the third if we start counting it may affect the mother's younger brother, sisters etc. adversely if Rahu is not well placed in the sixth house or if it is badly affected by Jupiter.

Both Lal Kitab & and ancient astrology consider that any planet placed in the sixth house becomes inauspicious & give bad results. Lal Kitab considers *Budha* auspicious and important if placed in this house. In case the Sun is placed in the sixth house in a *kundali*the native is advised to feed unmarried girls. Lal Kitab considers Moon inauspicious if placed in the sixth house as it considers this house to be controlled by *Budha*& Ketu. Since the Moon is an enemy to both *Budha*& Ketu, the *jatak* is advised to feed 101 unmarried girls & give them some money as well. In order to satisfy Ketu, the native should feed 101 dogs or if it is possible he may keep a *double roti* in a small bag and go on giving one peace to every dog he meets on the way while going for a walk early in the morning. He may feed girls or distribute pen, pencils or note books to the needy students in a school. Our experience unfolds that if the Moon rises in the sixth, it is not auspicious to the native. Such a native may go on quarrelling with others without any cause. He may not be interested in any sort of work & does not enjoy his time during studies. The native may also be involved in some kind of bad habits like drinking or eating bad things which bring intoxication. The native certainly troubles his mother by his odd activities. As an *upaya* Lal Kitab unfolds to give away lot of water to drink to the most needy & miserable persons. It will certainly lessen the ill-effect of the Moon. If possible the native may also arrange some drinking facility in a hospital or at a *samshan ghat* (the place where dead are burnt or buried). It may help the *jatak* to get happiness and every kind of pleasure in life.

Mangal placed in the sixth house is adversely affected by Ketu.So the *jatak* has to do some *upayas* for Ketu. Lal Kitab considers that if *Mangal* is placed in the sixth house, the Sun in that *kundali* is supposed to be in its exalted sign. *Mangal*, therefore, rising in the sixth house will destroy enemies & sickness but it also represents elder brother so the *jatak* will

results indicated above would come true if the native is involved with good acts and possesses good conduct. To get good results from *Mangal*, the native should always help the poor girls & assist them when they get married.

Lal Kitab considers *Budha* in the sixth house quite auspicious as it considers *Budha's* own house. As an *upaya* Lal Kitab suggests that the

goddess with bowed head. It will help to start the work well as *Budha* represents business. Though *Budha*& Ketu are enemies, but if they rise together in the sixth house, they will give good results.

Lal Kitab reckons Jupiter in inauspicious in the sixth house. Therefore, the native should use Jupiter related things as little as possible & try to keep away from father, grand-father & children. Lal Kitab unfolds that in case Jupiter rises in the sixth house, and Ketu sits in the eighth, such a native hardly gets an issue (child). As an *upaya* he should distribute pencils & note-books to the school children.

Venus in the sixth house is considered in a debilitated state according to Lal Kitab.Venus represents wife or Goddess Laxhmi, so the native may have problems related these two—wife as well as money. As Venus is considered *jatak's* wife, so his wife should keep money tugged in her hair with a gold clip. Though gold represents Jupiter, but by doing such an *upaya*, the wife of the *jatak* may have no hair in the long run. She is advised not to get her hair trimmed and try to keep them as long as possible. It is because of that that our *rishies&munies* have suggested that while offering prayers one must cover one's head. It will get help from Jupiter, which may give favourable results. Some people also keep a small hair-tail just behind their head. It is

use a gold clip in her hair and keep her hair long, it helps her husband in getting progress in business and at work place. It will also help keeping good relationship between husband & wife. But if the woman (wife) gets her hair cut and keep them short, she gets *Mangal's* adverse effects& that may cause quarrels between both, man & woman. A *Sikh*, a Hindu and a Muslim wear some kind of covering on their heads. It helps them to get good effects from Jupiter. It is also advised by Lal Kitab that the native should keep a small silver ball in his pocket, which will help him in many ways. Roundness of the ball represents *Budha*& silver represents Moon. It will also help the native to get good effects & progress in business or work.

Lal Kitab suggests that the *jatak* must feed small birds. It will help him to get favours from *Budha*& Venus as well. Lal Kitab considers that Saturn in the sixth house is not auspicious because this house represents sickness and enmity& Saturn also supports these matters—sickness & enmity. So whenever Saturn rises in the sixth house, the native may not be happy related land & property, and if he involves with the oil, gas, stone, raw soil (*bazri*) or transport business, he will get losses. When Saturn transits in the sixth house in *gauchar* (in the orbit) during any year, that year the native must not buy leather or iron articles for him. He may give a leather pair of shoes to a poor beggar, leper, or a labourer instead, to get Saturn's good effects. Lal Kitab also suggests the *jatak* to put six earthen-built bottles

will help improve *jatak's* health. We have observed that this kind of *upaya* is very useful to the *jatak* in many ways. Lal Kitab suggests that in case Saturn rises in the sixth house in a chart right from birth (nativity), that *jatak* must give a leather pair of shoes to a needy, poor person to ward off Saturn's ill-effect.

Lal Kitab considers Rahu's placement in the sixth house as good. The sixth house represents enemies, sickness, loans& losses. Rahu being the owner of this house will destroy all such odd things which will in turn bring peace and happiness to the native.

If Ketu rises in the sixth house, it may not do any good to the native. In that case Rahu will rise in the 12th house, which is the house of expenses and losses. Ketu gets exalted in Jupiter's ninth (Sagittarius) and twelfth (Pisces) signs/*rashis*. Ketu's rising in the sixth may not be favourable to the native. Itusually gives problems from his children as well as involvement in useless expenses. The only *upaya* for that will be that the *jatak* should not be an egoist, may not be hot headed and should not feel proud on his own things. He should always remember God to save him from odds in life.

The Seventh House

The seventh house represents husband/wife, partnership in business, opposition or opposite party, court problems, &litigations etc. It is the house that indicates the time of death of a *jatak*. It is also related tointer-national business, general audience, and the middle part in body, etc. Venus is the owner of this house. Venus &*Bhdha* are also considered *karak* of this house. *Budha* is considered *karak* as it represents business. Lal Kitab considers *lagna* as the soul & the seventh house as *Maya* (riches) because every native wants to be rich and wish to possess a beautiful & good wife or husband, get every kind of happiness in life that includes a good abode as well. He should also be famous & be friendly to every person of whatever religion he/she belongs to. Lal Kitab considers human life like two parts of a grinding machine in which all gets broken into small pieces. Thus, without caring for God, Who lives in all the living things, the *jatak*may go on grinding himselfoddly in the matters of life and gets into troubles.

Saturn in this house is considered in an exalted state, but the Sun in debilitated state. If there are planets in *lagna*& not in the seventh house, the planets will start helping the native after marriage. The native should keep a maid servant & serve cows by giving them food. But if there are no planets in *lagna* and but some are rising in the seventh house, the *jatak* is advised to wear in the neck a 2" squire piece of silver or gold, tied or

jatak's wife as

it will diminish the ill-effects of Venus. The *jatak* is advised (Lal Kitab) to make 100 *chapaties*

the ill-effects of several planets and get help from the planets sitting in the

The Sun is considered in a debilitated state in the seventh house. The native in whose chart the Sun rises in the seventh house his time of birth would be around the sun-setting. It is not considered a good time of birth as it creates differences between husband & wife's relationship. As *upaya*, the *jatak* is advised to sprinkle some milk on the stove after making *chapaties*. This *upaya*

that will come out when milk is put on the stove will bring freshness in the house and make the life of *jatak* happy. It will also help to invite gods to stay in that house as gods live in the places where things are clean& pure. Demons stay where there is uncleanliness and dirt. The Moon is

make the life of husband/wife happier and lovely.

According to Lal Kitab if *Mangal* rises in the seventh house in a *jatak'skundali,* it is quite auspicious. But the ancient astrologers consider that *Mangal* in the seventh house creates Manglik Dosha, which lead to a quarrelsome life between husband and wife. They may live away from each other or one of them may suffer from some kind of illness. In case *Mangal* rises in its friend's sign/*rashi* or if it has aspects from friendly planets, then *Mangal*/Mars given good results. But if it rises in its enemy's sign or has aspects from Rahu or Ketu or rises with them, it is going to do so many odd things to the native. In that case the native is advised to distribute some sweets to people on Tuesdays in a Shri Hanuman's temple.

Budha is considered auspicious if it rises in the seventh house, especially if it is in its own sign or in a friendly sign/*rashi.* Thenit will provide favourable results. Both husband and wife will leada friendly life and live happily. The partner of such a native will be intelligent & he/she

Lal Kitab does not consider Jupiter favourable if it rises in the seventh house.It unfolds that such a *jatak* should not give alms to a *mahatma* or *sant*

have also observed that if Jupiter rises in the seventh house it is quite auspicious. Both, husband and wife are generally religious & wise and abide by the law because it is one of the centers in a *kundali*. Therefore,

seventh house Jupiter will also have its aspects on the *lagna*, which is really very auspicious. As an *upaya* the native is advised not to indulge in drinking, or should eat meat or eggs. If the native leads such a life, he will be greatly happy.

Venus in the seventh house is considered very auspicious as it is its own house. So Venus will provide good results to the native.But ancient astrology unfolds that if Venus is strong in degrees or if it rises in its friend's house or sits with friends, it will give favourable results. In order to keep Venus helpful, it is necessary that both husband and wife should not quarrel and live amicably. As *Budha* is the *karak* of this house, the native is advised to speak politely to all to get good results from both Venus and Mercury.

Saturn in the seventh house is considered favorable if it rises in its own or friend's *rashi*. Lal Kitab unfolds that if there are no planets in *langna* it *lagna*. As an *upaya* the native should try to be religious, keep a *choti* (small tail of hair) at the back of his head, and should also wear a white or yellow coloured cap on the head. It will help to get good results from Saturn. We have observed that if in the seventh house Capricorn or Aquarius sign rise, the native will get married late in life. It is because of Saturn that things are usually delayed. In order to keep Saturn in order and make it favourable, the native must not indulge in drinking and eat meat, eggs or such things. He should also read *Laxhmi Chalisha* for forty days to invoke Saturn's good effect.

Rahu in the seventh house is considered inauspicious according to Lal Kitab. It may create a suspicious environment between husband and wife and would not let them live happily. If Rahu is in the seventh house, Ketu would rise in the *lagna*. As a result the *jatak* will not be able to stay at his home, will be away most of the time and go on changing his jobs. If Rahu rises in the seventh, one of the partners will be either in military, so will stay away from home or be constantly sick, so no amicable life will be enjoyed by the couple. Such a native will not keep any control on his eating & will become unhappy due to several sorts of ailments. Some consider *Mangal* bad in this house, but our experience unfolds that Rahu is far more inauspicious in the seventh house. Such a native, if he/she starts working with any partner, will soon be separated from his partner. If Rahu or Ketu are in *lagna*, such results are bound to happen & often the native stays abroad, get separated from the partner. If Saturn rises in the *lagna*& Rahu in the seventh, the native does not get good education. Both Rahu & Ketu are impediments in furthering one's education.

Lal Kitab does not consider Ketu auspicious if it rises in the seventh house. If Ketu is in the seventh, one needs to pacify Venus as it becomes inauspicious to the native. Ancient astrologers consider rising of Ketu in the seventh house unfavourable as it brings bad results. It does not permit husband and wife live happily. It mayalso create urinary related sickness. As *upaya* the native should always speak to others politely & not indulge in false promises, also becaue *Budha* is the *karak* of this house. *Budha* always demands the native to speak in a good and polite manner. If the native makes false promises or speaks impolitely to others, both *Budha*& Ketu will bring harm to him/her.

The Eighth House

Astrologically, the eighth house represents death, ditch, depth, dirty lane or dirty water, or an underground house. Ancient astrology as well as Lal Kitab considers this house unfavorable & gloomy. Therefore, no planet is considered auspicious in this house. According Lal Kitab, the sign Scorpio rises which is controlled or owned by *Mangal*. But Lal Kitab considers this house as the headquarters of *Mangal*/Mars & Saturn because these two planets usually give problems and bad results. For example, *Mangal*

military. Saturn is considered to be a very cruel and a low kind of planet which is mostly related to destruction & devastation. When a judge orders someone to be hanged, the *zallad*/hangman puts the convicted person on the gallows or hangs him & ultimately kills him. But neither a military person nor a hangman is considered guilty & no case in any court is considered against them. Though this house belongs to Saturn and Mars, these two planets don't give any good or favourable results if placed in this house.

Lal Kitab considers this house as a place where dead are burnt or buried & when there are no planets in the second house, this house is reckoned to be sleeping, not effective. Lal Kitab considers that when this house is in a state of sleep, it must not be awakened as doing so will be inviting

upayas suggested by Lal Kitab to make this house better or improve its effects. For example, if Jupiter is placed in this house, the *jatak* should plant a *peepal* tree in a

Jupiter will start giving good results and will become favourable to the native. Most thingsrelated to Jupiter will also start giving good results and the house will be favorable to the native. In fact, planting a tree in a burial/funeral place is a good act as it helps people to take rest or get into the shade when they reach that place to cremate a deadbody. Ancient astrology considers that when the *lagnesh*/ascendant rises in the eighth house or vice versa (the owner of the eighth house rising in the ascendant),

these houses, it makes the life of the native full of problems and he has to struggle a lot in life. When *lagnesh* sits in the eighth house, usually the

problems or goes to a foreign land away from his relatives. Such a *jatak* also become interested in astrology or some kind of secret science as this house is also a kind of secret house. As an *upaya* the *jatak* is advised to put into the running water some *gur*/sugar, which will lessen the ill-effects of the Sun to a great extent.

If the Moon is placed in the eighth house it will create danger from water for the *jatak*. But if such a *jatak* does not drown in water, he/she will have a restless heart which will go on bothering him for small things and he will get disturbed. As the Moon represents one's heart or soul, & if ill-placed in the eighth house, it will always create problems for the *jatak.* If in a native's *kundali* the Moon is placed in the eighth house and no auspicious planets rise in any of the *kendras* houses, it may cause death to the person when he/she is merely a child. For example, if the sign Cancer rises in a *kundali*, and the moon along with Ketu sits in the eighth house, and in the second house Rahu rises though Jupiter

does not do any work and he is 26 years old. Another example is of a native in whose chart the sign Cancer is rising. The Moon sits in the eighth along with Saturn. He lost around twenty lacks in gambling. What we mean by these examples is that the Moon which represents one' soul & heart, if it sits in the eighth house & does not have any aspects from the auspicious planets, such a *jatak* will not only be creating problems for himself but for others too. As *upaya* the native must seek advice of his parents before starting any work. If he goes on taking blessings from the parents his life may become much better. As an *upaya* the he is advised to carry some water from the place where dead are buried or burnt & keep it in his home. It will be just like getting blessings from Lord Shiva. It may happen so as the eighth house represents a burial place (or where dead are burnt) and it is the place where Lord Shiva resides. If the native keep his parents in good esteem, it will be a sort of blessings for him.

Lal Kitab considers *Mangal's* placement in the eighth house inauspicious. It will harm the relationship between brothers & may harm the children as well. The native may have blood related sickness or problems. As *upaya* the native is advised to wear a15 grams of a squire piece of silver in a chain. It will be much better if this piece of silver is obtained from one of the seniors of the family or may be taken from the parents. He should drive very carefully to avoid any accidents. He should also go on helping friends & brothers, and read *Sunderkand* chapter from the Ramanaya every day as well as feed dogs every day with the pieces of bread. Lal Kitab considers *Budha's* placement bad in the eighth house. It is because this house belongs to the enemy of *Bhdha.* If *Budha* rises in the eighth, it will disturb the nervous system of the native and may create problems in the mind as well. As the eighth house is related to 'death', *Bhdha* placed in it may give problems to the native's teeth and mind. For example in a *kundali* in which Virgo is rising &*Budha* sits in the lieighth house, such a native will go on possessing suspicion on the members of family without any sod reason & involve in quarrels. *Budha* as a *lagnesh* if rises in the eighth house, certainly make the native misjudge people & involve in quarrels on matters that don't exist in reality. As an *upaya, the jatak* should get his/her nose pierced and wear in it silver (small ring of silver) for 100 days. It will pacify the native mind and provide him/her the capacity to think better away from suspicious. When the native will wear silver, it will give peace to his mind and he may live happily without keeping any suspicion for others. Thus, he may start doing good things in life. If Jupiter is in the eighth house, it may give the native different sorts of problems & losses. One's valuables may be lost & the native may not get all the pleasures from wife or husband. As an *upaya*, the *jatak* should wear a small squire piece of gold to ward of Jupiter's ill-effects.

Venus represents wife & Goddess Laxhimi. Venus will not be favourable for the partner (wife/husband) if it is placed in the eighth house. As an *upaya* the native should feed the black cows with sweet *chapatis*

to the native.

Saturn in the eighth house is harmful and creates problems of different kinds. If the *jatak* starts business of oil, gas, stone or *bazari*/rough soil or becomes a contractor, Saturn will surely harm the native. He may get hurt or may get losses relating property/house or vehicle. In case Saturn is in the eighth and the second house has no planets, then let Saturn go on sleeping. He should not construct any religious place but can give alms at such a place. He may give leather shoes free to the poor & offer 8 kilograms of black grams in the running water & keep away from drinking, eating meat or eggs. The native should also wear a squire piece of silver in a chain. This upaya will lessen the ill-effects of Saturn to a great extent.

Rahu in the eighth house will give lotsof problems as it will also have its aspects on the second house, which will give sickness & quarrels in the family. The family may start splitting and dividing the property which will become a source of unhappiness to the native. He may go abroad & be separated from his kinsmen. He may have stomach problems or piles too. As an *upaya*, Lal Kitab advises the *jatak* to stay honest if he wants to be free from problems. Rahu placed in the eighth house may not permit the native to get education beyond tenth or twelfth standard & may become an impediment for further education. As an *upaya* the native should not wear black or blue clothes, must not accept free electrical goods or black & blue coloured clothes. He should also wear a squire piece of silver in a silver chain. It will help him save from the ill-effects of Rahu & Saturn. The Moon is related with one's mind & soul. Thus if one wear's silver, it will pacify both. *Mangal* represents squire sign. So the squire piece of silver will give the native courage to deal with his problems. The *jatak* should also offer 8 kilos of mustard into running water. It will help against the ill-effect of Rahu & Saturn as well.

Ketu placed in the eighth house may be harmful to *jatak's* children. It may give problems in his legs & urinary related problems too. If Ketu is in the eighth, Rahu will be sitting in the second house. We have already told some *upays* for Rahu. Ketu will also give results almost like that of Rahu. Therefore, the *jatak* should do similar *upayas* for Ketu as well. He should get his ears pierced and wear rings in them as well some silver rings in his ankles & thumbs of feet. It will save him from Ketu's ill-effects. In case *jatak's* children are not studying well, he should distribute bananas to all the school children & teachers & should give medicines to some hospitals tobe distributed free to the needy.

The Ninth House

In a *kundali*/chart it is Sagittarius sign/*rashi* that rises in the ninth house. Its owner &*karak* of this house is Jupiter. This house represents *dharm*/ dedication towards religion, luck, attachment towards the law, belief in God and His following etc. It also represents wife's younger brothers & sisters, or *jatak's* younger brothers & sisters and wife/husband etc. This house also represents higher education and father as well. Lal Kitab & ancient astrologers unfold that the twelfth from the ninth is the eighth house which is considered to calculate native's death. The ninth is related to *dharma*. A person stays in this world until he goes on performing his *dharmic*(religion & duty related) duties but he goes away from this world as soon as he is not able to perform his dharma. It is because of that that the eighth house (twelfth from the ninth) represents one's death.

Ancient astrologers reckon the Sun & Jupiter its *karak*/overall controller. Even if the ninth house is not very strong in a *kundali* but if the Sun & Jupiter are strong, the native would not suffer in life & his luck will provide good results. Ancient astrologers believe that every planet that sits in this house is considered auspicious, but Lal Kitab considers Mercury/ *Budha*& Venus inauspicious because both the planets are Jupiter's enemies.

If Venus rises in the ninth house, then *Mangal*/Mars gives bad results. Therefore as *upaya*, the *jatak* should avoid using a stone of the colour that is represented by the planet that rises in this house. For example, if

jatak's house. In case if there are no planets in the ninth house, no stone of the colour that is represented by the Moon (*rashi*) in the *kundali*, need

Budha

inauspicious in this house because this house is controlled by Jupiter. In case the *jatak* is not able to speak clearly, it is advised to do some *upayas* for *Budha*. For that, the *jatak* should get his/her nose pierced & feed cows with green grass. He can also distribute notebooks & pencils to school children to reduce the ill-effects of *Budha*/Mercury.

The Sun is considered auspicious in the ninth house. However, the native is advised not to use *petal*/yellow-material utensils in the kitchen. If the Sun rises in this house, then the native should have been born around 2 O'clock in the afternoon. As temperature at that point will be high, the native's behavior will be accordingly affected and he may be aggressive in conduct, but he will also be a religious kind of person. If he lives with in the code of conduct, he will stay happier in life as the Sun will provide good and faviourable results.

Jupiter. It will help the native to get good education & if he serves his mother, his luck will favour him. In order to get progress in life, the *jatak* should use a white sandal-wood*tilak* on his forehead. It will boost up the luck of the native, especially in the year, which belongs to a particular planet. If *Mangal*& Sun are in the ninth house the native should put a red *tilak* on his forehead to get their favour.

Lal Kitab considers *Mangal*/Mars to be auspicious if it rises in the ninth house. It considers that if Mangal rises in this house, all the other planets start giving good results. *Mangal* represents brother & courage, so it will provide good luck when the native reaches 28 years of age. The native is advised to put a red *tilak* on his forehead to get more favours from *Mangal*.

In case Jupiter rises in the ninth house, it is considered highly auspicious. We have observed that in whose *kundali* Jupiter rise in the ninth house, he/she is highly religious & always followsthe moral code in life. He possesses good thoughts & leads a simple life. Such a native will get a lot of progress in life if he goes on serving & helping others. Such a native must not eat meat or drink & avoid eating eggs. He should also not involve in back-biting if he wants his luck to boost up properly.

Venus is considered not auspicious in the 9th house but our experience unfolds that if Venus rises in its own or in a friend's *rashi*/sign, it will provide good results. As an *upaya* the native should help the poor

house, Lal Kitab unfolds that the native cannot died without constructing three houses. In our opinion, Saturn is responsible for the construction of houses and therefore, until the *jatak* doesn't complete them he will stay in this world. If the native goes on doing good acts & help the needy in the society, he will surely live happily. That will give him quite a long life too. The ninth house represents luck &*dharma*. So the *jatak* is forbidden to talk ill of others. He/she should not tell lies. Only then Saturn will provide good results. If one talks ill of others, it willlessen the good effect of the planets & make the native suffer. Lal Kitab considers that if Saturn sits in this house, Venus gets exalted in whatever place it may rise.

Rahu in the ninth will be affected by Jupiter. Jupiter and Rahu are not

If Rahu, Venus and Mercury (*Budha*) rise in the ninth house, Jupiter needs

native may be a doctor who treats mad people because Rahu is related to mad people, mentally sick as well as crippled. So Rahu is considered an inauspicious planet. Since Rahu & Ketu are shadow-planets, they create problems to the house which they occupy in a *kundali*especially if they rise in a good house or *trikona*. Rahu becomes highly inauspicious if it rises in the eighth house as the eighth house represents death. However, we have observed that Rahu, if sits in the ninth house, and if its *Mahadasha* starts in native's life, he/she gets lot of progress in life. When Rahu gets aspects

Ketu, being a friend to Jupiter, gives good results if it rises in

making certain *upayas* for Mercury & Ketu by doing *upayas* for Jupiter. Our experience betrays that Ketu gives good results in the ninth house. If Ketu rises in the ninth house, Rahu sits in the third. It is because of that that both the shadow-planets provide good results.Ketu also helps in getting salvation (*moksha*), so if such a *jatak* becomes a doctor, he will highly be successful & will be able to treat the patients very successfully. In return the *jatak* will get blessings which will be helpful to him/her to get progress in life. In the ninth house, Ketu makes the native helpful to the needy people. The more social-service the native does, the more progress and happiness in life he gets.

The Tenth House

In a *kundlai* the tenth house represents duty, work and once attitude towards work. This house is strongly related to work or duty. If any planets sit in this house they affect the *lagna.* It also represents heights or hills. That height also represents native's heights in life's success in work or business. Lal Kitab & ancient astrology consider this house very auspicious for *Mangal*. That means that if *Mangal* rises in it, it becomes very auspicious. According to the ancient astrology, *Mangal*& Sun are considered very strong but Lal Kitab does not consider the Sun very auspicious if it rises in this house because according to Lal Kitab the sign Capricorn rises in this house, which is detrimental to the Sun. If the Sun rises in this house, the native needs to pacify Saturn by certain *upayas.*

In northern India astrologers consider this house representing a native's father. But in the southern part of India astrologers consider the ninth house representing father. This house also represents the mother of one's wife as it is the fourth from the seventh house. Ancient astrology considers that any planets rising in it always become auspicious & help the native to rise in their profession & work. But Lal Kitab does not consider Moon, *Budha* and Ketu very auspicious if they rise in this house. However, our experience betrays that planets if they rise in the tenth house in a *kundali*, they provide favourable results to the native. We have also experienced that whenever planets rise in a *Kendra* (the 1st, 4th, 7th& 10th houses), they

to that extent & provide good results. But if planets sit in the 6th, 8th or 12th

that if two planets that are enemies to each other, if rise in the tenth house, they provide bad results & becomes harmful for business or work. If there are planets in the tenth but no planets are in the second house, in that case

upaya the native

needs to serve the blind people because of the tenth house the *kundali* becomes just like a blind person. All this becomes detrimental to one's business.

The tenth house represents one's work or business. Most natives are also eager to learn whether he/she will join some work or do some business. In case the signs/*rashis* of Mercury, Venus or Saturn rise in this house, or any of these planets sit in this house, the native invariably indulges in some kind of business, especially when there is no effect of any kind of the Sun, Moon, *Mangal* or Jupiter on this house. But if the Sun, Moon, Mars or Jupiter sits in it or if their *rashis* rise in this house, the native invariably indulges in some kind of service or job. Whether the native will indulge in a business, or take up a job—all will depend on the placements of the planets in a *kundali*. Therefore to decide all that one needs to study the entire *kundali* carefully before replying this kind of question 'that the native will be a businessman or will do any job somewhere.' To determine that kind of answer about a job or business, native's *lagnesh* as well as *dasha* periods also need to be studied carefully.

patrick/father's obligations. As a consequence Saturn may be harmful to all those objects which it represents, for example, property, house, shop etc. To ward off that obligation& to be saved from Sturn's ill-effects, the native must pay the laborers properly when constructing a house or any kind of property. As an *upaya*, the native

be offered to running water.

In order to keep the Sun favourable, the *jatak* is advised to keep his head covered with a cap or a turban which should not be blue or black in colour as these colours represent Saturn & Rahu. It is a general practice to cover one's head in India from the ancient times. Whenever someone prays or sits at a religious place, he/ she generally covers one's head. One's turban is like one's respect & whenever someone is in trouble &wants to get help from a senior person or from someone who is in command of things, the needy person would like to put his turban or cap in front of him who is capable to redeem/help the needy one. In the police depart or in the military, one's cap bears a lot of respect & responsibility. In olden times Maharajas would wear golden crowns on their heads & whenever any Raja or Maharaja desired to make his son responsible to take from him the reigns of the state, he would give him that crown to wear. Long back Muslims and Christians used to wear caps or hats & Hindu ladies usually wear saris & would cover their heads in respect of the seniors. Sikhs cover their heads with a turban. To keep one's head covered would get Jupiter's favour therefore, Lal Kitab recommends to keep one's head covered to keep one's work go on well.

The Moon in the tenth house will rise in Capricorn which is governed by Saturn. The Moon represents soul heart, water & milk, so Lal Kitab considers it a weak planet if it rises in the tenth house. The native is advised not to drink milk before going to bed. It will disturb one peace if one does like that. It is a common practice of astrologers to declare that Saturn's ill-effect will stay on the native for 'seven & a half years' if Saturn starts transiting one sign before the Moon's placement until it completes its transits to the next sign after the Moon in a particular chart/*kundali*. This period of Saturn's transit remain for seven & half years in *gauchara*.This kind of transit usually disturbs one's mind & peace in life. Thus, whenever the Saturn starts having its aspects on the Moon (Saturn has its three aspects, which are third, seventh & tenth), it

carrier & at his working place.

kundali. In case any of the bad periods (*dasha*) has been operating or there is an ill-effect of a planet on the *kundali* of a *jatak* or if planets in *gaucher* are unfavourably transiting, that person is bound to suffer heavily. H/she may even die at that time. However, it has also been observed that the seven & a half

happen only when the *lagna* is either, Taurus, Libra or Aquarius. Saturn is friendly to Venus & Capricorn as well as Aquarius are its signs/*rashis*. It

in whose*kundlai* at *lagna* either Gemini or Virgo *rashi* are rising because *Budha*

Saturn to be blind therefore after the Sun is set the Moon will hold the command. It is because of that, that Lal Kitab demands people not to eat rice, curd or drink milk during night, as it will create problems to one's

mild will become dull & thinking crippled.

When the Moon rises in the tenth house, Saturn is usually unfavourable. As an *upaya*
into running water or feed 100 labourers at a time. It is our view point that if the Moon rises in its own sign/*rashi*, or in its friend's sign, it will

should serve his/her parents or senior persons whole-heartedly, give full wages to the labourers & help the needy & the poor. If he/she does so, the Moon will give good results and make the native's life happier. But if he/she does not give full wages to the labourers or troubles the parents, he/she will surely suffer in life.

Mars/*Mangal's* aspects from the tenth house on *lagna* will provide courage & fortitude to the native & he/she will be able to perform every work successfully. If *Mangal* sits in the tenth house, it usually makes the native a doctor or an engineer in a government department. Lal Kitab as well as ancient astrology considers *Mangal* to be highly auspicious in this house. Our experience betrays that *Mangal* in the tenth house at times is troublesome to the native's parents. If the native desires to keep *Mangal* favourable, he should pray to Hanuman Ji & distribute sweets (*bhoga*) on Tuesdays in Shri Hanuman Ji's temple& regularly *Hanuman Chalisa.*

Mercury/*Budha* placed in the tenth house will be adversely affected by Saturn. But if Saturn is well placed, Budha will also give good results. We have often observed that if *Budha* is placed in someone's tenth house, it makes the native a successful businessman.In order to keep Saturn good, the native should not eat eggs, meat or drink & permit the Sun rays to enter

Lal Kitab considers Jupiter in the tenth house inauspicious. But we consider that Jupiter, rising in one of the *kendras,* will provide good results. But if Jupiter is in its debilitated sign or in its enemy sign, it may trouble the native. If such a *jatak* goes on doing social service & help the needy & poor, it may provide unfavourable results & bestow progress in life. If Jupiter rises in the tenth house in a lady's *kundali*, she should not get her hair cut & keep her head covered. If she does so, Jupiter will give good results.

Venus in the tenth house will be adversely affected by Saturn. But Saturn being a friend to Venus, bothSaturn & Venus may give good results. Such a *jatak* will be highly successful if he starts business relating 'marriages, relating law, decoration of houses or buildings etc. In these

have its aspects on the fourth house from the tenth, it will give the native lot of comforts & happy life.

Saturn rising in the tenth will provide good results as it is its own

others advise or opinions. But the more one does good & hard work, the more progress he/she will get in life. Leading an honest life, will surely give a lot of progress and happiness to the native in whose chart Saturn rises in the tenth house.

Whereever Rahu sits in a *kundali* it generally creates problems to the native relating that house. As the tenth house is considered relating to work or business, Rahu will give sometimes a lot of progress & at times losses or problems to the native relating work or business. The *jatak* will lead a strange life as at times Rahu will take him to the great heights in life but at other times will drag him down from the ladder of progress.We have observed that Rahu in the tenth houseusually rises in the politicians' *kundali*. A politician wins in an election at one time but also losses on the next time.It is also seen that a politician at times also may go to prison when sitting with the opposition. Rahu in the tenth house may send a native abroad. When Rahu rises in the tenth, Ketu sits in the fourth. It is the reason that the native has to go abroad on account of Ketu as well as Rahu as he will get a job outside his own country. The same thing happens to a politician. After winning elections, he/she has to quit his home-town & need to go to some other place or town to live on account of the duty or need of the situation. Rahu is a shadow-planet but if such planets rise in a *Kendra*, they don't provide bad results. However, our experience conveys that if Rahu rises in the tenth it is usually unfavourable to one's parents. In order to please Rahu, the *jatak* is advised to keep a *choti* (small tail of hair at the back of head) & wear a cap not having blue or black colour & serve the blind. It will please Rahu & help the native get good results from it. The native is advises not to take bribes or he may go to jail.

In the tenth house Ketu will be affected by Saturn. As Ketu represents native's feet, he will be more involved in a work which would demand lot of walking, travelling or physical movements. For example, he may be a driver, sales representative, a sports man or involved in politics etc. Rahu being in the fourth house (as Ketu is in the tenth) will not let the person stay at home quite often due to various reasons.In order to keep Ketu in order, the native is advised to keep his conduct clean so that he may not be troubled by Ketu.

The Eleventh House

sign rises in it according to Lal Kitab. Its owner is Saturn but Jupiter is considered its *karak*. As Jupiter is an auspicious planet, it is bound to take a *jatak* to great heights in life. We also reckon elder brother's status or position

therefore, takes the native very high in life if it is placed in this house. Lal Kitab considers all planets to be good if placed in the eleventh house. No planet is considered in a debilitated state in this house. On the contrary any planet rising in it usually lessens the ill-effects of its enemy planet. If Ketu rises in this house, the Moon's effect is diminished. If Saturn rises in it, it will diminish Sun's effect. But if Mercury, Venus or Rahu rise in this house, Jupiter may become inauspicious to the native in whose *kundali* such combinations take place. If Sun or Moon sits in this house, Saturn's ill-effect

various *upayas*
certain good acts, it may affect the progress of the person and may not give any children. The native may also not get good education & not rise in life.

his feet & if he takes up a machinery business, he may not be successful as Saturn is the *karak* of machinery. Our experience betrays & also it is accepted by the ancient astrologers that whatever sign rises in this house, a person's luck rises in the same direction. For example, if in a *jatak's kundlai* the sign Capricorn rises in the eleventh house, the native's luck will favour him in the Western direction as Saturn owns this sign. Lal Kitab advises *jatak* to get up before the Sun rise as the rays from the Sun help to get riches

house cleaned so that the rays that come from the Sun, may bring riches,

the blessing from the Goddess Laxhmi.

One's income is represented by Jupiter. So If Jupiter is good and favourable, the *jatak's* income will be good. But if a *jatak* invokes Rahu, his income will be dull. If a *jatak* uses intoxicants, drinks, smokes or eats meat, eggs etc., he is supposed to be in Rahu's camp & bound to lead unhappy life. His health & income both will be adversely affected by those bad habits. In case the enemy of the planet that sits in the eighth, if sits in the eleventh, the native is advised not to buy things that are related to that planet (that one sitting in the eleventh) but should give such things free to

jatak. If auspicious planets sit in it, the result will be favourable, if not then it will be against the native. If the Moon & Saturn sit in this house, the native is advised to put a pitcher full of water in the house or shop to ward

If the Sun rises in this house, it will be adversely affected by Saturn. To get good effect from Saturn, the native is advised not to tell lies so that his income is not adversely affected. The Sun represents soul, so keeping good

this house will be affected by Saturn. So the native has to do some *upaya*

small balls made from 400 grams of thick milk & put them in running water. It may help improve the native's income. *Mangal* will provide good result in if it rises in this house provided it is not in its enemy sign.

Budha

it is friendly to Saturn. But *Budha* is not a friend to Jupiter. If *Budha* rises

should not wearin his arm a or a thread related to , instead he

give good results.Jupiter is considered auspicious in this house as it hasits

considered very pious and auspicious. Whereever Jupiter has aspects, it provides highly favourable results. The third house is related to neighbours

is concerned with husband or wife, partnership or business etc. So Jupiter will boost up all these in favour of the native. It is advised by Lal Kitab that to get further good results from Jupiter, the native should give a sheet of cloth to cover a dead person to please Jupiter further.

If Venus sits in this house it will be adversely affected by Jupiter. So the native should do some *upaya* to please Jupiter. Only then Venus will give favourable results. If Venus rises in this house, the native should make 121 cotton sticks to offer to the Goddess Durga & pray Her for his happiness and progress. Only then Venus will be favourable to him.

Saturn will be favourable in this house, so the native should put a pitcher full of water in his house or shop before starting any work. Jupiter is the *karak* of this house so the *jatak* should always serve others to get

machinery, wood, mines and takes up work related to transport, computer,

So it is necessary to do some *upayas* for Jupiter to make it favourable to the *jatak*.So the *jatak* is advised to offer corn & coconut into running water (river) & try to establish Jupiter by praying for it & should also wear a golden chain & put a *tilk* of *keshar*on the forehead to invoke Jupiter's favour. The tenth house represents father. The tenth is the twelfth from the eleventh house, so Rahu may give adverse effect and the native may not get father's property. The second house represents one's mouth, so *jatak's* father should not drink and sue intoxicants to help his son live happily. He should also wear a silver chain in his neck to help his son in life. If

favourable for the children of the native. Rahu may also trouble the wife or husband of the native if it sits in the eleventh house. So the native is advised to distribute 11 *mulees,* a bitter longish fruit to the poor who live in straw-roofed houses & also distribute the fruit at certain religious places which will help in restoring husband & wife relationship.

Ketu in this house will be adversely affected by Jupiter & Saturn. *Mangal&Budha* are Ketu's enemies. When these planets will rise in the

native should distribute freely the articles related to the planet with which Ketu sits. He should also give free 11 *mulees* for 11 days to the poor & lame people or distribute the fruit at a religious place to get good results from Ketu. If the native wears ear rings, Ketu will become favourable & will provide good results.

The Twelfth House

It is the last *rashi* of Kal Purusha that appear in the twelfth house. It is Pisces & its owner is Jupiter. It is the last *rashi* of Kal Purusha that appear in the twelfth house. It is Pisces & its owner is Jupiter. Lal Kitab considers Rahu as the *karak* (functional) of this house. But ancient astrologers consider Ketu as the *karak* of this house. Both Lal Kitab & the ancient astrologers have their own reasoning behind the argument that Rahu or Ketu are the *karaks* of this house or this sign. As Ketu leads one to get *moksha* which

to be the *karak* of this house. Since Rahu leads one to indulge in court matter, sickness, problems, in quarrels, expenses as well as spending time in hospitals as a sick person, Lal Kitab consider Rahu as the *karak* of this house. However, the fact is, that both Rahu & Ketu could be the *karaks* of this house as the house implies and involves all what has been covered by Rahu or Ketu as the *karaks* of this house.

The twelfth house is related with the second, sixth and the eighth houses. The second house belongs to Venus (Lal Kitab). It relates to one's attachment with money, *maya*, property, wife, and land etc. In this world

The native goes on struggling to get a high chair (position & status), riches and women throughout one's life. The fourth house represents property,

& impediments. The twelfth represents *moksha* hospitals, prisons & expenses. Ancient astrology indicates that any planet rising in the twelfth house does not give favourable results. Lal Kitab considers the twelfth house as one's bed on which one rests, & also the roof of one's house. It suggests that if a *jatak* wants to improve the ill-effect of the twelfth house, he should then take one thing (something) from the house of a relative who died recently and keep that in his own house, or pluck a small plant from the house of the dead relative and plant it in his own house. It will reduce the ill-effects of the twelfth house.

We have observed carefully that when the *dasha* period of the twelfth house starts, it brings certainly some kind of problem.If *Chandra Kundali* or *Surya Kundali* (when you place the Moon or the Sun as ascendant and make a *kundali*) is powerful or strong, the twelfth house does not create problems. If the owner of the twelfth is sitting in the twelfth house &

create any problems to the native. In that case the native's job is connected with hospital. He/she may be a doctor, a nurse, a chemist, may be connected with prison work or court, or he/she may go abroad, away from home. We have often observed that when there is an exchange between the owners of *lagna*& that of the twelfth house, the native usually go abroad. If the owner of the twelfth sits in the sixth or eighth house, it makes Vipreet Raj Yoga, which is also a very strong favourable yoga in a *kundali*. That means

carefully that whichever planet rises in the twelfth, the native spends his/her money accordingly. For example, if Jupiter rises/sits in this house, the native will spend money on schools, *dharmshala*/rest-house for the poor, or on making temples. If Rahu rises in this house, the native usually involves in quarrels, sickness & spends money on such things which are not worthwhile. However, one needs to examine carefully the entire *kundali* to give correct predictions on all these matters.

If the Sun rises in this house in Pisces sign (*Meen Rashi*), of which the owner is Jupiter &*karak* is Rahu, it may help the native to get *mokcha* for the Sun is considered *atman*& the last mission of *atman* is to reach God's house. The sign of *Meen Rashi*

either the native is involved in money-race or will try hard to get God. It

busy in doing good work, go on help the needy, serving the poor,the more he/she will be nearer God. But if he/she is involved in unholy work or activities, he/she will suffer in life. It will only happen when the native is

wrong things & not to involve in giving wrong witness in a court, or to deceive anyone. If he/she does so, Rahu & Saturn may affect the native's eye sight. He/she may be blind or lose the eye-sight. Both Rahu & Saturn represent darkness & the Sun represents light. So if the native is involved in doing wrong things, he/she may lose the eye-sight and darkness will prevail in his/her life.

The Sun represents light & brightness. So the native is advised to keep some open space in his house to let the Sun light get into the house. It will bring new hopes in his family, which means his children will grow and get success in life. Ancient people believe that God Brahma live in the middle & if the Sun light comes in the middle of the house, the entire house will

house which open space conceives from the Sun. Jupiter also loves to live at such a place where there is the Sun light. To please Jupiter, the native should put a *tilak* of *keshar* on his forehead & in the middle of his stomach to please Jupiter. It will make Jupiter strong in the *kundali*, and will start giving favourable results. The cleaner the native will keep his/her house, the better life he/she will lead.

The Moon in the 6th, 8th& 12th houses in a *kundali* is not is not considered auspicious. When someone is going to be married, the *pandit/ purohit* who performs the marriage ceremony would like to examine the Moon's position in the chart that is made at the time of the marriage. If the Moon is placed in the 6th, 8th or 12th houses in that marriage related *kundali*, that time is not considered auspicious. So some other time is chosen to perform the marriage so that both, the bride & the bride-groom may lead a happy life. The Moon is considered representing one's soul & is responsible to give riches, happiness & property. If the Moon is weak in someone's *kundali*, it is most likely that it will not let the native live happily when he/she is very young. But if the Moon is sitting even in the 12th

friend's sign (*rashi*), it may not give bad results. If the moon is placed in the 12th house, the native may be involved in prayers & such activities. It is also observed that when the moon is placed in the 12th house, the native often resides outside his/her country. It also involves in making expenses. Lal Kitab advises such natives in whose *kundali* the Moon is placed in the 12th house, that the native should go on collecting rain water on the roof of the house. It will help him not get disturbed by wrong thoughts & will help keeping a peaceful life& will do his/her duty honestly & carefully.

Rahu is considered as a *karak* of the 12th house. *Mangal* is considered as the chief-commander of /gods' army whereas Rahu is the commander-in-chief of the demons' army. Rahu is scared of *Mangal*. So if *Mangal* sits in Rahu's house, *Mangal* usually keeps quiet, but stays there give any kind of ill-effect. But our experience unfolds that Rahu, like its nature, does not relinquish its bad nature and whenever gets a chance, it does something unpredictable and bad. It does give problems to the native. Mangal in the twelfth house makes the *jatak's kundalimanglik,* which means that it gives problems at the time of one's marriage or disturbs the married life of a *jatak*. It is therefore advised that *jatak'skundli* should properly be matched with the other *kundali*

We have added one chapter on Manglik Yoga in this book for the reference of the interested reader.Ancient astrology unfolds that when Mangal rises

kundali is supposed to be Manglik. Some astrologers consider that if Moon, Jupiter, Saturn, & Rahu sit in this house Manglik *Dosha*

agree with kindof argument. In the Southern part of India some astrologers consider Manglik yoga when *Mangal* sits in the 2nd house, as it becomes the eighth house from the seventh house of both, the wife & husband. When *Mangal* rises in *lagna*, it has aspects on the eighth & spoils the seventh house. Likewise it will spoil the seventh if it sits in the fourth house. As the eighth house indicates age, it is going to give some kind of physical ailment to the native.

Some astrologers reckon Manglik *Dosha* from the Moon. Since we were discussing the position of *Mangal* in the twelfth house, we will limit our discussion to that only. In case *Mangal* rises in its own *rashi*/sign or in its friend's sign or has aspects from its friends, its unfavourable result will be lessened.Astrologers consider helping the native from the birth if *Mangal* is well placed in the 12th house. It will help increase wealth in the house & give happiness to the native from the beginning. In our opinion, if *Mangal* rises in Jupiter's house (sign), it will be favourable to the native

Sun everyday in the morning. He/she should also not keep any arms & ammunition in the house& keep it very clean. In case *Mangal* sits in the twelfth house, the native may not get any happiness from his elder brother

Mangal represent strength & power. Any planet sits in the twelfth, makes the native spend money according to one's own conduct & behavior. *Mangal* may also help in spreading bad things about the native if placed in the twelfth.

Mercury/*Budha* in Pisces sign is debilitated & becomes Jupiter's enemy. So Lal Kitab considers *Budha* to give bad effects to the native &

Budha rising in Pisces sign in the twelfth house may affect the native's wisdom to a great extent. If someone's wisdom/*budhi* is badly affected, it will surely

it has been observed that if someone is wise, he/she may not only earn a lot of money or get rich but may also reach a very high position in life. There are examples of natives who by their wisdom have reached very high positions in life. Some have reached so high like a king or a *raja*& have enjoyed all the pleasures of life. But those who don't possess wisdom may soon be lost in this world and destroyed. However, if *Budha* sits alone in the twelfth house, it will provide different results, but if it sits with the Sun or other planets, it may give all the different results. If *Budha* is not auspicious, it will spoil the native's teeth & nervous system. It will also be bad for sisters and aunts. When one involves in predictions, one must see carefully the chart of the native & specially judge the position & rising of the planets in the eighth & sixth houses. If inauspicious planets rise in the sixth or eighth houses, the native needs to get his/her nose pierced &wear a silver ring in it for at least 100 days. The native should keep courage and thinkthat all what has been happening is the wish of God. The native is also advised to distribute notebooks & pencils among the poor school students & whenever he/she visits sisters or aunts places, must carry some sweets to their houses.

If Jupiter sits in the twelfth house, the native may spend a lot of money on good and kind activities, such as making some public guest houses (*dharma shala*), temple, shops, houses for the needy, or may spend money on the marriages of the poor girls. No one can get *mokcha/*salvation in life

according to the effect of the planet rising in it. As Jupiter is an auspicious planet, it will involve the native to spend on good deeds and in public service. It leads the native to help the needy and the poor. If Jupiter rises in the twelfth house, it helps the native to get a good house, a vehicle, a shop etc. It also has its aspects on the sixth house which will diminish enemies & by its eighth aspect will provide a long life to the native. In order to keep Jupiter as an auspicious planet, the native should serve his/her father, saints &*brahmans*& offer water to the *peepal* tree on Thursdays. It will help both the native's health as well as his/her mind. It will also provide progress in life.

Venus in the twelfth house in Pisces sign gets exalted & it gives every kind of comfort & happiness to the native. Venus is considered a cow or partner (wife). Such a *jatk* in whose *kundlai* Venus rises in the Pisces sign, will have a good and serving wife who will stay attached with her husband

and serve him wholeheartedly. If a native serves cows, *brahmans*and crows, God always helps him/her. If Venus rises in the twelfth house, the

be obtained.

Saturn in the twelfth house will rise in Jupiter's sign. As such it will inspire the native to help the needy, poor and downtrodden. If Jupiter & Saturn combine in this house, they will lead the native to serve the poor.

sanyasi that means he/she leaves everything of enjoyment in life & lives like a hermit. The native will lead a poor life & have no attachment towards property & money. The twelfth house is considered as a prison, hospital, court etc. So the*jatak* may work in any of these places in different positions. Since Saturn rises in the twelfth house, the nativeneed to do lot of social service & help the needy. The more he involves in such things, the less he will be affected adversely by Saturn but get good results from it. But if Saturn rises in an enemy sign, it will not let the native construct his/her own house and will create constant pain in the legs of the native.Therefore, the native should go on helping the poor & needy to keep away from physical ailments.

When Rahu rises in the twelfth house in Jupiter's sign, it is debilitated. When Rahu rises in the third or the sixth houses, it is considered to give good results. Rahu in the twelfth affects adversely the married life of the native, he/she is not able to sleep well in the night, & the native involves in spending money uselessly. Lal Kitab recommends that such a *jatak* should keep some *sauf*(a kind of soft & sweet material that people like to chew after meals) under his/her pillow after tying it in a red cloth. It might help him/her not to spend uselessly. In case the nails of the native start falling down, it is an indication of an inauspicious Rahu. As an *upaya*, the native should help a poor girl in her marriage so that such problems don't encounter him/her & ill-effects of Rahu can be spared. If the native eats inside the kitchen as an *upaya*, it will help to get peace. The twelfth house is also related to the sub-conscious mind & day-dreaming. So such a native will go on dreaming to get rich immediately. Rahu is also considered mind's thinking waves. So when the *jatak* will try to sleep, he/she may not get sleepas he/she will go on thinking & making castles in the air. Before he/she goes to bed the following*mantra* need to be repeated by the native to go to a sound sleep.

Boley bihas Mahesha tab gyani muudh n koi;
Jehee jab jas Raghupati karahee, so taahe tey chan hoi.

That means that in this world no one is wise & none is stupid but God makes one like that—a wise or stupid & accordingly one acts instantly in the world. It was uttered by Lord Shiva to Mata Parvati when He was narrating some *katha* (real legendry story) to her. Sri Tulsi Das wrote it in the Ramayana. Our experience betrays that at many a time a judge, a minister or an administrator, may act in such a way that even a mad person may not act that way.But on the contrary at times a mad man may act in such a way that even a wise person may not do so. Therefore, whatever has been happening in this world, it happens on account of God's will &desire.

Ketu is considered in an exalted state in the twelfth house. In case Ketu is in Jupiter's sign in this house it will be very strong. So Ketu in Jupiter's sign & Rahu in *Budha's* sign will give excellent results. Lal Kitab recommends that any *upayas* to be done for Ketu & Rahu, they need to be made through Jupiter &*Budha* respectively. The twelfth house refers to *mokcha*, so Ketu also indicates *mokcha* if rises in the twelfth house. The better the conduct of the native, the more he/she will rise in life. Ketu also represents children & thus, if Ketu is well placed it will be favourable to the native after the birth of a child. The native will get lot of progress in life. Ketu in the twelfth house may also send the native to foreign lands. As an *upaya* the native is advised to suck his/her thumb after putting it into a sweetened milk. Our experience conveys that the bigger is the thumb, the native will get equally big progress in life & he/she will get a lot of property & money in life. This process of sucking the thumb may also lessen sickness of the native if there is any. If a dogs are fed by the *jatak*, it will help pleasing Ketu & it will start giving favourable results to the native.

So far we have described the placements of nine planets in the twelve

*kundali.*When two-three planets rise in a house, its (house) results differ. If any planet or house provide ill-effect, it is better to make some *upaya* for that. In case a house supports the native, better not to disturb it and let it operate as it is. However, to provide good result and to give correct predications, one is advised to read the entire *kundali* very carefully, thoroughly and with concentrated mind. Only then one will be able to say things correctly.

Results conveyed after studying a few houses or by observing a couple of planets, will be half -cooked results and may not come true. If one observes a *kundali* very carefully & with concentration, one can only see various combinations &*yogas* that lie within the frame work of a chart/ *kundali*. We are sure that our able readers will like to follow our humble advice before they come to any conclusion on certain particular matters or issues relating a *jatak*.

In the following chapters we will discuss the problems of marriage making and on the factors that need to be examined carefully when we try to calculate someone's marriage or when we advise someone to go ahead to marry someone.

Contemplating on the Issue of Marriage according to Lal Kitab

At the time of marriage of a boy & a girl, usually the *pandits* match the *kundalis* of both, the boy & the girl who are likely to be married to each other.Some people don't possess any *kundali*& they are also unaware of the time of their birth. It is because of that that our *rishis*&*munies* have made certain traditions that at the time of a girl's marriage the parents of the girl give in gift or in *dan* certain articles which are highly useful to her in her in-laws place & she can live most happily there. At the time when an engagement is made, certain ornaments or a golden or silver ring

which she wears it has its relation to her heart. It helps her to stay strongly with her new family. A *Mangalsutra*(an ornament to be worn in the neck by the bride) made of gold or silver is also given to the girl at the time of

attached with her new family.

Astrologers hold that woman & wealth are related to Venus & therefore, wealth & all the worldly facilities are obtained by the family of the bridegroom through the bride's luck. So at the time of marriage,

time the groom takes the lead. The secret that lies behind this tradition or custom is that it is the responsibility of the bride to sustain *dharm*, wealth & work/activity in the family. The groom is responsible for getting *mokcha*/salvation. Therefore, all what is done at the time of marriage is

purohit, who performs the marriage ceremony, puts some rice, sweetened *sindur*&*haldi* at the forehead of both, the bride & the bride groom. Then these things after being tied in a red piece of cloth are tied on the arm of both the persons by the *purohit*. Both, the red colour & arm represent *Mangal*. It means before starting an auspicious activity (marriage), auspicious planets are established in the family (of the newly married couple) to help the couple to live happily throughout their life. Then they take a vow by holding some water in their hands that 'O Lord, help us throughout our lives'.Water represents the Moon. Our *rishi&munies* usually would take water in their right hand to bless or to curse someone when they were pleased or angry. When people go to *dharmic yatra* (holy/religious journeys), they would offer so many things into the river (usually Ganga or Yamuna). Lal Kitab considers water to be very important as it helps to sustain human life.

Lal Kitab advises that one should not keep bad or inauspicious things with him/her& only keep those things which are of absolute necessity & importance. In case Rahu is not well placed in a native's *kundali*, it will

time of the native's marriage, the parents of the native should give him 60 grams of a square piece of silver piece which may be 5" long & broad in

the couple. As silver represents the Moon & square represents *Mangal*, so they both (Moon &*Mangal*) will diminish the ill-effect of Rahu & let the couple live happily in future. In case Ketu has its ill-aspect on the seventh house or sits in the seventh, the parents of the girl usually give a bed to the groom in gift to ward off Ketu's ill-effect from the lives of both, the girl & the boy. As long as the bed (cot) stays in their house, Ketu's ill-effect will be removed from the house. Lal Kitab unfolds that at the age of 22nd years Sun, at 24th Moon, at 25th Venus, at 28th*Mangal*, 34th*Budha*, at 36

a great impact on the native's life. In case any of these are not auspicious, the native is advised to stay away from the things that are related to them during those particular years. It will help him/her to stay away from any kind of ill-effect of these planets.

For example, in a native's *kundali* if Rahu is placed in either in the 1, 3, 7, or 11th houses, or if Venus sits with Rahu, then at the age of 22nd year on account of the Sun & at 25th year on account of Venus, the native should not get married to keep away Rahu, Sun & Venus's ill-effects. Even if Venus & Sun rise together in a house, then Sun will affect adversely Venus. When Saturn affects a native adversely, it usually passes that ill-effect to Venus & let Venus take care of bad things in the life of such a native. As the Sun represents day & Saturn represents night, it would be really bad if they meet at a place. That means both, the Sun & Saturn, if rise at one place (house) in a *kundali*, they will give bad results. Such a combination is extremely bad for a marriage.

The seventh house, usually is supposed to belong to Venus. If the Sun rises in that house & if Venus is in *lagna*, marriage should not be performed at the 22nd& 25th year of the native. Lal Kitab considers that Venus in the 1st, 6th, 8th, & 9th houses is supposed to be bad. Therefore, no marriage should take place until 25th year of the native as various sorts of problems may crop up in the married life of the native.In case Venus & Rahu rise together in a *kundali*, the native's wife should not keep her nails long. Besides, the native should offer a silver ring to his wife, who

ill-effects from their lives. If the Moon sits in *lagna* of the native, he/she should not get married at the 24th year as it belongs to the Moon, which will affect adversely by its aspect on the seventh house.

In case Venus sits in the fourth house in a native's *kundali*, then such a native should remarry his wife once again & give her two names & call her with different (two) names time to time. The fourth house belongs to woman (wife) & Venus in that house tends to indulge in two marriages. So if the native remarries his wife once again, it will diminish the ill-

to remarry his wife once again to keep off Rahu's ill-effect. Rahu is a naughty & negative planet & creates bad ideas in the native's mind. So if the native remarries his wife, the bad effects of Rahu will be reduced. Lal Kitab also suggests to remove all the ill-effects of the planets in a *kundali* at the time of marriage when both, the bride & the groom are inside the *mandap* (temporarily made shelter) through *mantras*(chanting of sacred verses) by the *purohit*. It will help remove the ill-effects of the planets. It is believed that after the marriage the groom's *kundali* becomes effective, so instead of concentrating on the girl's (bride's) *kundali*, the *purohit* should concentrate on the boy's so that if any planet is producing its ill-effect on Venus, its *upayas* should be made and the ill-effect should be removed, so that both may live happily. In case Venus is affected by Jupiter's aspects or meeting it in the same house, as an upaya the parents of the boy should give two plain pieces of gold to both, the boy & the girl at the time of

the other piece need to be put into the running water. Those parents who cannot afford to give gold, they should give two pieces of *haldi* (a kind of yellow herb usually used in cooking), & may put one of them into the running water within 10, 15, or 20 days.In case she losses one of the pieces by chance, she may buy another one & keep it the bedroom.

In case the Sun, Venus or Mercury/*Budha* sit at one place (in one house) in the boy's *kundali*, then the boy should give a cow & its calf to a poor *brahman* at the time of his marriage. In case this *upaya* is not *moongdal* (a kind of pulse that is usually eaten) in a small copper pot, cover it and put it into the running water. The secret behind this *upaya* is that by offering *moong* in this manner, the ill-effects of the planets is reduced & the native gets piece. As far as possible the boy should give a milk-giving cow to the poor *brahman* to satisfy the ill-effects of the planets. In the groom's *kundali*, if the Sun has its inauspicious effect on Venus, then he should take two square pieces of copper & put one into the running water & the other should be kept by the bride with her during her whole life. If *Mangal* has its ill-effects, one piece of *moonga* (a kind of red coloured jewel) should be put into the running water and the other should be kept with the bride. If *Budha* is not well placed in the *kundali*, then one piece of *panna* (greenish jewel) should be put into the running water & the other need to be kept with the bride.In case *Budha* is in the twelfth house in the boy's *kundali*, then two iron or steel rings should be given to the bride & groom. One of them need to be put into running water & the other should be kept with the bride.In case Venus is affecting adversely, then a real pearl should be put into water & the other piece should be kept with the girl.

If Venus is placed in the sixth house in the boy's *kundali*, then at the time of marriage, the parents of the bride should give her a gold-hair clip, which she needs to use in her hair. The reason behind this *upaya* is that Venus in the sixth house is supposed to be debilitated & the golden clip will improve the Jupiter's positive effect on the native. It will improve

ill-effects, the bridegroom should get two square pieces of iron, one should be put into running water, & the other need to be kept by the bride in her sleeping room. It will help providing happiness to the couple.

Lal Kitab concentrates on Venus' placement in the groom's *kundali*, & in the bride's *kundali* for getting respect & love from her husband it concentrates on Jupiter's placement in a *kundali*. The ancient astrology considers houses, placement of the planets & their effects on the houses & planets when it considers the happiness of the couple. It also considers important the position of *Mangal* in a *kundali* as to a great extent *Mangal* is quite effective to determine the happiness of a couple in a *kundali*. But Lal Kitab also holds that small *upayas* can help reduce 50% ill-effects of so many problem given by the planets. Thus, both, ancient astrology and Lal Kitab concentrate on how the couple should get as much happiness in their lives as possible and stay peacefully in their lives. It is also quite surprising that those who don't have any faith in astrology, go on wearing gold, which is helpful in reducing the ill-effects of so many planets on account of Jupiter's positive effect. Lal Kitab & ancient astrology are complementary to each other. The following *kundali* contains some details about *upayas*& other matters described here above. The native was born on 21st April in 1963. We are not mentioning the place of birth on account of certain reasons.

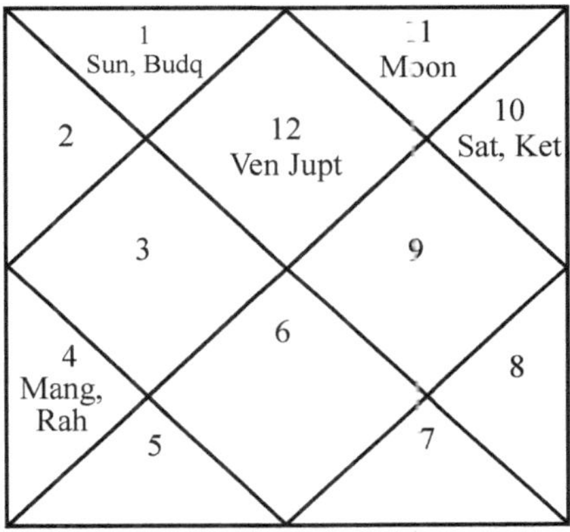

In the above *kundali* the conduct of the wife is adversely affected by *upaya* the parents

to their daughter out of which one she should have kept with her & the other she would have put into the running water along with the chanting of *mantras* (chanting from the Holy Scripture by the *purohit*). Whenever the Sun, Rahu & Ketu sit together or sit in the seventh house, Venus becomes inauspicious and some kind of *upaya* is required to be done for it.So that it may not create problems in getting happiness with the wife.

In the above *kundali* the Sun rises in the second house, so it is necessary to make some *upayas* for Venus. The *jatak* should make 100 *chapaties* every year for several years & offer one *chapati* to one cow to eat. It will not only pacify Venus, but cows will also be served by the *jatak*. It is a kind of social service, which will help satisfying the ill-effects of certain planets. We would like to say more about certain planets at this occasion, especially about Venus.

There are certain *upayas* which will lessen the ill-effects of the planets like Venus, as well as, the bride & the groom will lead a happier life in future.In case Venus rises in a *kundali* having very low degrees in strength&

if *Mangal*& Rahu rise in the seventh house, it will be a bad combination. They may provide a very bad effect on the lives of the couple, resulting even in a divorce among them. So at the time of the marriage two small pieces of copper of equal length & breadth should be given to the bride by her parents to help her save her from the ill-effects of Venus & the Sun. Out of the two, one she should put into the running water & the other she should keep with her. It will help her to get favours from Venus & the Sun..

gives ill-effects to the native. According to the ancient astrology if *Mangal* rises in the seventh, it creates *Manglik dosha*. Our experience unfolds that both, Rahu &*Mangal*

problems for the couple to live happily. Such a native should keep patience & try to lead a happy life with a wife who may or may not be very suitable for him. He should take it God's desire and live with her happily. Lal Kitab suggests simple & inexpensive *upayas* to mend the ill-effects of the planets on the seventh house. If these precautions/*upayas* help the native to some extent, they should be practiced peacefully & with full efforts as

Reasons that Disturb a Marriage

Our experience betrays that the parents of a girl are so disturbed at the time of the marriage of their daughter that they are even unable to sleep for days. As the marriage is done and the parents have spent a lot of money during the marriage of their daughter, they are again not able to sleep properly after the marriage of their daughter. Why are there so many problems even after the marriage of a daughter? Astrologers unfold that if in the girl's *kundali* Jupiter is of very low degree (*asta)*, or if it is debilitated, she will not get at least 35% happiness in her life. In case the Sun or the Moon rise with Rahu, all such problems crop up. In case both the states of the planets exist, she will not get up to 70% happiness from her husband & will receive only 30% favours from her husband. Her husband may be quarrelsome, may often get sick & ill, may not do any kind of job & sit idle at home, may stay far away from home or live abroad, or their ideas don't match, often resulting in quarrels etc.

Behind all such problems, the only cause is the ill-effects of planets. They don't let her live happily & up to 30% of her happy life is curtailed on

Mangal, Ketu which

often rise in the seventh house of the *kundali* of the *jatak* and give problems. Likewise if in the *kundali* of a boy Venus is of very low degrees in strength, or debilitated, he may not get at least 35 % happiness from the wife. If the planets rise in it, he may not get up to 70% happiness from his wife. She may get constantly sick, may be quarrelsome, or may possess a bad temperament. In case the Sun, *Mangal*, Saturn, Rahu or Ketu rise in the seventh house or even if the *lagnesh*

least 30% happiness from his wife. If the *lagnesh* is debilitated, he may not be happy with his wife or it will create impediments during his marriage and later on after the marriage he may not let him lead a happier life.

If the girl's hands are tender, the palms are quite broad, & if the line of heart, head and life are long in the hands, & if the hands' thumbs are

boys & girls are quite suitable for marriage. To marry such a girl or boy would bring every kind of happiness to both. In case the owner of the seventh is Jupiter, Venus or Mercury, and may rise in a friend's sign or

But if the owner of the seventh is placed in the sixth or eighth house from

Mangal, the married life

owner of the seventh rises in its friend's sign at *lagna*, or if it has aspects on the seventh on its own sign, the married life of the native will be happier.

How Much Happiness a Husband & Wife May get from the Marriage?

Every parent of the girl desires that their daughter should get a good husband who would take good care of hers & be employed or involved in some kind of work or business. He may also be well known in the society & belong to a good family. Besides, his *kundali* should also be

one car & an impressive house. But the parents usually don't think about how much happiness she will get from her married life. Is it not something primary that the parents must try to investigate through astrological investigations? Most parents try to know from an astrologer 'how their

kundali and try to learn whether it is weak in degrees, debilitated or retrograded. If this exists in the girl's *kundali*, she will not be able to get happiness from her husband. In case

the twelfth house, even then the girl will not get any happiness from her husband. Many astrologers consider such placements in a chart providing widowhood. We hold that if planets are auspicious from the position of the

In the boy's *kundali*

Venus. In case Venus is in low degrees, debilitated or retrograded, he will not get all the happiness from his wife. Our experience unfolds that if a native's *lagnesh*
good *yogas*
things cause unhappiness in his married life.

If *Kalserp dosha* (all the seven planets placed in between Rahu & Ketu) exists, it takes away many sorts of happiness from one's life. It may not let the native get parents' happiness, or keep him/her away from getting the parents' property, or the native would leave for foreign land and would not get happiness from one's wife/husband. Such a native will never have all things in life and will feel that certain things always lacked in life. *Kalserp dosha* may bring death to someone in the family when the native is very young. This yoga, according to Lal Kitab, is even worse than that of *Manglik Yoga*. Many people get scared by *Manglik Yoga*, but there are so many other *yogas* in a *kundali* that are even bad than it. It is also possible that *Mangal*

kundali is Aries, Cancer, Leo or Pisces. *Mangal* represents blood according to astrology. If blood is ever needed by a native, the doctor transmits the same blood from the group which the native possesses. If native's blood group does not match with the blood that is donated to him/her, the doctor does not transmit that blood in the body of the native.

In case the blood groups of a girl & boy match, and if they marry each other, their off springs will also be good. So *Mangal* has been considered so important in astrology. However, there are different opinions of astrologers about the placement of Mangal in a *kundali.* Some consider that if *Mangal* rises in the fourth, seventh, eighth or twelfth houses, it makes *Manglik Yoga* as it has its aspects on the seventh house from all these places. Even its aspects on the eighth house make *Manglik Yoga*. The fourth house represents one's happiness (*sukha*), the seventh represents wife/husband, & the eighth represents 'death'. So *Mangal* tarnishes all these houses. If *Mangal* rises in the fourth house, it has its aspect on the seventh house, if it rises in the seventh house, it spoils the *langna,*& if it rises in the twelfth house, it spoils the seventh house & consequently tarnishes husband/wife relationship.

The astrological calanders (*Panchang*) that are published from Kurali & from Jalandhar by Devi Dayal Ji, state, that if in these houses (the fourth, seventh & twelfth) Moon, Saturn, Rahu or Ketu rise, the *Manglik Yoga* is

Mangal rises in its sign/*rashi*, or takes a different position in a *chalit kundali* (*kundali* made according to the degrees of planets in which they rise at the time of a native's birth), even then *Manglik Dosha*

dosha is not totally

much problem as it should. Some astrologers hold that *Mangal's* good or effect stays up to 28 years only & then it becomes less effective. Our experience conveys that every planet provides good or bad effects during its *dasha* periods & whenever the native gets *Mangal's* period (*dasha*) in his/her *kundali*, he/she will experience its effect accordingly. If *Mangal* is inauspicious, its effect will also be the same.

If the *lagnesh* rises in cups (*sandhi*) that means is in its last degrees in a *rashi*/sign, even then planets don't provide good results. If the owner of the sixth, eighth or twelfth sits in the seventh house, it produces ill-effect & diminishes the native's happiness. If the owner of the seventh house rises with the owners of the sixth, eighth or twelfth house, it does not let all the pleasures in life and creates some kind of problems.In case *lagnesh* sits with the owners of the sixth, eighth or twelfth, it is bound to create problems. If Sun, Saturn, Rahu or Ketu rise in the seventh house, some kind of problem is created in the married life of a native. If the Sun or Moon rise as the owner of the seventh house & Rahu or Ketu sit with them, some kind of problem is bound to come in the native's married

the married life of a native may come. Similarly, if the Sun or the Moon rises as *lagnesh* in a native's *kundali*& are not well placed or rise in an inauspicious house (6th, 8th, or 12th houses), problems in the married life

Ketu if sit in the second house, married life of a native will be adversely affected. The second house represents family. So such combinations or placements may give various kinds of physical ailments to the members of the native'sfamily or keep him/her engaged in quarrels. As the second house also represents money& wealth, it may affect the sources of income adversely.

gunas) of a boy & a girl through *nakchatras*. That implies that both have quite akin behabiour. For example if one desires to take tea, the other would also like to have it at that time. Besides comparing their behavior, we also need to compare their ages and see that anyone of them is not suffering from any serious ailment or have any hurt. The nativeis involved in some kind of business

know about whether there they will have any children or not. All this can be found out with the help of the planets posted in the *kundalis* of both, the boy & the girl. When all these aspects are thoroughly examined by the astrologer about the boy & the girl, only then their marriage should be done. Otherwise there is no use just to talk about *Manglik Dosha* in the *kundali*. In case there are certain problems relating the marriage of the boy when we examine his *kundali*, it is advised that he should read daily **Laxhimi Chalisha** & if there are problems in the marriage of the girl after examining her *kundali*, she is advised to read daily to ward off the ill-effects of certain planets that create problems in the marriage.

How will Husband & Wife meet & Which Direction will the Marriage take Place?

The *jatak*often possesses a question in the mind, which he/she asks at the

her companion, how much will he/she be educated & in what direction the marriage will take place?'

Whenever an astrologer examines a *kundali* for marriage, he examines

kundali he examines the placement of Venus and that of Jupiter in the girl's *kundali*. Our experience betrays that in whichever sign the owner of the seventh is placed, it provides the effect of that sign/*rashi* up to 30%& it gives the results up to 20% of the place (house) in which it rises. It also gets upto 15% effect of the aspects it has from any planet. Just like there are twelve signs, the seventh house of each *jatak* when calculated from *langa*, provides the effect in that manner. But when it rises in different

one's marriage is delayed. But if *Budha*

takes place earlier. According astrology 1,3,5,9,11 signs are considered *purush rashi* (manly signs), and 2,4,6,8,10,12 are considered *ishtri signs* (womanly signs). In case the owner of the seventh rises in *sam rashi*, both the husband and wife will be handsome/ beautiful.

tatwa

they rise in the east direction; Taurus, Virgo and Capricorn represent earth and rise in the south direction; Gemini, Libra, Aquarius represent air & rise in the west direction; Cancer, Scorpio & Pisces represent water& rise in the north direction. In whatever signs the owner of the seventh rises, the native bears the same kind of conduct, behavior & possesses the same sort of complexion. The Sun & Venus indicate east direction; the Moon & Saturn indicate west direction; *Mangal*, Rahu & Ketu indicate south direction; *Budha*& Jupiter indicate north direction. 1, 4, 7, &10 signs are *char-rashies* *rashies*/signs; 3, 6, 9 & 12 are the *rashies* that possess dual signs. In case *char* (movable) *rashi* rises in the seventh house & its owner also is placed in a *char rashi*, the girl will get the boy from a distance place. That means she will be married far away & stay away from her father's home town. In case the owner of the seventh house rises in the twelfth house or if it has aspects from Rahu, Ketu or Moon, the marriage will take place further far away from her

rashi), the marriage will not take place far away from her home town. In case the owner of the seventh rises in a dual sign, the marriage will take place not very far but also not so close from her home town.

tatwa(element) *rashi* rises in the seventh house or if the owner

and wife. They will have medium body structure & possess aggressive conduct. If the seventh possesses earth *tatwa rashi*, & conjunct with cruel planets like Rahu & Ketu or has their aspect, then both the husband and the wife will cruel or very aggressive attitude towards life & others. Such a native is always aggressive, full of anger & is an egoist, laden with proud temperament. In case the seventh house possesses airy *rashi*/sign & is

possess an intelligent outlook of life. But if watery *tatwa rashi* rises in the seventh house & Moon & Venus rise in it, both the partners possess a calm temperament but are heavier in body.

If *lagnesh*& the owner of the seventh rise in the same house, and/or have mutual aspects, then both the partners love each other. If they rise in a *Kendra*/Square or *Trikona*/triangle, they provide good results. In case *lagnesh*, & the owner of the seventh sit in the sixth, eighth or in the twelfth from each other, both the partners will have a different way of thinking, consequently both will often differ in their opinions. If Rahu, Ketu or Sun rise in the seventh house, even then both the partners will differ in their opinions or stay away from each other. But if there is an exchange between the owners of the *lagna*& the seventh, both will live amicably. If both, the girl & the boy have Cancer *lagna*, both will lead a friendly life.

At the time of marriage if good *dasha*
are rising in good signs in the orbit, & the astrologer, who is comparing both the *kundalies* takes care of the & keeps in view the Moon *lagna*, & if Venus is well placed in the of the boy's *kundali*& Jupiter in the of the girl's *kundali*, then the marriage
lagna,
the marriage will be delayed. If Jupiter rises in its weak degrees in the girl's *kundali*, it will not let her enjoy married life upto 40% &her husband may not care so much for her. The husband may be sick for a long time, or may go abroad on account of duty or job, or may be a drunkard, or there may be a difference of opinion in both of them. So, in case Venus rises in weak degrees, or is debilitated in the husband's *kundali*/chart, he may not be able to get a good wife and both may not lead a happy life.There may bee various causes for this kind of ill-effect. Either the man may not be in a job, & so may stay away from the woman, or she may be sick most of the time. Thus, only after examining the entire chart/*kundali*, one should give any predictions. The astrologer must keep in mind, the ,
Chandra *kundalui*& the position of the planets in the orbit before giving any predictions about the marriage of a boy & girl.

We, therefore, insist upon the *pandits*/astrologers that when they compare both the *kundalies*, they must examine the positions of the owners

the position of the owner of the eighth house, so that neither at the time of marriage nor even afterwards, any problems occur &should not limit their decision about a marriage on *Manglik Dosha*only.

10

Love Marriage/Inter-cast Marriage or More than One Marriage Yogas?

Marriage is an approved custom of a society in which a husband & wife are like two wheels of a cart. The systems & customs about performing a marriage differ according to the place, people and their way of their leading lives in a particular place or country. It is therefore, imperative to learn through a *kundlai* how much two charts/*kundalies* match with each other & both, the boy & the girl proposed for a marriage, will compete with each other favourably as far as their future union in a marriage is

kundali indicates 'love-marriage', & the seventh house represents husband & wife. When there is some kind of union among *lagnesh*

to a 'love-marriage'. Some astrologers reckon that when *Mangal*& Venus rise in one house or have their mutual aspects it leads to a 'love-marriage'. Rahu is considered as a tricky planet & may have its contribution in such activities. Our experience conveys that often Rahu plays a role in creating an environment for a 'love-marriage'. A 'love-marriage' may take place

in a certain position in *gauchar*(movements of planets in the orbit), or its *dahsha* or *maha-dasha* is operating.

their positions in the *kundali* or they are rising in each other's *nakchatras*, or if Rahu has its aspects on the Moon, *lagna*/ascendant, or the owner of the ascendant, a 'love-marriage' may take place.Our experience betrays that quite often natives make 'love-marriage' when '*kalserp-yoga*' (when all the seven planets are placed within the placement of Rahu & Ketu in a *kundali*) exists in their *kundalies*

& Ketu develop atheism in a native & leads to anti-reasoning attitude. In

it done. When they rise in the *kendras*/squares in a *kundali,* theyhelp the native to act that way. When Venus and Jupiter, Rahu & Ketu rise with the

inspire the native to go for a 'love-marriage'.

In a girl's *kundali* it Jupiter which indicate about the native's husband & in boy's *kundali* it is Venus refer to the status of a wife. When Jupiter is

place. Then the native does not care for the parents' advice or order and go

dasha starts &*gaucher* is also good

a 'love- marriage', the society doesn't approve of such a marriage. When Jupiter & Venus have their aspects on the seventh house, or if the owner of

of the sixth, eighth or twelfth houses, the native goes for an inter-cast marriage. The following *kundali*/chart support many things indicated just here above.

The native's birth took place on the 9th June, in 1964. The nativewas involved in a 'love-marriage'. In his *kundali*, the owner of the *lagna*,

Budha, rise together in one house in the *kundali*. All the planets sit within the placement of Rahu & Ketu & hence that makes *Kalserp yoga.*

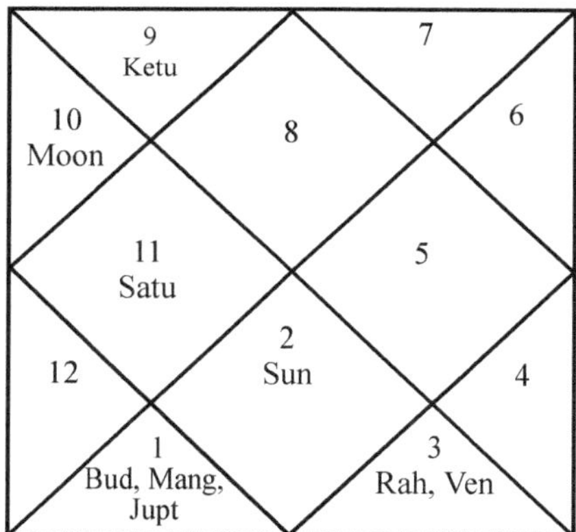

In this *kundali* Venus is retrograded &rises with Rahu in the eighth house. If we consider matters from *Chandra lagna* (Moon *lagna*), the Moon has its aspects on its own sign. It indicates wife's (good) temperament. In the above *kundali*, there is *Gajkeshari Yoga,* which ultimately reduces upto 50% the ill-effects of *Kalserp Yoga*. The native is interested in the study of astrology. *Gajkeshari Yoga* makes the native God fearing; he regularly prays & keeps a sane and pious conduct. His wife has been working in the Income-tax Department as a clerk. The owner of the seventh, Venus, rises in Gemini sign. It has connection with writing, education, clerical & book-keeping job. Rahu is connected with short-hand writing, expert in

in the Income-tax Department. She also knows how to operate computers.

We are providing another *kundali* for the readers' reference. The native was born on the 4th October in 1968. This native married three times and all the three marriages failed. None of the wives stayed with him. In the *kundali*, *lagneshBudha* is retrograded & in the seventh house retrograded Saturn is rising. Some astrologers don't approve or accept that a retrograded planet may do any harm to the native. However, the result is that after three marriages he is without a wife. He is trying for the fourth

lagna& does not permit him to stick to his work.

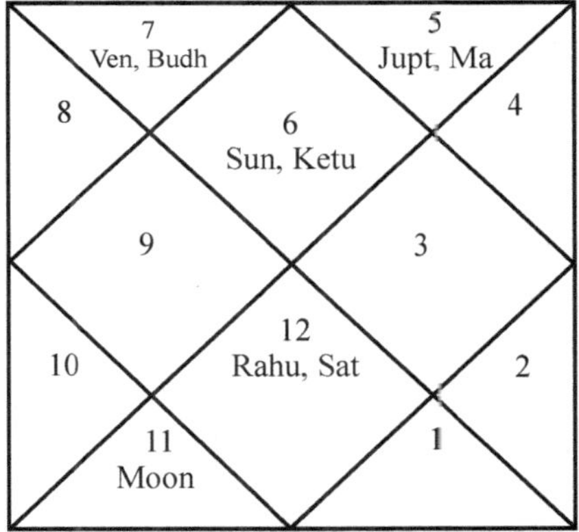

The *jatak* whose *kundali* we are now presenting for your reference was born on 2nd August in 1966. He made a love-marriage. This native

department. In the *lagna*

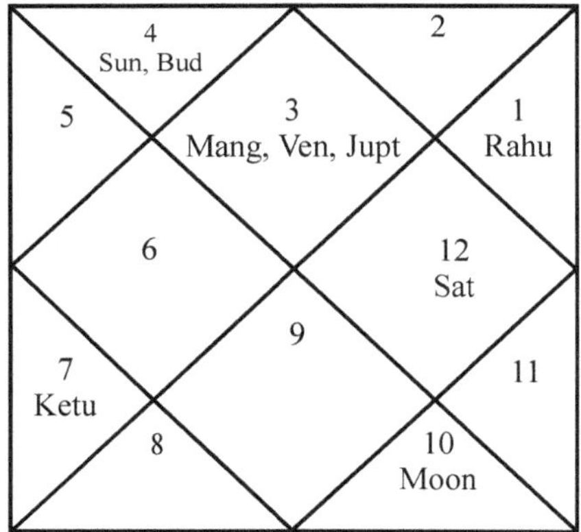

lagna. Mangal in *lagna* rises in *Budha*'s *rashi,* which is favoured by Rahu. That was the reason that the native married outside his own cast. *Mangal* is also the owner of the sixth house.

The native's wife works in a bank. The owner of the seventh house, Jupiter, sits in *lagna* in *Budha's* sign/*rashi.* Jupiter bestows money/wealth & sits with *Mangal* in *lagna.Mangal* is also the owner of the eleventh

Though the native is quite happy with his marriage, but quite often there are quarrels & differences in their opinions as Venus and Jupiter sit in the same house, *lagna*. It was also the reason to marry outside the native's cast as both the enemy planets, Jupiter & Venus, rise in one house, especially when Jupiter is the owner of the seventh house& Venus is of the

a few miscarriages have taken place.

Thus, Venus and Jupiter, when rise in one house they create problems relating those houses. As Jupiter has aspects on its own house (seventh) that relates wife/husband, the native's wife is good, but does not agree

it. That is the reason that the native has yet no children but may have one or two a little late in life. Keeping all such discussions in mind, the progressing astrologers are advised to predict on all matters only after studying the total chart of a native & keeping the entire *kundali* in mind.

Calculating from Kundali whether there will be Anybrothers/sisters, and Children?

When a *jatak* gets his/her chart examined, he/she often asks questions about the work/business of senior/younger brothers & sisters & also about their behavior & relationship towards the native. The third house in the *kundali* refers to brothers & sisters & the eleventh house refers to senior brothers & sisters. But the native puts questions relating all the brothers & sisters.The following *kundali* belongs to a native who was born on the 20th April in 1963.

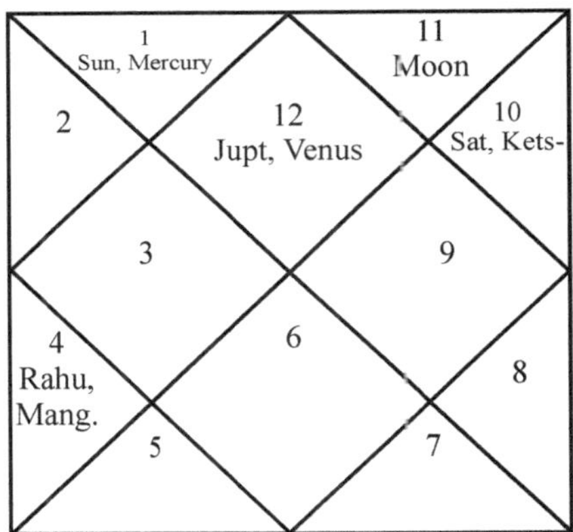

The third sign counting from the sign Cancer is Virgo. Its owner is *Budha* which rises in Aries sign of its enemy, *Mangal.Budha* rises in the eighth house from Virgo sign which belongs to *Budha. Budha* is also rising with the Sun. The Sun, the owner of the 6th rises in the second house, is ineffective & it also weakens*Budha*further. The third sign from Virgo is Scorpio which has affected adversely the education of younger brothers & sisters. The younger brothers are not able to earn their livelihood. The third sign from Scorpio is Capricorn in which Saturn is rising. Saturn is *Mangal* resulting in not giving any chance for further education to the younger sister.She is not even married. When we the ninth house, & from the eleventh house &*lagna*

Lal Kitab considers that if Mangal rises in *lagna* it is not auspicious to the native in whose chart it is rising. If Rahu sits in *lagna*, it spoils the Sun

upaya, the native should put 4 kilos of corn (*jaoo*) and 4 coconuts in the running water. If the Sun

few drops of milk on the stove which has been extinguished recently. The smoke which will come out from it, will make the entire house pure & the native will get blessings from God as He lives in the places that are pure. The Sun willnot harm the native by this *upaya*

& Moon represents milk. The seventh house is represented by the evening

milk, it will passify the Sun &*Mangal.*

The third house belongs to *Mangal* according to Lal Kitab. It refers to courage, fortitude & effortful nature of the native. If Saturn, which is the enemy of *Mangal*, rises in it, the native should make *chapaties*&feed dogs to ward off the ill-effect of Saturn. The eleventh house belongs to Jupiter, but if Venus is also there with Jupiter, it is necessary to remove the ill-effect of Venus. For that, the native is advised by Lal Kitab to make 121 small cotton sticks which should be burnt at a sacred/religious place on Fridays.

Rules & Precautions Regarding Residence

After the 'Stone-age', men always built good houses to live in them. Since then their families live in houses but how to lead a good life & how to live happily in them with one another, our *rishis &munies* developed certain rules & regulations. These rules & traditions have helped us live amicably with one another. The *rishies* always considered the planets important in that respect and studied them thoroughly to ascertain what ways would be useful to make us live happily. They discovered certain factors & rules based on the movements of the planets in the orbitto help us live peacefully with one another. Even today those rules & customs are important for us & help us lead a happy life. We write here below those regulations for the readers' kind reference.

One of them is that before moving into a new house it must be discovered that in the front portion of that house there was no big

(*bhatti*) was closed with mud and soil for good. If it is not checked, then when a child is born in that house whose who has the Moon rising in Scorpio sign of *Mangal*, he would destroy the family when he grows young and the members of the family will suffer a lot & would say abruptly that 'all has been burnt in our family. We are totally lost & destroyed'. So, in order to save the family from that kind of destruction, that place should be dug out & the soil of that *bhatti*) should be dug out and thrown into a river. It will help save that family from destruction.

It is also inauspicious to make a stone statue in a house and install it in a small for worshiping.The bells that chime in that house for worshiping will not permit any child born in it, especially when someone who has the predominance of Jupiter in his *kundali*and enters into a house having number 7. Such statues are good to be kept in the religious temples only. Only pictures of God & Goddesses would be useful to be kept in a house to provide good environment & family-peace, not the stone made statues.

In the houses made during olden days, there used to be a dark room at the place where the house-boundary ended & it had an entrance into it. There used to be no ventilator or a window for the light to enter into it. In such small rooms if a new ventilator or a window is made or created for air or light, it will destroy the family for good. Even if a new roof is to be made on that dark room, precautions must be taken before constructing the roof that no light enters into it.

Formerly in the olden times, people would often dig some small holes to put their money & ornaments into them. In case if such a dig has been discovered in a house where one is shifting to live

something, like dry fruits etc., one should not then trust the man

& live peacefully.

In case there is no place in a house where there is no open space which is unpaved, then that house is not blessed by Venus. Saturn

and health of the residents of the house. In order to save from the ill-effect of Saturn, one must establish things related to Venus. It would be good to keep a cow in the house & plant a potato plant as well.

The main door of the house where one lives should not be facing the south. It is considered inauspicious for the women as well as for men. Therefore, the main door in a house should not be facing the south.

Precautions about the Corners in a New House

It is imperative to check the corners of the land before actually constructing the house. If a land possesses four equal corners, each corner having 90 degrees' angle,& if a house is constructed on it, is considered good from all respects.The following number of corners should not be inside the house, such as 9, 3, 13 or 18

5 or 8 corners, they are also not acceptable. The description about various corners in a land on which a house is not permissible for construction, is given below for the advice of the readers.

(i) Where there are 8 corners in a land. It will be affected adversely by Saturn which will cause illness & death in the family.

(ii) Where there are 3 & 13 corners. A house constructed on such a land will bring bad effect from *Mangal* which will create problems for brothers & relatives& may destroy them

& relatives & someone in the family may also be hanged on account of some crime.

(iii) Where there are 18 corners in the land.A house made on such a land will bring ill-effect from Jupiter, which will affect the income of the native as well as affect the children adversely.

(iv) Where there are 5 corners in the land. It will bring destruction to the owner & his children. There is a sayingcommonly uttered for such a house made on the land having 5 corners in it. Its sense is that if someone makes a temple on a land that has 5 corners, then even God cannot save him from destruction. So anyone who wants to construct a house must see that such corners don't exist in the walls of his house before the construction of the house.

A house having some kind of bulge in the land like the stomach of *rishies.*It may reduce the number of the family (some may die early) & the owner of the house will die without any children. Consequently no one will be left out after him in the family.

House without any Sides

A house without any sides or corners is just like a deadbody, in which people only wail & witness death. If someone is married in such a house, either the man or woman will be left out without the partner (he/she will die soon after the marriage).

The Walls of the House

After examining the corners of the house, the owner of the house should measure its area (without measuring its foundation) & also measure the areas of each room separately by the length of his own arm, whether the

the elbow until the corner of the palm of the right or left hand of the native.

The Effect of the Planets on a House

In order to observe the effect of planets on a (new) house, astrologers often reckon it with the help of mathematics, which I as follows.

$$\frac{[(\text{length}+\text{breadth}) \times 33] - 1}{8}$$

Whatever is left out will be considered the effect of the planets, such as: length ¾ 15 and breadth ¾ 7 measured with the hands. Only then its length and breadth will be considered good.

$$\frac{[(15+7) \times 33] - 1}{8}$$

If only 1 is leftout, it will be considered good. Thus, in case 1, 3, 5, & 7 are left out as a result of subtraction, it will be considered good.

inauspicious.

A detailed description of the effect of auspicious & inauspicious planets, rising in the *kundali* of different newly constructed houses is given here below from the point of view of Lal Kitab.

kundali of a house, that house, it will be considered very auspicious & display all the favours of these planets.

If Jupiter & Venus sit in the 6th house, it is considered very inauspicious (just like a dog) and it brings poverty. In case Ketu sits in the sixth house, some *upayas* need to be done to get the favour of Jupiter.

In case *Mangal* & Jupiter sit in the third house, it will be like a lion & will be auspicious for men, their business or some sort of shop, but not as good for children & women. In this kind of a house,

matters. If husband & wife are without children when Venus rises in the third house, it will be useful to live in a house where Mangal rises in the *lagna* of the *kundali* of that house. However it may not be as good for the children. In case the man (husband) & the woman (wife) must to live in that house with the children, they should plant

husband & wife don't live there with the children.

If Saturn & Moon rise in the fourth house, that house is not considered auspicious. It just like a donkey, not of much use & dull. Someone, who lives in such a house, works like a donkey but does not get as much returns as he much he works. The native is advised to do some *upaya* for the Moon & Saturn.

cow. In such a house, women & children will be totally happy. Even Venus will support such a person. If such a house is broader from the back side, it will be considered auspicious.

If the Moon & Venus rise in the seventh house, that house is

house'. If animals are reared in it, it will be useful to the owner/ native.

If Saturn & Sun rise in the sixth house, the inhabitants of that house will just be like passengers/travelers & will never be able to stay in it for long. On account of Ketu's ill-effect the native will neither get the blessings from mother nor from father. The children will also not be able to live in it happily & there will not be any cooperation from friends. Such a person will go on moving place to place like a traveler on account of problems.

If *Mangal*& Saturn rise in the eighth house, that house will be like

upaya

for *Mangal*& Saturn need to be done in relation to the eighth house.

The Main Doors in the House

The main door in a house is always considered very important. It is said that through that door good & bad luck enter through. Laxhimi & poverty also track through it. Therefore, the main door of the house should be well tuned with the planets *&dashas* so that no inauspicious things may happen in it. The analysis about the main door of the newly constructed house is presented here below.

If the main door of the house is towards the east it is considered to be highly auspicious as through that door time to time some good person may come in and bless the house. It will bestow happiness to the inhabitants of the house.

If the main door of the house is towards the west, it is considered the second best in comparison to the one which has its main door towards the east.

If the main door of a house is towards the east it is auspicious and the owner of thehouse gets plenty of blessings through prayers & good acts in which he/she is constantly involved.

If the main door of the house is in the south, it is inauspicious & is

not get any happiness in it. Fire often gets erupted in it & the natives may also go to jail at times. In order to get away from its bad effect the native is advised to give away a lamb to some needy person & may also give away things, to the needy, relating *Budha* when it is evening. No alternations need to be made in the house to check unexpected expenses.

Planting a Sahateer Tree

sahateerplant

Venus, will always be good for the inhabitants of the hosue. A roof created in according to Saturn's impact, will cause illness or death in the house.

The Number of Rings in the House

If total number of the rings used in the house when divided by 4 gets to 1, that house will be considered auspicious. It will foster environment just

brings *Rajyoga*to the native & gets him/her a lot of happiness.

Analysis of the Entire House on Principles

If air comes straight into a house through its main door, it is considered auspicious for children & would save them from problems. During the night at the time of taking sleep if the head of the bed lies towards the east or south, it is considered good and auspicious. It helps the native's mind work well during the day & the Sun helps such a person. The Moon also helps during the night by providing strength to the soul of the native. It is inauspicious to keep one's feet towards south or east. So it is imperative to work with entire heart & soul and do good deeds for the people.

Things that are placed inside the house also have their good effect on the inmates of the house when they are placed in the right direction.

is burnt in the east or south direction in the house; water is kept in the north-east corners in the house where worship is also done. To keep a native's valuables in the south-west corner of the house & if guests are accommodated in the west side of it, it is considered auspicious. While

place is placed behind, it is considered auspicious.

In case there is a *peepal* tree is near one's house, it will provide good results only when it is worshiped regularly. If it is watered regularly, it

neglected. The same good & bad may happen if there is a well near one's house. In case some milk is poured into it regularly with faith, it will help the members of the house grow well, but if neglected it will bring devastation to it.

Permanent Places of Planets in a House

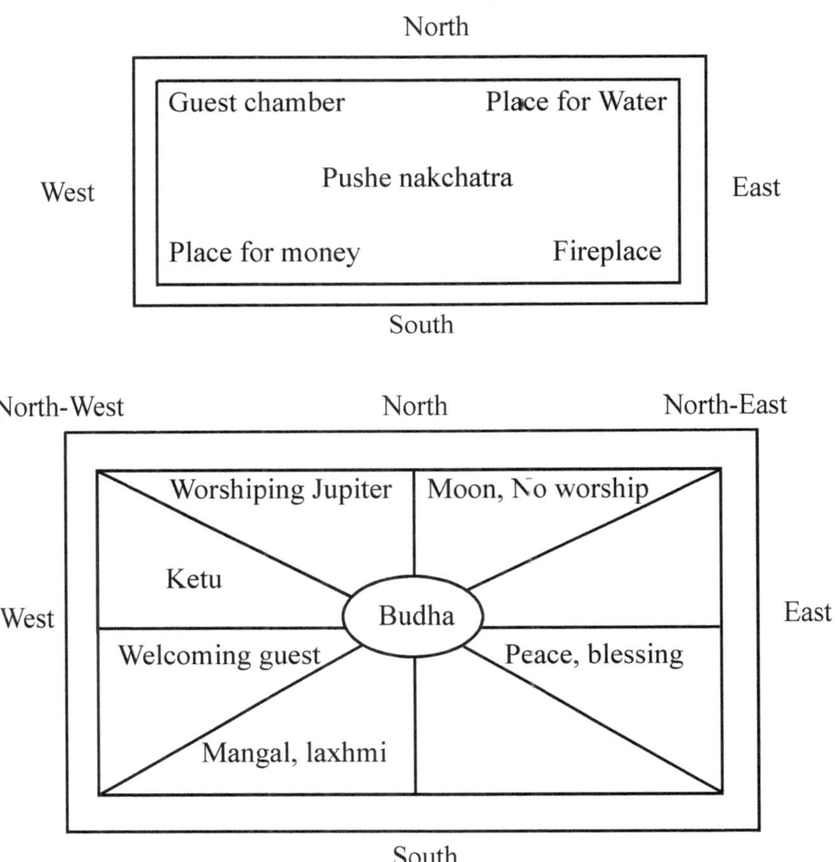

If one plants a *keeker* tree in the house, it will not let the children survive in it. To save its ill-effect one needs to water it for 40 days on Saturdays

provided here above indicate that in every corner & place in the house there is a place meant for different planets. That means that if the native puts things belonging to the enemy of a planet in a particular corner or place, it will bring ill-effect to the native in various ways. For example, if a box is kept in the north-east corner which belongs to the Moon in a house, it will diminish the good effect of the Moon. So better use things that belong to the Moon and put them in the right place or appropriate direction.

A house constructed on a land where the dead are cremated or buried, it will make the native childless. The best *upaya* for it would be to sit on the roof of the house in the east direction and dig a well within 40 to 43 steps measured from there in the ground. It will be auspicious for the native. The house that stands at the end of the street or in which there is a direct entrance from the main road, it is considered bad for the children as bad souls keep coming and going through that route. It brings bad-effect on the women & children of the house. Rahu & Ketu also have their ill-effect on such a house. Such a house will always bring ill-effect on the

there each day or frequently. That house will be terribly bad for women & men to live in but will be good only to the blind people.

13

Serious Thinking on Kalserp Yoga

When all the seven planets are placed between Rahu & Ketu in a *kundali*, astrologers reckon it to be a Kalserp Yoga. Some astrologers consider that when certain planets sit with Rahu & Ketu & in degrees the planet is more than Rahu & Ketu's degrees, the bad effect of kalserp Yoga is diminished. However, we think that this *dosha* (Yoga) does not end completely. It stays to a certain extent & so also its ill-effect.In a native *kundali* when this Yoga appears, his/her luck & body are supposed to be tied down with snakes. Rahu is considered as the head of snake & Ketu as its body. In whose *kundali* this Yoga appears, there are ups & downs in his/her life frequently.

Astrologically there are twelve kinds of *Kalserp Yoga* that starts from

kundali, the *dosha* is reduced or does not exist, but different astrologers have various views in this context.

Anant-Namak Kalserp Yoga

This yoga makes the native a non-believer. It may also create health related problems, especially in the throat & mouth & neither husband nor wife can lead a happy life.

Kulik Kalserp Yoga

When Rahu is in the second & Ketu is in the eighth house, this yoga is formed. It creates problems to the native relating education, money & family.

Vasuki Kalserp Yoga

When Rahu rises in the third house & Ketu in the ninth, this yoga is formed. It affects native's relationship with family, friends, brothers & relatives adversely. The native is constantly in struggle with his/her brothers.

Shankpal Kalserp Yoga

When Rahu is in the fourth house & Ketu in the tenth, this yoga is formed. On account of this yoga, the native does not get any happiness from parents or in-laws. It also creates poisonous wounds in the native's body, makes the native irritating and keeps him/her constantly unhappy.

Padam Kalserp Yoga

It does not let the native have children, affects his/her thoughts adversely, &indulges him/her in unnecessary expenses as well as in love affairs, which keeps him/her unhappy throughout life.

Mahapadam Kalserp Yoga

If Rahu is in the sixth house & Ketu in the twelfth house, this yoga is formed.The native has to suffer on account of false accusations against

in the sixth house, it defeats the enemies ruthlessly & gets the native free from any accusations.

Kerkotak Kalserp Yoga

When Rahu rises in the seventh house & Ketu is in *lagna*, the yoga is formed. This yoga brings bad events to native's life & he/she has to face several wicked incidents in life. The native is constantly worried on account of family & liver problems as well as sex problems. It may lead to several operations. The native may suffer from small-pox while he/she is very young. It also affects the native's thinking capability and personality adversely. As Ketu rises in *lagna*, it constantly indulges the native into negative thinking & infuses jealousy in the nature. The yoga also affects the native's married life adversely.

Takchak Kalserp Yoga

It is formed when Rahu is in the eighth house & Ketu in the second. It delays the growth of native's luck-time & does not let the native get a good job early. It is also bad for long life, & often indulges the native in operations. It is the yoga which does not let the native have friends, may also get an early death, & the native may constantly suffer on account of lack of money.

Shanknad Kalserp Yoga

This yoga is formed when Rahu sits in the ninth & Ketu in the third house. When this yoga is formed it checks the growth of good luck, & the native is often deceived by his friends & relatives. It also makes the native a non-believer in God. The native may be involved in unfruitful journeys which leads to useless expenditure. It may also affect native's relationship with the father adversely.

Ghatak Kalserp Yoga

It is formed when Rahu is in the tenth house & Ketu in the fourth. Such a native hardly gets the father's property or it becomes a barriers in getting children & jobs. The native is constantly involved in changing jobs, which makes the native a debtor. Such a native constantly suffers on account of heart and other severe problems. He/she may have troubles relating breath or heart. But Rahu being in the tenth house rising in Saturn's sign, may

department. It also affects relations with the father positively.

Vishakta Kalserp Yoga

is formed. Such a native often suffers on account of children, stomach ache & attainment of education. Such a native suffers from an ailment that constantly goes on for quite long.

Sheshnag Kalserp Yoga

When Rahu is in the twelfth house and Ketu in the sixth, this yoga is formed. Such a native suffers on account of sleeplessness & is involved in unnecessary expenses. The native often suffers from headaches & is involved with negative thinking. But the native loves to visit sacred places and isoften involved in useless expenditures.

has been stated here above, does not go exactly as stated. Certain things are not applicable to all the natives except that in principle many things are applicable to all or most of the natives. It is also observed that a native in whose *kundali* Kalserp Yoga is formed he/she lacks something important in life.It could be anything like not possessing good health, or he/she may suffer constantly on account of some illness one after another. At times the illness is of the kind that no medicine is effective against it. The native may not have children or may not have a good married life or lead a pauper's life.

It is also observed several times that a native may have lots of wealth, say up to two-three million rupees, but all is lost all of a sudden and he is ruined. It may also happen that during his childhood the parents are gone to God's house or he may live away from them due to certain reasons. Or he/she is adopted by someone immediately after the birth. When we examine Kalserp Yoga in a *kundali*, we also observe thatdeath visits the native's family several times when he/she is very young, or the native does not get any parental property. He may also earn his livelihood far away from his birth place. Such a native, though gets good education, is not able to take its advantage in life and luck is never with him/her. The native is often troubled by his/her children or the children are usually unproductive or characterless. Such a native may also lose a good job on account of certain reasons & becomes jobless. To provide more information on Kalserp Yoga, we present a few *kundalies*for so that the reader may understand the problems imposed by Kalserp Yoga.

Date of Births: 10th April, 1943

The native was married for twelve years but he had no issues (children) or even later on.Later on he involved himself in *puja-path* (worshiping) and served *sadhus&brahmins* sincerely but nothing blessed him with a child. Some people in his family suffered from cancer & supreme court sue against him on account of some happening for which he was accused. The native has not been keeping on well health-wise and he stays pretty disturbed mentally. As the mother-in-law of this native offers Rs. 2000/- to the poor and the needy each month, he is still alive. However, after twelve years of his marriage, perhaps on account of the mother-in-law being so kind and religious, he got a son, but unfortunately the child has not been keeping on good health.

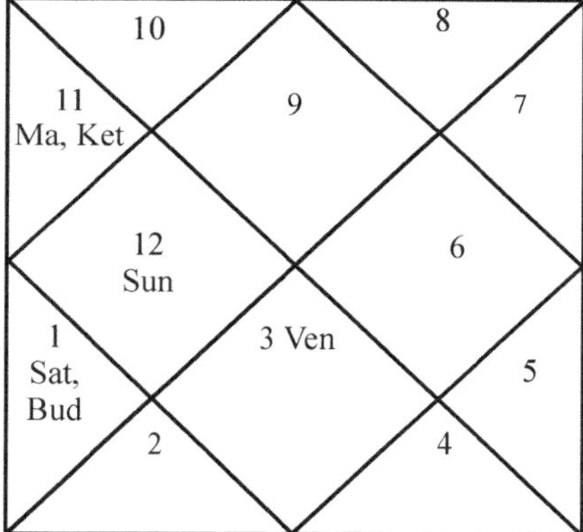

21st April 1946

This native's son suffered from cancer & he spent around Two Lack

heart disease & had to stay in bad for 9 months & got himtreated in All IndiaMedical Hospital, New Delhi, but could not totally recovered. He lived in a rented house until he survived. He died on 20 Augustin 1999 in spite of taking regular treatment from doctors. Though the native was slightly aggressive in conduct, he was very religious & kind-hearted. However, he had a short life-span &died early inspite of all medical help.

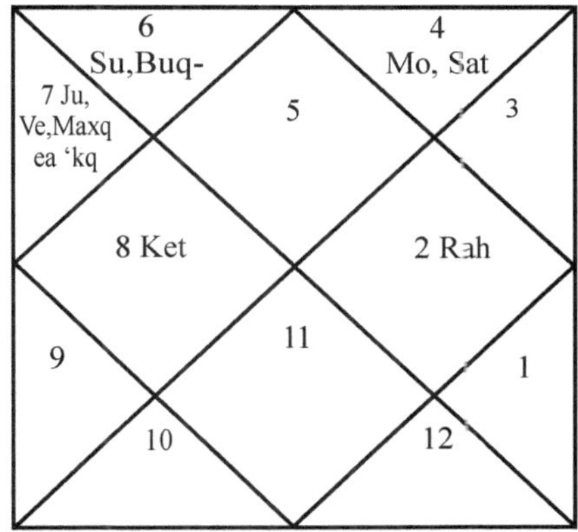

13th January 1988

There is partial Kalserp Yoga in this native's *kundali.* The health of the native is not as good as it should have been and his father died in June

the younger son when he grew young, did well in life. The Kalserp Yoga could not do much harm to the native as Jupiter, sitting in its own sign in

and alsohas its aspects on *Mangal*, which is the *lagnesh* in this *kundali.*

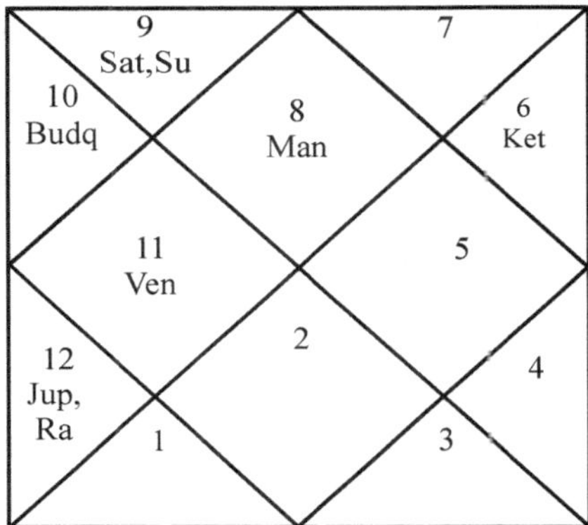

6th March 1963

This *jatak* has no son but has a daughter only. His liber also has gone weakened. As one of the doctors in a civil hospital is his friend & classmate, he went on treating him but of not much use. Then he got himself operated in Apollo Hospital, New Delhi after consulting a few doctors but along with his liber, his heart and *gurdey* also went bad. Doctors tried their best to treat him but he died during 2000 after spending around 20 lacks of rupees. However, he left a lot of wealth for his family which helped in the wedding of his daughter and running the family well after him.

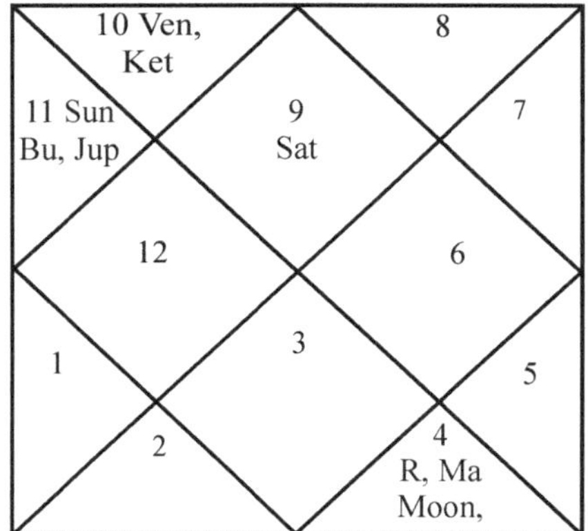

This is indicated from the chart as Saturn sitting in its own sign in the second house with Ketu, has its aspects on the 11th house, the house of wealth. Thus, Kalserp Yoga is reduced to a certain extent by the aspects of a planet rising with Rahu or Ketu, though it has its other effects on the native.

17th August 1947

This native worked in Merchant Navy but resigned from job 20 years before due to his family problems. Since then he has taken some small jobs and earns small amount of money. Sometimes he gets Rs.1500 or a little more but it does not help much to run his family. If he were still

rupees monthly. But currently he is passing his days in a poor state. Since Jupiter rises in its enemy sign in the seventh house, he is not getting much pleasure from his married life, though a good son & a daughter are indicated by his chart. As there is Kalserp Yoga in this chart/*kundali*, the entire life of the native has been wasted struggling hard though he has been very effortful.

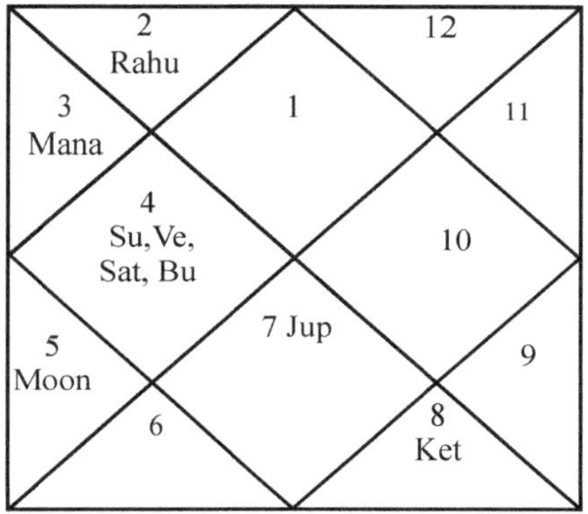

7th May 1968

This native has good education but his father's health is weak. His one sister was married successfully but was divorced after two years of her marriage. She has been living with the native since then. She was divorced after three months of the native's marriage. So far the native earns only Rs 1200/- or 1500/- a month, serving in private jobs. Now since one year he is jobless sitting idle at home. It leads to several problems & constant quarrels in the family. Though there is a Gajkeshari Yoga in the *kundali,*he is unable to do any *upayas*or he gets a job. It is also a result of bad placements of planets in the *kundali* that his wife's health is constantly unwell, so his even married life has not provided him any happiness.

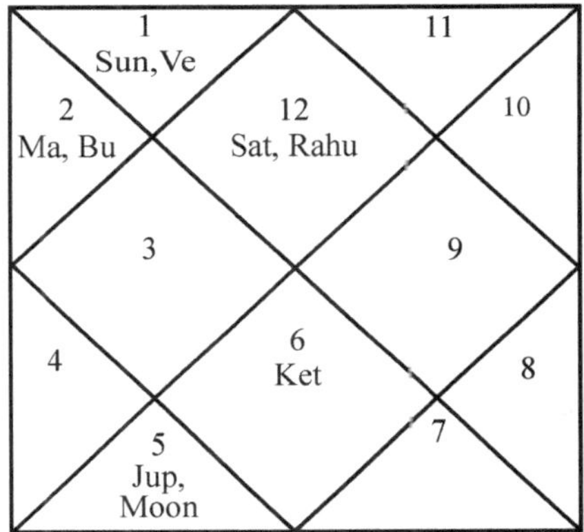

23rd October 1946

The native worked in an ordinary position in Food & Supply Department. He was removed from the job on account of certain charges against him. As the charges were false, he fought for his

or worshiping. He is also not interested in any kind of job. Besides Kalserp Yoga, his ascendant Moon, has aspects from Saturn. It has led his thinking adversely affected. Consequently he has tried to kill

house, it has not created much love for his children though he goeson quite well with his wife.

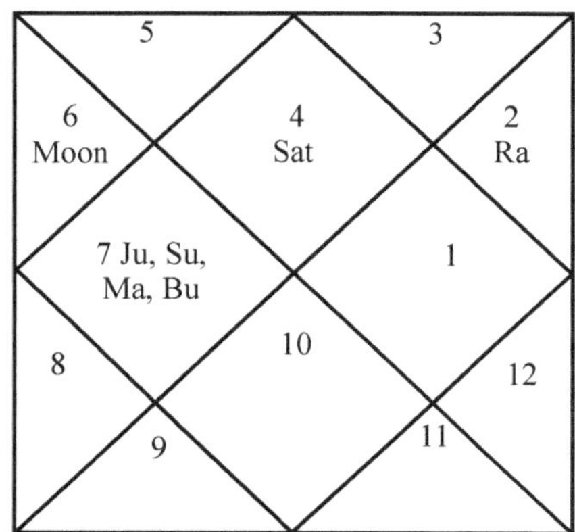

22nd March 1964

for thirteen years but did not have any issue (child) though every kind of treatment was taken by her. Her health is also not good andshe once suffered on account of T. B.As the Moon, the owner of her luck & ninth house, is eclipsed by Saturn & Rahu, her luck has been adversely affected. She gets often failures in any work that she undertakes.

She has also grown as a suspicious kind of person, so she never gets any pleasure in company any outside or inside the house. Her health is also not good and she has not been pulling on quite friendly with her husband as well.

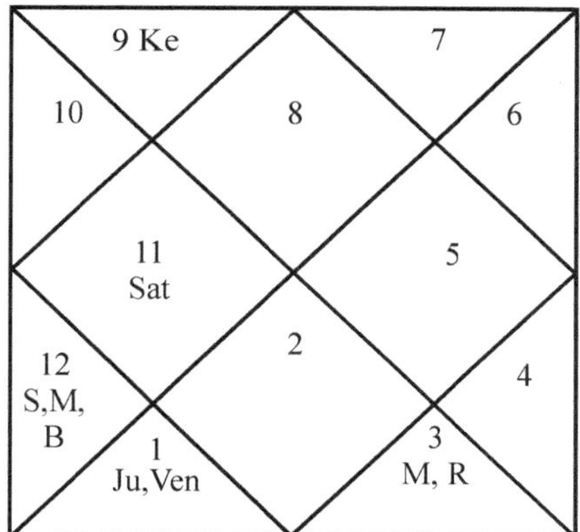

24th October 1946

The native possesses good health & as he is born in a good family he is always inclined to help others when need arises but there is Kalserp Yoga in his chart probably on account of his previous life's activities & bad

property worth several lacks is in danger. His own brother has captured his property. Besides, he is involved in two-three other court cases. His son has been suffering from certain kind of mental ailment (*mirgee*). Though the native is a good person, he does not do any *upayas* to get the effect of Kalserp reduced. Consequently he has been suffering in life.

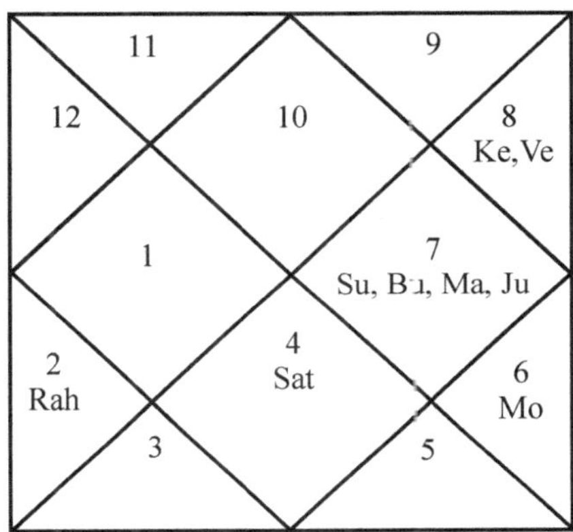

Our Own Opinion on Kalserp Yoga

Some people consider Kalserp Yoga very inauspicious and some consider that it has no impact on the individuals.Our experience say that every *kundali* has good & bad yogas. Therefore, one should make predictions after considering both sorts of yogas because certain yogas affect adversely on other yogas & end up their effect. At times certain people who have Kalserp Yoga in their *kundali* reach very high positions in their livesthat all that is not easily imaginable. However, at times something important lacks in their lives. Considering all that we indicate here below how one can try to save oneself from the ill-effect of Kalserp Yoga.

The Yogas that Redeem Kalserp Yoga

1. When a native has a good position in life, it is seen that in his/her chart auspicious planets rise on both sides of the Sun in the *kundali* of that *jatak*. Ancient astrological books also unfold that planets sitting on either side of the Sun form Beish Yoga. But neither Rahu, Ketu nor the Moon should be placed in the 2nd& 12th houses before & after the Sun to make a successful *Beish Yoga.* When the Moon rises near the Sun, its good effect ends, but if other auspicious

which is very auspicious. If planets rise in the sixth & eighth houses from the position of the Sun, they are considered very auspicious.

2. In case Rahu, Ketu & Sun don't rise on either side of the Moon in a *kundali*, they provide good effect on the native.If the Sun rises on its either side, it reduces the good effect of the Moon.
3. In any *kundali* if planets rise in seven houses each, it is known as Saptrishi Yoga.Such a native rise very high in life & gets most of the things that give happiness and prosperity.
4. Gajkeshari Yoga is formed when the Moon rises with Jupiter or when Jupiter rises in a *kendra* from the Moon.
5. In any *kundali*Adhi Yoga is formed when auspicious planets rise on both sides of *lagna* or if they fries in the sixth, seventh or the eighth houses.

of Gaj Keshari Yoga.

7. The Moon & the ascendant rise in *lagna* or if *lagnesh* has its aspect on the Moon, it is auspicious.
8. If Jupiter, Moon & Saturn rise in one house or if *Mangal*& Moon rise at one place or have aspects on eachother, it is auspicious.
9. In case a native is born during day time & the Sun & the Moon rise in *Visham Rashi*, the Yoga is known as *Maha Bhagyawan Yoga.* Deeru Bhai Ambani has this yoga in his *kundali* although he also Kalserp Yoga in his *kundali.*He is a famous industrialist. Similarly if a native who is a woman,is born in night and *lagna* is in *sam rashi*, and the Sun & Moon are also in *sam rashi*, *Maha Bhagwan Yoga* is formed. This yoga was found in Srimati Indra Gandhi, Shri Morarji Deshai, Shri Rajeev Gandhi & Shri Chandra Shekher's *kundalies*.
10. Similarly, when many planets have exchanged there places (*rashis*), like *Mangal* is in *Kark*/Cancer sign, and the Moon is in Scorpio, such a yoga (bearing great luck) is formed.
11. When planets are rising in all the four *kendras* of a *kundali*, or of if planets are rising in all the four *kendras* from the Moon, or if 4,5,6 planets rise in any one house of a *kundali*, it is also very auspicious.
12. When *lagna* is Vergotam, that means when the *lagna*& Navansh in the *kundali* have the same sign/number, it is also very auspicious.
13. When the *lagnesh* rises in the second (*dhan asthan*) or eleventh houses (*labh asthan*), or the owner of the eleventh rises in the second house or vice versa or the *lagnesh* is sitting in the eleventh

house or vice versa, or the owners of the second & eleventh have aspects on each other, it is very auspicious.

14. If in any *kundali,* 3-4 planets have digbala, that means *Budha*, Jupiter are in, the Moon is in the fourth house, Saturn is in the seventh house, & the Sun &*Mangal* rise in the tenth house, the *kundali* has *digbala*.

kundali, it is also highly auspicious.

16. When Jupiter, Venus & Moon rise in one house, it is highly auspicious.

17. When *Vipreet Raj Yoga* or *Neech Bhagna Yoga* are formed in a *kundali*

represents sickness/illness, impediments, and loans or debts, & the twelfth house indicates expenses. If the owner of the sixth sits in the twelfth or the owner of the twelfth sits in the sixth, it makes Vipreet Raj Yoga. Like that the eighth house represents life, death or poverty. If the owners of the sixth or twelfth sit in the eighth, the Yoga is formed. This Yoga forms several kinds of Raj Yogas.

Neech Bhagna Yoga is formed when any planet which rises in an exalted or debilitated sign in a chart/*kundali*, and it rises in a *Kendra* from the *lagna* or Chandra *lagna.* This yoga is more than a Rajya Yoga &

manner in any *kundali.*

18. When many or great number of planets have their aspects on the ninth or tenth houses.

19. When a planet rises in its own sign and Rahu or Ketu also rise with it, it forms a Neech Bhagna Yoga as both Rahu & Ketu, which are shadowy planets, also work like that planet with which they sit.

20. If the owner of the sign (*rashi*) rising in *lagna* and the *lagnesh* sit in *Kendra* from each other's position/ placement or if the Moon rising in one of the signs owned by the *lagnesh* and *lagnesh*& the Moon sit in *Kendras,* this yoga is usually found in the *kundalies* of successful people. In such a *kundali* at least one planet rises in *Kendra.*

    (a) In case there are planets in the third, seventh and eleventh houses from *lagna*, Chatra Yoga is formed.This yoga provides every kind of facility in *jatak's* life. Even if there are no planets in the seventh house, most of the needed amenities in life are received and life runs smoothly.

(b) If planets rise in the second, fourth & the sixth houses in a *kundali*, they also provide e very kind of happiness to the native.

(d) Similarly if planets rise in the eighth, tenth and the twelfth houses, good results are produced. There are some other general rules that need to be kept in mind.

21. Ketu placed in the ninth house provides good result.

22. The owner of the sign rising in *lagna* if it rises in its own *rashi*, or is exalted and sits in a *Kendra*, it is known as Kahal Yoga. Similarly, the owner of the sign that rises in *lagna* if rises in *Kendra* or *trikona* and is in an exalted sign or in its own sign (*rashi*), it is known as Parvatakhya Yoga. One who is born in *Kahala Yoga*, he/she

Yoga enjoys a kind of Rajya Yoga, rules on land and enjoys life. Such natives get several great positions in the world, enjoy great status in life and get famous.

23. When the owners of the 9th and the 10th houses rise in one house in a chart, it also provides every kind of happiness to the native in life.

24. When one is born at the time of full Moon, and if auspicious planets sit in *Kendra* or *Trikona*, it is considered auspicious.

25. Similarly if more planets sit in *char rashi*, it is also considers auspicious.

26. If the owner of *lagna&lagnesh* don't rise in *sandhi* (cups), and the *lagnesh* in not debilitated, it is also auspicious.

27. The owner of the sign in which Rahu & Ketu rise in a chart sits in *Kendra* or *Trikona* from the positions of Rahu & Ketu, good results are provided to the native in whose chart such placements occur. If the owner of a good & auspicious sign sits in the 6th, 8th or 12 house, then Rahu & Ketu don't give good results. If the owner of the ninth house sit in a *Kendra*, it brings success in the native's life when he/she reaches 25 to 28 years of age. If it rises in the third, second or eleventh house, the native gets success when he/she reaches 45 years of age. If such an owner sits in the sixth, eighth or twelfth house, success comes hardly by the end of native's life.

28. If most planets sit in the ninth, tenth or eleventh houses or have good aspects on them, it is very auspicious. The reason behind it is that the ninth house is the house of luck, the tenth represents *karma*

a fact that planets when they rise in these houses they have aspects on the 3rd (house of good efforts), 4th (house of happiness, property & facilities), and the 5th house (house of wisdom & intelligence). So

native. Therefore, if planets don't rise in the said houses, it weakens those house in several ways.

29. Parijat Yoga is formed when the owner of the sign controlled by the*lagnesh*if rises in a *Kendra.*It is also highly auspicious to the native. We are providing a few *kundalies* having this yoga for the reference of the readers.

Dr. Rajendra Prasad's Kundali

The native whose *kundali* possesses this yoga, rises in life to a great extent.

so that some clear undersnading may come to the reader about it. The following *kundali* belongs to First President of India. The Sagittarius sign rises in *lagna* and its owner is Jupiter, which is rising in the ninth house in the sign Leo owned by the Sun. The Sun rises in *Mangal's* sign & *Mangal* is sitting in *lagna*. This is creating Parijat Yoga.What else one would like to become more than that in one's life. The said Yoga took Dr Rajendra Prasad to a great height. He became the First President of India.

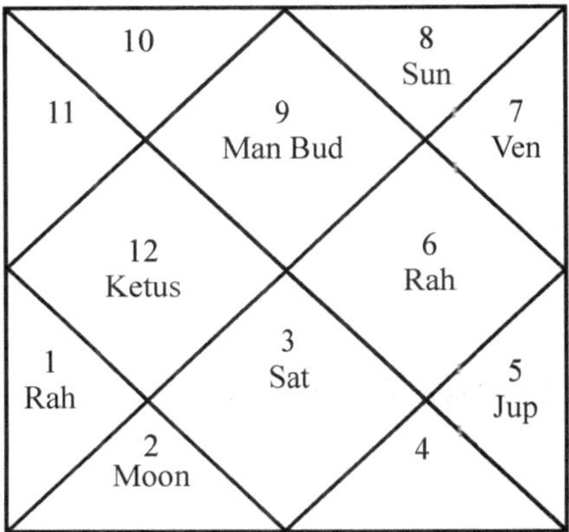

Sachin Tandulker 24th April, 1973

In this context we are providing here below the *kundali* of Sachin Tandulker, who has been one of the the most famous & successful cricketer in the world. Though there is Kalserp Yoga too in his *kundali*, he became most successful *kundali, Mangal* is exalted & it has its aspects on the exalted Sun rising in the eighth house.

of the most famous cricket players in the world. Very auspicious yogas exist in his chart. There are planets on both sides of the exalted Sun. It forms Vaish Yoga which provides riches and fame. Both, the Sun & Venus rise in *Mangal's* sign Aries, which controls sports & courage. The Virgo *lagna* is rising in the *kundali*. *Budha*, the *lagnesh* and the owner of tenth, sits in the seventh house and has aspects on *lagna* which is helpful & provides riches to him. Both the Sun & Venus have aspects from *Mangal*& Jupiter. *Mangal* controls games & sports.Its aspects on the Sun rising in eighth provides extreme courage to the native. Saturn rises in the ninth, has aspects from *Mangal.*

The tenth house has aspects from Rahu & the Moon. So the 9th& the 10th houses have become very strong in the *kundali.* The Sun owner of the 12th, is rising in the 8th. It forms a Vipreet Raj Yoga & provides unusual strength of character to the native.

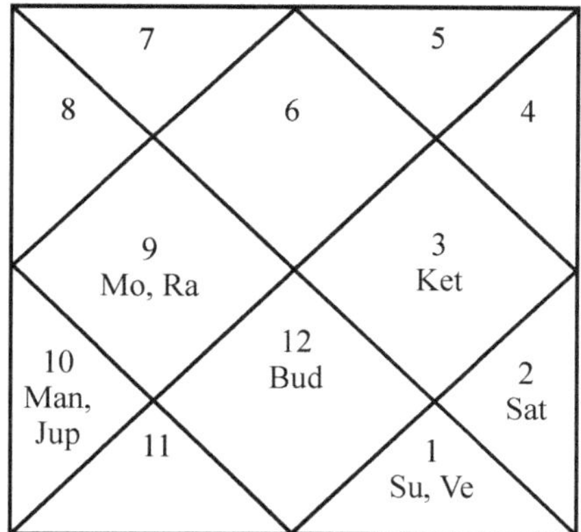

Successful ENT Doctor 07.01.1955

Now we provide here below a *kundali* of a very successful ENT doctor for the reference of the readers.

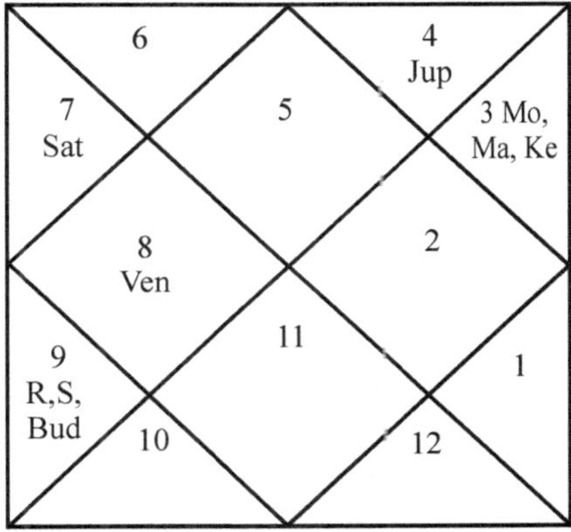

In the above *kundali* both the Sun & the Moon are adversely affected by Rahu & Ketu. *Budh* is rising with the Sun &*Mangal* is with the Moon. Both Ketu & Rahu have their aspects on the Sun which is *lagnesh* in this chart. It affects the doctor's income &prestige to some extent. Besides, most planets are rising within Rahu & Ketu, which make Kalserp Yoga and which affects doctor's income, prestige etc. although he is one of the best ENT doctor in a big town in Rajasthan. However, *Mangal* is the owner of the ninth house (house of luck), and has its aspects on the Sun. So the doctor has to stay out of his own town but he became head of the department in a big government hospital in his own state.

Manglik Dosha & Its Precautions

In the Indian society Manglik Dosha or Manglik Yoga is one of the most discussed issue as far as astrology is concerned. However, our *risies* especially Parashar, Barahmahir etc. whose famous legendry books named 'Parashar Hora Shastra', 'Saravali', 'Jatak Parijat' etc. have never made any reference of Manglik Dosha or Manglik Yoga in their books. But astrological books that were written after them, contain dreadful account of Manglik Dosha.

Even these days in whole India several kinds of varied information regarding Manglik Dosha is rampant. It is quite surprising that our ancient *rishis*

modern Indian society this issue is very popular & people do strongly hold their belief in it. Even if someone does not possess any knowledge about astrology, he/she claims to know much about this Dosha/Yoga. The impact of this Yoga is so much that girl's mother & father are often prepared to have no alliance with a boy (proposed bridegroom) in whose *kundali* this dosha occurs. So this Yoga has become an important aspect of astrology as far as marriage alliance is concerned, although such decisions are not totally acceptable or important. Any sort of knowledge about certain unknown aspect should be to dispel ignorance, remove darkness & confusion but not to spread fear. So such ignorance about Manglik Dosha need to be well guarded and adequate knowledge about it must be gathered before anyone talks many things about it.

It is because of that we would like to discuss on the issue of Manglik Dosha so that many sort of prevalent fearsome information about it should

& how much it is harmful? These are some of the important matters that must be understood clearly before breaking down a marriage alliance when this Dosha is discovered in a *kundali*. One also needs to discover its *upayas* before breaking already decided alliances. There are so many other important matters that need to be understood if a happy married life is to including on Manglik Dosha & also on how far this Dosha needs to be considered before and after making or breaking a marriage alliance.

Its very name indicates that it is a *yogkarak yoga*
as the meaning of *Mangal* is *subh* or auspicious. Then how can this Yoga be considered providing bad effect?What is Manglik Yoga? Before understanding the Yoga one needs to understand the qualities of *Mangal*that make this yoga. The term '*Mangal'*
certainly not 'bad' or harmful. So before starting any auspicious deed we pronounce/chant the following *sloka/mantra*invariably.

मंगलम् भगवान् विष्णु: मंगलम् गरूड़ ध्वज:।
मंगलम् पुण्डरीकाक्ष: मंगलाय तनों हरि:।।

Therefore, *Mangal*
can bring unhappiness and ruin. Keeping all this in mind we need to get more information about the planet *Mangal*.

Form & Qualities of Mangal

When we look at *Mangal* from a distance it looks red hot, so we also call it *Lohitang*. We also call it *kunja*. The Meaning of *kunja* is related to the earth. As *Mangal* separated from the earth, it is known as *Mangal*. Besides, it separated from the earth after a lot of struggle, it also indicates struggles, quarrels and problems. In the family of planets the Sun is like father & the Moon is like mother. *Mangal* has both the qualities that of the Moon & the Sun. The qualities that *Mangal*
by many ancient astrologers as follows.

Acharya Varahmiher
each day & looks fresh. It contains more of its father's qualities, it has an instable mood and conduct, it is narrow-minded & possesses thin waist.

Rishi Parashar considers that *Mangal* has good qualities & is very powerful as a planet. It is a leader in the row of planets. It is tall in height & its colour is red like blood. It worships Kartikey as its god. It represents
Mangal is a worrier or
a *chatriya* by conduct. It possesses aggressive attitude. A native having *Mangal* as a predominate planet in the chart like bitter taste. It resides in the south direction. It is very strong on Tuesday, in its own *hora*& in the month that it controls astrologically as per one's chart &placement of *Mangal* in it. *Mangal* provides ideas to have a family or it loves to possess a family. Red & pictured clothes are liked by the native in whose chart *Mangal* dominates. It rules the summer season too.

The Summary

Keeping all the above information in mind one comes to conclusion that *Mangal* provides energy. It possesses a sharp &naughty character. It makes the native clever to perform acts and jobs quickly, provides courage &

implicit with right code & conduct. The native in whose *kundali Mangal* is predominant leads a physically aggressive life, the native believes in hitting and killing, he is courageous, competent to defeat & kill enemies, possess agitated bearing, very active in sex related activities, kind hearted and obliging but also idle at times. In whose *kundali Mangal* is exalted placed in its own *mool trikon rashi*, own sign/*rashi*, it becomes *yog karak*, which means very auspicious. In case *Mangal*
planets or sits with such planets in auspicious houses, it provides extremely fortunate results.

Having cruel conduct, be violent and to act according to the situation, are some of the characteristics of a native in whose chart *Mangal*/Mars is

work in police or military departments, be a mountain rider, and involved in mines business etc. are the departments that belong to *Mangal*. If a

aspects of *Mangal* in the chart of a native.

Manglik Yoga

In case *Mangal*
second, fourth, seventh, eighth or twelfth houses, Manglik Yoga is formed. In the north in India if Mars is placed in the second house no Manglik Yoga is considered to be framed but in the south of India astrologers consider the second house also to frame Manglik Yoga. Some astrologers reckon that Chandra Lagna and *lagna* starting from Venus, should also be considered to take into account Manglik Dosha. In case Mangal & Moon are in *lagna*, or they rise in second, fourth, seventh, eighth, or twelfth houses, Manglik Dosha is created. As an example we provide the following *kundali* for the reader's reference.

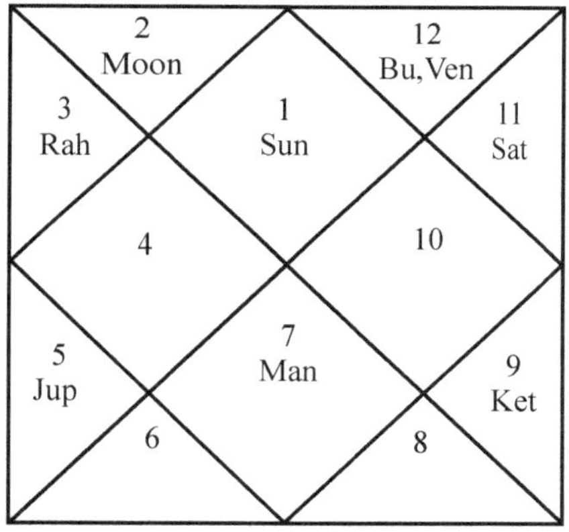

In the above *kundali Mangal* is rising in the seventh house. However, *Mangal* is placed in the sixth house if we examine the chart/*kundali* from the Moon *lagna*. So the native's chart is not Manglik if we examine it from the Moon *lagna*. But if we observe the chart from Venus *lagna*, it is Manglik. Certain books display the following *sholaka* relating Manglik Dosha.

लग्ने व्यये च पाताले जायित्रे चाष्टमें कुजः।
कन्या भर्तः विनाशाय भर्तोः कन्या विनाशकृत ।।

That means that if *Mangal* is placed in the 4th, 7th or 8th houses in wife's or husband's *kundali*, it is considered inauspicious. But it is also commonly accepted that if a Manglik girl is married to a Manglik boy, that *dosha* is redeemed.

Parashara Hora Shastra displays the following *sholoka* about Manglik Dosha in its *Istri Jatak* chapter.a

लग्ने व्ययें सुखे बालि, सत्यमें वांडष्ट में कुजेः।
शुभ दृग्यों हीने च पति हन्ति न संशयः।।

That means that in a girl's *kundal*i if *Manga*l is placed in the 4th, 7th, 8th or 12th house and *Mangal* has no aspects or company of good planets, the girl may ultimately bring disaster to her husband. Similarly if *Mangal* is placed in the same houses in a boy's *kundali*, it may end up in the death of wife.

Although *Mangal* is a cruel planet but it also not true that its impact or effect is always inauspicious in every *kundali*. Logically, it may not provide similar results if placed in different houses out of ones indicated

st, 4th, 7th, 8th& 12th and results need to be discovered.

The native may suffer

worried on account of varied reasons. He/she may have regular headaches, or have eye troubles, and get lots of impediments in completing jobs or tasks.

Rishi Varamahir writes:

"लग्ने कुजे क्षततनु"

If *Mangal* rises in *lagna*, the *jatak*
get killed.

Rishi Mantreswara indicates:

"क्षततनु: अतिक्रूर : अल्पायु तयौ धन साहसी"।

In case *Mangal* rises in *lagna*, itmakes the native very cruel & dauntless, but such a native may not have long life to live and may get hurt or wounded.

Shri Ved Nath Writes:

"क्रूर साहसिकों डटनोति चपलों रोगी कुजे लग्न में ।

If *Mangal* is placed in, the native becomes very cruel, be courageous, likes to wander about, possess a clever temperament, and also has various diseases in the body.

Shri Mahesh indicates:

अति मति भ्रूमतां च कलेवर क्षययतं बहुसाहस मुग्रताय।
तबुमृता तनुसंस्पितोडव निसूतो गमनाममनानि च।।

If *Mangal* is placed in *lagna* in the *kundali* of a native, he/she is disturbed on account of ego relating wisdom. (The native thinks that he/ she possesses more wisdom and this thought keeps the native always disturbed on account of ego.) Often such a native gets wounds on the body & is very dogged in nature. The native is constantly wandering over & always go on worrying.

When Mangal is placed in the second house:
Acharya Varahmiher unfolds:

"धनगे कदन्न"

If Mangal is placed in the second house, it provides money related losses.

Rishi Parashar says:

"स्वे धननाशय"

It is harmful relating money.

When Mangal is placed in the fourth house:
If in a native is placed in the fourth house, in that case even if other planets are favourably placed in the *kundali*, he may not get any happiness in life except that he/she may be honoured by the rulers and get land and dresses in honour from the government.

"सुद्राति विसुहन मातृ–सुखालय वाहन "

In case *Mangal* rises in the fourth house in anative's *kundali*, the native is often without a mother (she may die immediately after the native's birth), without any friends, he may be landless, without a home/house, and without any vehicles or transport.

Acharya Varahmiher says:

"विमुख: पीडितमान सुश्रतुर्थे

If *Mangal* is placed in the fourth house, the native never gets any happiness in life & keeps on worrying constantly.

Shri Ved Nath Says:

"भौमे बंधुगते तु बधुरहित: स्त्रीनिर्जित: शौय्रवान।"

If *Mangal* is placed in the fourth house, the native is without any family and wife but he is very effortful and dauntless.

Shri Garg expresses:

"कुजे बंधौ भूम्मा जीवोनर: सदा।"

If *Mangal* is placed in a native's *kundali* in the fourth house, it makes him earn his livelihood through cultivation.

Rishi Parashar unfolds:

"बन्धुमंरणं शत्रुवृद्धि र्धन्यव्यय:।"

Mangal in the fourth house increases the native's enemies, brothers die and money is lost.

When Mangal is placed in the seventh house:

If *Mangal* rises in the seventh house in a native's *kundali,* it provides

native usually stays away from home and does not come back soon. He/she is troubled by enemies and often defeated by them. *Mangal* in the seventh house often destroys man and woman after their marriage.

Rishi Varamahir states:

"स्त्रीर्भिगत परिभवय"

The native in whose *kundali Mangal* is placed in the seventh house,his wife alwaysdishonours him.

Rishi Parashar says:

"स्त्रियां दारमरण नीच सेवन स्त्री संगम।
कुजोक्ते सुस्तनर कठिनोर्ध्वकचा ।"

The native's wife dies early, he enjoys the company of the women

his wife's breasts have some sort of problems, like not getting a proper shape as required.

When Mangal is placed in the eighth house:

If *Mangal*rises in the eighth house in a native's *kundali*, such a native does

house in the *kundali*. *Mangal*

Mangal

that that though the native is honoured by the people, he does not behave properly and acts like enemies towards them. Even after constantly *Mangal* becomes a barrier to

Mantri Ver Says:

"कुतनुरघनोंडल्पायु: छिदे कुजे जननिन्दित:।।"

If *Mangal* rises in the eighth house in a *jatak's kundali*, it makes the native sick and he is constantly unwell on account of certain diseases. The native may not have a long life, may keep a badcompanyand is implicit with unhappiness.

Rishi Varamihir states: A native in whose chart Mangal rises in the 8th house, has hardly any sons.

When Mangal is placed in the eighth house:

Mangal placed in the twelfth house in a chart provides money related losses to a native. It may also get the native some wounds signs of which are visible on the body. The native is usually involved in telling lies and goes on spreading gossips about others. Such a native is always worried on account of wounds in the body, often involves in quarrels, and remains unhappy on account of job involved in.

Kalyan Verma holds:

The native is often sick on account of eyes, hurts his wife, is usually dishonoured and may stay in a prison.

Rishi Parashar States:
A native in whose chart *Mangal* rises in the twelfth house, is usually blind and without a mother or his/her mother dies early.

The Effect of Manglik Yoga on Marriage : If Manglik Yoga rises in a chart in 1, 4, 7, 8, or 12thhouse, it affects a native's married life. In south India Manglik Yoga is also formed if *Mangal* rises in the second house besides in the other houses mentioned above.

When Mangal rises in the First House: *Lagna* indicates a native's countenance, complexion, dimensions of the body, conduct, personality, character, health, energy in the body. When *Mangal*
house, it has aspects on the 4th, 7th and 8th houses. *Mangal* in *lagna* gives temperament (angry moods), and makes the native easily agitated, creates blood related illness and may involve in accidents. The native may have wounds on the forehead and be aggressive. But if *Mangal* rises in its own sign or is exalted or belongs to *mul trikona rashi*, it works positively and give good results but it may still create angry temperament, jealousy, irritating nature etc. in the native.

The seventh aspect from *Mangal* on the seventh house creates impediments in one's married life. In case *Mangal* owns the 6th, 8th or 12th houses in a chart, it usually leads to break husband and wife relations.

If *Mangal* has its seventh aspect where its own sign is rising, it may help in the native's married life go better, but *Mangal* from *lagna* will have its eighth aspect on the eighth house, which is considered the house of life. It may affect that house adversely and cut native's life short. It may also affect adversely married life to a certain extent. Thus, *Mangal* having its aspects on the seventh house, may tarnish the married life of the native.

When Mangal rises in the Fourth House: The fourth house indicates happiness and comfort in life. Family happiness and happiness through relations, home, land, vehicle, things that give enjoyment in life and make life easier, all are considered from this house. In case an inauspicious *Mangal* rises in the fourth house, it not only affectsnative's home, property,

things, whatever reasons may develop on that account. When fourth aspect of *Mangal*will be on the seventh house,it will affect the native's married life adversely.It will affect wife/husband relationship adversely in some respect. The native will often get into angry moods, which will affect native's health unfavorably and it because of that also native's married life will go on unpleasantly.

When Mangal rises in the Fourth House: The seventh house indicates married life or relates to husband and wife relationship. It immensely indicates about native's married life. Seventh house can also tell about wife/husband's being handsome, about their body complexion, physical dimensions and health etc. This house also indicates partnership in business. If *Mangal* rises in the seventhhouse, it does affect one's married life to a great extent & goes on affecting the temperament of the life partner. It also has its impact on the private parts of the body and can lead the native astray in lifeas far as character is concerned.

When Mangal rises in the Eighth House: The eighth house, which relates to native's age or life span, if *Mangal* rises in it, it may bring death, disturbances in native's life, impediments, unhappiness etc. If *Mangal* rises in the eighth house, it will affect adversely native's life-span and surround

from the seventh house, *Mangal* in this house (eighth house) may distort the speech of the life-partner leading to bad relationship between husband and wife. Consequently, it may affect married relationship adversely.

When Mangal rises in the Twelfth House: We consider native's happiness, enjoyments, expenditure, imprisonment, hospital and foreign visits etc. from the twelfth house.In case Mangal is rising in the twelfth house, it will reduce the native's happiness relating married life. It may also develop dependence on others. The twelfth house is the sixth house from the seventh house. So it may affect adversely the health of the life partner. It may reduce the happiness that one gets from married life. It

& conduct. It may indulge the native in unsocial activities. The native may even go to jail on account of his unsocial deeds or he/she may visit hospitals because of ill health. Mangal rising in the twelfth house will have its aspects on the third house. It will create impediments in regular work & duties & develop enmity with brothers & friends.

Mangal rising in the twelfth house will aspect the sixth & seventh houses. The seventh house is related to wife/husband, so it may bring problems to married life creating differences among the couple. In case *Mangal* is auspicious in the twelfth house or has its auspicious aspects on the seventh, its bad effects may be reduced to some extent.

Considering all such situations, it is clear that *Mangal* rising in the 1st, 4th, 7th, 8th and 12th

Mangal *Mangal* sitting in

the second may affect one's life span. Mangal rising in the 1st, 7th, 8th and 12th

Married life of a native could be adversely affected if some of the following combinations of planets or their aspects happen occur in a *kundali*.

In case the seventh house, or the owner of the seventh, and Venus, *kundali*, one's married life is likely to be adversely affected. If *Mangal* is in a better state in Navmansh, and even if Manglik Yoga appears in the *kundali*, it

Mangal is not the only planet that usually destroys one's married

As *Mangal* a native with lot of energy & enthusiasm, its aspects and placement in certain houses, may affect most of the factors that are related to one's married life and may reduce the good affects or issues related to that.

connected with the houses mentioned here above, native's married life is likely to be affected adversely. *Mangal* will also affect the native married

seventh or its owner.

When Manglik Yoga is cancelled! Manglik Yoga in a *kundali* is considered cancelled in the following situations.

1. If *Mangal* rises in Aries or Scorpio signs in the 1st, 2nd, 4th, 8th or 12th houses.
2. Jupiter, rising in any sign or house, has its aspects on *Mangal.*
3. Saturn rising in any house has its aspects on *Mangal.*
4. If Rahu has aspects from Jupiter,or Saturn & Rahu has its full aspects on *Mangal*
5. If *Mangal* is in the fourth or seventh house where Aries, Cancer, Scorpio or Capricorn signs are rising.
6. In case strong *Mangal* rises in 1st, 2nd, 4th, 7th, or 12th house along with powerful Moon, Jupiter or Mercury.
7. If *Mangal* rises in Taurus or Libra signs in the fourth or seventh house.
8. If *Mangal* rises in Gemini or Virgo signs in the second house.

9. If *Mangal* rises in Cancer Leo or Capricorn signs.
10. If *Mangal* rises in the eighth house in Sagittarius or Pisces signs.
11. If *Mangal* sits in Aswani, Magha, Mool Nakchatras.
12. If *Mangal* sits in the 12th house in Libra or Taurus signs.
13. If *Mangal* sits in the eighth house in Cancer or Leo signs.
14. If *Mangal* and Saturn rise in one house.
15. In boy's or girl's *kundali* in whatever sign *Mangal* rises and if it rises in the same sign in either of the *kundali*, the Manglik Dosha is cancelled.
16. If *Mangal* rises in the seventh house.
17. If the *lagna* is Leo or Taurus & Mangal rises in Scorpio sign.
18. If *Mangal* rises in the 12th house in the signs owned byMercury or Venus.
19. When *Mangal* rises in its own sign in the fourth house.
20. If *Mangal* rises in Leo sign.
21. If *lagna* rises in Capricorn or Aquarius sign &*Mangal* rises in the seventh house.
22. *Mangal* in Saturn's sign rises in the eighth house.
23. If case Saturn rises in the 1st, 7th, 8th, or 12th house in a *kundali.*

24. If bridegroom's *kundali* has Manglik Dosha & if in the bride's *kundali* Saturn, *Mangal*

    & weak Moon rise in the same house where *Mangal* is rising in the groom's chart, the Dosha is cancelled. For further reference, in case *Mangal* rises in the eighth house in the bride's *kundali*, and in the bride-groom's *kundali* Rahu, Saturn, Ketu or Mangal rise in the eighth, the Manglik Dosha is cancelled.
25. If there occurs Manglik Dosha in the groom's or bride's *kundali* & if from Moon Lagna or *lagna*, *Mangal*, Saturn, Rahu, or Ketu—any

    st, 4th, 7th, 8th or 12th house, the ill

    effect of Manglik Dosha in either of the *kundalies* is reduced.

    kendra or *trikona* in the bride's or groom's

    kundali
27. In the groom's chart considering from the Moon Lagna the number

    st, 4trh, 7th, 8th or 12th house & in the

    bride's *kundali* considering from the Moon Lagna if the number of st, 4th, 7th, 8th, or 12th houses, Manglik Dosha is cancelled.

28. In any *kundali* if *Mangal* has aspects from its friendly planets or rise

Manglik Doshas which are very harmful when marriage matters are decided. Let us examine some of those *doshas.*

When Mangal is Inauspicious!

1. In case Mangal is debilitated in the 1st, 2nd, 4th, 7th, 8th or 12th houses it becomes more inauspicious.
2. If *Mangal* rises in Aries or Scorpio sign in *lagna*, it is harmful to the seventh house (married life to the naive).

or planets combinations or because of their aspects, *Mangal* may be harmful to a native. For example, if it rises in its debilitated or exalted sign in the seventh house, it becomes inauspicious for the seventh house.

4. In case *Mangal* owns 6th or 8th house & is related to the seventh house, it becomes more harmful.
5. If *Mangal* has its alliance with Saturn & is connected to the seventh house, it becomes more inauspicious & provides much harm to the seventh house (married life of the native).

The Ill-effects of Manglik Yoga

The following are some of the ill-effects of Manglik Dosha.

1. It may delay the native marriage.
2. Married life of the native may be disturbing and may involve the native in quarrels & expenditure on the partner.
3. Besides quarrels, it may lead to cruelty and different sorts of injustice cropping up in the native's life.
4. Though married life of both the partners may go on but on account of bad health of either of the partner, there may not be any enjoyment in their lives. If *Mangal* rises in the 1st, 2nd, 4th, 7th, 8th or 12th house, some sort of problem may continue in the natives' lives.We are providing a few examples indicating some such yogas and ill effect of *Mangal*in view of those yogas.

Example 1. The following *kundalis*belongs to the natives whose married lives have been greatly disturbing as *Mangal* is sitting in the 1st, 2nd, 4th, 7th, 8th, or 12th house in their charts.

The following chart belongs to the lady, whose husband tried to kill her but any how she was saved and currently she has been living with her parents.

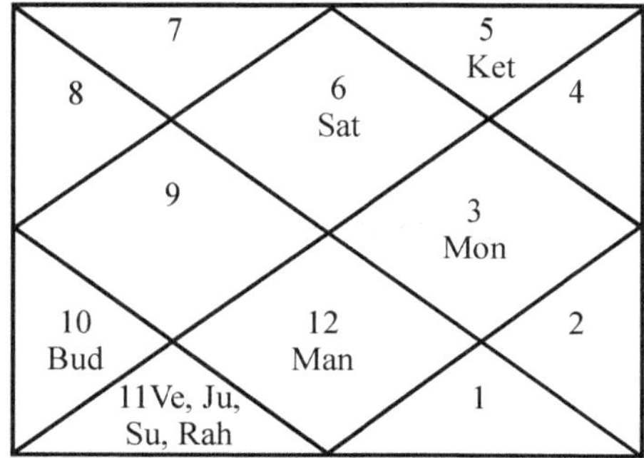

After suffering for quite long time both husband & wife separated and their married life ended. *Mangal* is placed in the lady's in the seventh house in Pisces sign & Saturn has its aspect on *Mangal* from *lagna.Mangal* is also placed in the second house from Venus. All such combinations & aspects have become instrumental in making Manglik Yoga strong and consequently husband and wife got separated.

The following is the   of the ladywhose *kundali* has been projected here above.*Mangal* is placed in the 12th house in the husband's chart. Saturn &*Mangal* are placed in the fourth house calculating from the Moon. As Saturn is placed in the 12th house with *Mangal*, it is making Manglik Yoga more strong. Consequently, neither the man nor the woman could have a happy married life.

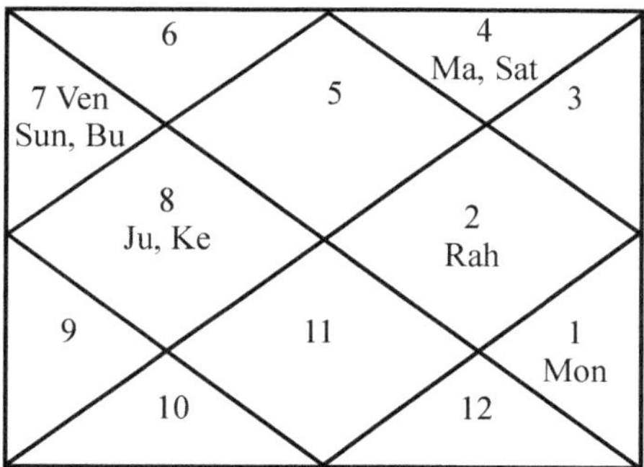

Example 2 : The following kundalibelongs to a native in which debilitated Mangal rises in Virgo sign in the seventh house. Since the native's chart is Manglik right from birth, he could not get any happiness from his married life.He was married when he was thirty years old but on account of problems with wife, he committed suicide. He was married when the Mahadasha of Venus was operating and Moon'ssub-period (unter-dasha) was going on. But when the sub-period of Mangal started under Venus's, he died.

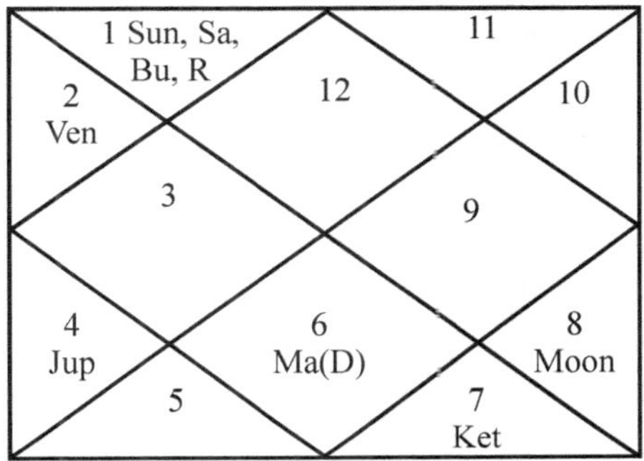

Example 3 : In the following *kundali, Mangal* is rising in the eighth house in Scorpio sign. It is situated in the 12thhouse from the Moon. Saturn rises in *lagna*. Though *Mangal* is in its own sign, there is no cancellation of Manglik Dosha. Just after a few months from her marriage, the lady has to leave her husband's home and started living

sake & she enjoyed married life only for a few months and then she ahd to leave her husband's home.

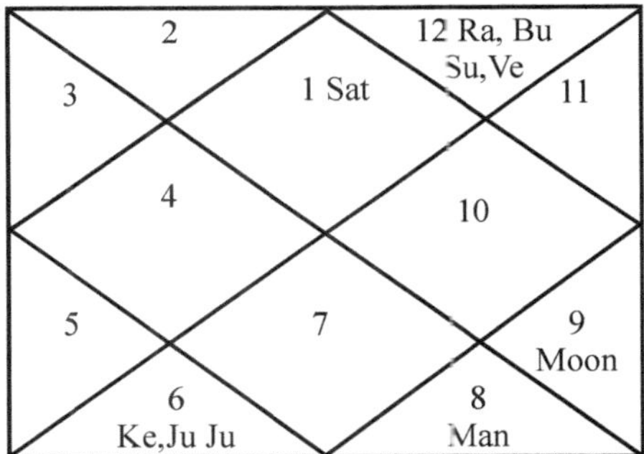

Example 4 : In the following *Kundali, Mangal* rises in its debilitated sign in *lagna*. Saturn rises in the seventh house in its own sign, Capricorn.The native married twice but both the marriages did not provide him any happiness in life.

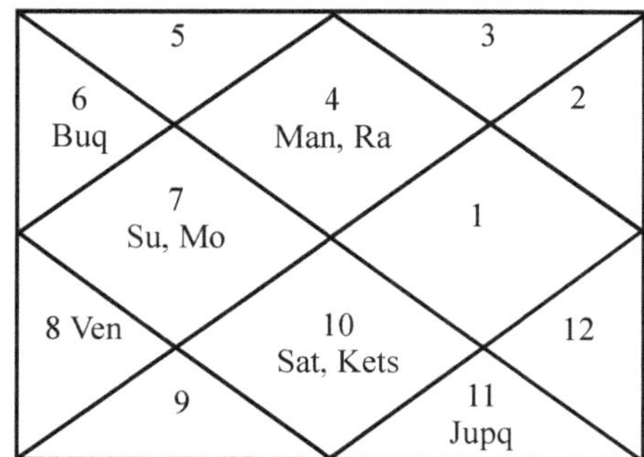

Example 5 : The Native was born in December 1990 but he was divorced in 1993. In his *kundali Mangal* rises in Gemini sign in the eighth house. Jupiter sits in Kendra and has its aspects on Mangal from there but his married life simply stayed for two-three years & divorce took place.

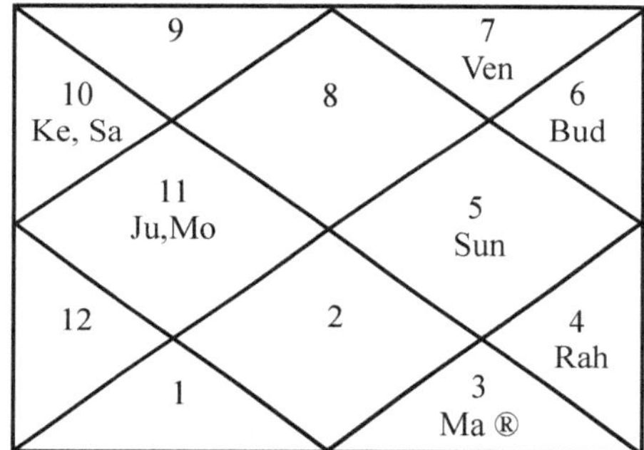

Example 6 : Sanjaya Gandhi died after a few years when Shrimati Menika Gandhi was married to him. He died in an air crash. In her *kundali* debilitated *Mangal* rises in the eighth house in Aquarius sign which though has aspects from Jupiter but could not reduce the ill-effects of Manglik Dosha.

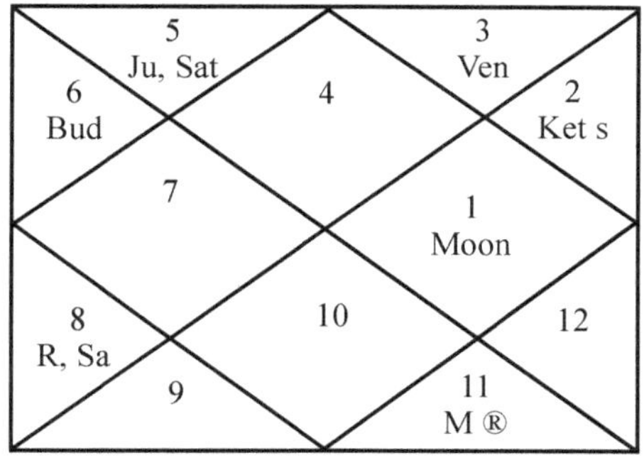

Example7 : The *kundali* given here under belongs to a lady. In the *kundali*, rises in the eighth house which indicates husband's death or bad health. When *Mangal's* Mahadasha was operating both husband & wife got separated and started living separately for seven years. It was at this time that the husband's one leg got injured and was cut off. As *Mangal* is in the eighth house in the wife's chart & Saturn,rising with the Sun, has its aspect on it. So she could not get husband's love, live with him happily

also suffered physically and his leg was cut off.

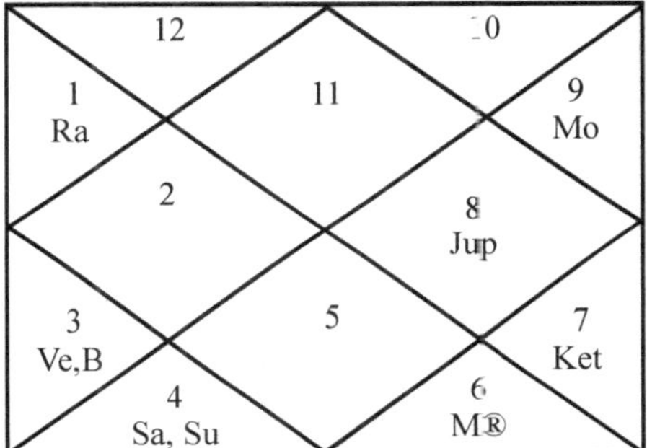

Example 8 : The following *kundali* belongs to Shrimati Indra Gandhi. She was born on 19-11-1917 around 11.11 in the night in Allahabad. In her *kundali, Mangal*rises in Leo sign &sits in the second house which is the eighth house from the Moon. Saturn rises in her *lagna*and has aspects on its own house. It is because of all that, that she was not able to get any happiness from her married life.

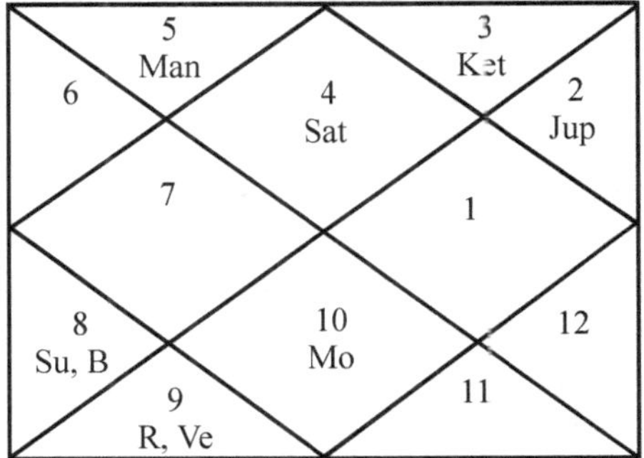

How to lessen Mangalik Dosha?

In case Manglik Dosha occurs in a girl's or boy's *kundali*, then to reduce its ill-effects is possible to a certain extent. One of the possible ways is that both the *kundalis* should be matched properly. It will help cancelling the ill-effects of the yoga persisting in the eachother's*kundali*. We provide here below two charts in which though Manglik Dodha is there but the boy & the girl lived happily in their lives. It happened as in both the *kundalies* the Dosha persists and hence got cancelled as both the charts had their effect on each other.

Example1 : In the wife's *kundali* in the fourth house *Mangal* rises in Libra sign. But her husband's *kundali*is also Manglik as *Mangal* sits in the fourth in its own sign, Scorpio. In the lady's *kundali*, Saturn sits in the eighth house and *Mangal* sits in the fourth house & has its exalted aspects on the seventh house. Even then the lady has been living happily with her husband.

Lady's Kundali

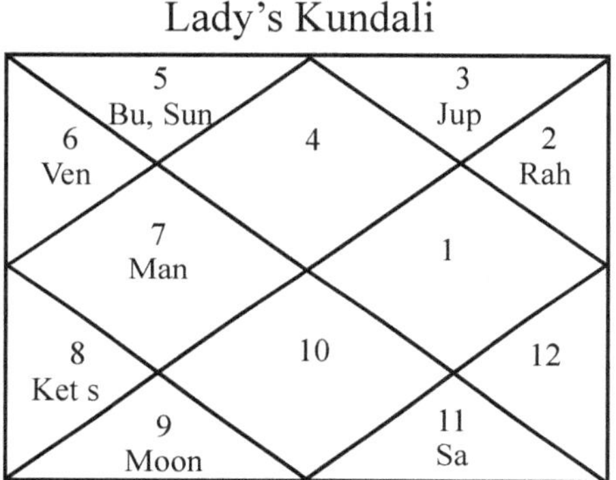

Example 2 : In the following *kundali,Mangal* rises in the fourth house counting from the Moon, Venus and *lagna*. In both the *kundalis* of the man and the woman, *Mangal* skits in the fourth house. In the wife's *kundali,Mangal* rises in Libra sign, and in the husband's *kundali* it rises in Scorpio sign. It has its aspects on the seventh house in both the charts. In both the *kundalies* Saturn rises in the eighth houseand Manglik Dosha exists. There is one & a half years' difference in age of the natives (wife being senior in age), but their married life is running very smoothly &happily. Both have extreme love for each other. Thus, these two examples, and many more like that,suggest that if are matched properly before the marriage,the Manglik Dosha can be cancelled. Therefore, matching the horoscopes before deciding a marriage, is absolutely important. Therefore, match them properly and thus avoid or cancel the Manglik Yoga. Thus, though *Mangal*may rise in the seventh house or has its aspects on the seventh house in a chart, it may not do any harm to the natives.

Husband's Kundali

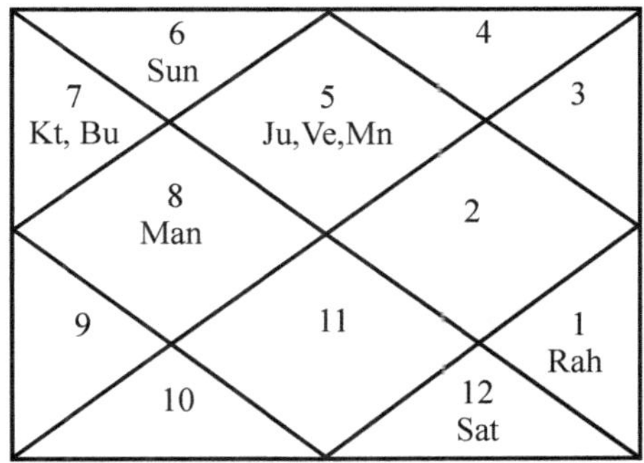

The Effect of the Nine Planets Placed in Different Houses

The Planet Sun

The Sun is a very important planet & none can think about life on the earth without the Sun. The light on the earth from the sky & warmth on the earth, life of a beggar and that of a king, living and cradling as well as continued progress in life-- all such things cannot be imagined without the power of the Sun. The Sun gives light and day starts when it rises in the sky, the night falls when the sun is set. Man soul and story of kindness as well as help to others are attributed to the Sun when it is placed in one's chart in an auspicious sign or house or degrees. To go on constantly without getting tired& provide day light as well as night, all such acts are caused by the Sun only.

favourable results in life. If the lines of Mercury & Venus join Sun line in a hand, the native usually construct a rest-house for the travelers, digs wells for the thirsty, & such a native is famous like a king. He/she also takes care of Dharma (religion), stays away from unethical activities and drinks, &

The parts of body of the native are very strong, and always without any ailment. The native is happy on account of children and married life. Now we write the results of Sun's placement in the twelve houses in a *kundali*

The Sun in the First House

will not only help his father but serve him too. If the native does not even

for his/her own children when he/she dies. Such a native will have two different kinds of conduct. He will cradle anger like a snake but even if rich by his/her own hard work and earnings. If native possesses all such

in his/her *kundali.*

However there are also ill-effects of the Sun if it rises as an inauspicious

native is just a child and may also suffer from T.B. as he/she grows. Such a native will like to enjoy the company of a woman/man when it is day.

other planets also don't support such a native and he/she is ready to commit suicide. Lal Kitab suggests some *upaya* for such negativity of the Sun in a *kundali*. These are: The native should get a drinking water tap installed in

two years good results of such an act could be seen by the native.His/her

The Sun in the Second House

When the Sun rises in the second house in a native's chart, the native gets

of good name and fame in life.The native also earns a lot of money from the sales of articles in a business. If a native possess all such things in life, the Sun in his/her chart should be rising in the second house.

However,inauspicious effectsof such a Sun would also be immense. These could be that it would give money related losses. The native may lose wife/husband or lover. He/she may get losses in the business especially related to oil, butter, potato, camphor, aunty, mother, mother's sister, buttocks or buttock-hole etc. The native will remain involved in land and woman cases and will lose money and respect. The number of women will go on reducing in the house and will have problems with sisters and brothers. The native will be greedy and will not have enough money even he/she put any efforts in life.

Lal Kitab suggests certain *upayas*for such problems caused by the inauspicious Sun in the second house. It would be better to invoke Saturn's favour to reduce the ill-effects of the Sun if placed inauspicious in the second house. The native is suggested to offer coconuts, almonds, oil at some religious place to reduce the ill-effects of the inauspicious sun in the second house.

and will be able to defeat the enemies easily. *Budha* & Venus will also be favourable to such a native. The native may get some special position in

work and activity and the children will live long. In case some of these things happen to the native, it should be considered that the Sun rises in the native's chart in the third house. Accordingly the hand lines will also project all such things in the native's hand.

In case the Sun is **inauspicious in the chart** it would result in thefts in the native's house even during day time. The grandfather and father will become moneyless and poor & his/her maternal uncle's home will almost be destroyed. Lal Kitab suggests certain *upayas* to ward off such inauspicious effects of the ill-placement of the Sun. It is simply to keep one's conduct in line with the norms and lead a composed life.

The Sun in the Fourth House

If the Sun rises in the fourth house in a native's *kundali*, he/she will be like a king whether the father of the native may be or not be a king. Such a native will serve the parents whole heartedly. The native may get losses in business or at work place but he/she will not like to give any losses to others. In case the native possesses some of these qualities or characteristics and leads the life in the manner as suggested here above, it should be considered that the Sun is rising in the fourth house in the native's *kundali*.

If the sun gives any **inauspicious effect**because it is not well placed or it is inauspicious in the *kundali,* it may affect the native's life adversely in many ways. The native may be miser and eager to get more money. It will lead the native to bear lots of burdens in life as he/she goes on avoiding the right path. The native may involve in theft cases & will destroy his/her own property in wrong activities. The native may also suffer from night-blindness. If he will keep someone else' wife with his he will be destroyed and will have no children of his own.

The native would need to do certain *upayas* to remove the ill-effects of the Sun. The native need to feed the blind beggars in his/her parental house.

The Sun in the Fifth House

The native will work according to one'sown desire & convert the luck in one's own favour. As the native will grow in age, the amount of incoming wealth will also increase. The more the native will spend, the more money he/she will earn. Such a native will be considered a *kuldeepak* that means someone who actsexcellently well in all things and matters in life for the

be done successfully by him/her. The native's family will just be like a temple in which all have been happening in a good manner. In case if some of these things are happening in someone's life or family, it should be considered that in the native's *kundali*
Lines in the native's hand will also project the same.

However, there may be some **inauspicious effect** also if the Sun in the

jatak. These could be that he/she may need to marry so many times, native's children may die one after the other & he/she will bear lot of unhappiness in life. Such a native will also have to bear money losses time to time.The Lal Kitab suggests certain *upayas*

house. These are: The native would need to feed the red-faced monkeys with jiggery & serve them well.

The Sun in the SixthHouse

If the Sun rises in the sixth house in a *jatak's kundali*, it will help him/her ending up all the miseries from life. The native will possess good health

he/she will also get it. The native will shun down one's enemies and will travel abroad. The native may get a new jobs. He/she may be successful in making some new medicines. The native's luck cannot fail under any circumstance even if someone tries to do so. No one can stop such a native

There may be certain **inauspicious effects** also in case the Sun in the sixth house is not sittingauspicious. These are that up to twenty two years of age either the father or the son—only one out of them, will be able to get a government job. The native's planets will not favour the father to live long & women folk will go on dying in the family. It may also not be favourable to children.Either the *jatak* or his wife will be blind with one eye. There are certain *upayas* for the ill-effects of placed in a native's *kundali*. The *jatak* is advised to do some *upayas* to get the favour of *Budha* if not placed favourably. The native should give some alms early in the morning. He/she should also offer food to dogs at some religious place like a temple or so. To help the native's maternal uncle, some sweets (*gur*) may be offered to monkeys.

The Sun in the Seventh House

If the Sun rises in the seventh house in *jatak's kundali*, it will appear at the time of birth of such a *jatak*that someone lighted a hundred watts bulb. That means a *kuldeepak* is born in that house. Such a native will be

and business, gains from lottery and through unearned money, gain from one's wife and the native will get great respect from the seniors in the job.

However, there will also be several **inauspicious effects** if the Sun is not well placed in the seventh house. Some of these may be that the native will have a very small family & will have no gold in the house. The

also break out in the house. The native may not be trusted by the people and his/her father may suffer in different ways. As an *upaya*, the native is suggested to serve a black coloured cow which has no horns. It will give him/her good results. The native is also suggested to put into the earth a small squire piece of copper and in the evening after cooking, the stove should be extinguished with milky water. All this will help in reducing the ill-effects of the inauspicious Sun if rising in the seventh house.

The Sun in the Eighth House

In case the Sun rises in the eighth house in a *jatak's kundali*, he will be highly honest and as he will be highly true and honest, bad things will run away far from him. The enemies, who will try to hide away from him, will soon be discovered and caught. The native's relives will also feel safe & secured on his account. Such a native is expected to be very rich in when he reaches 22 years of age and because of the Sun's good placement, the native will be free from Manglik Dosha.

In order to check the **inauspicious effects** of the Sun when it is not well placed in the eighth house, the native may have do the following things if certain things are not well placed or not correctly made in his house. Some of these are that the main door of the house is in the south

affected. It will also affect the native's eye-sight adversely. Some of the *upayas* to get away from the aforesaid ill-effects will be to serve a black or red coloured cow. Before starting a new job or task, the native is advised to eat some sweets (*gur*) and then drink some water. It will give good effect to every sort of work that the native will like to start for his earnings. The native should throw some coins into a burning dead body. All such efforts (*upayas*) will reduce the ill-effects of the inauspicious Sun if rising in the eight house of a native'*s kundali.*

The Sun in the Ninth House

In case the Sun rises in the ninth house in a *kundali*of a *jatak*, then he/

determination & will be able to take care of his family comfortably and decently. Such a native will be able to help others and will stand in their

native's parents & grand- parents will live long and will bear long and happy life.

There may be some **inauspicious effects** also if the Sun is not favourably placed in the ninth house in a native's chart. The native will not able to tolerate more cold or heat and suffer on that account. As the native will like to enjoy life without any serious efforts or being involved in any work, all that will lead him/her to ruins in life. As *upayas* the native is advised to give silver, rice and milk as alms to the needy and poor..

The Sun in the Tenth House

If the Sun rises in the tenth house in a *jatak's kundali*, the native will own a great property and will be extremely rich. Success will always be gained by him and he will be able to take responsibility of big projects and mighty tasks. He will always be successful in any business and will always be a winner in any task, examination or tests. The native'slines in hands will also indicate such conditions, if observed carefully.

The **inauspicious effect** of the Sun in the tenth house,if placed in bad degrees or inauspicious sign, will be that the native will spend more money on house-hold articles, will not observe dharma & some of his children may die. The native's father may also die when he/she is very young. The native will neither get any happiness in life nor will get any position in *darbar* or in government. However, there are certain *upayas*to lessen its bad effects. One is that the *jatak* should throw some copper coins in the running water of a river for 4o days. The *jatak* should drink river water or use it after taking it out from the ground (well). The native should cover his head with a white or red coloured turban and should never wear black or blue clothes. He also needs to throw some *shilajeet* (a kind of herb) into a river.

The Sun in the Eleventh House

If the Sun rises in the eleventh house in a native's *kundali* then the *jatak* gets

gets a lot of money all of a sudden.The native is usually religious and likes to enjoy life to a great extent. If all this happens in the life a native, one should take that the Sun has been rising in the eleventh house of his *kundali*. All this

However, if there are any **inauspicious effect** of the placement of a weak Sun in a *kundal*i, it will be that the native will talk ill of others,

to others.Quite often dead children will be born in his house. There are certain *upayas*to lessen the bad effects of the Sun. These are that the native should keep *mooli, saljam* and carat near his pillow before he is going to bed and when he gets up should give all that to the needy or to anybody.

The Sun in the Twelfth House

When the Sun rises in the twelfth house in *jatak's kundali,* the *jatak* will enlighten the world with his knowledge. He will be rich and live for 100 years. He may not give alms to anyone but will progress even if he is hurt or dejected. He will be earning lot of money just when he is only 22 years of age. He will defeat his enemies and will get lot of progress in life and enlighten the name of his forefathers. He will observe the dharma totally and will be a good house holder.

There may be some **inauspicious effects** also of the Sun if it is not placed auspicious in the twelfth house in a chart. The native will not be able to sleep well in the night. He may be jealous of others, will like to live indark (lightless) houses, may involve in giving wrong witnesses, may be caught in theft cases, will never be trustworthy if any responsibility is given to the native. Thus, the native will go on harming oneself to a large extent. Lal Kitab suggests certain *upayas* to check the bad effects of inauspicious Sun if placed in the 12thhouse in a *kundali*. These are to

gur

(thickened brown sugar) to monkeys and practice dharma and may not involve in giving wrong witness against anyone in the court.

The Planet Moon

There is no exact translation of the following lines of poetry, but it means that the Moon rules one's heart and gets light from the Sun. But he Sun may provide any amount of heat to the moon, the Moon always stays cool and composed & wants to stay near the Sun.

बढ़े दिल मुहब्बत जो पांव पकड़ती ।
उम्र नहर तेरी चले जर उछलती।

place is just below the heart line and near the Sun line. Venus, represent wife, Moon represent brothers, brother-in law is represented by *Mangal* and Jupiter represents father in one's hand—all these lines are very near the Sun line and not far away from Moon's place in one's hand. It is the Moon that represents one's heart around which the entire world resides. On one side there are all relatives, members of family and on the other side native's own soul & body (Sun) eyes & head (Saturn, Mercury).Let us elucidate further the places and powers of different planets and the Moon as far as possible.

When the Sun sets down in the evening the ruler is Rahu in the evening& just before the Sun rises, the owner of the world is Ketu.Saturn rules the whole earth in the night. Let us now reckon what different houses are represented by the Moon. In case if we consider that the Moon represents 'water', it will represent all the twelve houses as follows.

1. If the Moon rises in 1st house, it will be pure like the water in a pitcher &will be drinkable.
2. If it is placed in the second house, the Moon will represent water that comes out of hills and trickles from the middle of the rocks.
3. If placed in the third house, the Moonwill represent water that comes from desert.
4. The Moon in the fourth house represents pure water that comes from springs.

helps the people to live happily as it helps to grow corn and make

6. If it is placed in the 6th house, it will represent water that comes from wells and hand pumps. It will also be considered good water.
7. If the Moon is in the seventh house, it will represent water that comes out from a river and makes everything green by its effect.
8. The Moon in the eighth house will be like poison or like nectar.9. The Moon in the ninth house will represent sea water which indicates impurity.
10. If it rises in the tenth house, it represents stored water that comes from the hills.

11. If it is in the 11th house, it could be like the dirty rain-water that

12. If the moon rises in the twelfth house, it represents water that comes from the sky that melts from the ice or dirty water that comes from the lanes.

Now we will discuss Moon's placement in different houses starting from the 1st to the 12th. The following couplet unfolds the basic qualities represented by the Moon.

हुक्म पूरा माता का गर तू करेगा।
उम्र रिजक माया न तेरा घटेगा।

The Moon in the First House

his mother and gets successful in life. He gets honour in the court and gains power and progress. Now we unfold the results narrating the placement of

When the Moon rises in the 1st house in a *kundali* of a native, he/she will have a new vehicle and a new house at the age of 24 years. When he/she will reach the age of 27, the native will have children & will also get all

necessary material required in a home. His/her body will have no disease,

lives until 90 years. This will also be represented in the native's hand lines.

However, there could be some **ill-effects** if the Moon rises as **inauspicious** in the 1st house. The native mother's health will not be good and she may die soon. The native may be so poor that he/she will struggle hard to get a few pennies. Due to ill-effect of *Mangal* his/her own brothers will be useless and unproductive. As the native will try to involve in romantic affairs or will like to develop friendship with different women,

believe in not doing any work and enjoy life at others' cost, so he/she will

upaya to lessen the ill-effects of a week or ill-placed Moon in the 1st house. It will be to bury *Mangal*related things into the earth. If such a native goes on respecting the mother and touches her feet regularly, it will help to increase his age or his

to get the blessings from the old women as it lessens the inauspicious effects of the planets.

The Moon in the Second House

The following verse represents the good effects of the Moon if placed auspiciously in the second house.

गले बनजे घड़ियाल मन्दिर जो ञर में।
बजा देंगे घंटा लावल्दी का घर में।

In case the moon is placed in the second house it makes the native very rich and places him in a commending state. The native will simple have brothers and no sisters. He will be very happy from his parents' side, will have children & horses to mount on them. The native will get success in

would give a lot of satisfaction and happiness. The native will get success

However, there may be some **inauspicious effect** of the Moon in case placed weak in degrees or in enemy signs. When the native reaches 48 years of age, his/her mother may get sick & it will keep him/her worried. The ill-effects of the Moon may not give him/her children & if he/she will get good education, there may not be any children to the native. But if there will be children, the native will not be able to get any education. The native will also remain penny-less from 25 to 34 years. Such a native will not be helpful to any one in life. Lal Kitab suggests certain *upayas* for some of these ill-effects created by an inauspicious Moon in the *kundali* of a *jatak*. The native is required to give milk & rice to the needy at some religious place or temple. He/she must obey the mother & should also give some green coloured clothes to girls continuously for 40 days & lessen the ill-effect of Mercury.The native is advised to take some rice & silver from the mother and keep it carefully in a small piece of cloth. The native is advised to put a small piece of silver under the foundation of the house. It will also be good if the native stores in a small silver box some old uncooked rice and keep that carefully. All such *upayas* may be helpful to a great extend to remove the ill-effect of the Moon if not placed auspiciously in the second house.

The Moon in the Third House

The following verse unfolds about the placement of the Moon in the third house.

भरा माया होगी जहाजों कोड़ा।
पिए दूध स्वयं बहन, भाई जो तेरा ।

When the Moon rises in the third house in a *kundali*, the native will have plenty of wealth but will be a yogi (mendicant) by nature. That means he/she will remain unattached towards riches. He may be a *sadhu* and will have the knowledge of *ridhi-sidhi*; if a house-holder, then very wealthy. The native will have a long life & will highly be helpful to the family from the very beginning. He/she will defeat the enemies & on account of the native's spouse get good progress in life. It is also expected that such a native will have Raj yoga in the *kundali*. The lines of the hand of the *jatak* will also display all these things in the hands.

However, there may be some **inauspicious effect**of the Moon also if not well placed or placed in its enemies signs. If theft is not committed, there is every chance to lose money. The native may be separated from his own kith and kins & enmity may be created with some people on account of ill-placed Moon. Both *Mangal*

on the relationships with mother & brother. If weak planets are placed in the eighth house, they may affect adversely the native longevity. Lal Kitab suggests certain *upayas* to arrest the ill-effect of the Moon if placed inauspiciously in the third house. In order to get more money, the native should give in alms certain things that are related to the Moon when a daughter is born in the house. The native should also worship *Budha* regularly & earnestly if it is not done, it will the results may be further bad. The native can also help his/her in-laws by helping any poor girl

The Moon in the Fourth House

The following verse is written to support Moon's placement in the fourth house when it exerts good effect.

शुक्र सूख में क्यों तू धन का करता।
कदर दुखिया जाने हो आहें जो भरता।

If the Moon is placed in the second house, the native will always be happy on account of mother's blessings. He will get pleasure from vehicle such as car etc. He/she will be able to support the family to a large extent.

Such a native will like to worship beauty or beautiful things. He/she may like to stay away from own town, will be a good writer and a leader among own people. The native will live until 85 to 95 years & it is because of the Moon is well placed in the fourth house & the mother of the native has always been kind to him/her and has been bestowing constant blessings on the native. Whatever business he/she does, it will be successful. The traditional business of the family will also grow to a great extent. If all this has been happening to someone, it should be considered that the hand lines of such a native also suggest the same.

However, there may be **some ill-effects** too if the Moon is not auspicious in the fourth house. This will be that if a native starts a business of selling milk, it will bring ruins to the family. He/she may also get punishment even when he/she will offer bread to others. The charges will be that he/she also gave poison to the people with the bread or the bread contained some sort of pision. Lal Kitab suggests some *upayas* too to arrest the ill-effects of the misplaced Moon. These are instead of distributing water to people the native should give milk free to them. The native must not involve in selling milk as it will ruin him & his family. If grand-parents, father and the grandson go to some religious place all-together, it will help them to lessen the bad effect of the planets if they are not well placed in the native's *kundali.*

The Moon in the Fifth House

The following verse also suggests that indicates good turn of the Moon in

प्याह नेक की जो, बुरा करके लेता।
भला उसे बढ़कर नहीं कोई होता।

jatak will be lucky like a king and will have long life to live. The native will possess self-respect and may like to die but will not compromise the self-respect and honour. Whosoever the *jatak* helps or gives company or stays with, he will never be away from that person even though he is broken into pieces. If he helps any one that person will surely win. He is capable to cultivate successfully the barren lands.Lottery, shares and business, all the three will be auspicious

jungles & hills green by his efforts. He will be as strong as to crush anyone whenever he would like.

inauspicious effects and the native may suffer on that account. The native's speech may be unpleasant and he may create enemies on that account. If the native is intelligent he would go on telling people about his intelligence so will get defamed as he will convey what he should not convey to others. Lal Kitab suggests some *upayas* to lessen the ill-effects of the Moon. It is that on a Monday the native should tie down some rice &sugar in a small white piece of cloth and put all that into the running water. The native is also

The Moon in the Sixth House

The following verse also suggests a few good ideas when auspicious the Moon rises in the sixth house in a native's *kundali.*

एवज तुझको दुनिया, है तेरी ही देती।
नहीं पहले की गर, तो कर देखने की ।

In case the Moon rises in the sixth house of a native's *kundali*, he will be good for the good people but will not spare the bad ones and will like to punish them. Thus, he will be good for the good and bad for those who are really bad. He will get riches, will be victorious on the enemies, possess good health, and will keep the company of good friends. He will be involved in religious and cultural activities. The native will get name and fame as a patron in the society and will be rewarded as he would wish to be rewarded. The lines in his hand will also support all what has been stated here above. If we examine the **ill-effects** of an inauspicious Moon

his father's family. Mother's family will also be destroyed until the native reaches 34 years of age.He or his wife either of them will be one-eyed. The native will lead a traveler's life—will not be able to stay at one place for long.If he drinks milk in the night it will bring bad effects and the native may not have long years to live. Lal Kitab suggests certain *upayas* to lessen the ill-effect of such a Moon. It suggests that the native should distribute water free to those who are thirsty and serve his father whole-heartedly. The native is also advised to give free certain things that are related to the Sun, *Mangal* and Jupiter to the needy. He may keep a male rabbit in his house and also give free milk and rice to the needy.

The Moon in the Seventh House

The following verse is also indicative to support the good placement of the Moon in the seventh house in a *kundali*.

नहीं दिन है परिवार बढ़ने को लगते।
भरेंगे खजाने जो अपने हीढंग से ।

If the Moon rises in the seventh house the native's mother will be like the goddess Laxhimi. Just after the birth of *jatak* the amount of wealth will go up very high in his home. The native will highly be educated and

native leads a life of a mendicant, then he will always keep busy in prayers and religious activities. His imaginative powers will be great and he will possess so many other qualities that normally people don't have. The

white things and die in his own house. Some of these things will also be

The **inauspicious effects** that may come to the native as the Moon is rising not auspiciously in the native *kundali* or it is weak or is rising in an

native will be involved in selling milk or water, it will affect adversely his income and number of children. The native's children may die when he/she is quite young. The native will always be involved in quarrels with the mother-in-law; his/her property will be destroyed & will be killed by a weapon. The *ypaya* that Lal Kitab suggests is that the *jatak* should not indulge in selling milk or water and avoid marrying until he/she has reached 24 years of age.

The Moon in the Eighth House

The following verse suggests that the Moon rising in the eighth house will be good to a great extent to the native and help him/her live for many more years.

बुजुर्गों के दिन चीज चन्द्र जो देता।
रुके न कभी सांस, जब तक हो लेता।

If the Moon rises in the eighth house in a native's chart, he will never be defeated until his mother lives. He will be free from every kind of

if he/she follows dance & music as professions. His prestige will increase and his circumstances will change in his favour all of a sudden. He will be quite happy with his wife and children. All such factors will also be indicated by the lines of his hand.

The **inauspicious effects** of the ill-placement of the Moon in the eighth house will be that after the death of the mother & when the well in the house will dry up, the native will suffer from short of breath& from heat strokes. He may need to travel without much reason towards hills and into forests. Enemies will be created without any reason & native's mother will suffer when such a native will get the birth. Simple *upayas* that Lal Kitab suggests to lessen ill-effects created on account of the ill-placement of the Moon, are that the native should get some rice from the mother and keep them safely in a small silver box which should be kept safely at some unknown place in home. Likewise he should get some rise and after drenching them in the water taken from a cremation place, keep them under the ground in his home.Likewise he should keep some milk in an earthen pot and put it under the earth in some remote place. The native is also advised to wear a few pearls in a golden chain.

The Moon in the Ninth House

The following verse suggests that the Moon, if rises in the ninth house in a native *kundali*

असर तुरब्म सोहबत, ढई कृतघ्र का।
फर्क दूध गाय जो होता थोहर का ।

If the Moon rises in the ninth house in a native's *kundali*, the native will possess great knowledge in mathematics. He/she will be involved in good acts and will always like to help others. He will always be ready to serve the poor and needy. His/her children will be kind and good. He/she may live

also get praise as he will be involved in public well-fare. He will always

However, there may be certain **inauspicious effects** of the Moon if placed in an inauspicious sign or weak degrees in the ninth house. If the

will suffer losses. At times the native may not be able to think properly and as such his plans will fail. His/her mother's eye-sight will become weak. Lal Kitab suggests some *upaya* to lessen the bad effects of the ill-placed Moon in the ninth. It says that the native needs to wear *pukhraj*(yellow jewel) in a golden ring to remove the ill-effects of the Moon.

The Moon in the Tenth House

The following lines convey a few good aspects relating the Moon if it rises favourably in the tenth house of a native's chart.

कब्र मुर्दों की कौन जल्दी भरेगा।
उसी ठेकेदारी को तू अब पूरा करेगा।

If the Moon rises in the tenth house in a native's chart, it will help the *jatak*

native may live until 90 years and get lot of respect in the society. The native will also get a lot of success in different kinds of competitions and

uncompleted tasks/jobs. The native will usually be involved in supporting the poor and needy in the society.The heart line in his/her hand will usually end up near the Jupiter mound.

If the Moon is placed in its enemy sign it may have some **inauspicious effects** on the native. One of that will be that if the native has animals

case there are things related to the Moon in the native's house, they will bring losses and problems.If the native drinks milk at night, he/she will suffer health-wise.Such a native will be defamed as a cheat. The native

main cause of his death.Lal Kitab suggests certain *upayas* to lessen such ill-effects of inauspicious Moon placed in the tenth house of a native's chart. It says that the native should not drink milk in the night. He also needs to put some poisons in the running water & take help from Jupiter by giving some of the things related to Jupiter to the needy. Such a native needs to serve his/her aunt to remove the ill-effects of the weak Moon.

The Moon in the Eleventh House

The following lines of poetry convey how the Moon could be useful in case placed in the eleventh house in a *jatak's* chart.

दिए दूध है पूत दुनिया में मिलता।
नहीं दिल तू खाक दुनिया में र्जता।

If the Moon is placed in a chart in the eleventh house in a *kundali* it will help keeping the *jatak's* health good as well as his progress. The native will be able to see his/her friends regularly will get happiness from the spouse, and get good food usually. Great celebrations will go on in his house time to time and will get unexpected gains.The native who will not remain unemployed at all & get soon some job when required. The native

these features.

However, some **inauspicious effects**may happen in case the Moon in the eleventh house is not auspicious on account of rising its enemy sign or weak in degrees. Some of these effects will be that the grandmother and

no male child will be alive. The grandmother will become widow early in

jatak's life.

1. If a sister is born to the native on Wednesday or *Budha* related things' business starts on Wednesday.
2. Either the native or any relative gets married on a Friday.
3. If the native buys a house or dismantles it on a Saturday.
4. Either the native accepts things or starts some business of the things that are related to Ketu during early morning which is Ketu's time before the Sun rises.
5. If the native likes to listen to his guru's advice or teachings and involves in any business relating things with Jupiter during the evening time which is known as Rahu's time, the native will suffer in life.

Lal Kitab provides some *upayas* to lessen the effect of such inauspicious things if they happen in *Jatak's* life on account of bad placement of the Moon in the eleventh house in a *jatak's kundali*. These are that when a child is born to the native his/her mother should stay away from there and should not visit the child for 43 days. The native is advised to give in alms sweets made from milk to 11 children or should pour out milk into the river which would be enough for 11 people to drink. The native is also advised to give milk to the needy in Bheron's temple & wash the grandmother's eyes with milk.

The Moon in the Eleventh House

The following verse unfolds some thoughts that are related to the Moon if it rises in the twelfth house of a native's chart.

छोड़ी याद मंजिल बुढ़ापा उजाड़ा।
गया जल, बिका उससे तेरा ही क्या था।

If the Moon rises in the twelfth house in anative chart, the native will possess sharp intelligence and will be famous in his family on account of his quick progress. The native will earn a lot of money from foreign lands also be very happy & successful. If all this happens to a native, the lines of hands will also support these things. When such things happen to a native, it is usually observed that the Moon and *Mangal* mounds will be raised in the *jatak's* hands.

However some **inauspicious effects** of the Moon's placement in the 12th house in its enemy signs will disturb the native's life to a certain extent. All that needs to be known. If the native usually keeps quiet, t will harm him and bring disaster to his/her life. If the native has some land,

native by the parents that will bring losses and accelerate misfortune in him/herlife.The native will get losses at every move that he would make. His own wife will be one-eyed lady. As *upaya*, the native should drink rain water and before starting any work he should drink some water out of it. He should put some *kapoor* into running water or offer it in a temple and serve his/her mother-in-law properly.

The Planet Mars/Mangal

The following lines are well expressed to indicate the power and auspicious effect of *Mangal* in a *kundali.Mangal* *jatak's kundali* as it can usually give good effect if placed in its own signs or in its friends' signs.

दो रंगी अच्छी, न इक रंगा हो जा ।
सुर असुर तू हो मोम या पतथर हो जा ।

In case the Sun and Mercury rise in one house in a *jatak's kundli*, *Mangal* usually provides good results. On the contrary it provides just opposite results if Saturn and Venus rise in one house in the *kundali*. *Mangal* becomes inauspicious at that time andeither physical ailments or quarrels in run for 20 years in *jatak's* life. Such things go on as all that period belong to *Mangal.Mangal* also rules the middle part of one's body. If the Sun's direct rays fall on that part, they bring good effect to the native's health.

If *Mangal* rises in the fourth house in a *kundali*, it has some special effects on the life of a native. Such a person will serve the humanity & offer food to millions of needy as well as serve the mendicants. If *Mangal* is well placed in a *kundali*, it will act like a lion & when its auspicious period will start, it will make the native's enemies run miles away from him. But if *Mangal*& Venus both are placed with equal strength in a *kundali* or rise in one sign, they both will act as inauspicious planets. But if the Sun & Moon rise with *Mangal* or are well placed in a chart, then *Mangal* will also act in a favourable way in the chart. When Mercury gets weaker in a chart, *Mangal* also becomes inauspicious.

We will present now *Mangal's* effect placed in different houses in a chart.

Mangal in the First House

The following verse elucidates *Mangal's*
a *kundali* of a native in a poetic manner.

थमे कटती तलवार शहजोर हो कितना।
रुके दांत ३२ ना बोल अपना।

If *Mangal*
in his family. He will have either a senior or junior brother with him. He will be a rich man at the age of 28 years by his own efforts. He will always act on right lines and be a courageous person. The native will be a simple

accordingly. Such a person is very lucky but such a native will have no

If *Mangal* **inauspicious effect** when not placed well in a *kundali*, it will provide several from his family.If he will keep any company of mendicants, it will bring him losses. The native by mistake if start taking responsibility of others' problems, it will be injurious to him. His married life will never be happy. If he likes to enjoy on others money, it will bring him losses. The native will be inauspicious to his parents. When he is young one of them may go to heaven. However, Lal Kitab suggests some *upaya* to check some of these bad effects of ill-placement of *Mangal* in a chart.The native is advised to take care of Jupiter& keep some of the thingsin his house related to Venus. He should use *sonf* time to time and keep things that are related to the Sun and Moon.

Mangal in the Second House

Mangal's
position when placed in the second house in a chart.

गिरे नजर से भाई अपने जो तेरे ।
पहाड़ा दो दूनी दो तुझको घेरे ।

If *Mangal* sits in the second house in a native's chart, the native will either be the eldest brother in the family or take responsibility of the eldest brother. He will always be dealing in iron & steel business and will be the head of a clan or tribe. As he will help others, it will help him too get more riches in life. He will never suffer on account of lack of money and will become rich by his own earnings. His whole life will be happy and contented. The native will get money from his in-laws and will have

his hands. However, there will also be **some ill-effects** of *Mangal* if placed inauspicious in a chart. Others will be highly jealous of him & he will die ultimately being involved in quarrels. Such a native may stay sick for nine years in life & if he will help others, it will affect his money income adversely. Lal Kitab suggests some *upays* to remove such bad effects created on account of adverse *Mangal* placed in a chart. It suggests to put some *rewri* in the running water, keep deer and help his brothers.

Mangal in the Third House

The following lines of verse suggest the quality of *Mangal* when placed in the third house in a *jatak's kundali*.

झुकी सर कलम कटती तलवार मिरछी।
पड़ा खम ना जालिम पकड़ तेग जिसली।

If *Mangal* is placed in the third house of a *kundali*, the *jatak* will surely possess brothers & sisters. Such a native will be happy to support others at his own cost. He will take care of his family and friends equally, but if such a native gets annoyed, he would not spare anyone whom he considers enemy. Otherwise he will sit silently like a lion who sits that way in its cage. His in-laws will be rich. He will not like if others are put to problems. He will always favour justice & will do the same to others. The lines of his hands will also convey the same.

If *Mangal* is placed **inauspiciously** in a native's chart in the third house, it will make the native very clever & cunning. The native will like to enjoy life wrongly and as a consequence he will be lacking money. Physically the native will have a small head but his stomach will be heavy & fat. His children will also be rouges. Lal Kitab suggests some *upaya* to lessen the ill-effects of an inauspicious *Mangal* in the third house. It suggests that the native should keep toys made of elephant's tusk and serve his senior uncle. All that may reduce the ill-effects of an ill-placed *Mangal* in a chart.

Mangal in the Fourth House

The following lines of verse suggest the quality of *Mangal* when placed in the fourth house in a *jatak's kundali*.

पकड़ हौसला तो मुसीबत सब कटती।
मगर लेख उलटे में हिम्मत ना हो बनती।

Lal Kitab suggests that *Mangal* placed in the fourth house in anative's chart is never inauspicious and if people hurt the native, the he will always

or Saturn rise with it, Ketu always gives right results to the native. Such results are received only when *Mangal* is placed in the fourth house in a chart. It always helps the native to go high in life. His brother's wife and hidden riches always support him to go high in life. If *Mangal* is placed in the fourth house in anative's chart, the lines of his hands also suggest these things and the money (luck) line in his hand will cross starting from the Moon's mound, and will go straight towards the top.

However, if *Mangal* is **not placed favourably** in a hand, the native will be very cruel by nature. By its bad aspects it will destroy everything. A well settled family will soon be destroyed by the rage of *Mangal*. A rich man will become a beggar. Such a native often becomes the cause to destroy a well-settled family. As such a native is not very intelligent, he is constantly serving others and destroys his whole family ultimately. He is always inauspicious to his mother, mother-in-law and grandmothers as well. Lal Kitab suggests some *upayas* for such an inauspicious *Mangal*. It would be better to take care of Moon and consequently the native should clean his teeth with alum. The native should offer milk mixed with sugar to the *bargad* tree & put a *tilak* of soil on his forehead. In order to save his children from calamity, the native should take in an earthen pot some honey and put that pot under the earth in a burial place. In order to save oneself from illness, the native is advised to use deer skin to sit upon it & keep some small squire pieces of silver with him. The native is advised to keep a small piece of tusk with him & feed birds regularly.

Mangal in the Fifth House

The following verse suggests how *Mangal*
native's could be useful and effective.

भरा सुख से सागर, जहाजों का बेड़ा।
खुश्क दम में न कर दे महबूब तेरा ।

If *Mangal* *jatak's kundali*, most of the planets will provide weak results except the Moon and Venus, which

results in view of their placement and strength in degrees in a chart.

If such a *jatak* will start any kind of work, it will increase favourably

good knowledge relating medicines, he will either be a doctor or a . If he serves his parents, he will get great progress in life. His children will be good and work well. The native will like to do justice to others & serve the people. Though he will be rich but have nc proud and will get respect from the people. His hands' lines will also project all such facts.

If *Mangal*
sign, it **may be inauspicious** to the native. It will lead to some problems and ill-effects. There may be thefts committed in the house, and sometimes

of the parents may die early but such ill-effect will not disturb aunt, sisters etc. It is also possible that the native may stay away from his house for a long time. Lal Kitab suggests some *upayas* to arrest some of the ill-effects of*Mangal* thus placed in the *jatak's* chart. The native is advised to keep a small pot full of water under his cot before the native goes to bed. At the time of *shradha* (when late ancestors are offered food etc.) the native is expected to give milk to the needy & offer milk to unmarried girls & should also give some silver and rice to them. He is also advised to serve his sister's husband.

Mangal in the Sixth House

The following verse related a few ideas that are connected to *Mangal's* placement in the sixth house in a native's chart.

जे नाम लड़के वे बाजा जो शार्द ।
गमी देर न करती उस जगह पे आती ।

If *Mangal* is placed in the sixth house in a native's chart then the native, even if he is not very lucky, will highly be dutiful and follow the code of conduct in his life. Good effects of planets will shine his life like the Sun. Such a native is very courageous and is able to do impossible things in his life. He is the leader of his family and takes care of every member of the family. But he leads a very peaceful life like a mendicant. His family will

However, there may be some **ill-effects** of *Mangal* if placed in its enemy sign or if it is weak in degrees. The Moon, Mercury, Venus, and Ketu may be harmful to the native's relations. Such a placement could

his mother may die. If the native uses any gold on his body it will highly harmful to him. When weak periods of planets will run in his *kundali*, the native will not be able to express any happiness as his children may suffer health-wise at that time. Lal Kitab suggests some *upayas* to arrest *Mangal* in the sixth house. It suggests that when there is a birthday of a child in the family, the native should distribute certain salty things instead of sweets. The native's brothers must bring a few things and offer them to the native to lessen the bad effect of *Mangal*. The native should also take care of some unmarried girls and help them time to time.He should do some *upayas* to console Saturn, Mercury and Moon to get good results. It may help his children to grow well in life.

Mangal in the Seventh House

The following verse unfolds certain thoughts related to *Mangal* if placed in a native's chart in the seventh house.

मलेगा सभी कुछ जो दरकार घर में।
शर्त सिर्फ इतनी, दोबारा न तलबे।

If *Mangal* is placed in the seventh house in a native chart, the native is born in a high family and is greatly kind to the people who need his help. He will get a good name among his family &people. If he eats sweet food it will be helpful to him most of the time. The native will be expert in mathematics. Such a native may be a good accountant or a lawyer and earn a good name & fame. If there is no *macha* line in his hand, he may not have any children. However, overall results of this kind of placement of *Mangal* in the chart, will be very fruitful. If *Mangal*is auspicious in the native's chart, the line indicating *Mangal* will be long and good in the hand. But if it is bad, it may start from *Mangal*'s mound and may end up on Mercury mound.

There may be certain **inauspicious effects** if *Mangal* is not placed good in the native's chart. These may beleading to the death of *bua's* (father's sister), sister's husband, and niece's husband at some time. His house may turn into a barren place or the native may involve in base activities to ruin his family. As *upaya* Lal Kitab suggests to give red coloured clothes to aunt (*bua*) or sister. In order to get good results from Saturn, he should make a new wall in his house. The native should keep some silver in his pocket and give rice full of a pot in Hunuman temple to the needy.

Mangal in the Eighth House

The following verse unfolds certain thoughts related to *Mangal* if placed in a native's chart in the eighth house.

वचन बेवा देती जो नेकी का तुझको।
बुझी आग खुद ही जला देती घर को।

If *Mangal* is placed in the eighth house in a *kundali* it makes the *jatak*

the capacity to win over his strongest enemy. He always possesses good & strong health. The lines on the hand of the native also suggest all that.

However, there are some **inauspicious effects**too if *Mangal* is not placed as auspicious in a native's chart. Consequently it will disturb the life of his younger brother and a widow's curse will ruin his life. Mangal,

kundali, may lead the native to be hanged. Lal Kitab suggests some *upayas* to reduce such ill-effects of *Mangal*. During

for cooking inside of the house. He should feed a black dog for 43 days by offering tandoori roti & wear silver in his neck. He should also wear a ring made with three metals. i, *Btashai*, and *Mashoor* dal should be put into water by the *jatak* and wear some silver after obtaining it from his grandmother.

Mangal in the Ninth House

The following verse unfolds certain thoughts related to *Mangal* if placed in a native's chart in the ninth house.

बड़े भाई की ताबेदारी में जो रहता।
जमाना गुलामी न तुझे कोई कहता।

When *Mangal* is placed in the ninth house in a native's *kundali*, he leads a just life and loves honesty & justice done towards people. His brother's wife becomes the cause to boost up his luck The Sun always gives him good results. The mound that belong to *Mangal* in the native's hand will be good enough to give him good results and help him to grow further. When the native will reach the age of 28 years, he will get great

person in life. The lines of his hand will also display some of these things.

However, there may be some **inauspicious effects** also if *Mangal* is placed in its enemy signs or weak in the chart. It may lead to so many problems such as that the native will not be God fearing or will be an atheist & his parents will also not help him in any way. The native could have lived like a lion but now he will act like a person who is afraid of everything & die also like that. Lal Kitab suggests some too to improve the condition of such a native. It suggests that the native should keep a red-coloured handkerchief with him & worship Hunuman Ji on Tuesday and serve him, give *prashadam* (sweet offerings) to the poor and needy. He should also wear *mooga* (red-stone) in a gold ring.

Mangal in the Tenth House

The following verse unfolds certain thoughts related to *Mangal* if placed in a native's chart in the tenth house.

बिके घर से सोना तो हो दूध जलता।
रहा जब न चन्द्र तो परिवार घटता ।

If *Mangal* is placed in the tenth house in the nativity in a *jatak's* chart, it helps riches to come into his house after his birth. By the time he becomes young he is very rich. Because of Saturn's good effect the native will behave like a lion or he will behave like a kind dear in life. The line of Saturn on the hand of the native will also indicate such results.

However, there may be some **inauspicious effects** on Mangal in case placed in an enemy sign or is weak in degrees. On account of need of money he may be required to sell gold of his house & his family will suffer a lot. His children, mostly sons, will go on dying & he may also lose one of his eyes sometime. As his father may die earlier, he may stay at his grandfather's place (mother's father—nana). Though such a native is seldom a thief, he may be blamed as a thief by people& will suffer on that account. Lal Kitab advises the native to serve Hanuman Ji, eat sweet food & should keep some deer at home and serve his uncles.

Mangal in the Eleventh House

The following verse unfolds certain thoughts related to *Mangal* if placed in a native's chart in the eleventh house.

मिले कुत्ता दुनिया, कि हर दम जो होते ।
असर शेर देंगे चाहे, कितने ही सोते ।

If *Mangal* is placed in the eleventh house in a native's chart then the native will courageous, will love to do justice for all. He will have patience and may belong to a middle class family. He will get victory over his enemies & will be considered as a lucky person. Such a native will get

Jupiter, Moon or the Sun. It is also expected that by the time he will reach 28 ears in age, he will be highly rich. He will lead a very comfortable life.

marriage. Such a native is often an engineer, a mathematician or a great sports man. Such a native always keep in mind what is right and what is wrong and only then follow the right track in life. The native is always

needy. The native knows how to converse with others so he often surprises

However, some **inauspicious effects** will also prevail in case *Mangal* is not placed in its own or friendly signs in the eleventh house. The native will incur loans on him & family and as a consequence parents' good-will and blessings will go waste. Such a native may sell his parental property cheaply.When he reaches the age of 45 his maternal uncle and other relatives will turn into his enemies. Lal Kitab provides some *upayas* to lessen the ill-effect of such a *Mangal*.The native should keep white &black coloured dog at his home & serve Hanuman Ji regularly.

Mangal in the Twelfth House

The following verse unfolds certain thoughts related to *Mangal* if placed in a native's chart in the twelfth house.

दिया मीठा लोगों, चाहे मीठा खिलाया।
कमी नजर दौलत की , सब कुछ हो आया ।

When *Mangal* is placed in the twelfth house in a native's chart, it is said that such a native will be very luck and a happy luck going person.

person and be very strong & will always defeat his enemies who will usually live in prison due to him. Such a *jatak* will be a religious kind of person who will always be serving *sadhus* and his gurus/teachers. His family will always be full with needful material and riches. The lines in

how he will stay protected by such a *Mangal* against all dangers.

There may be some **inauspicious effect** of *Mangal* in the 12th house if it is not in its friendly signs or weak in degrees. It may lead him to death at an early age& later on his mother will also die. *Mangal* is just like a

from him all the happiness relating his wife. Well, such a *jatak* may have two eldest brothers who may go to God's house when he is only 28 years old. Quite often such a native has no children. Lal Kitab suggests some *upayas* for Mangal if it is inauspicious in the native's chart. These are that the native should keep some rice and silver with him all the time. If he eats sweets and offers them to others, it will useful to get a long life. The native is advised to offer sugar mixed water to the Sun early in the morning. He should feed dogs with *roties*. He should give milk to others by adding honey to the milk and instead of water he should offer milk to the people.

The Planet Mercury/Budha

The following few lines of verse unfold certain thoughts related to Mercury/*Budha*if placed auspiciously in a native's chart.

खुला करते सूराख, मैदान बढ़ाता।
बढ़ी अक्ल इसकी, खर्च खुद जो करता।

Mercury/*Budha* gives wisdom and usually helps or destroys in jobs/ acts that need one's intelligence or wisdom. Mercury is considered controlling wisdom, mathematics, business, astrology, speech, intelligence and thinking capability, etc. In 2,3,4,5,6,7,8,10& 11th houses if Mercury is placed in a *kundali*, it is usually considered good.A native backed by Mercury usually deals with jobs that involve wisdom &therefore, such a *jatak* is either a writer, a wise person, a literary person, an astrologer and a doctor. The native endowed with the powers of Mercury will be a sane person and whichever task he takes in his hand, he is always successful. If Jupiter also supports such a person, his wisdom will be doubled. Such

which are impossible to be unmasked. Such a native is always considered possessing good thoughts, a worldly &friendly person who always deals with others very gently. Now we will deal with Mercury/*Budha* rising in different houses in a *kundali* and unfold the results of Mercury's placement

Mercury in the First House

The following few lines expressed like a short poem convey certain

Mercury.

मिला तख्त औरत को कितना ही ऊंचा ।
जवानी में तोहमत का खतरा ही होगा।

and walks along with the things that are common with the current times. He does not like the systems that belong to olden times, & neither the

that belongs to the olden days. Such a native may not believe so much in *dharam & karam* (rituals). The native changes his temperament time

kundalis.Such a native may go on changing his mind every minute. Whatever house the Sun rises in the chart of such a native, his relatives relating that house become rich all of a sudden. The native is so intelligent that he can make a stone swim or stay on water if he so desires. It happens especially when the native's complexion is black. One can see such a line in the hand of the *jatak* running from the Sun line to the mound of Mercury.

inauspicious effectswill be so many. Some of them are projected here under.When *Budha*/Mercury is not active (in the state of sleeping or weak in degrees etc.), the native's wife though she may be very rich, but when she is young, is defamed & accused in some way. Likewise, Mangal may cause a lot of destruction but the Sun is never inauspicious in such a chart. The native may be involved in drinking and as such his eating & drinking habits destroy him. Lal Kitab suggests some *upayas* to check such ill-effects created by Mercury. These are that the native should not use green colour in any form or way. He should also not keep the company of the wife's sister or he will be defamed.

Mercury in the Second House

The following few lines expressed in verse convey certain characteristics

पता उसके पिता, अगर मौत चलता।
दुआएं पैदाइश, न लड़के की करता ।

If Mercury is placed in the second house in a chart of a native, the

a different religion or cast. However, he is liked by his family and he works hard to increase the riches of his family. Such a native acts like a minister of a king or head of armed forces.The native is capable to write very well and also keeps his words. He is also expert to hide his misconduct and quite wise to deal with different things at different occasions. The lines in his hand also depict all such matters & qualities.

In case Mercury is not well placed in the second house being in its enemy sign or weak in degrees, it may bring or create problems for the native. The native may lose his respect &riches as well if Mercury is **not auspicious** in the second house. He will be fond of involving in gambling and drinking and consequently lose everything. He will not be considered as an auspicious child for his family & father especially when the father

further. The native may have illegal relations with his sister-in-law (wife's younger sister). It will create problems between husband and wife & their relations will be strained. As a result native respect in public & his wealth –all goes away. Bad combinations of the planets in his *kundali* take him to a very low level in life. If he keeps a goat or a parrot in his house, they bring bad results and his income and peace are badly affected. Lal Kitab provides some suggestions to boost up the badly placed Mercury in the second house of the *kundali* of the *jatak*. It suggests that the *jatak* should give in *dan*/almscertain things that are related to Moon. If he gets his nose

should also serve some unmarried girls & take care of the Moon & Jupiter by certain *upayas* such as keeping fasts or giving alms to the needy & poor on Mondays & Thursdaysfor 21 days.Such *upayas* may bring some of his lost riches and prestige back.

Mercury in the Third House

indirectly about its qualities/characteristics.

चरण धरते घर में लगी न कुछ देरी।
चल सब गए, आयु बाकी है तेरी ।

If *Budha* is placed in the 3rd house in a native's *kundali*, the native also support him in such acts. The native usually lives for 80 years. He is far away from serving others, or doing any religious activities & is usually an atheist. But if such a native is involved in a business in things that are

also be indicated by the lines in his hands.

However, there are some **inauspicious effects** too in case Mercury is not well placed in the chart of a native on account of weak in degrees or rising in an enemy sign. The native will be very stubborn, possess low wisdom, be a leper, & will be very clever. As such the native will not possess good conduct &will lose his family & riches too. Rahu & Ketu will also give bad effect & help him destroy. If the *jatak* has 32 teeth in his mouth, he will destroy several families on account of his bad language and low talks. If any planets rise in the ninth house of the *jatak's kundali,* they

Kitab suggests some *upayas* to arrest such bad effects of Mercury when placed inauspiciously in the third house. These are that the native needs to burn yellow *kaudis*& put their ashes into a river. A few leaves of *dhak* after washing them in milk need to be put into a river. The native may also wash

alum. He may also give to the needy goat's milk time to time. All such *upayas* may help him restore his peace of mind as well as riches.

Mercury in the Fourth House

indirectly about certain characteristics that Mercury possesses.

जन्म तेरे पर हंस माता क्यों रोई।
पता उसे लगा आयु बाकी न कोई ।

If Mercury is placed in the fourth house of a native's chart, the native will pay respect to each lady and elders. He often takes others responsibilities. If such a native possesses 32 teeth, *Mangal* also provides good effect to him. His family will rise in all respects. The native will be lucky to get his parents' blessings and as such a lot of family peace and happiness will exist in the house. The line of head in the hand of the native will meet the mound of the Moon. It will also indicate family happiness and a good married life.

However, there are some **ill-effects** too if Mercury is placed in its enemy sign or is weak in degrees in the fourth house. Mercury, if placed

mother. In case a parrot, horse, goat are kept in the house just after the native is born, then they may cause death to the native's mother as all these things are related to the Moon. Even if she does not die, she will stay in a bad condition health-wise. The native will suffer on account of loss of money and poverty. Saturn & Rahu will also be detrimental to the native's

native even to commit suicide. Lal Kitab suggests some *upaays* against all such odds. It suggests that the native parents should make some *upaya* to improve the Moon. For that they need to wear a silver chain in their neck. They are also advised to use *kesar*-oil for 43 days & put 40 grams *gur* into running water on a Sunday as well as one uncooked pitcher should also be put into the running water.

Mercury in the Fifth House

indirectly about certain qualities Mercury possesses.

जबान से पता नस्ल तेरा जो चलता।
उसे काबू फिर क्यों न तू अपने करता।

jatak's kundali, he will have a beautiful wife, possesses riches and lots of property. He gets progress regularly. Whatever he says will comeout true usually. By the grace of the Sun not only he will be greatly helpful to his family but to the state as well to which he belongs to. Such a native will highly be a good natured person, will be honest and kind to others. His family, business and work will go very well. After 34th year of age the Sun will be auspicious to him and it will help boosting up his luck. His children will also support his luck. Such

However, there may be some **inauspicious effects** too in case Mercury

get good education & by his ill-talks and criticism of others, he will make friends his enemies. Most people will like to stay away from him. Lal Kitab suggests some *upaya* to lessen the ill-effects of Mercury. He should keep things or articles that are related to the Moon. The native should also do some *upaya* for Venus which will be helpful to his wife also. The native should wear some copper in his neck and should not get his nose pierced

Mercury in the Sixth House

indirectly about certain qualities that Mercury possesses.

निकले सुख न मुख से जो पूरा तो होगा।
जबान मीठी तेरी भला दूसरों का ।

If Mercury is placed in the sixth house in a native chart, it makes the native honest as far as his promises are concerned. Whatever he would

world. Such a native is like a *sadhu*, or *sanyasi* whose heart is simple and

and is considered as a head of a clan, leader of people and he gets respect

Budha
press or news-paper, paper as well as government work. His hand –lines will also indicate some of these things.

There may be some sort of **inauspicious effects**too in case Mercury is not rising auspiciously in the sixth house on account of weak in degrees or placed in its enemy signs. In that case Mercury will give bad results. Suh a native will always deceive his master and if he makes a new house or new door to his house, it will bring ruins to his life & family. He should not marry his daughter in the north direction from his house as it will bring ruins to her and she will be never happy in life. The native may be a greedy /doctor, it will surely bring him ruins. Lal Kitab suggests some *upayas* to arrest some of the ill-effects of inauspicious Mercury. The native should take care of *Budha* and keep certain things in his house related to the Moon. He should take *gangajal* (water from the river Ganga) or milk in a bottle and bury the bottle far away in a jungle. His wife should wear a silver ring in its left hand. All that will be highly useful to him.

Mercury in the SeventhHouse

indirectly about certain qualities Mercury possesses.

मरे कफन पहन के, खुदा के घर जो चलते।
भला फिर भी जाएंगे लाखों का करके।

When *Budha* is placed in the seventh house a native's chart, it is always useful to others and as he takes care of them even if he neglects his house and interests. He may be helpful to anyone, even to those whom he doesn't know thoroughly. His wife will be honest and sincere and sister will love him too much. His sister-in-law will always assist him. He will always think good of others. He will be very intelligent and will write

marriage in his hand, which will indicate two marriages.

However, there may be some **inauspicious effects** of Mercury if it is weak in degrees or rises in its enemy signs. It may bring his business down in bad periods of planets. Home will not look attractive & all will look barren to him. The native will lead an unhappy life. His work and agriculture—all will be ruined. Lal Kitab suggests some *upayas* against such ill-effects of *Budha*. It says that the native should help his neighbour's or his brother's daughter when the need arises. He should also serve a black-coloured cow. All this may restore some good effect and may make native's life better.

Mercury in the Eighth House

about certain qualities Mercury possesses.

कब्र तक की लानत, फरीश्ता भी भागे।
जले आग ऐसी, जो नजर न आए।

If Mercury is placed in the eighth house, the native is often disturbed by his family matters but if he keeps things related to the Moon, it helps to save the native's mother from ruin and death. But the native leads a simple and ordinary life. Though such a native is intelligent and highly educated, he leads a poor life. All such is indicated by the native's hand-lines too.

The **inauspicious effects** in the native's life caused on account of

poisonous snake the inauspicious planet will work and spoil the native's

conspiracy. For example, a corrupt woman may involve him or trap him in a conspiracy that the native tried to molest her. Or the daughter of his

against him of that sort which will defame him to a large extent. Even when he grows older, he may be involved with the things of that kind and get defamed. Such a *jatak* is like a dead man before he is actually dead. Lal Kitab suggests some *upayas* against such defames. It says either on the birthday or a day before, the native should put an earthen pot full of honey inside the earth in a remote place. He should also give Moon related things to his relatives or animals. 24 pieces without sugar made from milk should be given to dogs to eat or may be put into a river. Similarly other planets need to be taken care of &wheat, *gur*

be given to the needy to lessen the ill-effects of other planets. Such efforts will be greatly helpful to the native.

Mercury in the Ninth House

about certain qualities Mercury possesses.

अजब भलू भुलैया जुबानी तमाशा।
दिखाते बहरुपिया ले बिस्तर ही भागा।

When Mercury is in the ninth house, the native is a leader and head of his family and of a community as well, but at times he is unable to earn his livelihood properly. Mercury rising in the ninth house sometimes acts like the planets that rise in the 11th house & is highly useful to the native as far

by the lines of the native's hands.

When Mercury is **inauspicious** in this house it has different kinds of bed effects. If it is a girl or a woman, she will ruin her father's house and bring problems for her parents. Such a native is shameless and can go to any extent to satisfy her physical desires. It happens because Saturn has its

bad luck. He/she is like a well which has no stairs and if anyone falls into it, cannot come out of it. Anyone who could take care of him/her goes away early in life, so there is no one left out to take care of him/her after some time. Such a native is very harmful to father and none who wants to help him/her can ever do so. Thus, as Mercury is not well placed and the native's luck is bad, nothing can be done to help him. If the native is a woman, she roams in the world like a mad person. None likes him/her as he/she is branded as a deceiver. Lal Kitab suggests some *upayas* to lessen the bad effects of Mercury in the ninth house when placed inauspicious. The native should get his/her nose pierced. He/she is also advised to wash a yellow piece of cloth in river water and then wear it. It will be good to put some piece of silver into the earth and also put a small piece on hjis body in the shape of a ring or a bangle. If the native uses mushroomsit will be good for him/her and the bed effect of mercury can be lessened.

Mercury in the Tenth House

about certain qualities Mercury possesses.

भला यार दोस्त न मक्कार होता है।
बचेगा कहां तू खामोश सोता।

Lal Kitab considers that if Mercury rises in the tenth house in a native's

from the native or to repay him/her for the acts that are done by him/

involves in business dealing with heavy things. However, if the native

for the person. The lines of the hand of the native also suggest some of these things clearly.

When Mercury exerts **inauspicious effects**on the native in whose chart/ *kundali* Mercury rises as an inauspicious planet as it is weak in degrees or rises in its enemy signs, it may create different kinds of problems for the native. The native may indulge in drinking and eating wrong things which are unhealthy and which may create health related problems. All this may

greedy as far as eating is concerned and it will create different kinds of problems for him/her.Lal Kitab suggests that to arrest such ill-effects, the native should make *upayas* for Saturn and feed cows regularly.

Mercury in the Eleventh House

-

rectly about certain qualities Mercury possesses.

सोना भाव बढ़ता लगे जब कसौटी।
समय नाश अपने अक्ल पहले सोती।

If *Budh*/Mercury rises in the 11th house in a native's chart, the native

native starts getting good income. The native leads a very simple life but he/she is quite talented and knows so many things which normally

the eleventh in the orbit (*gauchar*), it becomes very useful to the native things clearly.

If the native wears a , (a device to protect the native) it will not be favourable for him/her and bring problems of different kinds. Mercury if rising inauspiciously in this house, the native is likely to waste money in various useless jobs/acts, which ultimately disturbs him/her. Lal Kitab gives some suggestions to improve the bad state of Mercury rising inauspiciously in the eleventh house. It suggests that the native should wear a copper coin in his/her neck & serve unmarried girls. The native is also advised to use alum to clean the teeth.

Mercury in the Twelfth House

about certain qualities Mercury possesses.

ई रात न आधी, वह क्यों रो रहा है।
लिखा सब फरिश्ता, उलट हो रहा है।

If Mercury is placed in the twelfth house in a native's *kundali* it helps him/her from every kind of losses.It works like a nectar and helps the native in many ways. Such a *jatak* can bring life even in a dead person. Relations, in whose *kundali* Mercury is placed friendly, are usually helped by such a native except that those relations in whose *kundali* Mercury is not auspicious or placed in an enemy sign, will not be helped by the native. These things are also indicated by the lines of the native's hands.

However, there may be some **inauspicious effects** too if Mercury is not placed well in the twelfth house on account of rising in its enemy sign. Though the native will be well respected in the society, theft may be committed in his/her house and losses may occur on that account. The

her expectations often turn into disappointments & such a native often disturbs the neighbours as he/she is expert in involving with lies and wrong things. He is used to tell big lies so that people may believe in him/her. Thus, Mercury in the twelfth house is a great curse to a person. Such a native must not wear things related to Mercury lest they may bring bad results. If Rahu also rises with Mercury in the native's *kundali*, it involves

causes him/her lot of problems in life. Such a native often has to go to a prison or a mad house. The native usually involves in thefts, deception and cheating others which makes him/her unhappy further. The native's mother's luck is also badly affected by him/her.Lal Kitab suggests some *upaya* to lessen the bad effects of Mercury when rising in the twelfth house in a native's *kundali*. The native is advised to consult an astrologer time to time and keep a dog in his/her house. The native shouldn't get the nose pierced, use a *kesher tilak* on the forehead, wear gold & also wear a steal

pitcher in running water & avoid getting angry as far as possible.

The Planet Jupiter

The following few lines of verse unfold certain thoughts related to Jupiter if placed auspiciously in a native's chart.

दो रंगी दुनिया के, रंग दोनों देखो।
मगर आंख दु:ख जाए, अपनी आंख न देखो।

Jupiter is considered as the guru of all the planets and it also reigns both the worlds. It is tall in height, possesses golden complexion, and a bread *forehead*. Such a native never suffers from short of breath. If Jupiter is in its exalted state in a native *kundali*, the native gets honour, wisdom and good education. At the end of luck line in the native's hand there will

Such a *jatak* will enjoy all the privileges like that of a king, and even if he/

house is the house which involves a native to struggle hard to gain wealth & riches. It also brings success and failure in a native life. Though its owner is *Mangal*, but *karak* is the Sun,which represents the entire physical body of a native. The Sun, traditionally according to astrology is considered

exalted state but if Saturn is there it is considered as debilitated. Now we will provide here under two sides that Jupiter represents when placed in

Two Sides of Jupiter

House	Auspicious Dasha/Period	Inauspicious Dasha
First	Famous king	Great mendicant but kind and good.
Second	Jagat Guru who gives to everyone	Kind leader who destroys his own house.
Third	Great hunter of lions	Coward & possess bad luck

Fourth	Like Indra & Vikrama-ditya	One who destroys himself
Fifth	Happy with child's birth	A dead child born
Sixth	Gets everything easily	Extremely poor
Seventh	Involves in good acts	Even his adopted son is unhappy
Eighth	Can give all to others	Owns nothing
Ninth	True to his family	Owns nothing
Tenth	Never walks straight	Poor & unhappy
Eleventh	Even Snakes salute him	Possess nothing, extreme-ly poor
Twelfth		

We shall now present before the reader the results of Jupiter's

Jupiter in the First House

The following verse unfolds certain characteristic that may belong to a person in whose *kundali* Jupiter is rising auspiciously.

इल्म राज तेरा खजाने की चाबी।
फकीरी पूर्ण या पाएगा नवाबी।

good education to the native. The native is riche and possesses respect and honour from others as well as gets a good positions in government. His wife conceives soon, he gets success in examinations, and given responsibilities by the government. If such a native is not educated, he is honoured like a *sadhu*. He is separated from father at the age of 27 and

some of these things and at the mound of Jupiter there may be signs of that nature.

However, there may be some **inauspicious effects** also if Jupiter is not

deeply drenched in God's love & respected thus, but when he is only 12 years old most of his riches will be gone and even gold will convert into yellow metal (brass). Things that are related to Venus (like woman/wife) are mostly gone, and many unfortunate events may happen in the family of the native. His own property and big buildings are lost. His children will become the cause of his sadness. Lal Kitab suggests some *upayas* for it. These are that the native should give yellow clothes to sadhus & feed them too.

Jupiter in the Second House

The following verse unfolds certain characteristic that may belong to a person in whose *kundali* Jupiter is rising auspiciously.

जर्द माया गोदान से तेरा बढ़ता।
मगर सेवा उत्तम मुसाफिर जो करता।

If Jupiter is sitting in the second house, the native gets riches, honour, position etc. He possesses different kinds of knowledge, his family gets every kind of happiness, already earned name and fame get more strength and progress, gets gain in business and the native gets mental peace as well as happiness from his/her children. If there is any kind of loan on the native, he/she is also free from that. The lines of native's hands also suggest some of these things clearly.

However, there may be some **inauspicious effects** too if Jupiter is

remain sick, his health will be weak, and his nights will be restless. The *jatak* will possess jealousy against his own people and will be surrounded with troubles and problems. Lal Kitab suggests some *upaya* to arrest such bad effects created by Jupiter. The native should keep some gram *dal* in a yellow piece of cloth and give it to the priest of a temple. He should give milk to snakes, serve guests & help others so that the native may get

Jupiter in the Third House

The following verse unfolds certain characteristic that may belong to a person in whose *kundali* Jupiter is rising auspiciously.

गरजना शेर व खानदानी गुरु।
ज्योतिष व आशीष का स्वामी।

In case Jupiter rises in the third house in a *jatak's kundali*, the *jatak* usually lives for 75 years. Such a native provides happiness to the mother, and his luck is always in his favour.The native gets money from his relatives and his wife's health is usually good. His family always remains happy and children are attached to him. Such a native earns his livelihood by serving in the government or in a private sector. Jupiter placed in the third house makes the native very powerful and provides him many responsibilities as

There are also some **inauspicious effects** if Jupiter is not well placed in the third house in the *kundali* of a native. Such a native is usually a coward & possess bad luck. Such a native is either a great friend or a strong enemy. The native usually likes the company of women & wants to be rich by others' riches. Most of his relatives often face problems of different nature on account of him. His body emits bad air. Lal Kitab suggest that such a native should worship the Goddess Durga and serve unmarried girls

Jupiter in the Fourth House

The following verse unfolds certain characteristic that may belong to a person in whose *kundali* Jupiter is rising auspiciously.

पड़ा माया बन्द पानी दुनिया जो सड़ता।
फले बीज दुनिया जो बन्द मुट्ठी करता ।

When Jupiter is placed in the fourth house in a native's chart, the native is usually connected with construction business and is involved with high quality of work. The native gets progress and promotion as he desires & gets happiness from his mother and brothers. His whole family always stay happy. The lines of the native's hand also suggest these things.

There are some **inauspicious effects** too in case Jupiter is not placed

him, they start opposing him and deceive him. He is usually involved in wrong activities. He starts drinking and destroys his prestige, family peace and happiness. That leads him lose his gold and property as well. He may

runs away towards forests. Lal Kitab suggests some *upaya* to lessen the ill-effects of Jupiter if placed weak in the fourth house. The native should take care of the Moon, establish things related to the Moon in his house and never stay without clothes in the presence of others.

Jupiter in the Fifth House

The following verse unfolds certain characteristic that may belong to a person in whose *kundali* Jupiter is rising auspiciously.

धर्म नाम पर मांग, दुनिया जो खाता।
इसासा ही है बेच, अपना वह जाता।

kind to him. The native is also a businessman who deals in valuable jewels & ornaments. The native also loves to keep animals. His luck shines at the age of 16 and at the age of 36 a son is born to the native. The lines of the native's hands also depict such things.

There are some **inauspicious effects**

for alms in the name of dharma. It makes him childless & often he does not get any *kafan*(the cloth that covers a dead-body) at the time of his death. At times his children are born dead and the native digs his own well to be drowned into it. That means the native creates situations that ultimately drown him in loans and indulge in calamities. He often runs to get alms and creates problems for him all-round. Lal Kitab suggests some *upayas* to

the native to take care of Ketu & worship Lord Ganesha. He should also keep dogs at home, and serve his teachers. The native should put some *kesher*into the running water sometimes.

Jupiter in the Sixth House

The following verse unfolds certain characteristic that may belong to a person in whose *kundali* Jupiter is rising auspiciously.

मुफ्त रोटी तुझको हरदम मिलेगी।
मगर माया तो ढूंढनी पड़ेगी।

from his maternal uncle, his mother's sister and sister-in-law. He also gets

servants supports him and he gets success in elections. He soon becomes free from loans if taken earlier and gets so many valuable things in life. Such a native need not to work very hard to earn his livelihood. Most of things he gets without asking for them. His maternal uncle is always helpful to him in boosting up his luck. Though he may not get money in abundance, he will still be very rich. It is also seen that such a native is

above.

There are some **inauspicious effects** too when Jupiter is placed in the sixth house as it is either weak in degrees or placed in its enemy sign.

his father and son. He will often like to eat unearned bread & will go on asking for alms from others. Lal Kitab suggests some *upayas* to lessen the ill-effects of Jupiter. The native should take care of weak Ketu. He should keep a dog at home and water a *peepal* tree regularly.He should also give 600 grams *chanadal* in a temple & feed a yellow coloured hen with yellow *mashoor dal*. The native is also advised to serve an old *brahman* and wear some gold on his body.

Jupiter in the Seventh House

The following verse unfolds certain characteristic that may belong to a person in whose *kundali*Jupiter is rising auspiciously.

धर्म माला थैली, न परिवार देगी।
बड़ी शान शौकत, बिलाहर्ष देगी।

When Jupiter is placed in the seventh house in a *jatak's kundali*, he/ she gets money-gains. Such a native gets married early or when he is only

When he reaches the age of 40-45 he gets children & after that the native

He always respects his elders who are also the owners of the family. The native always practices dharma and his luck is boosted up by his wife.

foundation of his life. The native may die at any place away from his home but he will be cremated at his home town. Such things will also be displayed by the lines of his hands.

However, when Jupiter is *not auspicious* in the seventh house, any of his children are devoid of happiness. He may give any amount of money to others, but he has to earn his living with hard labour though he has lacks of rupees with him. While he was young he went on searching for knowledge and did not care for his children, therefore in his old age he will go on seeking to get happiness from his children & money. His parents and grandparents will suffer from short of breath. He may lose gold or wealth, he may suffer on account of having no children or getting no happiness from his children. All that will bring lot of unhappiness in his life. Lal Kitab suggests some *upayas* seventh house of a native's *kundali*. The native is advised to keep some gold in a yellow piece of cloth & if dasha is not running favourable, he needs to take care of the Moon by keeping Moon related things in his house. The native should worship Lord Shiva & serve frogs.

Jupiter in the Eighth House

The following verse unfolds certain characteristic that may belong to a person in whose *kundali*Jupiter is rising auspiciously.

बृहस्पति के आठवें घर का भाव

बड़ों का हो साथ जब रात करता।

धन, सोना, माया, आयु सब बढ़ता।

If Jupiter rises in the eighth house in anative's *kundali*, he often goes

is a son. He gets good opportunities for his progress and besides possessing Vedic knowledge and developing his intellectuality, he also gets riches all of a sudden.The lines of his hand also suggest all that.

However, there may be certain **inauspicious effects**also when Jupiter sits in the eighth house in a native's chart. Such a native will be harmful to his father. His grandfather will die before his birth & so many unpleasant information and news will be rampant about him in public. He will lose his money quite often and even if would have money, he will be under debts. He will be like a night bird (*ullu*), wherever he would sit turn that place into a cremation. He will take birth again and again and will have less number of years to live. He will always be defamed as a bad lover. Lal Kitab suggests some *upyas* to arrest

native should give in *dan* things related to Jupiter or Venus. .

Jupiter in the Ninth House

The following verse unfolds certain characteristic that may belong to a person in whose *kundali* Jupiter is rising auspiciously.

माया छोड़ संसार को न धर्म बनता।

धर्म स्वंय उल्लंघन, सभी कुछ ही जलता।

When Jupiter rises in the ninth house in a native's chart, the native goes to religious journeys, involves in , meditation, intellectual growth, keeps the company of *sadus* and *sants*, etc. He is married at an his dharma and as well as keeps his words. He will never suffer on account of lack of money and will never experience any bad times in his life. The lines of his hand also display such things in his hands.

However, when Jupiter is inauspicious in a *jatak's kundali,* the *jatak* will

completed and work done. On account of the ill-effects of planets, the native will lead a poor life and will also be a non-believer. He may relinquish his

on that account. He may suffer on account of heart problem & the number of days in his life get reduced. Lal Kitab as an *upaya* advises the native to visit a temple every day and serve the old people.

Jupiter in the Tenth House

The following verse unfolds certain characteristic that may belong to a person in whose *kundali* Jupiter is rising auspiciously.

बृहस्पति के दसवें घर का भाव
लिखा माया दौलत न था जो त्रिधाता।
बनाएगा क्या तू ये आंसू बहाता।

If Jupiter rises in the tenth house in a *jatak's kundali*, the *jatak* is the head of several villages. He may be a great *pandit* and his forefathers owns so many villages. Such a native earns his goodwill as he meets his both

things.

There are certain inauspicious effects also if Jupiter is not placed as a

jatak will grow moneyless the more practice he will do.His childhood and old age both

not leave for him any assets after his death. He may have good dreams about having riches but will hardly be rich. None of his desires will be

upaya to lessen the bad effects of Jupiter

a yellow *tilk* on the cow and his turban & blow his nose regularly before starting a new work or business. In order to improve his father's status he should put a brass coin in a river for 40 to 43 days.

Jupiter in the Eleventh House

The following verse unfolds certain characteristic that may belong to a person in whose *kundali* Jupiter is rising auspiciously.

कफन दूसरों पर जो तू देता रहेगा।
बिना कफन घर से न बाहर मरेगा।

When Jupiter is placed in the eleventh house, the *jatak* is very much interested in religious activities. It may also happen that the native's mother may not live long. The native usually lives until 80 years and is

Such a native also gets abundant of honour from people. The lines of the native's hands also depict these things clearly.

However, there may be some inauspicious effects too if Jupiter is not placed favourably in the native chart. As the father will die soon the native will feel weak and without any help. His/her character will not be sound & will wander in dirty places. At the time of death others will assist the native to complete the last rites of a relative. Such a native is usually jealousy of others & that will bring disaster to the family. There will be many death in the family and the native will lose lot of money time to time. Though the native will work hard and earn a lot but will incur loans usually. The native partner (wife/husband) will face problems and will be unhappy in life. Lal Kitab suggests some *upayas*

It suggests that when someone dies in others family, the native should help

advised to wear some copper in his/her hand.

Jupiter in the Twelfth House

The following verse unfolds certain characteristic that may belong to a person in whose *kundali* Jupiter is rising auspiciously.

प्रार्थनाएं भले ही सबकी अगर तू करेगा।
खजाना न शक्ति का तेरा घटेगा।

When Jupiter is placed in the twelfth house in a native's chart, the

if goes abroad. The native will get success in most of the tasks that he/she undertakes. Such a native's earnings and expenditure will almost be the same. The native will be highly wise, will possess the knowledge of ancient verses, will lead a contented life but will have a hard disposition. The lines of the native's hands will also display all such things.

However, there may be certain inauspicious effects too in case Jupiter *kundali*. The native will

ask for any favours, no one will oblige the native. The native will live in false beliefs and hope until 42 years of age. Though the native will be like a king but will live like a poor person. He/she will be wise and educated but all that will be of less use him/her. Neither the native will be

Lal Kitab suggests certain *upayas* to lessen the ill-effects of Jupiter, if placed inauspiciously in the twelfth house. The native is advised to wear a garland made with *tulsi*wood, put on yellow clothes and also a yellow *tilak*on the forehead. He/she should keep his/her nose clean and serve *brahmans* and *sadhus*. The native should keep his/her head covered and wear some gold on the body.

The Planet Venus

planet Venus.

बदी खुफिया तू जिसेस दिन–रात करता ।
वक्त मंदा वही तेरे सिर पर पड़ता।

As customary as well as according to the ancient astrology, Venus is considered o be the guru of demons. Guru Sukracharya was also known to be the guru of demons. This kind of thinking & imagination is based on different kinds of effects of Venus on the natives. But Lal Kitab considers Venus as Laxhimi. The meaning of Venus on the basis of its deeds is 'powerful', 'mighty' and 'strong.' Such a native is quite different and stands aloof from others. The native is also strong mentally,

indulging in business relating to different kinds of metal.

pleasures but is honoured by the society on account of possessing good qualities and merits. Even if such a native is less educated, he/she is good in conversation& therefore is able to get what he desires.

Such a native is good at talks and may hoodwink people. His wife makes a love-marriage. He is mostly involved in enjoying life. He/she daughters and sisters. He/she owns a state & is expert in some specially art. The native usually has big gardens, a bungalow and transport facility & is regularly involved in physical pleasures. Certain special signs also appear on his hands on the mound of Venus and indicate all such things in his/her life. .

Two-sides of Venus

In the First House:
she is totally involved in physical pleasureswhen he/she is young. The best time but was involved in love with her own slave-servant.

In the Second House: If Venus rises in the second house in a native's chart, the native is involved in improving her/his own health and beauty, does not like to have her/his own children, may act like a school teacher, who is liked by most of the people, but she keeps all of them away from her.

In the Third House: If Venus rises in the third house in anative's chart, he is as strong as a bull. That may lead to winning the love of any woman. If it is woman, she possesses a man's courage.

In the Fourth House: It indicates that Venus in the fourth house is like two men or two women, who though stay together but are totally apart from each other.

In the Fifth House: Lots of children in the family or children of the kind whom their parents may not advise any things in case Venus rises in the

In the Sixth House: If Venus is placed in the sixth house, usually the native is impotent and a woman does not conceive & minimum riches.

In the Seventh House: When Venus is placed in the seventh house, both the partners go on advising each other until they grow old.

In the Eighth House: Venus in the eighth house helps both the natives live happily and amiably until they live.

In the Ninth House: Venus in the ninth house may indulge the native in some kind of illness but the native possesses ample of wealth to enjoy life.

In the Tenth House: Venus in this house makes the native to possess more than one partner.

In the Eleventh House: When Venus is placed in the eleventh house,

desires. Such a native is usually a simple one who can change himself/herself under all circumstances.

In the Twelfth House: Venus in the twelfth house makes the native like a cow which is helpful to take the dead into heaven after death. That means

Now we shall provide the results of Venus' placement in the twelve

Venus in the First House

यदि धर्म दुनिया न स्त्री बिकता।
कोई लेख विधाता मंदा न लिखता।

enjoyment in life. Such a native can destroy enemies easily. The native gets every kind of facility and utility in life, like clothes, dresses, plenty of things that emit fragrance, and gets married soon. The native gets a lot of contentment and happiness in his/her marriage. Besides getting good education the native also gets a good name in the society. The native has children, gets rights and privileges that hardly one can think about. The

women and physical enjoyment with them. He/she also gets a lot of success in business and is always on the way of going up in life. These things are

However, there may be some sort of inauspicious effects if Venus rises

enemy sign or weak in degrees. Such a native is lose in morals, so he/she may indulge in sex activities and destroy him/herself as well as the entire family. The native's mother will die when he/she is very young. By the age 25 the native wife may die or may suffer from various diseases. There may be lots of death in the family. Not only the native but his/her friends will also get losses. If it is a *kundali* of a woman, she may be divorced by her man. Lal Kitab suggests some *upayas* against such odds. If the native is a man, then he should serve unmarried girls at the time of their marriage. If the native is a woman, she should give cows to the needy. If a woman at the time of her marriage gets some silver from her in-laws, it will help her family rise. The native is advised not to eat *gur*& avoid indulging with women sexually. The native should serve black cows, keep oneself away from other women and take bath mixing curd in water.

Venus in the Second House

the second house in a native's chart.

बने माया तेरी पशु जो मिट्टी।
तू मांगता क्यों, सोने की हट्टी।

If Venus rises in the second house in a native's chart, he/she gets lots of money, clothes, dresses, and things that give fragrance. The native is honoured by the government & he keeps the company of a beautiful wife. He/she gets early chances of marriage, gets children. The native also gets

of music & literature. His/her friends support him/her most of the time in

Venus in the second house of a *jatak's kundali* are also unfolded by Lal Kitab. It says that if the chart belongs to a lady, she will not conceive a male child or she may not give birth to any child. Without a woman or man, the native roams without any company in life and destroys one's life. His/her life will get no happiness in life without a suitable partner as often wrong company will lead to destruction. The native will also lose money in life. Lal Kitab suggests some *upayas* to lessen such odd effects of Venus

jatak's kundali in the second house. It suggests to make *upayas* for *Mangal*& lead a straight life implicit with moral code. It will help the native to ward off to a certain extent the bad effect of Venus. The native is also suggested to offer cows two kilospotato drenched in *haldi*/yellow powder & the native should also give 200 grams ghee made from cow's milk in some temple.

Venus in the Third House

the third house in a native's chart.

बुरा क्यों जो इज्जत तू औरत की करता।
वक्त पर है तेरे जो स्वंय मर्द बनता ।

If Venus rises in the third house, the native likes to love every woman he meets and so is the case of a woman. Such a native will be able to getting every kind of information from different sources easily. He will know about his on death beforehand. Different women will help him in varied ways,but his own wife will be sincere to him as well as attached to him. No theft will be committed in his home till he lives. His parents will live happily. If he goes on a pilgrimage on the tenth of any month, it will be highly suitable to him. The native will get abundance of honour, money, clothes and will win over his enemies. He will be respected in the society as well.The lines of his hand will also show all that.

However, there will be certain inauspicious effectsof Venus if placed

age of 34 years the native may earn as much money, may construct big buildings, or keep big vehicles or cars, he/she may not be able to sleep happily. His riches will go on reducing each day and he will have to work very hard to get his daily bread. His relatives will deceive him and his daughters may also not keep good relations with him. Neither he will be get any happiness in his home not he will get his father's property in life.

Venus. It says that the native should serve his elder brother's wife to reduce

Venus in the Fourth House

the fourth house in a native's chart.

नुक्स चार अपना इश्क औरतों का ।
चश्म पोशी करते भी लानत ही देखा।

When Venus is placed in the fourth house,the native gets name and fame, a good house to live in, gets lots of riches, vehicles and gold in abundance. He/she is likely to be married soon. But his wife may not support much his luck and will enjoy life herself without caring for her man. The native may have two wives at a time but both of them will be

is not employed he/she will soon get job. Such a native is either a lawyer, a writer, doctor, an artist, or a media person. Time to time the native will get good news & will enjoy his life regularly. In most respects his long

Venus will be going on to the mound of Moon in the *jatak's* hand if one observes the hand lines carefully.

However, there will be some inauspicious effects also in case Venus

will bring ruins to his family. His wife will not be favourable for his family and bring disasters. The native may indulge in drinking and start visiting other women and may grow poor gradually. Involvement in love affairs will also cause this kind of destruction. Number of children will be less in the family & if the native constructs a house on the top of a well after covering it, it will cause great losses and destruction to him. Lal Kitab

in the fourth house. It says that the native should keep a pot full with honey at the roof of his house & a very small silver box need to put into earth near a pond. The native should give curd/yogurt to the needy, serve cows, and make *upayas* for Jupiter.

Venus in the Fifth House

टाग जली न मिट्टी उड़े, उड़ेगी जिस दम वह ।
जे ग्रह पहलें नौवें, अंधा काना हो।

native a mendicant, a , a saint, a religious person, and one who loves his country dearly and family as well. The native possesses children. The native's wife is a devoted lady and helps her and family to her utmost. Such a native will always possesses lots of riches and if he/she is involved in a business that is related to Venus, it will bring riches. It is also possible that such a native will give lectures full of wisdom during the day time but will lead a sensuous life in the night. But if he/she serves cows there will be happiness in the family. If the native moral implicit life, the native will get great success in life. The native health will be good. Whenever

will be honoured by the society & his friends will support him in various ways consequently his enemies will keep away from him. The lines in the

However, there may be some inauspicious effects too in case Venus is

may bring disaster in the family. One of his elder brothers, if he has, will be either blind or be one-eyed. Business relating to Jupiter & Rahu will bring losses. The native's children will not be good for him and will never help him. Such a native will show of wisdom during day but he will waste his nights in immoral acts. In the name of dharma he will always deceive people. Native's children will never give him due respect. Lal Kitab offers some *upaya* to lessen the bad effects of Venus if rising inauspiciously in

body parts with milk or yogurt & keep milk, silver as well rice in the house regularly.

Venus in the SixthHouse

the sixth house in a native's chart.

जवानी तू नगर बच्चे भुलाता ।
बुढ़ापा न दुनिया में तुझको रूलाता।

If Venus is placed in the sixth house in anative's chart, the native is devoid of dharma, is an atheist, and indulges with women regularly. He talks always good with women to get their company. The native is never interested in earning his livelihood honestly but by cheating and false talks

As the Sun and Venus are not friends, the mound starting from Mercury and going up to the mound of Saturn becomes longer in the native's hand & the native's thoughts become cruel & hard against people. The native's wife's health is good and he leads a happy life during his old age. On the hands of such a *jatak*, the mound of Venus will have some signs indicating Rahu's presence & the line of Venus will go beyond the Sun line in his hands.

There are also some inauspicious effects of Venus if rising inauspiciously in the native's hand in an enemy sign or is weak on account of any reason. The native often may indulge in love affairs but he will not be happy with other women. His mind may remain disturbed but when such thoughts go away the native becomes a mendicant or a *sadhu*. Often thefts are committed in his house and animals, cash, all is stolen. This indicate a weak Venus rising in the native's *kundali*. It is also possible that the native may earn money by wrong means and will like to distribute that money among poor people. The native will hardly get any happiness from his wife & his children may stay away from him. Such a native usually gets some diseases relating to his sex organs & possess more number of daughters than sons. Lal Kitab suggests some *upaya* to lessen the bad effects of Venus. It advises the woman *jatak* to keep gold in her hair & the wife of such a native should always wear socks so that she does not touch the ground with her bare feet. The native should keep some silver with him, feed birds, and give (*dan*)curd in a copper pot to the needy. For six Fridays the native should put pieces of white stones into the running water

Venus in the Seventh House

the seventh house in a native's chart.

शुक्र के सातवें घर का भाव

एवज गैर पतिव्रता अपनी जो भूली ।

जली माया घर की यह,क्या नार आग ले ली।

If Venus is placed in the seventh house in a *jatak's kundali*, the native may have long life to live, keeps away from indulging with low things, is a good natured person and inorder to earn his livelihood, he has to live abroad or stay away from his home throughout his youth, including involving in lot of travelling. He hardly stays at home and keeps the company of parents. He is also involved in romances & is inclined towards beautiful women. If such a native tries to lead a moral life, he can stay in the world for 93 to 96 years. The wife of such a native is usually a good person who likes to lead a respectful life, is devoted and possess a lot of qualities. She is also a good house-wife. The native 25 years in life are very fruitful, he surely comes back from foreign land if has gone there & usually dies in his own land. The lines in the hands of such a *jatak* will also predict some such things.

However, there may be some inauspicious effects too in case Venus *kundali*/chart.It will lead to destroy his happiness, his personal property, his name & fame—all by his own mistakes as Saturn and Rahu both combine to destroy the native. If the native leads an amoral life, he will be going downwards in all respects in life as *Budha*, *Mangal*, Saturn & Ketu will accelerate his sexual or romantic feelings. It will usually indulge him in a bad company, consequently the native will keep wrong company which will bring him a bad name.

The native also losses money and thefts are committed in his house. It may also happen that man or woman may be impotent or devoid of children. Since the native will involve with different women, it will lead to his destructions. Lal Kitab suggests some *upaya* against such a bad effect of Venus. It says that the native should do some *upaya* for *Mangal &Budha*,

be put into running water, serve a red colour cow, take blessing from parents, and on Fridays the native should give copper utensils to the needy in a temple, and always follow the code of conduct in life.

Venus in the Eighth House

eighth house in a native's chart.

शुक्र के आठवें घर का भाव
कब्र दूसरे की जब कोई न पड़ता ।
फिर कसम पर जमानत तू क्यों करता ।

When Venus is placed in the eighth house in a *jatak's kundali*, such a native earns his livelihood with hard labour and honesty. His wife bears a

down before him & such a native knowingly suffers in life as he does not want to trouble others. The lines of his hands will also suggest some of these things.

But Venus, if placed inauspiciously will also give bad results to the native especially when the native reaches 34 years of age. The *jatak* is advised not to marry until 25 years as a weak woman or weak man spoil each other's life. The native should be give anyone's bail in a court case and take care of his seniors in the family. Lal Kitab suggests some *upayas* against a weak Venus. These are that the native should put a few blue

andvisit temples to pay tributes, take blessings from mother, sister and brother, put some corn into the earth and give some carrot to the needy in a temple for eight days.

Venus in the Ninth House

the ninth house in a native's chart.

शुक्र के नवें घर का भाव
गिना है बेहतर चाहे, मेहनत का खाना ।
मगर शेखी क्या, खून हरदम बहाना।

When Venus rises in the ninth house in anative's chart, the native may be rich from his father's side, but he has to earn his own livelihood with hard work. If he does not do so, he would need to go far away from his

Venus may also bring inauspicious effects when placed in an enemy sign or is weak on certain reasons. Most of the things relating Venus, like cultivation, relations and milk-giving animals—all will be destroyed at his 24 years of age. The native becomes fond of drinking and so losses all. His wife gets so many serious diseases and as *Budha* is not auspicious, the native also losses money. Lal Kitab offers some suggestions to arrest

square pieces of silver under a *neem* tree. Venus may be 9 times favourable to the native after that. He may also put honey in a small silver box under the *neem* tree & serve a black or red coloured cow. At the occasion of certain celebrations like *rakcha bandhan*, (when sisters tie a thread around their brothers' wrists to pray for her brothers' long life), the sister should wear red bangles. All such *upayas* may lessen the bad effects of Venus, if

Venus in the Tenth House

the tenth house in a native's chart.

सदा फूल औरत जवानी पर मरता।
गंवा खाली औलाद पीरी तरसता।

When Venus is placed in the tenth house in a native's chart, the native has a big and happy family and both the native-man & woman possess good and sane thoughts. The native will have great gardens& the native's wife will have good health and be lucky. Every kind of misfortune will disappear on account of the kind and good woman who is the wife of the native. If the fourth house of the *kundali* has no planets then Venus provides the results like Saturn. Then the native wife is quarrelsome and

native is clever but Saturn gives good results. Venus also helps such a native and he roams in forests and different places in the quest of a woman & gets success in getting one. But *Mangal*& Moon then turn away from the native and does not let him enjoy all that totally. If the native can abandon the quest of a different woman other than his own, he may live happily until he grows older. The native's hand lines also suggest all that.

However, there may be some inauspicious effects too on account of

kundali. It will delay

in having children & if any child is born, he/she will die soon. The wife of the native is more demanding (sex-wise) because of that the native suffers from vulnerable diseases. The native seeks for love when he is young but also weeps for children when he is old. If such a *jatak* is a woman, she loses her eyesight. Lal Kitab suggests some *upayas* to lessen the bad

sex-related diseases, the native is advised to clean his private parts with

away cows to the needy and keep cows and goats in his house. The native should also give some cotton to the needy & poor in a temple & make *upaya* to get the favour of Saturn.

Venus in the Eleventh House

the eleventh house in a native's chart.

शुक्र के ग्यारहवें घर का भाव

इश्क लहर और तन हो इतनी बढ़ती।

चिमट बाद जिसके हो जाती नामर्दी।

If Venus is placed in the eleventh house, native is very greedy and is surrounded with love towards money & always desires to get more and more in life. In all such matters he is so much involved that he even forgets his family, wife and home, as well as relatives. He may have lots of wealth but his wife will never be happy. She will live like a captive in the family. She will have no attraction for her man right from the time of marriage. The native works secretly and the woman gives just a false smile to please him as she knows that her man is not a right kind of person. Such a native usually dies on account of getting hurt on his head. The lines of his hand will also suggest some of these things.

When Venus is inauspicious in the eleventh house, it may not affect his earnings and income, but he gets less honour from people. His daughters destroy his family and as a result of the ill-effect of planets, the native family go on reducing as frequent death occurs in the house. Lal Kita suggests some *upayas* to arrest such ill-effects of Venus. The native should serve a *kapila* cow to save his wife from death. He should also give away cotton and curd in a temple to the needy & give some oil too to save

a gold bar after being heated eleven times, has been cooled down.

Venus in the Twelfth House

the twelfth house in a native's chart.

शुक्र के बारहवें घर का भाव
लहर माया चलती फिरा कुल जमाना।
गया भूल क्यों फिर तू जिस घर को जाना।

When Venus is placed in the twelfth house in a native's chart, the

his marriage all goes very well. He becomes free from his poverty and stand on his own feet & gets all the honour, becomes the head of a good family & gets all the required honour. Such natives are attached to his family and wife as well and enjoys every kind of happiness from his family and stay very happy until 40 years in life. a The native gets high position and status from the governmentbut his own wife's condition is not as good as expected. She is constantly sick. The native, a man or a woman, is a poet or poetess, sings well, is deeply interested in literature, and enjoys life until 96 to 100 years. The lines of the native's hands also suggest all that.

in a native's chart. At times when the planets are ineffective and weak in a *kundali*
the wife suffers more as she covers her husband in many ways and wants him to stay good. But the native, though saved from so many bad effects, is totally destroyed after 25 years. Lal Kitab suggests some *upaya* to lessen the bad effects of Venus. It says that the native should give a cow to the needy

and put it under the earth in a remote place. The native should keep cows in home and serve them. The woman should put some *gur*(jogger), rice and corn into the earth in a remote place in a jungle or the man should give corn equal to the body weight of his wife and give it in a temple to the needy.

The Planet Saturn

planet Saturn.

जमाने में बदकार अक्सर जो रहते।
भले लोगों को बुद्धू अहमक है कहते।

Its white cum black complexion indicates that it is also helpful and kind and when it gets pleased, it makes a native very rich and gets him/her the position of a king. Most of the other planets also act as per his desire and act favourably, but in adverse circumstances, it makes the *jatak* a pauper

houses. All such work is sponsored by Rahu & Ketu which are its friends.

Though Saturn is not such a bad planet but if it gets angry, t may affect

them to provide bad results. It has its sharp aspects like the Sun & it can do whatever it desires. Therefore, most astrologers always consider Saturn's effect in a chart all the time when required to examine a *kundali*. As it does not travel straight, it is worshipped so that it may stay calm and may not exert its bad effects on a native. The following verse unfolds so many aspects about Saturn.

"वक्र चन्द्रमा ग्रसहिं न राहू, टेढ जान शंका सब काहू"।

The planet Saturn is competent to turn a native's life into heaven or hell at any point. Therefore, all are scared of it and pray that Saturn be pleased with him/her and provide good results. Now we present here under Saturn's placement in all the twelve houses starting from the 1st house.

Saturn in the First House

jatak'skundali.

भरे जन्म पर जो खजाने दबामी (पुराने)।
फरिश्ता अजल बोल देगी नीलामी।

native in most of his/her tasks and makes him/her rich. But if it is not

any extent. If the native would desire to get a son, it will give him/her a

the lines of hands of the native.

several bad results. As other planets are also weak, the native usually doesn't get good education & there are hardly any hair on the native's body. If the parents of the native make celebrations at the time of his/her birth, he/she becomes poor by the age of 18 years. Such a native is usually a drunkard, keeps a bad company oris involved in bad company which affects the honour of the person & if the main door of such a native opens towards west, someone in his/her family is constantly sick and doctors go on visiting the house regularly. Lal Kitab suggests some *upayas* to arrest some of these bad effects created by Saturn. The native is advised to put some *surma* (eye-ointment) in his/her eyes regularly and put a *tilk* of *dhak* milk on the forehead, offer *gur* to monkeys, give an*angeethie* (a stove to burn char-coal) and *tawa* (an iron round plate) to *sadhus*.

Saturn in the Second House

second house in a *jatak'skundali.*

पंव नंगे मन्दिर जो तू भूल कहता।
जहर बाकी कोई, बला का न रहता।

When Saturn rises in the second house in a native's chart, it provides

The native regularly prays and believes in God, is intelligent, keeps his/her routine and helps others. He/she may look not so bright but in facthe/she is very intelligent in calculations and mathematics. The native believes in performing dharma, loves to do justice with others and is usually happy in life. He/she has a lot of parental property, does not like to trouble others and respects his/her guru. Such a native always keeps the company of his conscience and never tries to do anything wrong in life. The lines in the

However, if Saturn is not auspicious in a native *kundali,* it provides many bad results. If *jatak's*

native is very weak in disposition, meek in thoughts and easily accepts his/

like a car, or any machinery that he buys or owns, becomes un-operative or go bad. The house of the in-laws also starts getting losses. The native starts involving in gambling, becomes suspicious in nature and by the time he/she reaches the age of 28 to 40 he/she starts getting sick. Lal Kitab suggests some *upayas* to improve such bad effects of Saturn. The native should regularly visit a temple bare footed for 40 days & pray to improve the bad effect of planets, especially of Saturn. The native should offer milk to snakes so

pepper, grams and sandal wood in a temple to the needy.

Saturn in the Third House

third house in a *jatak'skundali.*

मिले राजा दो शेर बकरी कहेंगे।
मगर मर्द माया जुदा ही रहेंगे।

When Saturn rises in the third house in a native's *kundali*, he/she may

the native is not a drunkard. The native can be a famous eye surgeon and may increase his/her riches. If such a native keeps some dogs, Ketu will be against the native and make him/her disappointed in so many ways. Such a native's hands will have the signs of Venus and Mercury on the moundsin the hands.

There may be some inauspicious effectstoo if Saturn is rising in its enemy signs or is weak in degrees. If the main door of the native's house opens towards south or east, it will bring the native losses. If a stone is

his/her family & will continue visiting the family. Thefts will be committed and money will be lost. Lal Kitab suggests some *upayas* to arrest the bad

water, cover that pot & put all that into the soil of a running river so that

black/white dogs in the house and the threshold of the house should be nailed with several nails. The native is also advised to keep things that are related to Saturn & construct a dark room at the end of his/her, where no daylight could reach.Some of such *upayas*/ways could certainly lessen the bad effects of Saturn if placed inauspiciously in a *jatak's kundali.*

Saturn in the Fourth House

the fourth house in a *jatak's kundali.* These characteristics indirectly

शुश्क जहर से मरने वाला मरेगा।
घुली वह जब पानी न कोई बचेगा।

gets parents' as well as his wife's sincere love. Besides either native father, uncle or grandfather—any one them may be a doctor. The native too may be a doctor to earn his/her livelihood. The lines of native's hands will also

However, there may be some inauspicious effects too in case Saturn

make him totally poor. Black creatures will be regularly coming out in his house, his/her will also remain unhappy. Besides, native mother's relations will also suffer in many ways. Lal Kitab suggests some *upaya* to lessen Saturn's ill-effects.It suggests to offer milk to a snake, offer milk & rice to a crow of a buffalo and such things should also be thrown into a well. The native is also advised to give oil, black pulse and black clothes to the poor and needy.

Saturn in the Fifth House

jatak's kundali.

चले माया धन,जान बचता रहेगा।
मरे बेटे पोते तो फिर कया करेगा ।

kundali, the native builds his/her career by one's own efforts and takes care of his/her own things sincerely. Such a native gets due honour in the society but he/she may have less number of children but the native will be able to make a house when he/she will reach the of 48 years. Only one male child will

in the native's hands.

There may be some inauspicious effects too in case Saturn is rising inauspicious in the native's hands. The native may destroy the family job or business & if there are plenty of hair on the entire body of the native, then the native becomes a thief, a deceit and possess bad luck. If all these signs are there, someone in the family may die or get losses. The native will be a good writer but will be poor. Lal Kitab suggests some *upayas* to

The native is advised to keep three dogs in the house, and establish things that are related to Saturn in the house. In the night when extinguishing the stove on which food has been cooked, should be extinguished with milky water. The native should also give some almonds in a temple to the needy and poor. The native is also advised to keep rice, silver, natural water, a horse and a bird in the house & also put some black *surma* (powder used as a medicine for eyes) in the running water.

Saturn in the Sixth House

the sixth house in a *jatak's kundali.*

बुरा लड़का चाहे,पैसा खोटा न अच्छे।
मगर काम फिर भी वह अक्सर ही आते।

When Saturn rises in the sixth house, native's own younger brother becomes his/her enemy. Neither the eldest son's behavior is good towards the native, though he is the one who helps him whenever needed. If the

The native may be a famous player & build a house when he will be 36 or 39 years in age. Native's hand lines also betray all such things.

There may be some inauspicious effect of Saturn if rising in the sixth house in an enemy sign or is weak in degrees. Things like leather shoes, boots & material made with iron or steel if used by the children in the family,

he will be ruined as all that involves him in quarrels. The native's mother will suffer and his maternal uncle's eyes may be bad. Lal Kitab offers some suggestions to stop such bad effects of Saturn. The native should put almond & coconut oil into the running water & keep black dogs as pets. The native should offer milk to snakes, put a pot full of mustard oil in the running water

should start his new business when it is *krishnapakcha* or when the Moon rises very late in the sky. The native should also provide shoes in a temple to a bagger or a *brahman* who has no shoes.

Saturn in the Seventh House

seventh house in a *jatak's kundali.*

उलट रंगी बोतल जो नाजनीन थी।
कफन खेंचने को वह तेरा खड़ी थी।

When Saturn rises in the seventh house in a *kundali*, it makes a native dogged in nature, and he/she believes in not listening but only after seeing or observing things. Often people get separated from him/her. Such a native is clever and lives longer. The native believes in *tantra &mantra* as

The native gets several already built houses. He may be poor at the time of his birth but by the time he reaches 36 years of age, he will become rich. His children will be well established and strong. All such things are also

There may be certain inauspicious effects too when Saturn rises as a

affairs, it will harm his children & he will lose every thing including his house. In case the native uses eggs, meat or starts drinking, he may go

head will be cut off. When a grandson will be born to him, he will lose all his property and money. Lal Kitab suggests some *upaya* to arrest such negative effects of Saturn. It says that the native should keep a pot full of

with sugar and put it at a remote place. He should serve a black cow & use white *surma* in his eyes.

Saturn in the Eighth House

eighth house in a *jatak's Kundali.*

हुक्म मौत मालिक न फरियाद कोई।
सिर्फ दादापन न दिलदार कोई।

When Saturn rises in the eighth house in a native's chart it makes a native aking at times but may also makes him a pauper. Such a state of indecisiveness which continues for a long time. Native's luck rises after

happily. The sign of Rahu in his hand will also display such things.

When Saturn rises as an inauspicious planet in the eighth house, the native's enemies troubles him and he losses all his ill-earned money eight times more than what he had earned as well as losses his respect. Rahu acts against him and *Mangal* as well gives bad effect. All his gold is lost and if he gets the roof of his house replaced. It also harms him a lot. Lal KItab suggests some *upaya* to lessen the bad effects of Saturn on the native. The native should put 8 bad coins regularly for 40 days into a river & put coconuts too into the running water. He should not earn money by fraud otherwise he will lose all. The native should avoid marrying until 21 years of age & keep a small square piece of silver with him. When the native takes showers he should use some milk in water and sit on a wooden piece when taking bath. He should put into the running water 800 grams of black pulse after mixing mustard oil to it & also put 800 grams of milk in running water. He should put milk in running water on Mondays and black *dal* on Saturdays or Wednesdays. The native should also wear silver on his body. .

Saturn in the Ninth House

ninth house in a *jatak's Kundali.*

धर्म तेरा ढोलक या बच्चों का जाती।
बचेगी कहां तक जो बजाता हो हाथी।

If Saturn rises in the ninth house, it makes a naïve kind hearted. Such a natives serves *sadhus* and saints. It may also happen that the native may pose to treat people who have unique diseases. Therefore, such a native indulges in serving others though he wants to get money through wrong means and desires to get a good name in public. All that usually puts him

so Goddess Laxhimi helps him to get riches.

One can see a well placed Rahu in *jatak's* hands to justify some of the above things.

The placement of inauspicious Saturn in the tenth house &Rahu placed in the ninth house is harmful. It is also harmful to the members of the family as well as in-laws. It leads to constant quarrels and unhappiness. It also disturbs relationship between the native's son and wife. Things like wood, bamboo etc. if placed on the roof of the house are also harmful to the native. The native is advised to make *upaya* for Jupiter& also for Rahu & Ketu to get happiness for the members of family & keep a black dog in the house.

Saturn in the Tenth House

tenth house in a *jatak's Kundali.*

करे दोस्ती जब हाथी या राजा।
अच्छा ही होगा रखना बड़ा दरवाजा।

When Saturn rises in the tenth house, it makes a native rich & such a

Rahu is also good it also provides good results. Rahu if placed in the tenth house (in Saturn's sign) is usually good to the native. These things will

The native is advised to make some *upayas* for the inauspicious Saturn rising in the tenth house. When Saturn rises as a weak planet in a native's chart, everything made from iron becomes harmful to the native. So they need to be removed from the house. The native should not keep his/her

native should make some *upaya* for Jupiter, serve his/her uncle and always respect his/her others to get respect from them. It will bring his/her lot of progress in life. The native should not eat eggs, meat and should avoiding drinking. He should also put black pulse into running water for 43 days. .

Saturn in the Eleventh House

eleventh house in a *jatak'sKundali.*

बढ़े नाम बदनाम जब सीनाजोरी ।
क्सम खाके बेचेंगे सब माल चोरी।

When Saturn is placed in the eleventh house it is inauspicious for father. The native becomes rich by his own earnings.It is useful and

be supported by the sign of Rahu at the end of life line.

When Saturn is placed inauspicious in the native's chart, it may bring so

if father has lot of wealth. It may lead to theft in the house, someone may

may also die earlier. Lal Kitab suggests some *upayas* to arrest the bad effects of Saturn rising in the eleventh house. The native should bear gold & should pour out some wine or oil for 40 days on the ground just when the Sun rises. Whenever the native goes out of his house, a pitcher full of water should be kept in the house. He should avoid indulging with other women except his wife and should not drink. He must not deceive others. The native is advised to make some *upaya* for Jupiter, Rahu & Ketu as *Mangal*. .

Saturn in the Twelfth House

twelfth house in a *jatak'sKundali.*

रहा भूखा दिन भर, कमाई जो ढोता।
खजाने भरे क्या न जब रात सोता।

When Saturn is placed in the twelfth house in a native's chart, he

his honour and never incurs any loans. He gets honour from his in-laws. Enemies cannot harm him. He is dauntless and does his duty well. Such a native lives majestically and gets plenty of honour from people. But he gets more number of daughters than sons. The lines of his hands will also display such things.

However, there are some inauspicious effects too when Saturn is placed

telling lies, keeps the company of different women, naughty, and talk ill of others which causes destruction. His wife dies earlier & he gets eye problems. As Saturn & Sun are enemies and are usually placed as enemies

losses. Lal Kitab suggests some *upayas* to check such bad effects created by an inauspicious Saturn. The native should always eat in his kitchen and sit on a seat. He should make some *upaya* fro Rahu &*Mangal*. In the dark room of the house he should put 12 almonds in a tin container or in a black cloth & should not drink and eat meat and should stop telling lies.

The Planet Rahu

planet Rahu.

मुबारक यही तू जो आंसू बहाता।
हुई मौत बीवी, चाहे शत्रु की माता।

Thinking about the world and making castles in the air, day-dreaming and always expecting some thing new to happen in life, are some of the

if the native has everything, he/she believes to have more, so nothing is there with him/her. It is the specialty of Rahu to provide such a disposition to a native. Rahu is such a planet which protects a native against enemies & brings disaster to them.His face possesses a big chin, his complexion is black and he possesses one eye or is one-eyed, but if Rahu is exalted,the native's complexion is not black. A *jatak*
children, doesn't walk straight, like an elephant in complexion, possesses

big eyes like elephant, naughty and clever in behavior, can destroy its enemies, loves to lead an easy life and eats too much. Now we will present

kundali.

Rahu in the First House

jatak'sKundali.

हुआ लेख अंधेर, बादल जो घेरा।
कोई पौंछें आंसू, पसीना न तेरा।

kundali, the native will behave like a king and walk like an elephant. The native will be rich but as this house belongs to the Sun, Rahu will not let the native prosper until 42 years of age. Most of his neighbours become poor and loose everything they possess. Such a native is unable to do anything permanently. Every time he starts a new business and close it after some, then starts another one. The sign of Rahu on the mound of Sun in the *jatak's* hand will display all about the native.

kundali will

different kinds of problems which keeps him/her disturbed. As Rahu is not auspicious, it will destroy the native's money & his relatives will face

as constant quarrels will continue there. He may spend money without any serious need. Lal Kitab suggests some *upaya* to lessen the bad effect

needy and poor *gur*, wheat and copper & also put in running water these three things after keeping them in a small copper box. The native should wear black & blue coloured clothes & make *upaya* for the Moon. One kilogram corn after washing it in four kilograms milk should be put into running water.

Rahu in the Second House

second house in a *jatak'sKundali.*

उम्र गुजरी मन्दिर, मुफ्त माल खाते।
मिले दिल कहां, फिर जो खैरात बांटे।

When Rahu rises in the second house, it surrounds a *jatak* with the planets that get him/her into debt. Money and family both get lessened. Such a native often dies when hit by a weapon. The native suffers from liber problems.He has a long life, is extremely very clever and behaves like clouds of rainy season—sometime rich & happy & at the other moment unhappy and poor. His family life will be quite satisfactory.Certain signs on the hands of the native, will display all such characteristics of the native.

Inauspicious Rahumay involve the native in committing theft and stealing. People don't trust the native. Such a *jatak* may plan to commit stealing even when he is sitting in a temple. He never hesitates for asking

house. The native collect some soil under the feet of an elephant & put it into a well. A silver or gold small ball should be kept with the native all the time. After marriage the native should never accept electrical material from his in-laws place. He should serve his mother and if his son has been suffering, he should put into running water corn equivalent to his weight.

Rahu in the Third House

third house in a *jatak'skundali.*

अकलमन्द कभी तेरा शत्रु बनेगा।
बुरा यार अहमक से कमतर करेगा।

When Rahu is placed in the third house, a native clearly knows about the future. His dreams come out true & he is competent enough to kill his enemies without any sword. The native has a long life. He will be rich & when he will die, he will leave lots of money and property for his children. Such a native, if involved in coal business, will be greatly successful. In the hands of such a native a sign of Rahu will be prominent on the mound of *Mangal*.

However, there may be some inauspicious effects too in case Rahu is not favourable in the third house of a native chart. Native's own relatives, brothers etc. will not repay him after taking loans from him. Thus his riches will be destroyed. When he will reach the age of 34 years, either his sister or daughter will become widow. Lal Kitab suggests some *upaya* to lessen the bad effects of Rahu when ill-placed in the third house. The native should keep ivory toys in his house but when Sun and Mercury rise in the third house, such material should not be kept in the house.

Rahu in the Fourth House

fourth house in a *jatak'sKundali.*

भला कहते स्नान गंगा जो करता।
वही तेरा स्वयं अपने घर का ही बनता।

When Rahu rises in the fourth house, the native is usually rich & religious. He will love to see dreams during day time about his success & get a good vehicle to transport him. After his marriage he will get money from his in-laws. He will earn money from the government and provide help to his father. If such a native takes regular bath with the water of the Ganga, he will always stay happy and successful. It will give him a son and his parents will lead a happy life. If all these things are true there will be a sign of Rahu at the mound of the Moon in *jatak's* hands.

However, there may be some inauspicious effects too if Rahu is not

affected adversely. But after 22 years of his age when the Moon's effect will be lessened, he will get riches. Lal Kitab suggests some *upayas* to lessen the ill-effect of Rahu. The native should wear silver on his body, & 400 grams *dhania*should be put in running water for seven days on Wednesdays by him. He should also put 400 grams of almonds in running water for seven Saturdays.

Rahu in the Fifth House

jatak'sKundali.

खुशी दिन त्यौहार का फिर जो बनता ।
निशानी लावल्दी की पैदा वह करता।

saint and possess a lot of godly knowledge. In case Saturn rises in its

birth to one child, she will not be well physically for 12 years. The native's father may die when he is 42 years. Such a native may have four sons but whether they will be intelligent or not cannot be predicted. The native may not possess much property or money. The sign of Rahu on the Sun line in the hands of the native also suggest these things.

However, there may be some inauspicious effects also in case Rahu

die in its mother's bomb so the native will not be able to see it. His father-in-law will also die because of weak planets in the *kundali*. Rahu may also affect adversely the grand children in some way. Lal Kitab suggests some *upaya*

his house & remarry his wife to remove the bad effect of Rahu. He may keep a silver elephant (toy) in his house & stay away with the company of

mule under wife's pillow in the night & give them to someone in a temple.

Rahu in the Sixth House

sixth house in a *jatak'sKundali.*

गिरे तुझसे जब खनू भाई का कतरा।
नस्ल बंद तेरी का बढ़ता खतरा।

When Rahu rises in the sixth house in a jatak's kundali, it makes the *jatak* very brave, strong to sustain problems, as well intelligent. Such a native is usually very rich and possess good luck. It also takes the native abroad in case Rahu is sitting all alone in the sixth house, but sometimes he may keep bad company of friends. The lines of native's hands will also suggest all that.

However, there may be some ill-effects too when Rahu is placed as an inauspicious planet in the sixth house in a *kundali*. It may trouble brothers, friends & the native also in many ways. He may lose his wealth all of a sudden. His elder brothers and sisters if any, may be ruined of their own. It will also affect the native's children adversely. When planets in the twelfth house are weak, the native is destroyed in many ways. Lal Kitab suggests some *upaya* to arrest the bad effect of Rahu rising in the sixth house. The native is advised to keep a gray dog in his house & keep small black glass balls with him & worship the goddess *Sarswati* for six days.

Rahu in the Seventh House

seventh house in a *jatak'sKundali.*

फर्क बीवी बैठी या हो नजर आता।
बढ़ेगी दिमागी ख्याली खुशी का ।

When Rahu rises in the seventh house in a *jatak's kundali*, it makes him rich and provides a job in a government department. He may be employed by the intelligent department of government and hold a good post and gets good salary. But he may not get happiness from his wife. Most his friends

dealing with silver ornaments. If Mercury and Venus rise in 2 & 11 houses respectively, they support the native very much and he gets lots of riches and respect in the society. On the mounds of Venus or Mercury, the sign of Rahu can be seen in the hands of such a native.

There may be some ill-effects of Rahu's placement in the seventh house. If it is woman's chart, and if she is married at the age of 21, either she may die early or may be divorced or her husband may die soon after the marriage. Even in normal circumstances both, man and woman, will go on quarrelling or one of them will run away from home. Her man will keep suspicion unnecessarily against her & native's sister, aunt or son may be lost or ruined. The native will have a second son only at the age of 42 years.

Lal Kitab suggests some *upaya* to lessen the bad effect of Rahu is placed in the seventh house in a native's chart. At the time of *jatak's* marriage, his father-in-law should give him silver which he gives back to his wife who keeps it with her carefully throughout her life. It may help both to live happily in life. In order to help wife against health problems the native should give her a small silver brick which she will keep with her. The native should put coconuts or almonds into the running water on Saturdays & keep some Ganga water in a small bottle and keep it in his house after putting a small piece of silver into it.

Rahu in the Eighth House

eighth house in a *jatak'skundali.*

हुक्म मौत मालिक न फरियाद जोई।
सिर्फ दादापन न दिलदार कोई।

When Rahu is placed in the eighth house in a native's chart, it makes the native very brave and he goes on changing jobs frequently. Even if he possesses all, but in reality has nothing with him. In case Saturn rises in the sixth house in the native's *kundlai*, it will help his luck to boost up. It will alsohelp his riches to go further. But native's life experiences many changein many ways. Sometimes he goes high in status and at times goes down in riches and status. The sign of Rahu on the mound of *Mangal* in the *jatak's* hand will also support all that.

However there may be some inauspicious effects also if Rahu is not well placed in the eighth house in a native's chart. Whatever he has earned by dishonest means will be lost in greater quantity by him. Though such a *jatak* may belong to a good family, he will do wrong things and act like

due to a sudden bad happening. But if such a native possesses one eye or has no children and his complexion is like an elephant, the native will not suffer in any way. If the native marries at the age of 21 years and takes a job in a government forest department or electricity department or if he is not honest in his job, he may die soon. In case Rahu is in the 8th house and Saturn in 6th house, the native may die any time in life and his running business will suffer adversely.

Lal Kitab suggests some *upaay* to arrest the bad effects of Rahu placed in the eighth house. The native should keep a squire piece of silver in his pocket & put some copper coins or coal into running water. If there is any

almonds in a temple & at his birth day he may put some almonds into running water. The native is also advised to offer for 43 days bad coins in a temple & if possible these coins should be put into running water for 8 Wednesdays. He may also put such coins after breaking them into pieces into running water for 8 Wednesdays or Saturdays. .

Rahu in the Ninth House

ninth house in a *jatak'sKundali.*

धर्म तेरा ढोलक या बच्चों को जाती।
बचेगी कहां तक जो हाथी से बजती।

When Rahu is placed in the ninth house in a native's chart, it may make him a doctor who treats mentally sick people. He will achieve some thing in life by hard work and devotion only but he may also hurt his honour and respect by some sort of ill-deeds. Such a native will hardly believe in good acts or religion. Jobs related to Saturn will help the native & if the native involves himself in ENT related material business, it will in the native's hands.

However, there may be some inauspicious effectsof Rahu if placed

may have bad health. There may be frequently abortions to his wife, native father, grand father and in-laws will be destroyed & his children and money will be in problems. Lal Kitab has a few suggestions to improve such ill-effects of Rahu in the ninth house. It says that under the threshold of the main gate of the house from left to right a silver thin plate should be put & dogs should be kept in the house. Dogs will help the children to live safely. The native should keep a long tail of hair (*choti*) on his head & keep good relationship with his in-laws, put a *tilak* of *kesher*& wear gold.

Rahu in the Tenth House

tenth house in a *jatak'skundali.*

करे दोस्ती जब तू हाथी या राजा।

बड़ा रखना दरवाजा अच्छा ही होगा।

When Rahu rises in the tenth house in a *jatak's kundali*, it is highly

The native gets honour at all the places he visits. Such natives are very brave, rich and good businessmen if involve in the business dealing with

of Saturn, there may be a sign of Rahu on the hands of the native.

However, there may be some inauspicious effects of Rahu when placed

Rahu it will be very harmful and act like a snake whose all wishes are granted. If *Mangal* is not auspicious in the *kundlai*, Rahu becomes more

only Moon rises in the fourth house of the chart, it spoils native's eyes & he gets headaches regularly. He may also lose his property and money on account of keeping company of a person whose complexion is black. Lal Kitab suggests some *upaya* to arrest such bad effects of Rahu. The native should always try to keep his head covered & wear a turban of any colour other than black or blue colours. He should make some *upaya* to improve bad effects of *Mangal*. He should put *mashoor dal* in running water & also put brown sugar in running water.

Rahu in the Eleventh House

eleventh house in a *jatak'skundali.*

बढ़े नाम बदनाम जब सीना जोरी।
कसम खाके बेचेंगे सब माल चोरी।

When Rahu rises in the eleventh house in a native's chart, the native gets money from lower kind of people and is unable to see his father or grandfather living. The native keeps the company of cheat or bad people and after his birth father's income reduces to half. But such a native is good to get money until he is 16 years old. In case Saturn rises in the 3rd of 5th houses in his *kundali*, the native is a great sadhu, a sane person. Such a native never likes to take any help from his parents, instead become rich by his own income.There is a sign of Rahu on the mound of Saturn in his hands.

However, there are some inauspicious effects too when Rahu rises *kundali.*After 21 days, or 11th or 21st years of native's birth his father or grandfather will die as someone will shoot him or one of them will die because certain accident will happen. If they are survived, they lose their all the money. The native will be involved in useless quarrels & his money will be lost. Someone may deceive him and someone in the family will remain sick for long. Both,

brother will die as someone will cut his throat, and if *Mangal*/Mars rises in the second house, he will have untalented or useless children. Lal Kitab has some *upaya* for the native to lessen the bad effects of Rahu if rising *kundali*. The native should wear gold & put a *tilak* of *keshar* on his forehead. He should drink water in a silver pot & on Thursdays he should give yellow dal after putting it in a yellow piece of cloth to the poor and needy. He should not eat onions that day and give money to the sweeper as alms on that day.

Rahu in the Twelfth House

twelfth house in a *jatak'skundali.*

रहा भूखा दिन भर कमाई जो ढोता।
खाजाने भरें क्या न जब रात सोता ।

When Rahu rises in the twelfth house in a native chart, it makes the native very wise &carefree. His in-laws will be very rich and he will spend his money on noble deeds. He will take care of his sister or daughter to his best and as Saturn will be in its exalted sign in the chart, he will get every kind of happiness in life. But such a native will also like to day-dreaming.

However, there may be some inauspicious effects too if Rahu rises in the twelfth house in a native's *kundali.* The native may be involved in useless activities and waste his time uselessly. Some people will accuse him for no reasons. His enemies will destroy him& thefts will be committed in his house. Someone will fall sick in the family & if he will try certain yogic exercises, he will be crippled. His eyes may be hurt or go bad if he try to concentrate through them. All his dreams of life will be foiled and disturbed. Lal Kitab suggests some *upaya*to lessen the bad effects of Rahu

offer *muli* to an elephant & coal should be put in running water. The native should keep *saonf&moong* under his pillow at the time of going to bed & eat his dinner and lunch in his kitchen. He should give to sister or daughter some part of his income to help them.

The Planet Ketu

planet Ketu.

नजर पांव तेरे जो उखड़े पड़ेंगे।
सभी जेर रहते ही सिर पर चढ़ेंगे।

Ketu makes a man good and honest, it makes him travel long and provides good results in life. When Ketu &*Budha* rise in a house it may

Mangal are not together, Ketu gives good results. Such anative is honoured until 48 years and people like to take his advice in most of the matters. Yellow Jupiter, red *Mangal* and greenish *Budha* when are united in a *kundali,* they provide good results. In such *kunadli* Ketu provides good results. Just one child is always good for the native and that child helps the family a lot until the child lives. If there is any sign of Ketu on the mound of Jupiter in anative's hand all such things

a dishonest man and makes him moneyless though it may not give him death. If *Budha* *kundali*, Ketu's ill-effects get lessened. Now

house in a *kundlai.*

Ketu in the First House

jatak'sKundali.

रिजक तेरा जब तुझको है आज मिलता।
लंगोटा फिक्र कल का, तू क्यों ढीला करता ।

produces several children & without caring for today, he cares for the future. Such a native is very sensuous and desires to possess more and more wealth. He loves his father and takes care of him. If Jupiter has a bad *Mangal* in a chart, the native just uselessly travels in different directions to get something. Such a *jatak's* hands have some signs of Ketu on the mound of the Sun.

house in a native's chart. It gives useless worries to the native & if it is weak it affects native's father adversely. At the time of native birth, problem are created in his house & also in his neighbour's house. Lal Ktab suggests some *upaya* to lessen the bad effects of Ketu when rising in the *gur* to monkeys& make *upayas* for *Budha*. If children are suffering on some account, the native is advised to give red & black blankets in a temple as alms, wear silver in the both the thumbs of his feet & if native's health is not well, he should put a *tilak* of on his forehead.

However, the native has to be very careful to give alms when the Sun rises in the 6th or 7th house in the native's *kundali*. Then he must not give *gur*, wheat or copper in alms at the time of evening or at daybreak. It may disturb the life of the native to a great extent.

Ketu in the Second House

second house in a *jatak'skundali.*

हुई पैदा औलाद हर घर जो तेरी।
बुढ़ापे में तुझे कौन देगा दिलेरी।

When Ketu rises in the second house in a native's chart, it provides the native change in life and gives new directions to think and act. It makes the native travel to different directions and involves in different sorts of activities. The *jatak* is involved in a big business & deals in lacks of rupees. He gets honour from government, but at times he simply acts as a mediator years he earns a lot of money and leads a happy life. One can observe a sign of Ketu on the mound of Jupiter in the native's hands.

There may be some inauspicious effects also when Ketu rises in the second house. It will involve the native in romance and he will keep busy for long with different sorts of women and waste his time and money. Such a *jatak*

long. Lal Kitab suggests some *upaya* to lessen the bad effects of Ketu. It advises the native to put a *tilak* of *kesher* on his forehead and he needs to give some corn as alms in a temple to the needy.

Ketu in the Third House

third house in a *jatak'sKundali.*

बुझे प्यास न खून भाई का करते।
गले बाजू बांधेगें तलवार कटते।

When Ketu rises in the third house in the *kundali* of a native, it makes the native very sincere and devoted as well as a kind hearted person. He

good and happy homely life. After 24 years when he gets a son, his luck rises & he lives very long as is also shown by the lines of his hands.

There may be some sort of ill-effect also in case Ketu rises inauspicious in the third house. Such a native is mostly unhappy on account of his brothers and losses his property, wealth and all on account of different reasons. He wastes his money in court matters and spends a lot on his *jatak* has three children or three sisters & brothers & there are also three doors & three windows in his house. If

Lal Kitab suggests some *upaya* to lessen such bad effects of Ketu rising in the third house of a native's chart. It says that the native should make some *upaya* for Jupiter especially when someone is sick in the family.Things related to Jupiter should be put in the river, apply a *tilak* of *kesar* on his forehead, wear gold in his neck & if there is a gate in the house that faces south, it needs to be nailed by copper nails.

Ketu in the Fourth House

fourth house in a *jatak'sKundali.*

सब्र अपने का फल चाहे मीठा मिलेगा।
मगर बोझ देरी का सहना पड़ेगा।

When Ketu rises in the fourth house in a *jatak's kundali*, he gets a son

money. If such a native has more number of daughters, he remains very

God. There may be a sign of Ketu on the mound of the Moon in the hands of the native.

When Ketu is not auspicious in the fourth house in a native's chart, it is harmful for mother and children. It tempts the native with so many new ideas and makes him work hard to get lot of money by acting on those new ideas. Native's sons get more problems & he also suffers occasionally with different sorts of diseases.Lal Kitab suggests some *upaya* to help the native to earn more money. It says that to get more riches the native is advised to do some *upaya* for Jupiter, Rahu and Moon. He should put things related to Jupiter in the running water which will help to remove the problems related to his children. He should also keep a dog & wear silver to get peace of mind.

Ketu in the Fifth House

jatak'skundali.

हुए थे नेक जब जवानी पर चढ़ते।
मिले पोते इतने न थे जितने लड़के।

jatak's kundali, he has to take someone's help to earn his livelihood at the age of 24 years. But as Jupiter

He also gets three sons & three daughters & enjoys his married life fully. However, his wife has a hot temperament but she serves her husband well. And even if there are two women in the house, they don't usually quarrel with each other. The lines in the hands of the native suggest some of these things clearly.

However, there may be some inauspicious effects also when Ketu

a native starts getting older quickly and his many children may die after birth. He is hardly able to see his grandsons in his old age & as children die one after the other his house looks empty after sometime. Lal Kitab suggest some *upaya* to reduce the bad effects of Ketu. The native should give things related to the Moon &*Mangal* to the needy, give milk and sugar to the poor, and make some *upaya* for Jupiter as well. Al such *upayas* may be helpful to the native to lead a happy life.

Ketu in the Sixth House

sixth house in a *jatak'skundali.*

हजम घी अगर कुत्ता दुनिया में करता।
छुपे फिरता हर घर में बुजदिल न डरता।

When Ketu rises in the sixth house in a *jatak's kundali*, such a native has more number of sons as well as he has plenty of wealth. He takes care of his sister and never quarrels with her. His son is also very brave and puts an end to his enemies. In case Ketu & Jupiter both rise as weak planets

native's hands also display these thing and a clear sign of Ketu is visible at the palm of the native.

However, there are some inauspicious effects also when Ketu rises as *kundali* in the sixth house. It brings losses relating

travel which leads to unnecessary expenses. Such a native is like a stone

affect adversely native's maternal uncle's family. Lal Kitab suggests some *upaya*
house in a *kundali*. The native needs to wear a gold ring in his left hand

a dog in his house & also keep a male rabbit and take care of his grandsons.

Ketu in the Seventh House

seventh house in a *jatak'skundali.*

सब कुछ के होते जो रोता रहेगा।
तो यह नस्ल तेरी ही जाहिर करेगा।

When Ketu is in the seventh house in a native's chart, the native may get lots of money at the age of 24 years. His social prestige increases as well as his wealth. The eldest son of the native possesses hard temperament

& destroys his enemies.He is also sincere and takes care of his father. As Venus and Saturn are not weak in the *kundal*, the native is always gets new jobs if he likes, but if any enemy planet rise with them or if *Mangal* rises

peaceful sleep as combinations of planets are such in his *kundali* that they don't let him have total happiness in life. There may be a sign of Ketu at the mound of Venus in the palm of the native.

There are some inauspicious effects too in case Ketu is not auspicious in the seventh house in the *kundali*. The native gest losses after losses more so as he makes false promises to the people. Such a native gets different kinds of diseases & destroys his own family by his own bad acts. By his age of 34 years his enemies always keep him surrounded. Lal Kitab suggests that such a native should make *upayas* to restore good effects of Jupiter.

Ketu in the Eighth House

eighth house in a *jatak'skundali.*

मरे बच्चे इतने कब्र भर रही है।
गिला मर चुकों का तू क्या कर रही है।

When Ketu rises in the eighth house in a native's chart, such a native may get a son at the age of 34 years. The native lives until 70 years & any child born to him after the marriage of his sister, liveslonger. Before that hardly any son remains alive. There may be a sign of Ketu at the mound of Mangal on palm of the native indicating some of these effects.

There may be some inauspicious effects of Ketu, if rising in the eighth house of a native's chart. Most of relations suffer in many ways, his wife's health goes bad and he has to cry constantly on that account. He knows in advance about the bad happenings that may come in the future. That keeps him unhappy and disturbed. Lal Kitab suggests that the native should give a black & white blanket to the needy in a temple & certain articles relating to the inauspicious planets should be put at a desolate place by keeping them in a piece of a black & white blanket. He should put a *tilak* of *kesher* on his forehead and wear golden rings in the ears. He should keep his conduct in order so that his wife's health may stay well & good. The native is also advised to worship Lord Ganesha and offer bread to dogs.

Ketu in the Ninth House

ninth house in a *jatak'skundali.*

माता पिता एहसान हम पर जो करते।
आयु गुजारे सारी एवज उनका भरते ।

When Ketu rises in the ninth house in a *jatak's* chart, it makes him brave &he earns money by hard work and enthusiasm. He leads a peaceful life& supports all those who are weak and non -active in their duties or work. Such a native is usually helpful to others. Mostly he lives in foreign countries but serves his parentsas well his maternal uncle very well. When he reaches 48 years of age, his riches and wealth just doubles. There is usually a sign of Ketu on the mound of Venus on the hands of such a native.

However, there may be some inauspicious effects too in case Ketu is

he indulges in thefts& other bad acts& usually uses force to perform such

on his children as well. Lal Kitab suggests some *upayas* to make Ketu favourable when it rises in the ninth house. It will be good to keep a bitch along with small puppies in the house and the native should wear gold in his ears & put under the earth some gold at a place in the house. The native should worship Lord Ganesha also.

Ketu in the Tenth House

tenth house in a *jatak'skundali.*

उजड़े बृहस्पति मुआफी हो देता।
भरे पेट दौलत न कंगाल होता।

When Ketu rises in the tenth house, the native may not be poor though

problems are created by him only. It is also caused on account of Saturn *kundali*. On account of the

native's three children get losses but native's riches are not adversely affected and he is quite happy with that. The lines of his hand also display some of these things.

However, there may be some inauspicious effects of Ketu when placed

on the position of Saturn if it is weak in the chart. It creates bad plans in the mind of the native & as such his honour and wealth are usually at stake. Lal Kitab suggests some *upaya* to improve the effects of Ketu if it

at a remote place & keep a dog in his house only after his 48 years of age. He should also keep his conduct good.

Ketu in the Eleventh House

eleventh house in a *jatak'skundali.*

फिक्र छोड़ गुजरी का जो चली गई है।
नजर रख तू आगे की जो आ रही है।

When Ketu rises in the eleventh house in a *jatak's kundali*, the native doesn't care for things that have gone but takes care of his future plans. It happens because of Jupiter's changing its behavior. Such a native rises at the age of 48 years. In case *Budha*rises in the third house of the *kundali*, the native gest honour from the government. Such signs are displayed by the hand-lines of the native.

However, there may be some ill-effect of Ketu also in case it rises

native's mother's eyesight & age but his children get success as well

house & children badly. At times a male child is born dead to his wife. Lal Kitab suggests some *upaya* to lessen the bad effects of Ketu. The native is advised to keep a black dog in his house and eleven *mulees*, after keeping them under the pillow of his wife, need to be given to the needy in a temple for 43 days.

Ketu in the Twelfth House

twelfth house in a *jatak'sKundali.*

भरे जर कबीला चाहे बच्चों से तेरा।
एवज पर गुरू का तू जिस दम देगा।

When Ketu rises in the twelfth house in a native'*skundali*, it helps him get progress in his business regularly. If he deals with the material relating Ketu, he gets lot of success. Such a native is rich, and traditionally palm of the native.

When Ketu rises as a weak planet in a native's *kundali* in different ways. It harms native's wife & children and as a consequence, he has no children until he reaches the age of 28 years. When Venus rises in the sixth house along with Rahu, it does not give any happiness from the children & if he buys a house of a person who ahs no children, that also makes him childless. The native luck rises after twelve years of his marriage. Lal Kitab suggests that such a native should keep a black dog in his house, worship Lord Ganesha, make some *upaya*for Rahu & suck his thumb after putting it in sweet milk regularly for many days.

The Effects of the Two Planets Placed in Different Houses

The Planet Sun

Sun + Moon

Auspicious Effects

The owner of one's age Sun & the owner of wealth Moon, both keep native's company for 40 years of age. If both of these planets are well placed in a *kundali*, the native's old age is very peaceful and happy. His parental property helps him to stay cool and contented. Family happiness is provided by Saturn if well placed in the chart. Good job is provided

&have their aspects on the Moon according to their placements in 1—7, 4—10, 5—11 houses and help the native to become wealthy.

Now we will provide the results of the Sun & Moon's placement in

and will collect tax from others.

2. When rising in the second house:If the native is a male, he will get plenty of respect in the society. Even a woman will get such respect.
3. When in the third house: It will be good for a *jatak* but such a *jatak*

4. When in the fourth house: If tenth house has no planets, the native is like a jewel, has all the advantages of transport& lives like a lord.

happy.

6. When in the sixth house: If the Sun is not rising with Saturn, Rahu or Ketu, both the Moon & Sun will provide their own effect.
9. When in the ninth house: It may take the native to religious journeys; native will serve his mother well.

12. When in the twelfth house: Both Moon & Sun will give their own effect.

Inauspicious Effects

all the time, even if the native is rich, he will never feel happy. No chance of success or happiness in life to the naïve. Such a native is involved in extravagance & useless travels.

to the native.

If placed in the second house it may give losses & quarrels from women.

If placed in the fourth house, & Saturn rises in the tenth house, the native may suddenly be drowned in water. If the Sun is in the sixth house, it will give a moderate life span.

The both rise in the eleventh house, they may help the native live long

upaya to lessen the bad effects of inauspicious Sun. The native should put 800 grams of *alichi* in the running water and also give it to the needy in a temple.

Sun + Mangal

Both the planets give good results except that the Moon at times is not

Mangal provides

Mangal is exalted and rise with the Sun in any house, then the Sun will always give good result. In such *kundali*, mother's luck & money both, don't give favourable results. To lessen such bad effects, the native is advised to live in a house which is constructed on a squire piece of land. It will help the native and his elder brother as well. As the native grows in age, his income also grows.

Auspicious Effects

When Sun &*Mangal* are in the ninth house, the native gets high position.

In the tenth house both the planets help to increase wealth & riches and make the native lucky.

In the twelfth house both make the native good and clean hearted & stronger than his enemies. The years between the ages of 22 to 28, will be excellent for the native.

Rest of the planets will provide results in view of their placement.

Inauspicious Effects

When *Mangal* is not auspicious with the Sun, the native leads a tough life

and his relatives may die. It also has bad effect on the native's eyes.

may die after a lot of struggles, quarrels and problems.

In the ninth & tenth house in auspicious *Mangal* develops problems with the native's dear ones.

If it rises in other houses, its impact will be according to the house it rises in.

Sun + Mercury

If *Budha*/Mercury is weak along with the Sun, native's children suffer in many ways. The native gest progress if he has a shop to run, but his business is not very progressive until he does not reach 40 years of age. When the majour period of Venus starts, gets wealth & children. If Mercury is in its exalted sign, the Sun also gives good results.

Auspicious Effects

Sun & Mercury rising in 1,2, 7, and 10th houses give good results to a native. Both the planets are supposed to stay with each other until 39 years & give good results. But in any house if Sun rises as a weak planet, Mercury also becomes weak. At times Sun may give results as things related to Mercury are there in the native's house. A government job will be useful to the native & will have a long life but may die all of a sudden. Both native's education and writing power will bring progress and happiness to the native. Native's writings will always help his to grow and shine. When the native is young, his luck will shine, his wife's face may have some sign of hurt. The native will like to live comfortably with his own income & no problem will be created on account of Saturn's bad effect. The native will be self-made and will possess good health.

like a minister, his luck will be great & will have good relations with the government. If any problems occur, decisions will be in the favour of the native.

When both rise in the second house, native's mind and body will be great & strong.

If these planets are in the third house, Rahu cannot harm him.

If these two planets rise in the fourth house, the native's business will rise if he deals with the things relating to Jupiter.

the native, no bad effect of Mercury will be experienced by the native's & his children and ancestors.

When these planets rise in the sixth house and in native's *kundali's* second house has no planets, he will get honour by his writings & good publications in the government circles.

When these planets are in the seventh house, native's wife will be beautiful & she will belong to a rich family. Whatever the native will earn,

as his childhood will be very happy though to some extent his young age may not be so good. If the native learn astrology it will help him in many ways & Mercury & Ketu will provide good effect until he is 34 years old.

When both the planets are in the eighth house, and the second house is without planets, Mercury will give good results.

government until the native is 24 years old. He will progress until 34 years.

When these planets rise in the tenth house, Mercury, Sun & Saturn will give results according to their placement and signs they rise in. One

give results according to its placement in the *kundali*but if 1st& 2nd houses have no planets, Mercury and Sun will give good results.

Both these planets will give good results if good and religious people live in his parental house. It will also boost up his luck but if such people are not living in that house, the results will be just opposite.

If these planets rise in the twelfth house, they will give results according to the sign they rise in that house.

Inauspicious Effects

When both these planets rise inauspiciously, the effect of Venus will go waste until 25years. In native's childhood so many problems relating property will be experienced by him but decisions will be in native's

will remain greatly disturbed.

be quarrels and problems in government jobs and if Saturn is also with these two planets according to yearly calculations (*Versefal*), results will be just unfavourable to the native.

When they rise in the second house, the native will suffer on account of having no money or property.

When they rise in the third house, Rahu & Venus will give bad effects from 17 to 34 years of native's age.

die all of a sudden.

When they rise in the sixth house & if second house has become weak due to Sun's aspects, both may not give too bad effect. But native's age may be affected adversely & he may lead his life with less respect & dignity. When these two planets rise in the seventh house, native's wife may not lead a happy life & if children grow weaker in health, get less progress, native's in-laws may get losses. If some planets rise in the ninth house, they create hatred and dislike for other people in the mind of the native.

When these two planets rise inauspiciously in the eighth house, dealing with things relating Mercury will bring losses to the native. Planets in the second house will bring destruction to the native. In case Mangal is not auspicious, the native may die while quarreling with others.

When these two planets rise in the ninth house inauspiciously, and if Mercury rises as a weak planet, the native will have some kind of problems in life & will have no children until he reaches 34 years.

When Sun and Mercury inauspiciously in the tenth house, and when Saturn is weak, the native will get defamed on account of certain reasons & will not be able to get success in any of his errands.

When these two planets rise in the eleventh house, his parental house will bring bad results if unethical people live there.

When these two planets rise in the twelfth house, things related to Mercury will bring losses as the native will involve in extravagancy & he may be sick on account of some kind of mental disease. Mercury rising in the sixth house will destroy the native.

Lal Kitab suggests some *upaya* to lessen the bad effects of these two planets. The native is advised to put some *gur* in a glass pot and keep that pot at a cremation place. He should do some *upaya* for the Sun & Mangal but if a daughter is born to him on a Tuesday or a Saturday, he need not to do any *upaya.*

Sun + Venus

The native should not marry at the age of 22or 25 as it will prove

Native's father may not live long and he will have children quite late in life though the Sun rises in any house. Therefore, the native is advised to pacify the enemy planets through Mercury. Both, the Sun & Venus will

be inauspicious until then.

inauspicious & the native will not have a smooth married life. The native may be sent even to the jail.

Auspicious Effects

When these planets rise in the seventh house, he may go to a fruitful pilgrimage at the age of 20 years.

When these two planets rise in the ninth house, at times the native may enjoy riches in life.

When these two rise in the tenth house, the male planets (like Mars, Sun, Jupiter) sitting in the fourth house, will help the native. When the

Inauspicious Effects

When these two planets, Sun & Venus rise in different houses in a chart, there are inauspicious effects too. They affect adversely the life of grandfather and father as well. Either the father will live separately or may die earlier. A male child will be born to the native after 47 years of age & his wife may suffer from long illness, so he may have less family happiness. As the native is in the habit of believing everything he is told to him, he will be unhappy. There may be some kind of sign on the lips of his wife.

daily bread as most of the planets are weak in the chart. Native's wife may be mentally sick or a mad one, native's friends will suffer also.

Only Mercury will be effective instead of the Sun & will give results when these planets rise in the seventh house. The native may have constant quarrels with his wife, his health may be weak & luck bad.

When these planets rise in the ninth house, poor, sick and inactive kind of women will live in the native's house.

When both these planets are in the tenth house, on account of Saturn or ill-effect of other planets the native may not get much respect in the king's court & even if he is supposed to be a king, he will not be the king.

Lal Kitab suggests some *upaya* to lessen the bad effects of these planets. The native should give a cow with its calf in *dan*& after putting red *gajani* in a copper pot he suould put the pot into running water. He should give some milk to snakes, keep dogs and make *upaya* for the Moon.

Sun + Saturn

The Sun represents father, debilitated Rahu is the son of Saturn&*Mangal* is not auspicious, but at times on account of Mercury (representing sister

according to the Sun. When *Mangal* and Mercury are debilitated, they may create quarrels but if Mercury is exalted all is good. However, with Venus

inauspicious results. When the Sun &Saturn are against each other, Venus (representing woman) is less effective and woman's luck gets affected

combinations.

Auspicious Effects

results. The native will possess great knowledge about the world & if

business will be successful.

When these planets rise in the sixth house, the native will have a good married life but he will often be out of his home on account of business or work.

When both these planets rise in the ninth house, the native will be rich

When they rise in the twelfth house, both the planets will give good results. But in all the other houses they both provide results according to their signs they rise.

Inauspicious Effects

When Saturn and Sun rise together in a house, native usually loose most of his property and has no peace of mind. When he is young he is mostly sick,his health & wealth is gradually lost and his friends are not sincere. Though husband and wife live together, but mostly the woman suffers mostly when man wants her close company during the day time.

becomes weak on account of both of them constantly working against

business dealing with the things relating the Sun, he will get lot of success but if he deals with the things relating Saturn, he gets losses.

from the beginning until native's nine years creates problems of various kinds to the native & the native will suffer in many ways.

When these two planets rise in the sixth house, on account of Saturn Ketu will also give bad results and the native's children may suffer on that account. The native will lose money, Mercury & Moon will also give bad results but when native's children will reach 18 years of age, his riches will come back to him.

When these two planets rise in the seventh house, and if Mercury rises

sent to prison also.

When they rise in the eighth house, and if Rahu is in the eleventh, and Jupiter is in the twelfth,

and suffer in life. In case the native construct a house and deals in the mustard business, his children may die and he may lose all in business.

When these two planets rise in the ninth house and if *Mangal* is inauspicious & Mercury rises in the third house, then both the planets, the Sun & Saturn, will bring disaster to the native & provide bad results to the native.

When these planets rise in the tenth house, the native will be defamed uselessly and may also be sent to jail.

When they rise in the eleventh house, they will give effect according to the sign in which they rise.

Lal Kitab suggests some *upaya* for amending the bad effects of these two planets when rise jointly in a house. The native should put things like coconut & almonds into the running water when there is a Sun eclipse & if it is a woman native, she should wear copper, gold and *moonga* (red-coloured light weight stone) in her hair, the native should keep black dogs

glass & pearls at a remote place in a forest. The native is advised to put a heavy statue of Bherav in one of the walls of the house & make a hole in a walls so that fresh air may come into the house. It will help native's children live happy and live long.

Sun + Ketu

keeping its face towards the Sun near the native's house, it is harmful to the native. The native gets losses in journeys, & when Venus and Ketu are not auspicious, the native's wealth is lost & he is constantly on tours. When Venus is inauspicious, the Sun may rise in any of the houses, it gives

in everything told to him and it becomes the cause of his destruction.

Inauspicious Effects

As the Sun may not provide good results,the native may get losses in journeys & if he takes advice from others, it will give losses to him. His own bad habits may bring him disaster & native's own son will bring him money related losses & his wife will be quite hefty & will talk roughly to others & it is also possible that the native may not live long to see his grand-children.

When these two planets, Sun & Ketu rise in the second house, they will destroy maternal uncle's family. The native may have several physical & secret (sex related) problems, & on account of Ketu, the native will have a very rough and disturbed life.

Lal Kitab suggests some *upaya* to lessen these bad effects of Ketu. The native should sprinkle acow's urine in his house at different places, & at the time of Sun eclipse, things related to Saturn (Sun's enemy) such as almond, coconut and *til* should be given to the needy and poor by the native.

Sun+ Rahu

At the time when there will be a Sun eclipse, Rahu will not be much effective. In general, Rahu's period lasts for 42 years. During that period, Rahu will give problems to the native's children & they will suffer, his wealth will be lost and all the material relating to the Sun will bring bad

him. For example, Venus in 25th years, Saturn in 36th year and Rahu in 42nd year will be highly inauspicious to the native.

Auspicious Effects

from his *nana&nani* (grandparents from mother's side).

When they rise in the second house, he will be considered good like the soil taken under an elephant's feet.

When they rise in the third house, he will be taken like an elephant's tusk.

When these planets rise in the fourth house, the native will like to live in a dream world.

his children.

When these planets are in the sixth house, they act like a black dog.

If they are in the seventh house, the native involve in bats.

When both rise in the eighth house, native's body would go on shaking usually.

When they are in the ninth house, the native will from diseases and suffer a lot.

When these two are in the tenth house, the native will be considered just like a dirty drain.

When these two planets rise together in the eleventh house, the native will be very slow mentally, will not have happiness from children.

When they rise in the twelfth house, the native should keep a black dog, keep coal in his house, and if possible keep an elephant. Rahu will help the native to hold a big post until 42 years as it is the period governed by Rahu.

Inauspicious Effects

There will be more inauspicious effect of both when they rise in the ninth or twelfth house at the time when there will be a Sun eclipse.

house they rise, leaving that house, they will bring bad effect.

If they rise in the second house, they will give bad results relating that house.

When these two planets rise in the third house & if Mangal is inauspicious & has its aspects on Rahu, it will give bad results in the 21st and 42nd year, native's children will suffer & his luck will be affected adversely.

If these planets rise in the fourth house, the native's body may have black spots.

Lal Kitab suggests some *upaya* to remove the bad effects of these two planets.In order to save one's money, the native needs to put in a small piece of cloth some corn in a dark room under a heavy article. The native is advised to give corn to the needy or after washing some corn in cow's urine put that corn into the running water. He should also give things related to Mercury & Venus to the needy. He may also give (in *dan*) a cow or a sheep to someone who needs it. At the time of Sun-eclipse, the native is advised to give things related to Rahu, such as almonds and coconut, to the needy and also put them into running water.In order to lessen the bad effect of

them up in the morning to put them in a river or throw them in a remote place in a jungle. The native needs to be very cautious while carrying those

his children should face him for it may give bad effect. Such a native may be blind if Saturn and *Mangal* rise together,

The Planet Moon

Moon + Mangal

When *Mangal* and Moon rise together in a house, they act like honey mixed in milk—cool and give full of happiness, provide full life-span, lot

the native takes all his responsibility on himself and takes care of entire family. When these two planets rise in the same house say 2 & 4th houses where Moon is exalted, then both these planets stay together for 52 years and give good results. When Mangal is exalted, it provided good results until 38 years but when not good it gives bad results in 33th year.

Auspicious Effects

When these two planets rise in the third house, the native will be rich but none will like him as he will be cruel &possess bad conduct.

When they rise in the fourth house & Mercury rise in the 4—10 houses, the native will be wealthy in different ways.

When these two rise in the seventh house, native has a big family & very rich.

When Moon &*Mangal* rise in the ninth house, the native may not be good but will be lucky & his children will also be luck and good.

When they rise in the tenth house, then all will depend on the position of Saturn and its effect. If planets sitting in the 2nd and 5th houses are auspicious,

4th house, they may destroy everything that a native possesses.

When these two planets, Moon and *Mangal*, rise in the eleventh house, the provide peace and happiness like milk & honey together, and give every kind of comfort in the night and peace as well.

Inauspicious Effect

When these two planets rise in the seventh house and Saturn rises in the 1st, a native will not get any parental property or money, he/she will be a miser, & may die of an accident, or get hurt or may get any disturbing or sad information.

When these two rise in the ninth house, a native may die on account of any hurt/wound or accident.

When they rise in the tenth house, the results will be like that of the ninth house as stated here above.

When they are in the eleventh house, a native may not possess an intelligent mind and get different meanings of things he listens or receives. He will also be a miser.

In other houses, these two will provide results according to their signs and house they rise in.

Moon + Mercury

When these two planets rise in their own houses (own signs) they provide inauspicious results. If no aspects are there on them, and rise in other houses or signs, they provide bad results. When Saturn is of low degrees or weak,

bad planets are with these planets, both these planets stay together until 58 years starting from 29th. Mercury gives best results (in business) and Moon provides good result (in sea voyages) at native's 34th year and beyond. When these two planets rise in a house in which Mercury is exalted, Moon

Auspicious Effects

When these two planets rise in the second house, then until the native's father lives, no loss to father relating his property. Mercury will also help in that matter.

When they sit in the fourth house, the native will be excessively rich and will have every kind of happiness and peace.

When these two planets rise in the sixth house, the native will be a killer even though he possesses lots of property. When Mangal rises in the 4th or 8th house, native mother will suffer, he may be rich in cloth business & may possess a narrow outlook in life.

from sea-voyage, in business or during war time lots of movements will go on in the native's family.

When these two planets rise in the eleventh house, he will get good results from the time his daughter is married. He will go on getting wealth after that.

When they rise in the other remaining houses, they will give results according to the house and sign they dwell in.

Inauspicious Effects

When these two planets, Moon & Mercury, rise in the houses which are not auspicious for Mercury, they may give inauspicious results.

When they rise in the second house and if Saturn is inauspicious, Moon's helps the native to possess academic interests.

When they rise in the fourth house, and if *Mangal* is inauspicious, Ketu also gives bad results. Native maternal uncle's family suffers, he gets heart problems & losses by taking responsibilities of others. He suffers from hallucinations & he is often ready to commit suicide.

When they rise in the sixth house, such a native is a killer, and even if he is rich he suffers a lot.

When these two planets rise in the seventh house, he always suffers even though if he has riches & his mother is always unhappy & suffers.

When they rise in the eighth house, its results will be the same as when they rise in the fourth house.

When they rise in the tenth house, the native leads an unfortunate life, fear a bad death & his wife and children are usually not in his favour. When they rise in the twelfth house, Saturn gives very inauspicious result even though Saturn rises in its exalted sign in such a *kundali.*

Lal Kitab suggests some *upayas* to lessen the bad effects of these two planets if they rise inauspiciously. It suggests to do some *upaya* for *Mangal* or Rahu, if Sun & Jupiter are in the 2nd or 4th house and have aspects from Saturn, the native is advised to take some soil near a tube bell and put it into running water or put it in a temple.

Moon + Venus

When Moon and Venus rise together in a house, it is like mixing dust into milk. The native will have no luck. His mother will also be unhappy on account of her eyes andgrandparents from mother's and father's side will lead unhappy life. White cotton clothes will belong to Venus and white silken ones belong to Moon & both the planets will provide good result separately. The native will not be poor but will also not be very rich neither dead nor living & lead a life like a weak cow.

Auspicious Effect

When Moon & Venus rise in the second house, the native may be a chemist & Jupiter's ill-effect will indulge the native in romance in his old age. Whenever, he will like to get a well dig, his wife will suffer a lot.

If both the planets rise in the fourth house & if Saturn rises in the 10th house & Moon in the 4th, results will be favourable. When the Sun rises in the 10th house, the native will get all support from his father and if the Sun is in the 5th house, the native gets every kind of happiness from both—

is in the 3rd it will be bad fro mother. If the Sun rises in the 5th house, the native will have soft manners like girls but he will not be a stupid. When both the planets rise in the 7th house, the native will be kind and large-hearted, will respect others & if he spends money in good acts, it will be good or if he does it in wrong things, it will be wrong in its own way.

When these planets rise in the 8th house, the native will have good

grandmother.

When these two planets rise in other houses, they will provide results according to that house or the sign in which they rise.

Inauspicious Effect

Right from the time of marriage of the native both the planets will provide ill-effect. Native's mother may die or if she is alive, she will become blind.

that will be native's unethical conduct.

Native's mother may die & if she is alive, she would become blind. Both

unethical relationship on the part of the native. Native wife's health will go bad, or she will go mad or she will possess a weak mind.

When these two planets rise in the second house, it will be like mixing soil into milk. The native will have good luck but his involvement with other women will lead to his ruin.

When Moon & Venus rise in the fourth house in a native *kundali*, it makes the native heavy drug & wine addicted.

be lessened after the native's marriage & his mother's eyes will be affected adversely. When they rise in the eighth house, the native will be impotent, possess bad conduct & be slow witted.

Lal Kitab suggests some *upayas* to lessen the bad effects of Moon & Venus's placement in one house. It advises the native to keep a small silver ball with him. It will provide him peace & things related to Venus like woman & cow, will give him peace.

The native should do some *upaya* for Venus & Mercury. He should keep some curd in a small pot, cover it by a white cloth and put on it some ash. At the occasion of *rakcha-bandhan*(a festival in which sisters tie threads around the wrists of their brothers) only red thread should be sued to tie it on the hand, it will keep native's health good & help increase wealth.

Moon + Saturn

When these two planets are together in a house, they affect adversely the

Auspicious Effect

fear of theft in the house, &only after 36 years money gets coming into the house.

When these two planets rise in the second house, and if Sun rises

children adversely.

When these two planets rise in the third house& if the native keeps his money in a leather bag or iron box, it will be lost, go waste or bring destruction to the native.

When these two planets rise in the fourth house, they are detrimental to the native's mother.

in the 10th house.

When they rise in the sixth house, they may affect badly the things

money will increase, but to have three dogs in the house will bring bad results.

When they rise in the ninth house, they will help increase native's wealth.

When these two planets rise in the 12th house, the native will have not much interest with money and will be more religious.

Inauspicious Effect

will destroy native's love-life. When these two planets rise in the second house, all the business of things related to Saturn will be destroyed.

When these two rise in the second house in a native's chart, every kind of business or work related to Saturn done by the native, will go waste or destroyed.

When these two planets rise in the third house in a native's chart, and if the native brings things related to Saturn & Moon in his house, it will affect Jupiter & Ketu adversely and consequently those things may give bad results. The native may get hurt, his eyes may go bad & he may have heart related problems.

Moon in the fourth house will be dangerous for the native. He will die in the night& if he has relation with a widow or with any different woman, it will destroy him. His eye-sight will go bad on account of getting hurt. He will die outside or far away from his home town & his father will die by a gun shot.

When these two planets rise in the sixth house, three sorts of relationship if the native has with any of the following will cause problems for him—if a brother lives in his sister's home, a bridegroom lives in his father-in-laws place & daughter's son lives at his mother's father's place.

When these two planets rise in the seventh house, the native will waste his life in dealing with things related to Venus, especially if he interferes with the quarrels created by his wife. Thenhis life will go totally waste. When these two planets rise in the eighth house, native's eyesight will go bad during his old age.

When they rise in the ninth house, the native will not get any happiness in life & any good things done by him will turn into bad ones.

When these planets rise in the tenth house, the native will involve in a romance with a girl which may cause destruction for him.

When these two rise in the twelfth house, the native will have to run away from his house & he will have very little happiness from his wife.

Lal Kitab suggests some *upaya* to lessen the bad effects of these planets when rising in certain houses inauspiciously. The native should offer milk to snakes, he should work with one of his relations having the

running water & keep some Ganga water in a small pot and put it in an iron chest. When native's period is inauspicious, he should blacken the heads of certain animals, he should drink only water for 43 days after putting sugar, milk, lemon, or tea in it & at the time of Moon-eclipse the native should put almonds and coconuts into running water as well as he should put red alum in one of the walls of his house.

Moon + Rahu

When Moon & Rahu rise in one house, great problems in the native's life will continue coming until 45 years of his age. It means only after 45th years of completion bad effect of Moon and Rahu will be reduced.

Auspicious Effects

gradually it also gets disturbed. That means the native may plan to do big things and get losses as there was no proper planning.

When these two planets rise in the second house and if Mercury is also there, it given bad results.

When these planets rise in the third house, native in-laws may be rich but until 45 years the planets have not much positive effect.

In the fourth house if Rahu is inauspicious, Ketu will also give similar effect.

remain unhappy and suffer on account of various reasons.

When these planets rise in the sixth house, the effect of other inauspicious planets is always good.

When these two planets rise in the seventh house and if Sun is in the eleventh, Venus will act like an exalted planet.

When Moon and Rahu rise in the ninth house, Moon's effect is good & it will provide every kind of happiness in the native's parental house. Every kind of hope will start kindling.

Inauspicious Effects

When these two planets are inauspicious, the native may die after drowning in water. He may live only half way in life, his skin may suffer due to various diseases, and may have black & white spots, his in-laws may be

When they rise in the 3rd house, Mercury & Ketu usually give bad results.

When these planets rise in the seventh house, his in-laws are destroyed.

When they rise in the ninth house, the Moon give only partial positive effect.

When they rise in the 12th house, Venus is not favourable.

Lal Kitab suggests some *upayas* to lessen the bad effects of these two planets when placed as inauspicious. It suggests that the native should keep some rice in a blue piece of cloth & give in a temple for 7 days to the poor and needy. When there is a Moon eclipse, he should put almonds and coconuts (things related to Rahu) into running water.

Moon + Ketu

In case manly planets like *Mangal*, Sun and Jupiter are auspicious in the native *kundali*, they will provide good effects to the native or he will be very unhappy. His grandmother will be very unhappy & the grandson may not see his grandmother. Both may stay unhappy even if *Mangal* is with them but whenever there is an eclipse, it will bring adverse effect on the native.

to Mercury native's mother though she is religious, will be considered bad on account of Mercury as the Moon becomes debilitated.

When these two planets rise in the second house, the native has to deal with family quarrels.

When they rise in the third house, they will give similar results which Moon & Rahu combination will give in this house.

When they rise in the fourth house, the native will get urinary related illness.

Moon will not give bad results at the time of eclipse.

When these two planets rise in the sixth house,and if most of the manly planets are well established in the *kundali* of anative, in 28th year of the native most of the things turn into positive side and start giving him good results.

Inauspicious Effects

When Moon and Ketu rise in a house inauspiciously, they act like a blind horse, a lame mother who is very weak, native's son's life may be shortened, quarrels with the son& grandmother and the grandson may hardly be able to see each other, The grandmother before or after 43 days, may not be able to see her grandson, things like milk, may go bad in the native's house. These

If they rise in the second house, the native should not drink milk in the night for he may get diseases like gout or phenomena.

When they rise in the 4th house, and if the native is a religious person

If these two rise in the sixth house, at the time of Moon-eclipse, they will be inauspicious for both, mother and daughter.

If they rise together in the ninth house, they will give inauspicious effect but if are separate they may provide good results.

If these two planets rise in the 12th house, then if native earns a lot of money, all will be lost or spent & he may need more.

Lal Kitab suggests some *upaya* to lessen the bad effects of these two planets. Things that are white & red or red and black relating Ketu, will help the native in many ways. The native is advised to give things relating Mercury to the needy & to get good education he should give 3 bananas for 48 days in a temple to someone who need it.

The Planet Mars/Mangal

Mangal + Mercury

When *Mangal* is auspicious, Mercury will also give good results but if

operates, Mercury keeps quiet and does not give any losses to the native *Mangal.*

Native children will be good until 24 years & so will be native's wife and whatever he says will come true.

Auspicious Effects

brother-in-laws.

When these two planets rise in the second house & if the 2nd house has no planets, the results will be good. The native will be rich, will enjoy the company of his children, and his in-laws will also be rich.

When they rise in the third house & if native's elder brother lives with him, he gets company of his parents and stay happy with them. He may also get godly favours & will lead a reasonably happy life.

When these two rise in the fourth house, the native will be good for himself & his relatives but cruel for others.

When they rise in the sixth house, both the planets will give good results in their own way.

When they rise in the 8th house in a native's chart, both the planets will

destroyed & even if anyone is left without being harmed, he/she will live at a remote place.

Inauspicious Effects

When *Manga*

father may not support him and he may suffer from unpopularity on account of his misdeeds. Mercury will also give inauspicious results, death may visit his family, others may curse him &he may be defamed and will be surrounded with lots of worries.

When these two planets rise in the third house in a native's *kundali*, he will keep worried on account of money, his maternal uncle will be an impediment in every kind of his work, and the native will always like to involve in bad & immoral activities.

When these planets rise in the fourth house, it will be auspicious for the self & will not harm others, even then he will be inauspicious for others.

language & consequently will lose his family happiness & if Jupiter and Saturn are in one house in such a *kundali*, native circumstances becomes bad further. His luck will be bad and his wife will always suffer on account of various reasons.

When these two rise in the 8th house, native's maternal uncle's family will be destroyed & from the day the native becomes young enough to take care of own things, his maternal uncle will have bad circumstances. The only way will to stay good for other will be that the native should lead a very pious life or he will lose everything in life.

When these two planets rise in the 11th house, the native may involve in bad activities and start drinking which will spoil his eyes & destroy his property and wealth. His father will not favour him so will be his own house.

Lal Kitab suggests some *upaya* to lessen the bad effect of these two planets if they rise inauspicious in different houses. It suggests that the native should do some *upaya* for *Mangal*. The native is advised to put things related to Mangal such as honey & sugar in an earthen pot& put that pot in a remote place in a jungle & if that earthen pot is covered with *dhak*leaves, it may give better effect. The native is advised to take Ganga water early morning & wear a pearl in a gold ring & a *pukhraj* (yellow jewel) in a silver ring.

Mangal + Saturn

When these two planets rise in one house & if the Sun is weak in that chart & Rahu too is inauspicious & even if Jupiter is with these planets, the results will not be auspicious at all. Even if the native does not accept anything from his parents but if Jupiter is auspicious, he will earn a lot of money in life. But at times all that wealth may be looted by dacoits. Even if such a native deals in money landing & is very careful, he sustains losses. Such a native is a doctor, a dacoit, or a military personal. What kind of effect these two planets will give to the native is given here under in a

result. So the native is advised to give coconut and a dry fruit (*chuara*) to the needy in a temple to the needy.

House	Effect of Planet	Results or indicating sign
1	Mangal	Honour in Government
2	Venus	In-laws—Native's own marriage
3	Mercury	Ritudan—Marriage of daughter
4	Moon	Land for cultivation
5	Sun	Birth of Children
6	Ketu	Dogs, children, crows.
7	Venus	Happiness from wife
8	Inauspicious Mars	Deaths
9	Jupiter	Father's obligations
10	Saturn	Snakes may be seen during day in the house.
11	Jupiter	May not use father's, grand-father's property
12	Rahu	May involve in an *yagya*

position in the *kundali.* If Rahu is auspicious, both will provide good

Auspicious Mangal + Saturn

Lord Shiva & Vishnu will be very auspicious & Rahu as well. The native will get success and victory in quarrels & various problems. Rahu can exert its bad results and *Mangal* will also be weak but it will provide its

of an arrow on his hands, will be brave, possess good health and will command others, will boost up his elder brother's luck, will be like a lion. Those who will seek his forgiveness, he will forgive them but those who are rowdy and rouges, he will punish them severely.

Auspicious Effect

native's *kundali*, he should not cheat his wife or it will give bad results. Native's in-laws will get progress and riches will grow there & when the native will working at a king's place or in the government, both the planets

When these two planets rise in the second house, right from the time of

will grow & may get money from his in-laws. The native will be rich when his wife's planets are governed by Venus.

When they rise in the 3rd house, the native will hold a great position in Military, have lost of property & will be a brave person.

When these two planets rise in the 4th house, land-cultivation and

planets will give good effect in their own way.

native, it will help the native's luck boost up.

When they rise in the sixth house, and if a bitch gives birth to puppies,

When they rise in the 7th

Venus, he will be rich, get all the happiness through wife & will be greatly helpful to his relatives and his own family.

When these two planets rise in the 8th or 9th house, Jupiter will help the native to boost up his luck.When these planets rise in the 10th house and if ever a snake is seen in the house, it is a sign that his luck will rise onwards. If the snake is not killed or harmed, the native will then become rich and possess children. If native wife is lucky, the naïve will get progress immediately after his marriage & his family will have no sickness created by Saturn. Even if the members of his family may quarrel at times, but will have no losses and will not be harmed. When they rise in the 12th house, both the planets will give results according to their sign they rise in.

Inauspicious Effect

If *Mangal*

kundali, he will lose all his wealth & property,& will be ill constantly. Though his wealth may not be stolen by dacoits, but because of Saturn's adverse effect the native will surely lose his money and wealth.

native's wealth & property will be ruined by his wife & children. The native may have blood related illness & his interest in other women will ruin his life. Women having round eyes will bring him losses but someone who has gray eyes or is a widow, will help him in many ways.

When these planets rise in the 2nd house, and if the native goes out of his house with his mother or father-in-law in the evening or night, he may get accident or sustain lot of loss but if he travels with them during the day, nothing may happen to the native.

When these planets rise in the third house in a native's *kundali*, native's brothers and relations will oppose him in many ways. Any one of them such as brother's wife may poison him, native's property may be destroy & he may lose money as well as native's uncle or younger brother may have no children.

When these planets rise in the 4th

in the native's *kundali*, the native may lose his life.

age of 42nd year.

When these two planets rise in the 6th house, they make the native very

When these two planets rise in the seventh house, the native may go blind when he grows old. When these two planets rise in the 8th house & the native lives in a house made on a triangle-land, he will get losses &

he will gradually be involved in different kinds of bad acts. All that may destroy the native.

When these two planets rise in the ninth house in a native's chart, & if

When they rise in the 11th house, and this house belongs to Jupiter & also shared by Saturn, then even if the native may have good earning, the native will always go on incurring loans. But if he produces his own things & do some business of things made or produced by the native, he will get success and wealth as well.

Lal Kitab suggests some *upaya*
& Saturn when they rise inauspicious in one house. The native needs to keep a clear account of what he gives and takes from others. When a mare gets a cub, the native should keep its milk in a glass container. It will help increase the native's wealth. The native should also make some *upaya* for the Moon& obey his mother. It will save the native from getting cheated by others.

Mangal + Rahu

When Rahu rises with *Manga*l in a house, Rahu is not negatively effective at that time as Rahu is considered an elephant but Mangal is its driver who keeps control over the elephant. Therefore, Rahu does not give bad effect.

helps him to be like a king.

Inauspicious Effect

behaves like an unbridled elephant who has no controller. Then Rahu destroys the native in different ways.

Lal Kitab suggests some *upaya* to lessen the bad effects of Rahu. The native should sit on his cooking range & eat. Rahu will stop making any nuisance. When any weak period runs in the *kundali*, the native should put in running water some corn & mustard after putting them in an earthen pot.

Mangal + Ketu

When *Mangal* is auspicious in a *kunda*li, its effects just doubles when Saturn is also with Venus in that*kundali*. When a girl maturation period starts at the age of 14 and she iscapable to give birth to children until 48 years, children born to her are lucky and do good deeds in the world.When *Mangal* rises with Ketu in a *kundali*, the native suffers from (*Pitra-rin*) father's debts or obligationsas Ketu is not auspicious to the native. When the Moon rises with Saturn,Ketu also becomes like a debilitated planet but at that time *Mangal*

Auspicious Effect

When *Mangal*

and Saturn are exalted, the native should continue writing, to lessen the bad effects of *Mangal*. The native will get children up to the age of 24 years.

When these planets rise in the second house, both of them provide auspicious results.

When these two planets rise in the 3rd

condition of the native is changed at the age of 28 years, the effect of Ketu

upaya is need to be done.

When they rise in the 4th house, the native should do the *upaya* which is normally done for the 9th house when it is inauspicious. .

Inauspicious Effect

When *Mangal*& Ketu are against each other in a chart & Ketu is trying to lessen the good effects of *Mangal*, the native is advised to keep two different coloured dogs. It will lessen the bad effect of Ketu.

When they rise in the 6thor 10th house, until 28 to 45 years the effect of both these planets will be much less. The native will enjoy the effects

of Jupiter in whatever state or sign it would rise in theS chart. It is the 11th house and its strength according to which its good or bad effects are experienced by the native. The native is advised to make *upaya* for Ketu by taking care of things related to the Moon.

Lal Kitab suggests some *upaya* to lessen the bad effects of Ketu. It says that the native should collect seven different kinds of fruits and after cleaning them in seven different kinds of milk (cow's, goat's, camel's, elephant's & mare's milk etc.), the native should put them at a remote place or he will be sick in some way (like his hands and feet start trembling)& male folk will start dying in his family. To lessen such bad effects, the native is advised to keep some honey in a silver pot into the foundation of his house.

The Planet Mercury

Mercury + Saturn

When Mercury (*Budha*

native until 24 years & no enemy will be able to harm him until he is 42 years of age. The native will enjoy long & happy company of his father. His temperament will be good &he will possess good luck, but he will be too clever & will be able to read others' minds easily.

Auspicious Effect

When these two planets rise in the 2nd or 12th houses, native's relatives (related to Saturn) will give the native gifts that relate Saturn. He will get valuable ornaments from them & whatever he will do, it will turn into his

he is a drunkard, it will be harmful to him and his family.

When these two planets rise in the fourth house in a native's *kundali*, Mercury will exert less harmful effect & even though Moon may become *Mangal*& Saturn adversely.

When these two planets rise in the seventh house, the native will be rich and happy.

When they rise in the 11th

of wealth will continue until 45 years.

When these two planets rise in other houses, their effect will be according to the sign they rise and the house they are in.

Inauspicious Effect

When these two planets rise in the 2nd& 12th houses, native's father may die on account of Saturn related things like scooter, machine, liquor, car or poison.

When these two rise in the 4th house, the native will be a killer & will harm others like a scorpion who always likes to bite others.

When these two planets, Mercury& Saturn, rise in the 7th house, the native will be a drunkard, will eat meat such other things and will be ungrateful to others.

When they rise in the 9th house, the native will not do any kind of work or duty until 34 years of his age & will be dependent on others.

If there are no planets in the 11th house other than these two, then

view of the house & the sign they rise in.

Lal Kitab suggests some *upaya* to lessen the bad effects of these two houses. If the native plants trees in a temple, it will help the native to get good effect of these two planets.

Mercury + Rahu

Auspicious Effect

like a bird which destroys the tree on which it sits & of which it eats fruits.

When these two planets rise in 2nd
relating the 1st –6th
houses.

When they rise in the 3rd house, Mercury may lead the native to commit suicide.

When these two planets rise in the 5th
and gives bad results.

When the rise in the 6th house, both the planets give good results to the native.

When these two planets rise in the 7th, 10th& 11th houses, they are

is a foolish friend.

st, 4th, 8th& 9th houses are not very good for the native but he is good for others when these two planets rise in these houses.

When these two planets rise in the 12th house, Mercury will be totally inauspicious and everything relating the native, from a goat to elephant, & things relating Rahu, plus business & most of relations on his mother side will be destroyed & unhappy, unless both rise as favourable planets and provide good results.

Inauspicious Effect

will hamper in getting children born in the native's family.

When they rise in the 3rd house until native's 34th year Mercury and Ketu, both are inauspicious & his sister though she is rich, will be unhappy.

When these two planets rise in the 4th, 8th, 9th& 12th houses, these two planets will usually bring death to someone in the family & Rahu will usually bring destruction.

When these two rise in the 11th house, the native's sister, though she is very rich, but either on the 7th day, in 7th month, or after 7th year of her marriage, she will be widow or will be separated from her husband.

When these two planets rise in the 12th house, they bring losses to the native's family as well as to his in-laws. On account of native having no children or if he has children but they sufferendlessly.

The native's every word he utters out of frustration, will come true.

Lal Kitab suggests some *upaya* to lessen the bad effects of these two planets if they rise inauspiciously in different houses. The native is advised to keep things relating Moon at the cremation place & bring home some water from there. In case native's kitchen is towards the side east in

marriage, he has to take care of the 11th house in his *kundali.* To lessen his in-laws problems the native should make 100 round balls of soil and go on keeping one ball each day either in a temple, *gurudwara* or mosque & this routine must not be broken. In case the native need to go out of his town, he can keep the remaining balls in any of these religious places.

Mercury + Ketu

Auspicious Effect

it is auspicious and makes the native like a god's messenger or an angel. When Ketu rises in the 4th house, it makes the native very religious but if it rises with Mercury, it becomes inauspicious for the age of native's mother and children & Mercury also becomes weak.

When they rise in the second house, native will lose money through his children & mother & sea-voyages will inauspicious.

When they rise in the 3rd house & if *Mangal* rises in the 12th house, both Mercury and Ketu will have no ill-aspects of the 1st& 8th houses.

When these two planets rise in the 4th house and native reaches 17 years of age, it will be inauspicious for the sister's children & family.

When these two planets rise in the 5th house, & if in the 3rd, 4th, or 8th house (in any one of these houses) Venus rises & in the next house Mercury is there, it will lead to the destruction of the native's family & bring him great losses.

When they rise in the 6th house & have no aspects from other planets,

auspicious but if the house is inauspicious, these two can make it further inauspicious.

Inauspicious Effect

When these two planets rise inauspiciously in the second house in a native's *kundali,* they may bring destruction to the families of sister & maternal uncle of the native. They may bring different kinds of sickness/ illness to the native & make grandfather (Nana) physical cripple.

When these two planets rise in the 3rd or 11th house, both these houses will give inauspicious results to the native.

When they rise in the 5th house & if at the age of 17 years a son is born to the native's sister, the native is advised to give *dan*/alms for his long life.

When they rise in the 6th house, then the things related Ketu will bring

When they rise in the 12th house, both Mercury & Ketu will bring destruction to the native.

Both Ketu & Mercury, when rise in other houses, they will provide results according to that house or the sign they rise in.

Lal Kitab suggests some *upaya* to lessen the bad effects of these two planets. It advises the native to make some *upaya* for the Moon &*Mangal.*

The Planet Jupiter

Jupiter + Sun

Jupiter is considered as the father of the *jatak*& the Sun as its son. A *jatak*/ native's luck also rises with the help of his father and sons. When Jupiter & Sun unite, they become as the Moon. The Moon brings luck and is like a pearl. If these two planetsare exalted in a house and rise as auspicious planets, they can change *Vidhata's*(God's) decisions.

Auspicious Effects

person & collects tax from others. His age will be long but he may die all of a sudden. He will be an artist related some kind of hand-work.

When these two planet rise in the second house, the native will have a great & beautiful house, will live majestically, be straightforward, but be cruel.

When these two rise in the third house, the native may be a miser and will have lot of wealth.

When they rise in the 4th house, the native will indulge in business in Saturn related material/things, he will get money from his relatives & lead a happy life.

When they rise in the 5th house, the native's luck will grow better after the birth of a son, he will earn lots of money then & will also indulge in serving others.

When these two planets rise in the 6th, 7th, 10th or 11th houses, both the planets' good and bad effects will be experienced by the native only after his in inclining to grow old.

When they rise in the 8th

save the native from death.

When these two planets rise in the 9th& 12th houses, they will help the native in making his family

known to the people & will grow in all respects. Money and wealth

Inauspicious Effects

When these two planet rise an inauspicious planets in the 1st house, the native will always have the fear of getting disrespect from others & his wealth & money may be lost.

When they rise in the 4th& 10th hoses as inauspicious planets, both will not be much favourable & Ketu's 7 years period will bring losses to his grand-parents(mother's side), government connects will be fragile & if

in case it is weak in degrees or rises in an enemy sign.

If the Sun is in its weak sign or inauspicious sign in any house, it will tarnish the native's luck, he will experience impediments in every work &

If these two rise in the 3rd house & if the Sun is weak, the native will be greedy though he may have property worth lacks of rupees. He may bring disaster to his family.

Lal Kitab suggests some *upaya* to lessen the bad effects of these two planets. If the native gets a son, weak period will improve and he will be

will get losses. In case father and son are separated, the son should go on using the bed that his father was using before. The native should also keep pure gold &*kesher* in his house.

Jupiter + Moon

When any enemy planets have aspects on these two planets, Jupiter& Moon, then those enemy planets are destroyed by themselves. But if mother's or father's *rin* *kundali* of a native, then mother's & father's love is curtailed. Such a native also does not get happiness

education until 24years of his age, & his old age will pass comfortably and happily. Any business relating Mangal, Mercury & Sun will be helpful to the native &his relations, *bua*/aunt, sister, friends & brothers will help him to get progress in life.

Auspicious Effect

ordinarily.

When they rise in the second house, they make a native very rich, he gets all the happiness from mother & his agriculture land as well parental property increase.

When these two planets rise in the 3rd house, they make a native lucky, he earns lots of money & helps his brothers to make money.

When they rise in the 4th house in a native's chart, the native is very rich right from is childhood & material relating the Moon & Jupiter as well as most relations (grandmother, grandfather, mother & father) help him to

will be great writer & will help others too to grow. All this may also happen due to the good effect of the Sun.

When they rise in the 6th house, they will provide results like *Budha*& Ketu.

When these two planets rise in the 7th house, they don't provide much good result & if their enemy planets rise in the 1st house, native parents *dalali*/brokering.

When these planets rise in the 8th house, a native may have plenty of wealth but his brothers and relatives turn into enemies, but if one brother becomes his enemy, the other turns into a friend.

When these two rise in the 9th house, they provide very good results & if yearly astrological assessment (

the Moon.

When they rise in the 10th
an idiot who is unable to think properly.

When they rise in the 11th house, then at the time of birth of a daughter

when a son is born the situation changes and the native starts getting

person who will give all to others.

Inauspicious Effects

When these two planets, Jupiter & Moon, rise in the second house & if they have aspects from Rahu & *Budha*, they may affect the native's eyesight adversely, may give disappointment all round, provide unhappiness in old age & if the native keeps the company of his sister-in-law (*sali*), all will be destroyed.

When these two fries in the 3rd house & if Mercury is also there, they give poor results & affect adversely native's sister, sister-in-law & if he keeps things relating *Budha*, such as a parrot, a goat or clothes, they will give inauspicious results to the native.

When they rise in the 4th house, & if Saturn is weak in the *kundali*, the native becomes an atheist & is destroyed.

When these two planets rise in the 6th house, & if such a native gets a

well or pipe, are destroyed.

When they rise in the seventh house, then the native's childhood is full of problems, his parents are always unhappy but when a daughter is born

When these planets rise in the 8th house in a native's chart, then in case such a native starts enjoying on other's money, he is destroyed.

When they rise in the ninth house & if such a native accepts money as alms from others or from his own daughter, then both these planets give

When these two planets rise in the tenth house in a native's chart, he is destroyed even if his parents are extremely rich.

When they rise in the eleventh house, they simply provide losses to the native & his parents are usually unhappy.

When these two planets rise in the 12thhouse in a natives' *kundali*, the native will lose all at the time of his own marriage or when a daughter is born to him.

Lal Kitab suggests some *upaya* to lessen the bad effects created by these two planets. The native is advised to keep a small silver pot in one corner of his house under the earth, plant a *ber* tree in a temple, and after putting gram dal in a copper pot, put that pot into the running water, proper arrangements to supply water for the need of the people in a cremation place should be made by the native, some copper coins should be thrown into running water or into a river, worship some unmarried girls, put in a small cloth some *til &imli*&keep that cloth into the earth in a corner of the house, two coloured stones after getting them tugged in silver should be put on the body by the native-- are some of the *upayas* for the native to lessen the bad effects of these two planets, Jupiter & Moon.

Jupiter + Mangal

*kundal*i it rises like that. The native will be honest and will honour right decisions & like a king he will love God & will possess great worldly knowledge. When these two planets have aspects from Saturn, lot of wealth will come to native. The best time for the native to get a child is the 8th year after marriage. Both, husband and wife will live together until 72 year.

Auspicious Effect

but if Mercury is also with them, it will make the native useless and dull.

When they rise in the second house, the native will have good relationship with his in-laws & will support him to a great extent, ready to

When these planets rise in the third house, the native will take care of his parental property & hold strong belief in dharma & all performs rituals.

When they rise in the fourth house, it will help the native's family grow.

he gives alms but if he takes it, his wealth will be lost. Native's wealth will grow until 28 years.

When these two planets rise in the sixth house in a native's *kundali*, the native will be an elder brother in the family & the planets will give

When they rise in the 8th house, both these planets will give results according to their own sign and the house.

When they rise in the ninth house, riches will increase in the family & so will be family happiness.

When they rise in the tenth house, they will give results according to the planets that rise in the 4th or 6th houses. But if there are no planets in these two houses, theft may be committed in the native's house and he may get losses.

When these two planets rise in the 11th house in a native's *kundali*, and if his father and brother live with him, his riches will go on increasing.

When these two planets rise in the 12th house, the native will be happy in all respects, will have a big family & whomsoever he will bless, he/she will also be blessed and be happy.

Inauspicious Effect

When *Mangal* is inauspicious then until 33 years native's relatives will suffer &even some relatives may die. In case Jupiter is weak, then Saturn will be the sole contributor for the native.

When these two planets, Jupiter and Mangal, rise in the second house,the native will lose money even if he gives alms.

When they rise in the 6th house, & the native deals in a business with things related to Ketu & Mercury, it will bring bad effect on the native's children and relatives.

When these two planets rise in the seventh house in a native's chart, he will be under debt even if he will earn a lot of money.

When they rise in the 8th house, both the planets will act as inauspicious planets and affect the native's family adversely.

When they rise in the 11th house, they will give bad results and if the native keeps things related to them in his house, they will bring bad luck to the native.

Lal Kitab suggests some *upaya* to lessen the bad effect of these two houses. In case *Mangal* is auspicious (with Sun & Mercury), the native should use deer skin in his house. He should wear a ring made with three metals but if *Mangal*

should distribute & put some of these in running water as well as distribute sweets to the people.

Jupiter + Mercury

mutual aspects (1-7, 4-10, 5-11), then Jupiter becomes weak. When it rises it rises with the Sun, it becomes strong and effective. When Jupiter rises with the Sun, it provides certain results, especially for the native's father. We provide some of those results/effects.

When they rise in the second house, they lead to the destruction of native's riches.

When they rise in the third house, the native is wise, but is poor as well.

When they rise in the 4th house, they bring disappointments to the native.

When they rise in the 5th house, native gets a job.

When they rise in the 9th house, they lead to money loss.

When they rise in the 11th house, they bring destruction to the native.

Auspicious Effect

king.

When they rise in the second house, then native is very wise & rich & leads a happy and prosperous life until 12 years.

When they lead in the third house, the native is wise, brave, serious in conduct, but Venus becomes weak in the chart.

When they rise in the 4th house, the native has a Raj Yoga, but if he is involved in immoral activities, they become inauspicious. The native leads a very successful life until 24 years.

When these planets rise in the 5th house &if the native gets a child on Thursday, the native is lucky & leads a happy life for 60 years.

When these two planets rise in the sixth house, they involve the native in God's worship & makes him a pious person.

When they rise in the seventh house, they are good for the native's daughter but not for the son.

When they rise in the eighth house, Mercury is never weak and does

When they rise in the tenth house, the native is usually lucky & leads a happy life.

When they rise in the 11th house, the native gets lots of wealth.

When they rise in the 12th house, the native is an ordinary businessman but lives long.

Inauspicious EffectsWhen these two planets rise in such houses where

grandfather, father in-law & father get some kind of illness, usually related with breath. Native's words are not respected & he does not get father's love or happiness from him. He is usually unfortunate to himself and

by anyone.

a native's chart, he is reduced to poverty & lives like a foolish mendicant.

When these two planets rise in the second house, Venus exerts its inauspicious effect on these planets.

When these planets rise in the 4th house, the native is a coward, jealous of others, & acts impiously.

When these two rise in the 5th house, the native is usually indulged in sex activity & is highly ridden with sex feelings.

When they rise in the seventh house, the native is lives like a king at times, but then someday start living like a pauper on account of his bad habits & extravagant nature. He may have no children, live like a poor man & usually stays unhappy.

When they rise in the 8th house, the native mostly suffers from some kind of diseases.

Lal Kitab suggests some *upaya* to lessen the bad effects of these two

earth. He should get his nose pierced & wear a silver-ring in it & continue keeping it in the nose until 96 hours or days.

Jupiter + Saturn

In case Jupiter & Saturn both, rise in one house in a *jatak's kundali*, then the planets rising in the eleventh house on his chart, will decide his luck. If the 11th house has no planets, then Saturn will decide about the native's luck. The native may live until 34 years with his father& until 43 years of his age both these planets will go on helping his/herto get wealth & riches.

Auspicious Effect

recluse or a guru.

When they rise in the second house, the native will be highly educated,

When they rise in the 3rd house, the native will lead a simple life & his old age will be quite happy.

When they rise in the 4th house, the native will get good name & fame & will be honoured by the people.

When they rise in the 5th house, the native will get honour & respect from all. At times certain activities relating Jupiter may create some problems & quarrels may erupt, but every kind of decision will be in the native's favour provided he does not involve in drinking, eating meat & keeps away from other women.

When these two planets rise in the sixth house, the native will get every kind of happiness from his wife.

When these planets rise in the seventh house, all activity relating Saturn's sphere will be helpful to the native. His riches will increase, and if *Mangal* is well placed, the native will have a big family. There will be more number of men in the family than the women, often guests will be visiting his home.

When they rise in the eighth house, the native may not have much wealth, will have a bog family & live long.

When they rise in the ninth house, the native will lead a good life and help others too to live like that. He will have plenty of income in seconds & such a native will love money only even though he earns with fraud. He

native.

When they rise in the 11th house, then this house will mainly be

there are planets in the 3rd or 4th house, they will decide native's luck.

When they rise in the 12th house, only after marriage native's luck will rise & riches will increase. His family will rise after 28th year.

Inauspicious Effect

If the native will indulge in drinking, eating meat & will involve physically with other women, Saturn will start giving inauspicious results. If the native will use other's money without any returns, his old age will be unhappy & he may be affected adversely by ghosts etc.

When they are in the second house, keeps the native indisposed, and things related Jupiter brings problems to him, naïve health remains weak and father is constantly unhappy.

When they rise in the third house, Saturn usually makes the native poor.

When the rise in the 6th house & if Jupiter is weak or debilitated, native gets happiness from his wife but if Saturn is weak or rises in an enemy sign, native's wife comes from a poor family & he is usually unhappy with her.

When they rise in the seventh house, native's property is lost or business is destroyed after a son is born to him & either his wife, mother,

When they rise in the tenth house, then native's wealth will create problems for others. Money earned by him by fraudulent means will help him. He will have no wealth received from his father but things related to Jupiter will bring him honour from others.

When they rise in the 11th house, there is no guaranty that they may provide the native good luck. He will always be wanting for money & property.

Lal Kitab suggests some *upaya* to lessen the ill-effects of these planets if they rise inauspiciously in the native's *kundali*. It advises the native to make some *upaya* for Saturn & worship Lord Shiva constantly.

Jupiter + Rahu

When Jupiter and Rahu rise together in the *kundali* of a native, such a*jatak* is very sincere to keep his words and if ever he/she meets someone, he does not like to submit or yield before others in conversation or in any way. If the native gets hurt or wounded he/she is not disturbed at all. Such a native loves to live in two different ways or two kinds of worlds—at times he is happy and hopeful but soon he becomes unhappy and gets disappointed. Sometimes he is rich but at times he is extremely poor. After his 12th year his time is not good and after his marriagethe time will be unfaourable further. When he reaches 36 years of age, on account of Saturn, he will be rich & by the age of 48 years, the native will also have children and get lots of happiness. However, it is also true that if such a native is born even in a Raja's palace, he will be just like a *fakir* (poor man) who has no money at all but if he is born as a poor person, he will grow very rich & will be like a Raja. Such great changes will come to his life only after he/she gets a son.

Auspicious Effects

kundali, the native will be able to earn his daily bread comfortably even though he is born in a poor family. He will get money from the government to make his both ends meet.

When these two planets rise in the 2nd house, the native will always help the poor and needy and even if be is a poor person, he will have abundant courage to do great jobs.

When they rise in the 3rd house, such a native will be very smart and always live alert against his enemies, will be courageous & dauntless.

When these two planets rise in the 4th house in a native's chart, on account of exalted Moon, he will get all the advantages in his life.

When they rise in the 5th

government job.

When these two planets rise in the 7th house in a native's chart, either his father or father-in-law, any one of them will remain alive

When these planets rise in the 12th house, the native will be talented, wise, and will be expert in some kind of handwork but he may not get

If in the remaining houses if these two planets rise, they will give results in view of the sign they rise into as well as according the house they are in.

Inauspicious Effect

When these two planets are inauspicious in a native's *kundali*, they affect adversely his/her father's age, wealth & may give the father some kind of physical ailment. The native may lose gold and if he is involved in a business dealing with the things relating Rahu, he may incur losses. When these planets rise in the 2nd house & if enemies of Jupiter & Rahu are in the 8th house in that chart, the birth of a son may be delayed.

When they rise in the 3rd house, the favourable effect of Mercury & Ketu will be much less until the native has reached 34 years in life.

When they rise in the 5th house, Rahu will affect the birth of a child as and when Rahu if rises in the 5th house, does the effect.

When they rise in the 7th house, either native's father or father-in-law, any one of them will stay alive.

When these two planets rise in the 8th house in a native's chart, the native will experience disappoint and displeasure all round himself.

Lal Kitab suggests some *upaya* to lessen the ill-effects of these two planets. The native is advised to make some *upaya* for *Mangal*& Ketu& wear gold on his body. If his son is not able, then he should make *upaya* for the Moon. He is also advised to give alms of the things relating to *Mangal.* After washing some corn in milk the native should put that corn into the running water. He should take some silver from his mother and keep it with him & make some *upaya* for Jupiter as suggested above under the point No. 8.

Jupiter + Ketu

When these two planets rise together they provide good results. Ketu will hold control of all the matters that are normally controlled by Jupiter. It will help the naïve to get more wealth but Jupiter will stay as neutral without involving in any of the affairs relating the native. However, Ketu being a tricky planet, will not totally be free from making tricks, but Ketu

Auspicious Effect

kundali, they make the native religious & God fearing, following the moral code as prescribed. Where ever the native will go, all will be happy.

In case these two planets rise in the second house in a chart and if the 8th house has no planets, the native may get a high position in a temple.

When they rise in the fourth house, Ketu will be weak but Jupiter will be strong. Native's wealth will increase and so it is good for the children. The native will serve his parents warmly.

In case the second house has no planets, and if these planets rise in the sixth house, they may affect a native's luck adversely.

When they rise in the 7th house, the native may be poor and stay away from most of the life's comforts.

When they rise in the 8th house, they may make the native poor and he will be wanting things of utility in life.

When these two planets rise in the 12th house, they make the native

Inauspicious Effect

When these two planets rise as inauspicious planets in a *kundali,* the enemy planets trouble the native for 40 years in his/her life.

Ketu's Main Station/Position: If Mangal or Moon rise in the sixth house both are Ketu's enemies.

Jupiter's Main Station:In 9th or 12th house, Venus, Mercury or Rahu rise, they act its enemies. Similarly, things related to Jupiter & Ketu will be inauspicious for the native's father, grandfather & his children.

When these two planets rise in the 2nd house and the owner of the *lagna* rises in the 8th house, there will be mutual enmity between them.

When these two rise in the fourth house, a male child will be born late.

child will die & he will live like a slave.

When they rise in the 7th house, the native devotes his time in meditation

When they rise in the 8th house, the native leads his life like a dead person and is money less.

Lal Kitab suggests some *upaya* to reduce the bad effects of these planets. It advise the native to put 400 grams yellow lemon in running water or give in a temple as alms.

The Planet Venus

Venus + Mangal

If Mercury & Ketu are not enemies in a *kundali*,then both these planets create a situation of a Moon eclipse. However there are some auspicious effects of these planets when they rise in different houses.

Auspicious Effects

kundali is Manglik or if *Mangal*has

nd house, native's

bring auspicious results. Native's in-laws will be rich.

When they rise in the 3rd house, the native gets money which is useful to his family & brothers & sisters as well.

When they rise in the 4th

When they rise in the 5th house, both wealth and native's family will rise & will be useful to the native.

When they rise in the seventh house, the native will have children & grandchildren & will be extremely rich. He will also be very happy in life.

When they rise in the eighth house, the native will enjoy a good period of *dasha*

When these two planets rise in the 10th house, they make wife's brothers rich, native's brother-in-laws may have dark complexion but his wife will be white in complexion& the native will enjoy a good status in public.

When these two planets rise in other houses they will provide results according to the sign they rise and the house they are in.

Inauspicious Effect

native.

When they rise in the second house & if inauspicious *Mangal* is also with them, the native will just nothing who sits and hats to do any work,

always visits the native house.

When they rise in the 3rd house, the native indulges sexually with other women.

When these two planets rise in the 4th house in a native' chart, his in-laws' house is destroyed and sustain losses.The native will be unlucky for his own family & will destroy his maternal uncle's too.

When they rise in the 8th house, the native will talk ill of others& will deceive the person who will help him.

When these two planets rise in the 9th house, the native will be the eldest brother in the family and his wife's health will remain bad.

When they rise in the 10th house, native's wife will have Saturn's

be moneyless, quarrelsome & will regularly be involved in quarrels on small matters. Such a native may kill his brothers for the sake of his wife.

When these planets rise in other houses, they provide results according to the sign they rise in and the house they occupy.

Lal Kitab suggest some *upaya* to lessen the bad effects of these two planet. It suggests that the native should put at a remote place 700 *geru* (red coloured soft stone) under the earth, if the 7th house in the native' *kundlai* has no planets, he should make some *upaya* for *Mangal.*In order to help his wife get rid of illness he should offer red coloured bangles to wear & send medicine to his wife through his brother so that she may be cured soon.

Venus + Mercury

The native's luck will be great but his government duties will bring him

the native involves in a business with the things not relating with Mercury & Venus, it will bring him great success. His children will have no bad

Auspicious Effect

work and his family will be happy with that.

When these two planets rise in the 2nd house in a native's chart, and if both these planets rise with equal strength, they will stay together until 44 years and help the native. But if they rise in a debilitated sign or house, the native is advised to give a grinding machine (tool) in a temple or put it in the running water.

When these two planets rise in the third house in a native's *kundali*, he will be healthy & will get job regularly. When these two planets rise in the 4th house in a native's chart, his wife will give him all the happiness and pleasures in life, and when he reaches 37 years of age, he will have ample of wealth too.

When they rise in the 5th house, it may be like a half Sun eclipse & the native will get some small government job.

When they rise in the 6th

If the native has no sons, his daughters will help him & he will get help from women as well as enjoy happiness from his family.

When these two planets rise in the 7th house in a native's chart, he

use a balance. He may be a reputed businessman, rich and will enjoy full happiness from his wife and children. All will be good to him.

When they rise in the 9th house & where Moon, Ketu or Jupiter are also there, Mercury will never provide bad effect to such a native. Venus

When they rise in the 10th house, the native is wise & his health is good.

When these planets rise in the 1th house, native's health is good & he may live unto 100 years.

Inauspicious Effects

When these two planets, Venus & Mercury rise inauspiciously they may

various ways.

kundali, the native may have less number of years to live & may not keep animals as that will give him unhappiness.

When these two planets rise in the 2nd house, they make the native indulge in sex activities. When they rise in the 3rd house, & if the Moon is weak in the *kundali*, the native does not get any help from his stepmother.

his wife also dies soon. If such a *jatak* marries again, his wife and he will remain ill.

When these planets rise in the fourth house, both his in-laws and

native. Things relating Venus and Mercury, agricultural land, cows and corn business---all will bring losses to the native.

will get losses. If he makes a cooking place after digging the earth inside his house, his family will get losses.

When these two planets rise in the 6th house and the Sun is also there, the native will be opposed by the women folk in the family.

When they rise in the 7th house and if on account of Rahu & Ketu if Moon has become weak, then the impact of Venus and Mercury will also be weak. Native's children may trouble him regularly.

When these two planets rise in the 8th house, both man and woman will have different kinds of health problems. If the native will work without properly thinking, it will adversely affect his relations on mother's side as

will be arranged in the family so is the case of getting children.

When these two planets rise in the 9th house, *Mangal* will be inauspicious at the time of a daughter's birth & different sorts of inauspicious results will be experienced by the native. When these two planets rise in the 10th house in a native's chart, and if the 8th

then Mercury & Venus also provide bad results.

When these two planets rise in the 11th house, they create problems with the seniors in jobs, the naïve will have to leave company of friends

may go on shouting to save the animals.

When they fries in the 12th house, at the time of birth of a daughter, native's family will get losses, his luck will not assist him & he may encounter several kinds of problems which keep him disturbed.

Lal Kitab suggests some *upaya* to lessen the ill-effects of these two planets if they rise inauspiciously in a native's *kundali.*It advises to give a sheep in *dan*/free to someone who needs it. The native is advised to do some *upaya* for the Moon, offer a sheep some corn to eat, give his own daughter or any girl a sheep in *dan*& after dipping a gold necklace in milk, the native should wear it to redeem the bad effects of these two planets.

Venus + Saturn

Mercury will provide good results. If the Sun has its aspects on Rahu & Ketu, the native will feel the pangs of sorrow & native's relatives will

Auspicious Effects

kundali, both

When they rise in the second house, and if Saturn is in the ninth house, then Venus will give results relating the second house.

When they rise in the third house & if Venus has aspects on Saturn, it

stay together until 52 years.

When these two planets rise in the fourth house and if they have

When these two planets rise in the 9th or 12th houses & if Jupiter rises in either 5, 6th, or 10th

happiness from his wife & in agriculture or any other business he will

When these two planets rise in the 10th house in a native's chart, the native is saved from others' attacks & also from different kinds of problems. He spends lot of money on his son-in-law, during his youth he may be involved in drinking and with different women, his old age will be good and happy, he may construct a new house and have a long life to live & at the time of death he may not suffer much.

Inauspicious Effect

When these two planets have aspects from Mercury, then other people may enjoy his riches. As the native will be fond of eating different kinds of things, it will bring losses & problems to him. If these two planets are seen by the Sun, then Saturn will have its inauspicious effect & at the time of death, the native may suffer a lot.

the native will be sensuous, his body will suffer from burning sensation, his heath will be poor & in all respects he will be unhappy. .

When they rise in the third house in a native's *kundali*, others will enjoy upon the native's income, and native's uncle and his wife will have lose conduct.

When these two planets rise in the 4th house, his uncle will have physical relations with other than his own wife.

When they rise in the 7th house, the native will be an impotent, coward, will have bad conduct & his relations will use his money and income leaving him poor.

Lal Kitab suggests some *upaya* to reduce the ill-effect of these planets. It advises the native to put a few copper coins into running water to earn

Venus + Rahu

When these two planets rise together, only Mercury is helpful to the

rising with Rahu. As a result the native will have no sons. But if Sun &

can be obtained by the native. The native, on account of Mercury, will get respects from others.

Auspicious EffectThese two planets may rise in any of the houses,

neighbour's daughter may not be married for a long time but native's wife's luck will be good and favour the native.

When they rise in the 12th house, they will give somewhat better results

Inauspicious Effect

When the door the native's house will be towards south, Venus will give bad results. Native's wife will die soon and another wife will also die soon.

to colour his nails or put *surma* in his eyes to improve his appearance, his bad time will not go and until 43 years he will lead an unhappy life on

will affect adversely native's health and his wife's mind as she would be cruel & impolite.

When they rise in the 3rd house until 34 years Mercury & Ketu will

When they rise in the 7th house, native wife will have a short life,

inauspicious results. Ketu will destroy native's maternal uncle's house, the weak Moon will also bring bad results until 34 years.

When they rise in the 12th house, native wife's health and his money,

Lal Kitab suggests some *upaya* to lessen the bad effects of these two planets. The native should keep some rice after washing them in milk or

The native would need to do some *upaya* for the Sun and Mangal & a few copper coins & sugar should be put in the hcuse at a place where none could reach. The native is advised to do some *upaya* for Rahu & Venus & he should give milk, butter and coconut to the needy as alms. Native's wife should wear a ring in her left hand and she should put into the earth

these two planets.

Venus + Ketu

Auspicious Effect

kundali, the native gets all the happiness from his wife & children. He is also honoured in the society.

When they rise in the second house, and if any one of these two planets is exalted, the other one will also give similar results to the native.

When they rise in the 3rd house, the native may be surrounded by enemies until 40 years of his life so he has to take care of these two planets.

When these two planets rise in the 4th house, & Rahu may rise in a house before these two, then the native's son will not be married from the house where such a native has been living.

When they rise in the 9th house, and if Venus is weak then Ketu will give best results and consequently Venus will also provide good results.

When they rise in the 12th house, the native will have more number of sons, his wife will be courageous & his entire family will lead a happy life. He will also lead a very contented and happy life.

Inauspicious Effect

may not have children, especially when *Mangal* is rising in the 4th house. Native's children & relations may frequently die which will make him unhappy constantly. When they rise in the sixth house, both Venus & Mercury are left out unassisted by their friendly planets so they both exert

results. If Sun & Jupiter are also weak in the chart, native's wife will not give birth to any children.

Lal Kitab suggests some *upaya* against the ill-effect of these two planets. It advises the native to do some *upaya* for Jupiter. The native should take some gram dal, put it in a yellow cloth and then keep it into the middle of running water.

The Planet Saturn

Saturn + Rahu

Auspicious Effect

kundali

always help others.

When they rise in the 2nd house & if these is no aspect of these two on

When they rise in the third house, and if there is a black spot (*lahsun*) on his body, the native will be a mendicant or a sadhu.

When these two planets rise in the fourth house, and are in the 5—8 house, the native is wealthy and get honour from people.

Now we describe separately the effect of these planets when they rise in different other houses.

When they rise, in the 1st house: The native will have a big family.

When rise in the 2nd: The native may get lots of riches.

When they rise in the 4th-5th

When they rise in the 9-12: The native will like to suppress his wrong desires.

The Fifth house: When they are in the 5th house, the native will have a black spot bigger than his thumb on his body. In the native's left there may be a sign indicating a snake & if there is a sign of a snake on the native's

but if that sign can be covered with the thumb, then Rahu will favour the native.

If that sign is on the left side of the native's body, its effect will be auspicious but if it is on the right side (rising from 1—6), the native will be blind. If it is in 1—4, the native will be like a king, if in 5—8, that native will be like a Maharaja, if in the 9—12, the native will be a sadhu or yogi. In case there is a sign of *Saishnag*(the serpent king) on the left hand of a

Ninth House

When they rise in the ninth house, native's family will increase and so will be his riches.

When they rise in the 12th house& if there is a sign of a snake on the right hand of the native, it will be auspicious to him. He should not reveal his things to others & will act very cleverly.

Inauspicious Effect

When these two planets rise in the seventh house in a native's chart, his family will be destroyed, and so will be his wealth. His wife will be weak in health & his children will also not grow much.

When they rise in the ninth house, and if prostitutes live in the native's parental house, Jupiter will bring inauspicious results to the native. He will have to bear insults and he will be dishonoured by others. Native's grandfather will suffer from short of breath.

Lal Kitab suggests some *upaya* to lessen the ill-effects of these two planets. The native should put some rise in running water to keep peace in his mind. He should also make some *upaya* for Rahu & Saturn, but should not eat almonds or coconut after frying them as they will provide ill-effect. Therefore, instead of eating them, put them into the running water.

Saturn + Rahu

luck usually brises after 18 yearsbut ifany other planets also rise with them

them in the 9th house by certain *upayas*. Such a native gets more sons. The native is advised to keep animals having similar colour or they may affect the peace of the family adversely.

Auspicious Effect

When they rise in the 6th house in a native's *kundali*, he lives at least for 70 years.

When they rise in the 8th house, they give auspicious results and help saving the native from death, but if only one planet is there, the results are

The native possesses ample of wealth, a big family & plenty of wealth and property as well as grand & great-grandchildren.

When these two planets rise in other different houses, they give effect according to the sign and the house they rise in.

Rahu+Ketu

If Rahu represent head, Ketu represents tail. Ancient astrology unfolds that these two planets never rise in one house but they become one by their aspects. When Mercury's period in on in a *kundal*i, good deeds will be done by the native & Ketu will do the same when the period of Jupiter will be running in the *kundali*. These two planets are in fact the agents of

ones, then Ketu is helpless and Rahu is debilitated and ineffective.

Auspicious Effect

It is Ketu which in fact operates Rahu. When Rahu & Sun are together it creates Sun eclipse & if Ketu rises with the Moon, it leads to the Moon eclipse.

When these two planets rise in 1—6 houses, they don't run straight. They affect all the planets in their own way except Jupiter which move them as it likes. They also obey Mercury for good or bad results.

If these two rise in the houses before Venus & Mercury, Rahu then gives bad results, but if there is only Mercury in any of those houses, then Ketu does not give bad results. When Rahu & Ketu are in the 4th& 10th houses, Mercury & Saturn provide

In case Sun & Saturn rise together, then Rahu gives auspicious results.

Now we provide the effect of the combinations of different planets when they rise in one house. Moon + Saturn= Ketu becomes debilitated.

Mercury + Sun= Ketu gives auspicious results.

Venus + Saturn= Ketu is exalted.

Mercury + Venus= Native health is good.

Inauspicious Effect

When these two planets, Rahu & Ketu are inauspicious, they make the native ill-famed and he gets every kind of blame in life from others. The native himself creates problems one after the other. In view of their aspects, these two planets give bad results and all the things related to them, such as business etc. and native's relatives also get bad effects. But this bad effect will only be on the 7th and 10th houses not on the 5th and the 11th houses except the 1st& the 6th house which are exempted from their bad effects. The bad effect of these two planets stays only for 3 years—for

Such indications can be seen on the nails of hands and feet of the native.

for three years Ketu's signs will rise on the nails of the native's feet for three years. In general, bad effect of Rahu runs for 18 years & that of Ketu is for 7 years which are also their Mahadashas.

Lal Kitab suggests some *upaya* to lessen their bad effects. It advises the native to keep a small piece of silver with him. Either wheat, *gur* or copper, any of these, should be put into running water by the native. To improve Rahu's bad effect, the native should make *upaya* for Moon, and for Ketu the native should do some *upaya* for the Sun. Any *upaya* in the

th house for Jupiter, in the 7th house for Saturn, and in the 10th house that *upaya* should be done for *Mangal*.

Effect of Three Planets

Sun + Moon + Mercury

The effect of *Budha*/Mercury remains until 17—34 years and if it is not auspicious, it may lead to destroy a native's property, but also affect adversely relations with father, mother, and grand- parents. Any of them may die by a snake bite.In the night when it is full Moon and if the native mounts a horse, goes to his in-laws place, he may fall down the horse and may die instantly.

Sun + Moon + Venus

They lead to problems day & night, especially if they rise in the ninth house. At times the native is rich but the other moment he is poor but such a native is always a gentleman.

Sun + Moon + Rahu

As the Moon is not auspicious, it will affect native's mother and riches adversely. Instead of happiness the native will face problems and will remain unhappy. Native mind will work slowly, and he will lose money. As a result he will face problems after problems. Native's age is also short,

problems for the native's children. Even then the Moon will be kind and help native's family to grow.

Lal Kitab suggests some *upaya* to lessen the bad effects of these planets. It advises the native to take care of Mercury and do some *upaya* for it as well he should worship Goddess Durga.

Sun + Moon + Ketu

a native may be rich, but will remain unhappy in life. His mind will work at a slow pace &he will be unhappy day and night.

Lal Kitab suggests some *upaya* to lessen the bad effects of these planets. It advises the native to take care of Mercury and do some *upaya* for it as well he should worship Goddess Durga.

Sun + Mangal + Mercury

The heart & Sun lines will join at some point and there will be a triangle at the heart line. Such a native will be very strong from inside irrespective of his good or bad deeds.

Sun + Mangal + Saturn

Native will be rich, but he will be a liar, dogged in nature as a result his luck will go weaker.

Sun + Mercury + Saturn

Sun & Saturn will go on working in their own way. There may not be any quarrels among relatives and friends& if these three planets are weak, even though they will provide good results. Native's business will run very well & his wealth and riches will increase.

Sun + Mercury + Rahu

advised to do some *upaya* for the Moon.

Sun + Mercury + Ketu

Things related to Ketu will create problems for the native. His nephews will forget all the good acts done by him and will go on talking ill of him.

Sun + Mercury + Venus

If there are no good signs at the mound of Mercury will lessen the positive effect of Venus with the help of the Sun & native's family's welfare will depend on Ketu's *dasha*. If it is good it will provide good effect, if not it will give bad effect. Such a native may not have sons, & if the native gets any son, he will get him in his old age only. The native will be unhappy on account of money, wife and his physical self & he may be accused on account of right or wrong causes. After three years of native's marriage, his wife may get some accident during day time & if native's sister-in-law is married in his house to any of his relatives, it will bring bad luck to the native.

Lal Kitab suggests some *upaya* to lessen the ill-effects of these planets. It advises the native to put some almonds in a corner of a dark room in his

moong, cover it with a copper cover & pray hard for his welfare & later on put all that into running water.

Sun + Saturn + Venus

Such a combination of planets will make native's family life weak and put it in an unhappy situation.

Lal Kitab suggests some *upaya* to lessen the bad effects of these

pot under the earth in any corner of his house to satisfy these three planets.

Sun + Venus + Ketu

Native's wife's health will be weak and unstable, his mind will remain disturbed and weak and he will act like a mad person.

Moon + Venus + Ketu

Venus will also give adverse results.

Moon + Mangal + Mercury

If the Moon rises in an auspicious house, then the luck line will affect the

good shape.

Moon + Saturn + Mangal

These three planets are like three snakes having three kinds of colour. Native's wealth will be enjoyed by his cousins. The native may get some

native will be destroyed in different ways & death may visit his family some times. Such a native may be sick on account of leprosy or other kind of physical ailment, his skin will be white and black but he will get

Moon+ Mangal + Rahu

If such a native is born from legs instead of head, he will be unlucky for the father. Quite often such a native is born after father's death.

Lal Kitab suggests some *upaya* to lessen the ill-effects of these three planets. The native should make some (sweet dish) with milk and eat it as well as offer it to others.

Moon+ Mangal + Ketu

Moon & Jupiter will provide inauspicious effect and the native will be unhappy until 48 years on account of having no children. He will have no children.

Moon+ Mercury + Saturn

When these tree planets rise in one house, they make the native a killer but he will be rich and possess courage. He may suffer from heart disease& his maternal uncle's family will remain disturbed. The native will die as poor person.

Lal Kitab suggests some *upaya* to lessen the bad effects of these planets. It advises the native to pour some milk in a mango tree at its bottom.

Moon+ Mercury + Rahu

Native's father will die from drowning in water.

Moon+ Saturn + Rahu

At the native's age of 33-36-39,will suffer from accidents and unfortunate happenings on account of Saturn. He will get less happiness from his wife & mother, his children may not live long & such a native will always remain in want of his wife.

Moon+ Mercury + Venus

If the health line in a *jatak's* hand meets the heart line, the native will have headaches & disappointments. When a line starting from the Moon's mound goes up to the mound of Mercury, that will indicate delays in the marriage of the native or there may be impediments in his marriage. Both Mercury & Moon will behave like enemies. Native's relatives will get losses & it will also have adverse effect on the native's wife. Native may not have children and if there are some born to him, they will die soon. Such a native will also sustain losses in business.

Lal Kitab suggests some *upaya* to redeem the bad effects of these three planets. For the *upaya* of Rahu the native should give *dan* of a girl at the time of her marriage & for Ketu he should give a cow in *dan*. To improve the effect of Mercury, the native should worship Goddess Durga & keep

Sun rise and give them 1/10 part of the total food he carries to a river etc.

Moon+ Venus + Saturn

God helps those who help themselves. Native's riches will be enjoyed by his children & he will die in a foreign land. His wealth will look huge but

talk very high of him about his riches, but it will not be auspicious for the native. The in laws will be defamed later on.

Moon+ Mercury + Saturn

Native maternal uncle will be ruined and if anyone of them is left out in their house, he/she will become a sadhu & will leave the house. The native will have two kinds of conduct like Rahu. Saturn will be doubly inauspicious which may give two sorts of illness—one related to native's eyes & the other related blood.

Lal Kitab suggests some *upaya* to improve the bad effect of these planets. It advises the native to use deer skin to sit upon whenever possible & the native should give *dan*/alms of sugar made items & milk in a temple to the needy.

Mangal+ Saturn +Ketu

Mangal/Mars will be highly inauspicious to the native. Native's house made of bricks/stone or of mud, it will have a *neem* tree in it and a dog will also be there. All this will be on account of *Mangal's*

& bring destruction.

Mercury + Saturn + Rahu

Venus, Mercury & Rahu will give ordinary results and will affect the native just in an ordinary manner.

Mercury + Rahu + Ketu

Death will go on visiting the native's home often. If such a native's tongue & throat are black, he will destroy most of his relatives and will die without having any children.

Venus+Mangal + Mercury

The native will have a short span of life & his children will also have problems of different kind.

Venus+Mangal + Saturn

If *Mangal* *Mangal*& Saturn and Mangal & Moon if have their aspects on Jupiter, it will give a long life to the native and he will usually get help from the unknown people.

Venus+Mercury + Saturn

In case in the native's parental house if there is any ventilators & if Sun light enters through that,

it will lessen the native's riches & theft may be committed in the house. The native need to be very careful or he will get losses.

Lal Kitab suggests some *upaya* to safeguard against the bad effects of these planets. The native is advises to feed cows with grounded corn. It will help the native to keep peace in the family & his children will also live happily. He should keep a black cow and a black dog or even feeding them with roti will also bring good results to the native.

Venus+ Mercury + Rahu

The native may marry several times but he will never be happy.

Venus + Mercury + Ketu

encounter problems at the time of his children's marriage.

Venus + Saturn + Ketu

When these planets rise in one house, the native will pass his life in physical pleasures & sensual enjoyments. It will destroy him.

Venus + Rahu + Ketu

will not be married in the known families.

Jupiter + Sun + Moon
These three planets will give excellent results if they rise in one house in a native's *kundali*. They will make him a successful businessman; he may be a great writer and will be useful as well as helpful to others.

Jupiter + Sun + Mangal
All these three planets will provide the native courage and fortitude. The native will possess patience, enthusiasm, be a gentle man and a lucky person. All his relatives, his father grandfather and other kinsmen will be strong and bold & keep lot of courage. All his efforts will provide him great success. He will possess religious thoughts and all the three planets

Jupiter + Sun + Mercury

believe in dharma & will do right deeds. If his house is narrow at the face and broad from behind,it will make his both ends meet easily and his children will never suffer on any account. Even if he is captivated, he will live like a king.

Jupiter + Sun + Saturn
In case there is a dark room in the native house on the right hand side just after the entrance that house will give him good results.

Jupiter + Sun + Rahu
Though the native may have plenty of corn and lots of stored eatables, his relatives will be jealous on that account and quarrels will erupt with them. Most of the relatives know him that he is like a king, they will behave with him like thieves. All the three planets may not give auspicious results.

Jupiter + Sun + Venus

bring good luck and make his life happy & native's luck will rise after his marriage.

Jupiter + Sun + Ketu
Although the Sun may not be very much favourable, the remaining planets

Jupiter + Moon+ Mangal

Jupiter + Moon+ Mercury
The native will get advantage through broker, Mercury will be highly

favourable and so the other planets. At times the native may suffer even if he will have lots of money as his mind may not act as needed. Mercury

money & income is concerned.

Jupiter + Moon+ Venus

Sometimes the native may be happy and at times he may not. When there

will bear good temperament and help the native. Right from the time of native's marriage, his luck will go ahead but he may get some losses too and may lose some gold or silver.

Jupiter + Moon+ Saturn

Both Jupiter & Saturn both friendly & will help the native in every kind of work or business he will involve. But if all these planets rise in the

may commit suicide or someone may kill them.

Jupiter + Moon+ Rahu

When these three planets rise in any house in a native's *kundali*, they may not provide much happiness to the native & his wife.

Jupiter + Moon+ Ketu

The native may have several problems in life and the more he tries to earn money, the more desire to get money will increase in the native's mind.

Jupiter + Venus + Mangal

Involvement in love affairs will give several problems to the native & Venus may not give the native advantage to have children.

Jupiter + Venus + Mercury

The native may be involved in quarrels & he will have problems at the time of marriage and he so may not live happily with his family.

Jupiter + Venus + Saturn

Native's wife will create several kinds of problems for him as she will be very cunning but in other respects life will be easy.

Jupiter + Mangal + Mercury

The native's three sons may suffer from short of breath & may have problems with their legs.

Lal Kitab suggests some *upaya*

planets. The native should wear gold and do some *upaya* for Mercury.

Give food to some goat and worship an unmarried girl & offer almonds to her to lessen the bad effects of these planets.

Jupiter + Saturn+ Mangal

As Jupiter will not favour the native, he will incur loans even after selling the parental property. Constant illness and bad thinking will bring losses. Though Jupiter may not be as good as expected,it will help the native to get more money.

Jupiter + Ketu + Mangal

Native's luck will not favour him until 45 years on account of Ketu being

Lal Kitab suggests some *upaya* to lessen the bad effect of Ketu and other planets. The native should put a ring having the right stone for

of worshiping.

Jupiter + Mercury + Saturn

Native's bad speech & harsh tongue and his love to eat different kinds of food and drinks, will bring losses to him but his wealth will increase &so his family.

Jupiter + Mercury + Rahu

As the native will be a miser, he will not like to spend money. Though he will have plenty of wealth but just like a snake he will sit on his wealth and will not like to spend money at all. So he will not be able to use his wealth even for himself.

Jupiter + Mercury + Ketu

Native's luck will always favour him and he will have lots of wealth. His luck will favour him in all circumstances.

Jupiter + Saturn + Rahu

Jupiter will act like a thief, Rahu will induce deceitful nature in the native & Saturn will act like a poisonous snake. Such a native will have to live away from his family which will make him unhappy and bring him losses.

Lal Kitab suggests some *upaya* to lessen the bad effects of these planets. It advises the native to live with his united family.

Jupiter + Saturn + Ketu

On account of bad dasha/periods the native may lose some of his children & remain unhappy.

Jupiter + Rahu + Ketu

As Rahu & Ketu will act as inauspicious planets & Jupiter may also not help the native, his luck may not favour him on any account. Due to bad luck he will be defamed and unhappy for a long time.

Saturn + Rahu + Ketu

direction. As the number of enemies rise, the native will tend to do wrong

planets two may provide better results to the native.

Effect of Four Planets

Sun + Moon + Mangal + Saturn

When these four planets rise separately in the 2, 6, 8, 12then the dasha/ periods will be auspicious.

Sun + Moon + Venus + Mercury

The native will be a kind hearted person and will be a true descendent of his parents.

Sun + Moon + Mercury + Ketu

Native's father will die from drowning or will lead a very unhappy life being too sad on account of family problems.

Sun + Mangal + Mercury + Saturn

Even if these four planets may not provide any gains to the native, out of them any one may help him and bring back his happiness.

Sun + Venus + Mercury + Saturn

Even if the native may have two wives, he will not have children from either of the two. The native will involve with bad activities &collect a

waste &useless. At the time of his death none would be there to supportor take care of him.

Moon + Venus + Mangal + Mercury

All the four planets will give inauspicious results except that at the time of the marriage of native's daughter all will go well.

Moon + Venus + Mercury + Saturn

The native will lead a happy life and will live comfortably.

Moon + Venus + Mercury + Ketu

There may be death & births in the native's house at the same time.

Mangal + Mercury + Saturn + Rahu

results. In case native's house's outer wall is connected with somebody's house, no harm will reach to the members of his family but thefts may be committed in his house on account of Rahu &money could be lost. Anyone of native's brothers may have no children & although the native will be quite rich, his daughters may suffer & stay sick for long.

Jupiter + Sun + Venus + Mercury

Jupiter will be highly auspicious which will calm down other planets and they may not affect the native's luck adversely. In case Jupiter rises in the second house, the native's luck will be boosted. If the native bows down before the Sun in the morning after he gets up from bed, it will bring him riches.

Jupiter + Sun + Venus + Mangal

When three male planets are there Venus acts just like a cow. The native will lead a sane life and he will be lucky and happy and lead a comfortable life, being victorious on all.

Jupiter + Moon + Mercury + Saturn

If the native will have good company, he will act wisely and do good deeds, but if he does bad deeds on account of bad company, he will be unhappy.

Jupiter + Moon + Mercury + Rahu

Rahu will be inauspicious until 42 years & on account of Rahu, the other

were opposite to one another, they will start working like friends & will

Jupiter + Mercury + Saturn + Rahu

If these four planets rise in the 12th house, they will work together and make the native extremely poor. But if the native uses money of his uncles, he may be successful in life to some extent.

Venus + Mangal + Rahu + Ketu

At the time of marriage men and women will confront each other as they will differ in their opinions. The native is likely to spend uselessly and as a result there may be so many problems in the marriage.

Effect of Five Planets

without Mercury but Rahu or Ketu one of them is there. If in a native's *kundali* there are male planets & also female planets (without Mercury),

children, has a happy family life and possesses a long life even if such a native is simpleton and possess less intelligence. Saturn, Sun, Jupiter, Venus or Mercury if they rise in the houses from 1st to 6th

results , but they rise in the houses starting from 7th to 12th, they may not be so lucky for the native. Such a native will be very rich but cautious also &

Rahu, Ketu) then the good effect may not be much & the native may lose so many things in life.

Lal Kitab suggests some *upaya* to lessen the bad effects of these planets. Though the native will be religious, he needs to give dan/alms

corn and coconut for Rahu, bananas & things bitter in taste for Ketu, and almonds, wine, cigarettes, and other intoxicants for Saturn need to be given in dan by the native.

Assembly of Five Planets

them but that too has its aspect on them & in case Rahu & Ketu rise in the

Yoga. Their effect in different houses will be as follows:

If they rise in the 2nd house, the native will be a Raja.

If they rise in the 3rd house, the native will be like a Raja (not exactly a Raja)

If they rise in the 8th

help others to go ahead in life to get success.

feet are of equal length, such a native will never worry for tomorrow but if they are in order means big then small and smaller, such a native will have several children.

The Effect of Nine Planets on a Native's Life

Planet Jupiter

Right from the birth of a child and until 16years the time is controlled

without a human being is known as Jupiter or Jupiter's realm. Jupiter is known as the guru of all the planets and is the master or owner of all things

in a *kundali*

the golden Lanka but one is a faker/sadhu or one who has no money at all,

house. Such a native has no dharma or norm to follow. It is Saturn only *kundali*. The

Impact of Jupiter

When Jupiter rises with male planets (Sun or Mangal) or is conjoint with its aspects, it gives lots of wealth to the native. .

In case Jupiter is debilitated or is extremely weak in a chart, it is Mercury that restores its effect but it also depends on the strength of Mercury.

Even if Jupiter rises as a weak planet in a *kundali*, it will not provide inauspicious results to a native.

The Sun

Astrologically 21 years are considered to be ruled by the Sun in a *kundali*. The light in the sky, and heat that persists on the earth, the truth about a king or a faker/sadhu, to make one live or to provide progress to someone—all is known to be done by the Sun. When the Sun rises, it is day but when it sets, it is night or darkness. The soul in human body, to direct one's mind or soul, all is done by the command of the Sun. The intelligence in humans, progress in the world, and foundation of luck—all is controlled or done by the Sun. It teaches us to keep going, and not to think about one's end point. It teaches not to change one's path nor do any retreat and shine like it from the same place every day in the morning and evening. Is it not just a great wonder, which is made by the Sun every day? It is the Sun which provides encouragement to human beings to go on and on without being tired or changing the path.

The Moon

The Moon is the owner of man's heart & soul. The Sun may order it in heat (anger) several times or in a big manner, but the Moon takes it coolly & always stays near the feet of the Sun. That means it helps a person to keep cool under any hot (disturbing) circumstances or environment. The Moon owns night but just after the Sun set, the evening time when the Sun

little before the Sun rises in the morning, is the time which is controlled by Ketu. But this time is also controlled or owned by the Moon.

First 24 years of human life, are controlled by the Moon.

Mangal/Mars

In case in a native's *kundali* when the Sun & Mercury rise together,*Mangal*

*Manga*l becomes inauspicious. First 28 years of human life are owned by *Mangal*. Serving one's relatives & brothers and others, enjoying one's life, indulgence in quarrels & suffering physically on account of various illness, are controlled by *Mangal*. The middle part of human body is controlled or owned by *Mangal*. The colour of human blood also suggests whether *Mangal*

it is also indicated by *Mangal*. If someone is involved to give free food to the needy and people in the society & is involved in helping people, all that is controlled by *Mangal*. This planet helps all human couples to have children, and if *Mangal* is rising all alone in any house in a chart, it is as strong as a lion. So many things are indicated by *Mangal* in a *kundali*. If other planets are auspicious, *Mangal*

be understood by the things that are used or kept in a native's house. If *Mangal* is inauspicious, it may indulge a person in back-biting and doing wrong things to harm people. As honey & butter oil when mixed,their

second house in a *kundali, Mangal* becomes inauspicious. If *Mangal* gets aspects from the Sun & Moon or if Saturn and Rahu or Saturn and Ketu rise together in a *kundali, Mangal* is not inauspicious.

Mercury/Budha

Astrologically 34thyear of human life are controlled by Mercury. It is also the time to earn money. Most planets can work in alliance with Mercury.

To get education, deliver lectures, contemplate correctly, indulging in business, handicraft--all is controlled or completed by Mercury. If Mercury rises with auspicious planets, it gives good results but if it rises

Venus

25th year of human life is controlled by Venus. This planet representsphysical attraction, love for beauty, sensuous attraction & out of the two eyes of humans, one is controlled by Venus as it also has one eye. It is Venus that mends the situation/circumstances disturbed by others planets.This planet represents female, family life, children & in a male-native's *kundali*, Venus represents his wife & in wife's *kundali* it represents her husband. If Venus rises all alone in a house in a chart/*kundali*

SaturnThis planet represents 36 year of human life, which is the period of earning money for any human being. Except children, and family of a native, it is usually responsible to give disappointments, make one a *sadhu* or mendicants who has relinquished all. Saturn has two faces—one represents property, wealth & the other is cleverness and being crafty. Saturn is mainly remembered for all that.

Effect of Saturn

The following are various sorts of Saturn's effects.

When right period (*dasha*) is on, it provides good results. When it rises in 2-5-9-12 houses,which belong to Jupiter, Saturn never gives bad results Saturn's agent Ketu, which will support the native to live long.

Whenever Saturn gives bad effect, black coloured things that

with Rahu & Ketu, in 9-18-27-36 years Saturn will always give inauspicious results & provide losses to a native. If a native gives things in dan/alms representing Saturn like iron (things made of iron), *angeethee*/stove, disc for cooking *chapaties* to the needy or a bagger, they will always bring good results to the native. .

When Saturn is not auspicious in a native's *kundali*, the parson bears black complexion within and outwardly as well. Such a native may kill anyone during bright day light, the native represents death& instead of giving dan to a *faker*/sadhu, he can loot him. Such a native is never sincere in love. Saturn can be responsible to create

Rahu

42 year of human life is controlled by Rahu. It leads the native to think about the problems of the world, creates a tendency to copy others, and inspires to live in a world of thoughts and imagination. By 'world of thoughts' means to create the capability how to defend against the enemies

is considered an auspicious planet.

main door of the house is situated in the south direction. It not only

problems and losses.

When inauspicious period of Rahu is on, it may make the native very ill, like give him fever or he will suffer from fever, create enemies, may develop sudden quarrels and problems. When all such things happen to a native,the following *upaya* need to be done by him.

The native should make some *upaya* with the help of silver or by

ill-effect of Rahu.

Masoor dal (red coloured dal) should be given by the native to a labour who is involved with the cleaning of his house during early morning and he should also give a few rupees as dan to that labour for the use of drinking tea etc.

The native should also put into running river water corn as alms equivalent to the weight of the sick person.

Ketu

45th year of human life is considered to be controlled by Ketu. It is the time when a native has to perform so many duties of his family and run in different directions to handle his problems.

Ways (upaya) to Defend against Ketu's Ill-effect

When a native suffers from urinary problems, he should wear rings on the thumbs of his feet or wear white thread on the thumbs of feet. It will highly be useful to a native.

When a native health is adversely affected, he should do *upaya* for the Moon, but if native's son is ill, he should visit religious places and give black & white coloured blankets in dan.

If a native's sons die soon after the birth, then he is advised to produce children at a religious place. That son or sons born there will live long.

Inauspicious Effect of Planets & Their Upaya

First of all it must be understood clearly that in a native's *kundali* which

results. In case planets are weak or are inauspicious by sitting in the 6-8-12

upaya needs to be done.

providing auspicious results'. When a planet sitting in an auspicious house is not giving good results, it can be turned into an auspicious planet by doing some *upayas*.For that, a native has to wear certain jewels or valuable stones, he should do certain kind of worshiping and *jap*, chant regularly some mantras, so that bad effect of those good planets may be lessened

planets in a *kundali*, for their *upaya*, the native should give in dan certain things that are related to that particular planet and also put such things in the running water of a river. All such *upaays* will be highly useful to the native and may bring good results.

Characteristics of the Rashies/Signs

The cast allocated to each rashi/sign

Taurus-Scorpio-Pisces	Brahman
Aries-Leo Sagittarius	Chatriya
Gemini-Libra-Aquarius	Vaish
Cancer- Virgo- Capricorn	Sudra

A native born with the any of the above rashies/signs, bears usually the characteristics which have been allocated to the rishis here above.

For example if someone is born under the sign/*rashi* Brahman, he will be humane, good natured & God fearing in his conduct.Someone born *rashi*, he/she will live & behave like a Raja. A native born under/with Sudra *rashi*, will bear a haughty temperament. But such facts display that cast or category is simply man-made and not made by Nature.Therefore, a *brahman*can also take birth in a *sudra* family. In a *brahman* family a *sudra* can also take birth. In any *brahman* family if someone is born with Cancer, Virgo or Capricorn sign, *sudra jati*/cast, and if someone born with Taurus, Scorpio or Pisces *rashi* in a *sudra* family, will act & live like a *brahman.* It is such a fact which no astrologer can prove otherwise.

The entire earth is related to the universe and operates according to the rules of nature. The planets in the sky command the activities of human beings & in that respect astrologers also have their great contributions. When a human being is born and what characteristics he/she will possess & when he/she will die—all that could be foretold by the stars/planets. According to Hindu astrological system a year has 360 days & in view of that the entire universe is divided into 360 divisions. All such calculations were not so easy to be made in reality. Therefore, the 360 divisions of the universe, were ultimately divided into 12 divisions& 12 *rashies*. Each *rashi* has been allocated 30 points according to astrology. Twelve divisions of

rashies& accordingly in astrology different *rashies* rise in different *kundalis*. These twelve signs/*rashies* represent, in fact, twelve divisions of the universe. Thus, 12 *rashies* contain the effect or characteristics of the entire universe. Now we will narrate in detail most of the characteristics of each sign/*rashi*
reader.

Aries

The meaning of *Mesha*/Aries is *he-goat*
also seen in the sky when we look at the stars. If someone is born when that particular *nakchatra*is operating in the sky,astrologically that native will also bear such characteristics. A native born under Aries sign, is very

turmoil, such a native is able to win. Such a native takes his/her own

decision. A person born under the sign Aries, is more interested in technical

run big business concerns. Such natives are always free and independent while taking decisions. The native desires all work to be done as he/she wishes but if anybody else interferes in his work, often he quits that work and keep himself away from it & permits others to work in his place.

As far as success is concerned, there is no height which he/she cannot scale, provided such a native is able to keep control over himself. However, after some time or later on that sort of success may also cause

praise, he feels proud of his achievements. Consequently his judgments gets blurred and as he becomes dogged, and possess pride about himself, he starts getting losses in all direction, because he is unable to think about various plans that were possible at a particular occasion in respect of a particular business or work. He goes on judging others on the basis of reason but not with the existing circumstances. He lacks cautiousness,

hurriedly. Though, the native goes very deep in all matters, and is often large hearted, but open mouthed (speaks as he likes to), and says anything without properly thinking. All this brings disappointments & losses to him.

As these sorts of natives are not very clever in their behavior or conduct, they convert friends as their enemies. Such a native is often thinks to achieve very high, and he/she also gets great success. He also earns lot of wealth or are seated on high positions. If such a native possesses low kind of thinking, at times, he/she may reach a high position and attain his/her goals even though he/she has to adopt any kind of base means. At times such a native is very cruel, may lead to killings & often he/she dies as a result of heavy attacks from others. But a native who possesses high values, is also a great master, a good controller at the same time he/she also loves strict discipline. Such a native likes to get good work from others & he/she also possesses a haunch about future. Such a native always desires that he/she must always be consulted by others and his/her opinion should be taken as important. Either at home or outside, the native desires to be consulted by all and his opinion should be taken as primary.

Taurus

The meaning of Taurus is he-cow. Quite a big portion of the universe possess the shape of a Taurus or it is named like that. A native born

extent. Such a native's conduct, characteristics and behavior is usually

(out of 30), he/she may possess certain qualities of Aries, but if he/she is born in the later part of Taurus sign, he/she may possess some qualities/ characteristics of Gemini sign.A native who is born during the middle part of Taurus sign, possesses most of its qualities. One who possesses most of

does not depend on others as far as any work is concerned. Such a native tries to face most of his/her problems courageously & is able to turn any

(*rashi*) if possesses rage, he/she does not immediately attacks but goes on working gradually & attains the goal. Such a native is very determinant, dogged in nature, is a good host, knows a lot about food and can cook well if required. Such natives are also good in decorating houses or places &can arrange everything with care and in order. Such a native has ample of understanding about 'how to present things before others'.

Gemini

The meaning of Gemini is couple, which again means having a kind of activity that is responsible to produce this world of living by their physical togetherness. The sign indicates the process leading to the birth of an individual & engrossed in sexual activity. This sign primarily indicates man & woman's mutual attraction towards each other. Stars make that kind

a woman & man having a musical instrument (   ) in their hands.

A native born in this *rashi*, enjoys life to his/her utmost & if the native

he has unusual attraction towards women and tries to make all happy by his demeanor. Though he is quite sober from outside, he is sensuous by nature as he is born in Gemini sign. Such a native is also very strong and can do great jobs that many people can't even handle. He has good and

the early degrees of Gemini, he may possess certain qualities of Taurus as well. And one who is born in the latter part of this *rashi*, he/she may possess certain qualities of Cancer sign too. One born with full degrees of Gemini, he is very brave, he may possess some sign of black spots (*til*) or wounds on his body, his forehead is broad & so is his chin.

Cancer

The meaning of Cancer is a creature which resembles a scorpion to a

cancer, is known as Cancer sign. A native born in this sign is lucky but also unlucky at times, but such a native is very successful in turning every kind of circumstances in his/her . A native born in this sign is very emotional. His manner of conversation is very sweet & attractive, he has

is far away from lethargy, keeps busy in the job & whatever he/she says

not want to hurt others. As a result the native goes on bearing injustice against himself/herself.The native is good at conversation and with his/her manner of talks, the native is able to win others easily. Such a native is quite an expert to handle persons who are easily annoyed. He gets pleasure in such sorts of talks & so his/her intelligence is sharp & he/she always tries to balance things on the basis of situation persisting at that moment. Both man & woman having such a *rashi*/sign at his/her birth if married to each other, they enjoy their married life to quite an extent. They soon like to patch up if any bickering crop up between the husband and wife.

A person born under Cancer sign is quite often possess high hopes in life& tries very hard to go higher in life in comparison to others. Even if such a native is born in a smaller or ordinary family, but with his/her strong will & ability, he/she may reach high positions in life. The fact is others even they commit several mistakes.

Leo

The meaning of Leo is lion, who is a king of forests. The part of the universe that possesses the shape of stars like a lion, is known as Leo and that follows the name of the sign as Leo. The behavior of the man born

moods or disposition. Such a person gets angry on small matters and is not able to control his/her anger easily. The haughty temperament of the native is known throughout and at home or outside all usually fear his temper.

voice is very effective and quite usual the native remains in serious moods.

Whatever he decides in his mind, it stays with him/her for long &such personsalways try to keep others under discipline. He/she is also under

The native also does not like to be cruel to others & always keeps the feeling of helping others. On the basis of his intelligence the native is able to make himself/herself popular. It is also possible that such a native is usually acts with the wisdom & if one is a writer, then in his/her writings

Virgo

by the characteristics of a girl.Such a native is kind hearted and gets disturbed soon when he/she looks at such situations in which people are in

to help him. Such natives don't like to be harsh with others. If they see any other person behaving harshly, they get hurt but are unable to oppose that kind of behavior forcefully or openly. As such a native loves peace, he/she is usually away from quarrels, & is never interested in court cases. The native is capable to understand others' feelings & read the faces to know the inner feelings. Such persons are very polite and wise in looks but are very talented & full of wisdom.

Libra

The meaning of Libra is balance & the part of the universe in the sky

rashi

by showing a man holding a balance in his hand & a native born under

his/her conduct & love for being moral and honest in his/her decisions. Such a native does not want to charge someone more than required nor he/she wants to give more to someone. That means that this native is always honest in his/her dealings. A native born under this sign can be a successful businessman & though the person is not a miser, but tries to see everything with a careful eye & his/her sharp intelligence always checks from indulging in any problems. A person born with Libra sign is pleasant in his/her conduct, speaks in a sweet voice which often makes the opponents bow down before his/her.

Scorpio

The meaning of Scorpio indicates a kind of insect/creature which is ready to bite anyone by its poisonous back part. We call such insects a scorpion & a person born under this sign usually possesses conduct accordingly. Though a native born with this sign may be clean at heart, but possesses a biting tongue which mostly hurls bitter words/speech. Such a native may possess less energy but as his/her conduct is aggressive, he/she goes on hurting others by the vindictive nature. Such a native is used to talk sarcastically that makes the listener unhappy & gets disturbed.

The personality of a person born under the sign Scorpio is very attractive & anyone who comes in contact his/her becomes a friend. At times native's biting words hurt others but as soon the others learn that the person talks honestly, they start liking him/her.As many people like such a native, they also want to friendly to him/her. So a person born with Scorpio sign proves to be a good friend. The continence of such a native is mostly serious but is also pleasant. Someone born during the last part of degrees of Scorpio also consists of certain qualities of Sagittarius sign.

Sagittarius

The meaning of Sagittarius is a bow, is shown by a person with his strong thighs and holding a bow with an arrow in his hands. The part of the universe which indicates such a sign in the sky is known by the sign Sagittarius. A native born with this sign mostly possesses the qualities like that of a bow and an arrow. Such a native is mostly very strong physically, possesses lot of strength, courage and though he/she possesses a great physical attraction, but is also quite curt in talks. Such a native has a great as nothing. Therefore he/she does not like to stoop down before anyone & is always careful about himself/herself. A native born under this sign does not tolerate being insulted by others & therefore, is always charged with a feeling of taking revenge if someone insults his/her. As soon as the native gets a chance to hurt others, he/she never losses such a chance.

Such a native possesses a sharp eye with which he/she can judge others clearly. A native born with Sagittarius sign possesses a haughty temperament but he/she can also hide the anger within & the smile

may keep others in dark about the person & it is not so easy to understand what is going on inside such a native.

Capricorn

The simple meaning of Capricorn is a creature that lives in water. This sign has been represented by an alligator but its head by a deer. In the universe

that sort of a name. A native born with this sign possesses qualities of an alligator as well of a deer also. This kind of a native knows clearly how

success as well. The native may get lots of problems in life but he/she is capable to solve them carefully.

Aquarius

The meaning of Aquarius is a pot which may contain water.Such a pot is

in the sky is known as bearing the sign Aquarius. A native born with this sign also possesses qualities like that of a pot full of water.The face of such a native is full of attraction & those who come in contact with the person, becomes his/her followers.The native, because of leadership qualities, has so many people who like to keep his/her company. Such a native has to experience so many ups & downs in life as the luck at times favours and next time it does not. That keeps the native usually contemplating & worrying. Since the native gest lots of cooperation from his friends, he/she quite often leads easily on a path of success. The native's health is often broken & has liver problems, has indigestion, stomach pain and constant slight pain persists in the stomach. Consequently native's temperament is also affected by that.

Pisces

directions in the sky. A person born with this sign also possesses the conduct accordingly.Such a native his a kind heart & enjoys most when he/she helps others. Even such a native may get troubles, but most is ready to help others. As a result his family members start opposing the native. The native, even after helping friends, does not like to propagate about his/her good deeds or show any obligation on those who are helped by the native. Thus, all the *rashies*/signs about which we have talked so far, are closely related to the nature of a native born under those signs. These signs (planets bearing such signs) are at times exalted and debilitated also. We will like to give a clear picture of these exalted and debilitated planets and their signs.

Exalted PlanetsThe planets which are hundred percent strong in a sign are known as exalted in that sign. We shall identify them with the help of a *kundali.*

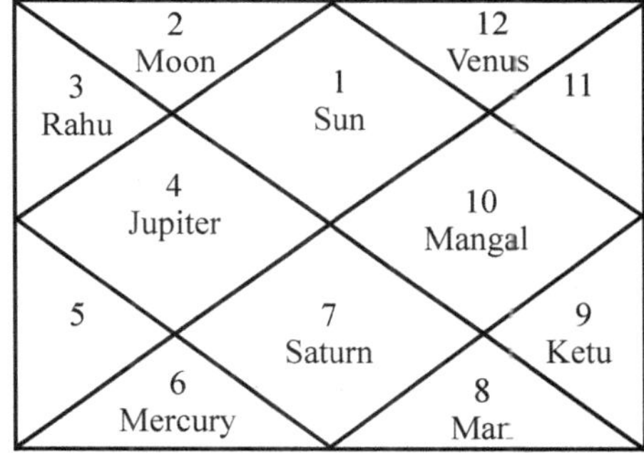

Special Remarks

Many a time exalted planets don't show their effect as exalted ones. Its main reason is that such a planet becomes debilitated by itself on account of rising in certain degrees in which it no longer remains an exalted planet. It may also happen on account of the conduct or behavior of a person in whose *kundali* planets are exalted. Some of certain things have been

Future Indicated with the lines of Hands

Before you examine someone's hands to predictthe future, it would be important to observe carefully the person's hands' colours. If the colour of hands is rosy, it is considered best astrologically. Such hands belong to good people who are morally high and possess high positions in the society

that the native will be very haughty in temperament; if it is yellow, the native's liver is bad or there is some kind of liver related problem with the native. Such a native gets nervous soon & starts crying on small matters.

If a native's hand is soft, he/she will work with mind; if a native's hands are hard and rough, he will do physically hard work. A native whose hands are soft, he/she is able to learn from time & change accordingly but whose

thumbs are very thick, the native will hardly be able to get any education.

lead a straight life & will act well in life without involving in wrong

if the lines are not straight and are twisted, the native will face so many

are put together, then such a native will face several problems in life, he/ she will get less happiness from the family. Ancient astrology indicates

long & there are knots on them, they indicate that such a native will act after lot of thinking & will be kind to the poor and needy. The native may act or work slowly but whatever he/she will do, will be done well after lot

everything before starting it. The native's nature will also become like that. Such natives are usually wise.

and thumbs are thick and broad, such a native will get little education but if they are broad from top and there are knots on them, then such a native will work to earn lot of money and will not waste any time to learn any art.

temperament but if the nails of hands are big, such a native will like peace

that such a native will be a thief and a cheat & such a native is usually involved with wrong & immoral acts. If the mounds on a native's hands are raised, his/her family life will run happy, but if the mounds are depressed, the native's family life will not be happy. But if all the mounds in a native's hands are raised & high,such a native will get high positions in life. If in a

a lot of wealth and riches, but if they rise in unequal length, the native will have to work very hard in life to earn his bread. We are providing a sketch of a hand showing some important lines in a native's hand.

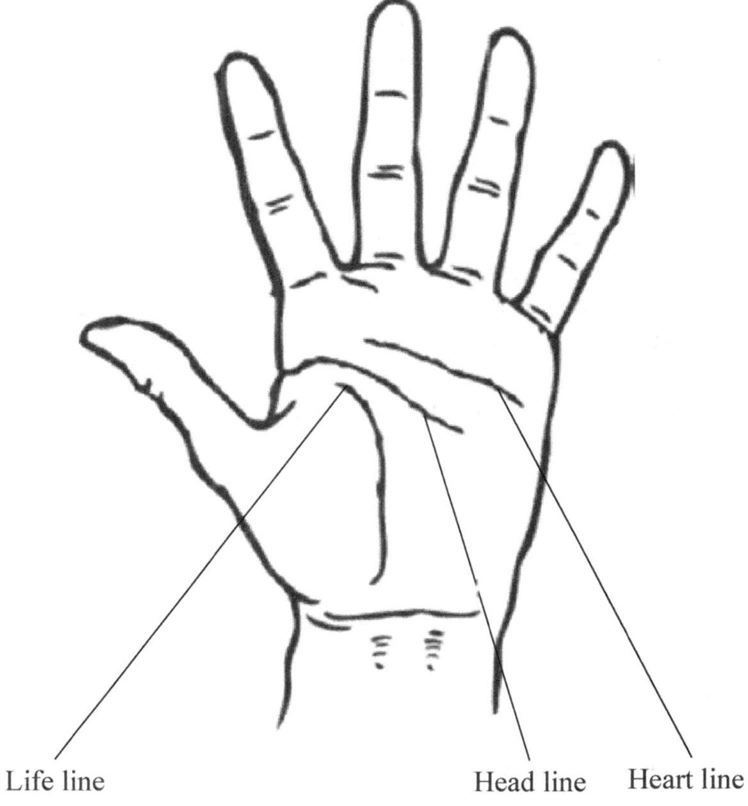

willed and courageous. Such a native will like to spend more and also earn lot of respect from people.

and will like others to offer him more respect. If a native's hands' thumbs are bigger, his/her luck will also support more; if the thumbs are long, such

the work which he will start to do. If the middle part of the thumb is long, such a native will think more. Often lawyers have such thumbs. In case third

Thumb in one's hand controls one's mind. If a native's thumb is straight, such a person has more technical knowledge. Such people like to spend time and money after lot of thinking. Such a native likes discipline & likes to hide or not tell others' secret things. If a native's thumb is not able to stretch fully, it is considered not suitable & such a native is unable to get more progress in life & their ides don't match with the others' ideas. In case a native's thumb open fully, such a native's temperament is cool & likes to meet different sorts of people. Such people also waste their time and money uselessly. If a native's thumb is smaller, such a person likes to

If a native's thumb is small and is raised high, such a native commit mistakes and spoils his/her life usually.If a native's thumb is thick and its nails are broad, such a native will get happiness from the family. If there are more islands in between the thumb, the native has the same number of children. If the island is bigger, it indicate number of male children and if smaller, it indicates female number of children. The islands also indicate about a native's riches and transport the native possesses.

Natives having broad palms of their hands are very bold as *Mangal* predominates in their lives. But if a native's palm is broad and Saturn predominates, such a native gets nervous soon & a native whose hands are big, often likes to go deeper in all matters of life & doesn't get disappointed

he/she belongs to a good family but if a native's hands are dry, he belongs to a poor or ordinary family & such a native is usually disturbed on account of certain things that may or may not be important for him/her in life. In kinds are often seen being projected on them, are considered good in all respects. Such hands belong to political persons, doctors, lawyers, professors, good

There are some other kinds of hands, that belong to wise, contemplative

native keeps patience and courage in every kind of job & becomes sad when

he/she often contemplates & often gets high education and loves reading a lot to gain knowledge. Yet there is a different kind of hands which resemble a

with hard labour. Such a native may be employed in police department. If a

discovery & may invent some new machinery. If a native's palm is broader towards his wrist, then such a native is more sensuous. He/she may be a lecturer, a writer, an advisor, an astrologer, a teacher or a social worker.

Yet there are some other kinds of hands, let us call them fourth

at the top. Such a native is fond of singing or wants to become an actor.

hands are really bad than the other hands. There are often three lines only on them—a life line, head line and a line of heart. Such hands are rough &

usually a labourer, a *cooli*(porter), a cultivator, a farmer and the native has a poor thinking capacity. Such a native possess less patience & gets nervous soon. But a native whose hands possess more lines, he/she also possess good mind & is also highly educated. Such a native also have knowledge of various kind in different directions. The native is usually employed by the government, is an astrologer, a lawyer or a writer. If lines in a hand are think, they provide good results but if they are thick, they don't give

and body & it also unfolds so many things about a native's father. If the

a straight line, it is considered defective and non-productive.Such a life line provides lot of struggles in a native's life & his/her stomach is always disturbed on account of something.Such a native does not get happiness from parents. The native has to change jobs frequently. If the life line is intercepted by *Mangal* or any line rising from the mound of *Mangal*, such lines are known Rahu lines. Many a times such lines involve a native in quarrels and court cases. But if any lines rise from the life line and goes if any lines go towards the mound of Saturn, even then they provide good results. Such a native earns a little extra in life.

If any lines rise towards the Sun line from the life line, then such a native possesses some kind of art & the native is respected widely. If any lines goes towards the mound of Mercury, they indicate success in business but if lines starting from life line rise upwards, they indicate impediments in work or job of the native. If a native's life line is cut in between, it indicates some kind of danger to the native's life but if there is any triangle or a rectangle on it, it indicates some kind of safety to the native against accident or bad happening. Some palmists consider a triangle or a rectangle indicates that a native will possess some property, house or a shop.

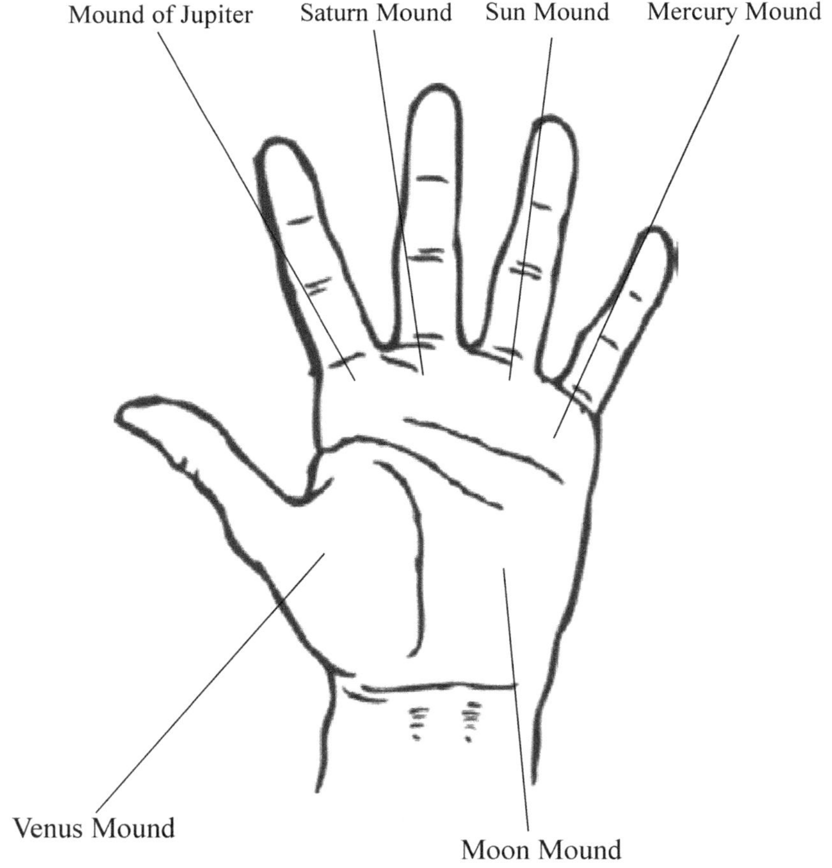

If the line of head and life line both are joint at the beginning, such a native is very wise and likes to take decisions from reason by involving his/her mind properly. But if the line of head is separate from that of the life, such a native usually works hard and rises in life by his/her own labour and intelligence. Such a native often starts his/her work or job to earn the livelihood. If the head life is a little separated from the life line, it is mostly considered good & helps a native to reach at some responsible position in life. But if there is more space in the lines of life and head, then it indicates that such a native possesses a free mind that means he/she is capable to think freely and likes to take his/her own decisions in most matters of life.

The bigger the mind line in a hand, the better it is understood. This line also gives idea about a native's riches. The bigger it is, the better a native's mind would be. In case the line of mind starts from the mound of Jupiter, a native is usually religious. If the line of mind goes straight to the mound of *Mangal,* a native's temperament is haughty, he/she studies logic but if this lines goes to the mound of Mercury, a native would like to indulge in business, if the line of mind is bent towards the mound of moon, a native may be more imaginative or keep busy in thinking. If the line of head is small, a native may not study more or get less education & will have troubles in earning money. If there is an island in between the line of head,

line is very small it indicates that the native may not live long and may die at an early age. If the head line and heart line both join at a point, the native will run after money an either his wife will be an earning member or he may get money in his marriage. If the head line is without any knots or any kind of impediments, the native's mother's health will be good and he will get happiness from his mother. If the head and heart lines are very to each other, they indicate that the native will be a miser. If the head line is divided into two parts at the end, it indicate double nature of the native& he/she may be interested in dancing and music.

It is also possible to examine about the qualities of a wife and husband by the heart lines in the hands of a man and woman.If the head line starts from the mound of Jupiter, is clean and ends at the mound of Mercury, then it is considered good. But if there are islands in it or of it is thick or broad,

Jupiter, it is always considered better. Often such a native is religious &

of Saturn and Jupiter, the native is very practical in his behaviour. But if such a line starts with the mound of Saturn, then such a native makes the other's happiness. Such a native's doesn't bent down on account of good or bad time in life.If the heart line is very straight and long, such a native's ideas don't match with others ideas. The native incurs enmity with so many people. Such natives are also very jealous of others.The line of heart also predicts about a native's destructive qualities. Such natives usually have only three lines in their hands, their hands are rough or very hard, and are of red colour, the thumbs are short and the heart line is very straight. Such native mostly destroys other people if they become their

him. To be friendly or to become his/her enemy, in both cases the other will sustain losses. If the heart line is short in a hand it indicates illness. If a line rises from heart line towards the mound of Saturn, it may help the native to get rises in life and he may also get good name in life. But if the heart line is very thick, it indicates that the native is very miser. If there is a cross in between the heart and head-lines, it indicates that such a native will not disclose his mind to others. Such a native ma also suffer from heart problems. If small lines rise from the heart line under the mound of Mercury, they indicate about native's children. The number of such lines indicate the number of children a native may have.If there is an island between the heart and mind lines under the Sun mound, it indicates that the native may suffer from eye troubles. If the heart line is divided into three parts going towards the mounds of Jupiter, Saturn and one towards the head line, it makes a *trishool.* Such a *jatak* will have plenty of wealth, earn good name and have children.

The Sun line, if it is there in a native's hand, is considered to be good. It is also known to an educational or success line. A native in whose hands such a line is there gets success in all directions—whether job or business. It rises from different points in a hand. If it rises from the luck line and goes up to the mound of the Sun, it indicates native's good luck as well as good name in the society. If it rises from the head line and goes up to the mound of the Sun, then such a native acts usually by his/her mind and gets a lot of success in life. If it rises from the mound of the moon and goes up to the mound of

The line of luck in a native's hand indicate about the luck of the native. If it rises from the wrist of a native's hand, it indicates that the native has been very lucky since his/her childhood. If it rises from the life line and goes up to the mound of Saturn, it indicates success in a native's life at the time it starts from the life line.If in beginning of this line there are islands or if it is divided into two branches, then such a native does not get any happiness or support from the parents or lives in poverty in the childhood. If this line rises from the Moon mound, it indicates that such a native will be a social worker and help the needy in the society & earn good name. If the luck line rises from the mound of the moon and goes up to the mound of Jupiter, it form Gajkehsari Yoga in the native's *kundali*, & makes a native very religious & he/she regularly worships God. Such a native is also wealthy and possesses lot of riches.

If the luck line starts from life line and goes up to the mound of Saturn, then the native gets success in life by hard work and perseverance. If it starts from one's head line, then such a native gets success on account of his/her good mind after 35 years of age. These lines should be thin & deep only then they are considered good. If they are very thick and broad, they

intercepted or cut in between by any other line, it indicates impediment at that age in a native's life. If it rises after some break in it then it creates problems for the native at that particular age in life.

If there is a squire on a mound in one's hand, it indicates success relating that mound. If a squire is considered as a sign of Jupiter, it would not be wrong as Jupiter is a planet that is auspicious for all. Therefore, were ever there is a squire, it gives good results. A triangle is also considered good in one's hand. If it is there on a mound or on a particular line, it provides

be the sign of *Mangal*. If it is formed on a native's life line it provides lot of property to the native. A star * in one's hand is also considered to be good but if it rises on the mound of Saturn it does not provide good results. A star is the sign of the Sun and both the Sun & Saturn are enemies, so if it

If there are crosses or nets on a mound or on a line that indicates problems and is considered inauspicious. Net is considered as Rahu & it created some kind of impediment where ever it rises. If there is an island on a hand at any place, it represents Ketu & on which ever mound or line it appears, it lessens the power of that mound or line. If there is a sign of a cross x on a mound or a line, it represents Saturn & is considered inauspicious as it reduces the power of that mound or line on which it appears. But if there is a cross on the mound of Jupiter, it is considered auspicious & indicates religious nature of the native.

When one's hand lines are studied it is necessary that one must try to observe both kinds of signs good and bad on it. Only then right predications should be made. If a native's thumb is long & thick, it should be given 10 marks: if it is long but broad from the top, give it 9 marks; if its second part

rises like a cushion, give it 5 marks.

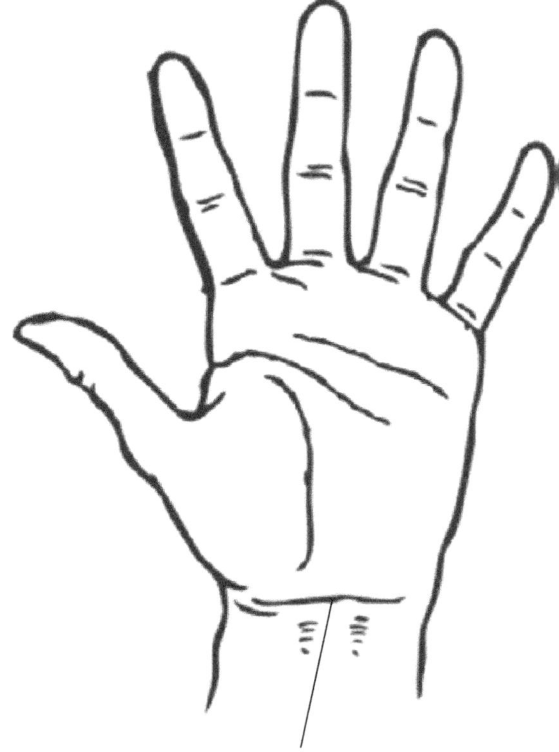

Mani Bandah (Indicating Age)

There are 9 mounds on each hand. If all the mounds are raised, give that hand 18 marks. That means 2 marks to each mound. If all the mounds are much raised, thy may not give good results. The truth is that each & everything has its own limit & if things go beyond that limit, it will not be

mark to each mound, but if they are depressed, don't give them any marks.

native's ascendant in his/her *kundali* is considered debilitated or weak. It makes the native's life full of struggle and unhappy. If the life line is smooth and long in one's hand, give it 10 marks, but if it is straight as if it is standing, give it only 6 marks. If the head line is long & straight, give it 10 marks & it is with the help of one's mind that a native gets success in life. The bigger this line is, the better work the native will do with his/her mind. He/she will also have plenty of wealth and riches. If there is any cutting or an island in between this line, it indicates impediments in the native's education, money and progress.

If the heart line is long and reaches the mound of Jupiter & it has not joined the line of mind, give it 10 marks. But if there is an island in between the line or if it is broad, or has joined the line of head, give it only 5 marks then. If the lines of mind and heart lines are very close, give 6 marks; if they end under the mound of Saturn, give 7 marks; if the head line is curbed like a bow and ends under the mound of Saturn, give 7 marks; if the line of head is like a bow and ends under the mound of Jupiter, give it 8 marks. If the luck line starts from the ***Mani Bandh*** (lines at the wrist) as shown in the sketch of a hand (given a little above) and goes up to the mound of Saturn, give it 10 marks, but if it starts from the life line, give it 9 marks only. If this line is deep but it has no cuts, give it 8 marks. If the Sun line is good in one's hand, give it 10 marks but if there

lines, give 10 marks to each, but if there are no lines give 5 marks only.

without cuttings, they will give auspicious results. But if there are islands

a hand one must see both sides and also try to observe the bad and good signs on it. Only then one's future should be predicated after examining one's hands & good& bad results should be predicated.

www.ingramcontent.com/pod-product-compliance
Lightning Source LLC
Chambersburg PA
CBHW060227100726
47907CB00003B/534
* 9 7 8 9 3 5 7 9 4 0 8 3 2 *